Praise for the Blake Sanders Series:

Night Drop

"Looking for an adrenaline rush? You'll find that and more in *Night Drop*. Blake Sanders is back, and that means the action is nonstop!"
—Alan Russell, author of *Multiple Wounds* and *Burning Man*

"I LOVED this story. *Night Drop* is a fast-paced, tension-filled thriller that will grab you by the throat until the very last page. Blake Sanders is one of the most intriguing characters I've read in years. This is definitely Sherer at his best."
—KT Bryan, author of *Team EDGE*

Night Tide

"A great, great read! Even better than *Night Blind*, and that's not easy."
—Timothy Hallinan, author of *The Fame Thief*

"A cracking good story and a first-rate thriller."
—J. Carson Black, *New York Times* and *USA Today* bestselling author of *The Survivors Club*

"A tight, well-constructed story and characters that leap from the page. I'll definitely be back for more."
—Robert Gregory Browne, author of *Trial Junkies 2: Negligence*

Night Blind

"An appealing, empathetic lead."
—*Publisher's Weekly*

"This is an exciting, well-crafted thriller and most certainly a satisfying one."
—*Mysterious Reviews*

"Thriller writer Sherer renders a sympathetic lead character and an

engaging . . . story line in his latest."
—Allison Block, *Booklist*

"Loved every page of it."
—Brett Battles

"A tightly paced page-turner that's impossible to put down. Terrific!"
—Allison Brennan

"Pay attention. You won't want to miss a word."
—J.T. Ellison

"Rich, complex, and deeply satisfying."
—Bill Cameron

BLIND RAGE

Also by Michael W. Sherer

Blake Sanders Series

Night Strike

Night Drop

Night Tide

Night Blind

Emerson Ward Mysteries

Death on a Budget

Death Is No Bargain

A Forever Death

Death Came Dressed in White

Little Use for Death

An Option on Death

Suspense

Island Life

BLIND RAGE

by

Michael W. Sherer

Michael W. Sherer

Cover Design: Anne Kaye-Jewett

For girls everywhere, young and old,

especially mine—

Anne, Megan, and Valarie.

Girls rule.

CHAPTER 1

Dreams might fade in the light of day, but reality doesn't disappear behind closed eyes. Tess felt a familiar sense of foreboding wash over her. As hard as she tried to push it away, it seeped into her subconscious, numbing her with fear. If she'd known then what she knew now, she would have changed everything about that day. She squeezed her eyes shut tighter, but still saw the same thing.

She leaned over and swiped at her snowboard bindings with her mittens. Normally, they would have popped loose right away, but not this time. She seemed to be all thumbs and she was tired, cold, and wet. Her frustration mounted as her goggles fogged; the tears she'd been holding back spilled unbidden down her cheeks. She yanked the goggles off her face and pulled them back over her head. The gesture was savage enough to take her hat off with the goggles—and along with enough hair to give her a second reason for tears.

Clenching the end of one mitten in her teeth, she pulled out her hand, bent down again, and dug her fingers into the catch of the binding. Wet, slushy spring snow had covered her boots and packed her bindings in ice—Cascade Concrete. Her fingers turned blue as she worked them in far enough to get the leverage she needed. With a mighty pull, she sprang the catch loose and stepped out of the binding. She blew on her cold hand before sticking it back into the mitten, then stamped her boots on the packed slope. Her mother swooped down next to her and skidded on her heel edge to slow. Tess turned her head and swiped at her face with her parka sleeve.

"Gosh, you're fast," her mother said, sliding gently to a stop a few feet away. "No way I could keep up." She looked back up the slope for a moment. "What a great last run."

Tess picked up her hat and stuffed it in a pocket, sneaking a glance at her mother from under a sheaf of hair the color of a raven's wing. Her mother had the same hair, the same exotically shaped face and features. But somehow, against all odds, Tess had gotten her father's blue eyes and a little bit of his nose. The cold had turned her mother into Rudolph, the speed of the run turning her nose cherry red and making her eyes water. Maybe she wouldn't notice that Tess had been crying.

"So," her mother said, "any thoughts about where you'd like to eat?"

Tess had a choice of where to go for a celebratory dinner.

Some celebration.

Eating was the last thing she felt like. The day had started out all right. Her parents had offered to take her up to the pass to go boarding after school and then out to a late dinner as a treat for scoring so well on her SATs.

"Not as a reward," her mother had said, "just an acknowledgement." Her parents—especially her "Tiger Mother" mom, but even her laid-back skater dad—expected her to get good grades, to get into the best schools, without the promise of any sort of reward. Tess didn't have a problem with that. She felt naturally driven to do well. Maybe it was the competition at school. After all, Tess was younger than most of her classmates, so had more to prove. Especially since this was spring of her junior year. Her combined 2240 on the college boards would help. So would her 3.98 cumulative grade average. And she could always take the SAT again in the fall and try to raise her scores.

That was all good, but the day had somehow devolved into a mess.

She looked up the lighted slope past her mother without answering. She spotted her father's plaid parka with the Olympic insignia on the front, the one he said Shaun White had given to him after the 2010 Winter Games. He flew down the slope, carving elegant curves, caught some air going over a small mogul, did a cab 360, then swooped toward them. Gnarly. It came naturally to him—he'd been almost as good a skater as Tony Hawk or Rob Dyrdek. Better than both, some said, even though Hawk was vert and Dyrdek was street. But Tess's dad had never been interested in going pro. At least that's what he'd told her. She sometimes wondered. He stopped quickly, showering them with wet snow, his grin stretching from ear to ear. He looked from one to the other, his smile fading like shadows do when a cloud passes in front of the sun.

"What's going on?" he said lightly.

"Nothing," said her mom. "Tess is deciding where we're going to dinner."

"Really?" her father said. "I could've sworn something's up."

Her mother flashed a quick smile and said gently, "She's miffed because I told her she couldn't invite Toby. I thought it should be just us tonight. I'm being selfish."

Her father shrugged. "I don't think that's selfish." He turned to Tess. "Your mom's right. We hardly ever get you to ourselves anymore, kitten."

Tess looked at her mother with daggers in her eyes, then turned an imploring look on her father.

It just blurted out of her. "She told me I can't go to prom, Dad!"

Her mother shook her head. "No, I said I didn't want you to go alone with Toby. I don't mind if you go with a group of your friends, but you're not getting into a car alone with someone when you don't even have your own driver's license yet."

"But that's not fair!"

She blinked back tears and turned to her father for help again. It wasn't her fault she didn't have a license. Not entirely. Between the pressure to keep her grades up and her extracurricular activities, she hadn't been able to find time to take driver's ed.

He wiped air with his hands. "Don't look at me, kitten. Not getting in the middle of this."

She'd always loved the idea of being his snuggly little kitten. Suddenly she hated the nickname.

"What do you mean, you're not getting involved?" she said, pouting. "You're a parent, too."

"I meant that I'm not about to countermand your mother," he said gently. "We have each other's back, especially when it comes to parenting. And it so happens that I agree with her."

"But why?" It sounded whiny, but Tess couldn't help it. She really wanted to go with Toby.

"For the same reasons your mother mentioned," he said. "I used to be in high school. I used to be just like Toby Cavanaugh. Heck, I *was* him. I know exactly what's on his mind."

Her mother positively beamed. Tess couldn't stand it. Her father and Toby were nothing alike. And she felt like she was losing her touch. She'd always been able to sway her father before.

"You don't trust me—is that it?" she said.

"Oh, we trust you," her mother said. "It's Toby we don't trust. Don't get me wrong. I think he's a nice boy, Tess. I just don't think it's appropriate for you two to be without some sort of chaperone."

"I can take care of myself."

"Maybe so," her father said, "but for now, think about going with your friends instead."

"It's just not fair!" she wailed.

Tess grabbed her board and stomped off toward the parking lot. She stood next to the big SUV under the lights and fumed, pacing, while she waited for her parents to slowly catch up.

They are so infuriating. She watched them surreptitiously, head bowed, as they approached holding hands. *Eewww.* She didn't know anyone else whose parents acted so sickeningly romantic in public. She glanced around the parking lot to see if anyone was looking. *If I did that with Toby in front of them, they'd just lecture me.*

Engrossed in conversation, they acted as if nothing was wrong when they came up to the SUV. Her father opened the tailgate and put his board inside, then took her mother's and laid it in on top. Almost absentmindedly, he reached over and grabbed Tess's board and stowed it along with the others, talking to her mother the whole time. He walked around to the passenger door and opened it for her mother, then circled around to the driver's side. Tess got in the back and flounced onto the seat. Her father climbed in, started the engine, and plugged his iPod into the stereo system. Soft jazz filled the interior.

"Dad, could you get some decent music on your playlist?" Tess said.

He glanced in the rearview mirror. "I'll get I.T. on it right away."

From the way his eyes crinkled, she knew he was smiling. She turned away and sighed. At least it wasn't the headbanger eighties punk rock he sometimes listened to when he wanted to pump himself up. "Reliving my ill-spent youth," he'd say, recalling his days skateboarding around the Cal Poly campus. She shook her head.

Parents are such a pain.

Five minutes later, they got onto the highway heading west toward the city. Tess stared out the window and watched the dark terrain zip by in a blur. A mix of light snow and rain had started falling, and the sparkling, lacy veil of flakes and drops mesmerized her. The season had run late that year. Normally, the ski areas closed by early or mid-April, but the cold, wet winter had provided plenty of snowpack. They might even get in another day of boarding in early May. It wasn't unheard of.

Tess's head nodded as drowsiness overtook her, and she jerked awake. She leaned against the door, wrapped her mittens in her hat, and put it between her cheek and the window as a pillow. Her mother craned her neck to look at her.

"Put your seatbelt on, Tess."

"Yes, mother."

Her mother smiled. "I love you."

Tess folded her arms over her chest and closed her eyes without responding. She must have dozed off. When her eyes opened, she immediately sensed something wrong. Her parents had stopped talking, but Tess felt rather than heard the unspoken communication between them. In the dim light from the instrument panel, she saw her mother's hand grip her father's arm. She felt the tension in it and slowly became aware of a sound other than the steady hum of the engine—a low rumble and loud hiss that almost sounded like a waterfall or a huge wave breaking on shore.

Tess swung her gaze out the window, eyes straining to see in the darkness. She suddenly realized with growing horror that a moving wall of snow was descending the mountainside ahead of them. They were driving right into it. Her father tensed and the SUV momentarily slowed, then spurted ahead again.

"James?" her mother said, a note of fear in her voice.

"No brakes, Sally," her father growled.

He gunned the engine, but there was no way the SUV could outrun the avalanche. As the lip of the rolling wave of snow and debris reached the edge of the highway next to them, Tess clutched the door handle, her heart leaping into her throat.

"Hang on!" her father yelled.

The roaring avalanche tumbled over the vehicle, blotting out the taillights of the few vehicles ahead of them. Tess heard screaming and realized the sounds came from her as the tsunami of snow flipped the SUV like a toy, rolling it over and over, burying it in an icy tomb.

Tess screamed again, the awful sound of her terror and pain lifting her from the depths of the nightmare into consciousness. It was the same dream she'd had for the past year, one that had recurred nightly at first. Lately, it haunted her with decreasing frequency, but with no less terror than when it had begun. She lay still, letting the tendrils of the nightmare dissipate like morning mist, willing herself to think of sunnier things. It wasn't easy.

When she came fully awake and the dream was no more than a fading memory, she slowly opened her eyes. And, like every other day for the past year, she saw nothing. Not darkness, or light. Not shapes or colors.

Nothing.

CHAPTER 2

One year earlier...
Captain Travis Barrett, US Army Special Forces, took slow, deep breaths to decrease his rapid heartbeat and focus his nervous energy. Sweat trickled down his side under his *qmis*, the traditional loose-fitting shirt that Pashtun men wore with full trousers called *shalwar*. He ignored it and opened his eyes wider to see more clearly in the dim light. He was acutely aware of the smallest sounds—the high, squeaky chirrup of a bat in the night, the faintest whisper of moving air, and somewhere up ahead, the low murmur of voices.

Travis kept up the deliberate, steady breathing, trying to keep his excitement in check. It appeared that they'd finally gotten some HUMINT that might pay off. He and his team relied heavily on two forms of information—HUMINT, or human intelligence that came from informers, eyes and ears on the ground, and COMINT, or communications intelligence that came from intercepted phone calls, text messages, and e-mails. And information was the currency Travis and his team traded.

He eased farther into the cave.

In a sense, Captain Travis Barrett didn't exist. An avowed adrenaline junkie, he'd felt rudderless in college, like there was no point to studying. Realizing he couldn't afford passions like skydiving and motorcycle racing on the wages of a burger-flipper, he'd joined the army. He figured Uncle Sam might as well pay for his adrenaline fixes. The army had definitely delivered. After 9/11, he'd immediately signed up for Special Forces, and the thrills, along with the opportunities to serve his country, had gotten bigger. His skills and fearlessness—along with a previously untapped facility for languages—had earned him notice from the top brass.

Less than six months after terrorists had brought down the Twin Towers by hijacking and flying jet aircraft into them, Travis had been recruited for a special detachment called the Strategic Intelligence Collection & Containment Unit. The army, like most government agencies involved in the war on terror, didn't want to rely on any other agency for help. That's why the Navy had its own air force, the Army had its own navy, and the Air Force, well . . . So the Army created a little version of the CIA within its ranks. And Travis was one of the unit's best spies.

For most of the past six years Travis and his team had operated in and around "the Stans"—Afghanistan, Waziristan, Pakistan, Kazakhstan, Kyrgyzstan, Uzbekistan. They'd also led incursions into other Mideast hotspots, like Yemen. But most of his time had been spent in Afghanistan, tracking al-Qaeda. Even though its leader Osama bin Laden had finally been hunted down and killed after nearly ten years, the organization and the terror it sowed still existed. Few people knew about his unit; fewer still knew what he and his teammates actually did.

Right now Travis was following a lead from an Afghani shepherd he'd been cultivating for months as a potential informer. He and his team, blending into the native population, had found the man veterinary care when his sheep had come down with a mysterious illness, and had brought in a midwife when the man's wife was due to deliver their third child after a difficult pregnancy. Travis had personally offered the man his friendship, sometimes sitting with him through late nights watching the flock, just talking with the man in his native Pashto language. Travis knew the shepherd's allegiance was to his family and tribe, first and foremost. The man had no love for the Taliban or al-Qaeda—both groups operated in ways foreign to his tribe's traditional way of life. Recently, he'd passed on information to Travis's team.

Travis eased into the narrow passageway, instinctively ducking to keep from banging his head on the low rock ceiling. He knew they never would have found the cave without the tip from the shepherd. Travis's excitement grew. His mission simply was to get in, verify the cave's occupancy, identify members of a particular cell if possible, and get out. If the information checked out, Travis would relay what he'd learned to another unit awaiting instructions.

The sound of conversation grew louder as Travis made progress through the confined space, and shadows flickered on the walls of the cave limned by dim orange light. Travis heard the low rumble of a generator, and along with it came the faint odor of diesel fumes. The light grew brighter as Travis negotiated a tight bend in the passage, and the volume of the words, murmured in

Arabic, not Pashto, told him he was very close. The passageway took another turn ahead of him, and Travis crept closer and snuck a peek around the edge of the rock wall.

Beyond the turn, the tunnel opened up into a larger cavern. Six men sat in a rough circle, some on the cave floor, a few on bedrolls, and one on an ornately carved wood Afghan chair. All were bearded and dressed in the traditional *qmis, shalwar* and *pagray*—turban— of the local tribesmen. Most also wore a long vest and a *chadar*, a scarf that doubled as a cloak, over their shoulders. Travis detected the mingled smells of sweat from men who hadn't bathed, horsehair, and damp earth and rock. The man on the chair appeared to be the leader. Travis would need a closer look to confirm his identity. Conscious of a soft whirring sound, he edged a bit closer, then closer still until the man turned his head and Travis could see his face in the light of the few dim electric bulbs powered by the generator. Travis held his breath.

It's him!

An al-Qaeda leader they'd been chasing for two years.

Quickly, he scanned the faces of the rest of the men in the group to see if he recognized anyone else. Just as he started to turn away, one of the men sat up abruptly and stared directly at him. Raising his arm to point, he shouted an alarm to the other men. Travis whirled and moved as fast as he could back down the passageway without waiting to see if the others spotted him or not. The tunnel walls flickered brighter with the glow of flashlights, and Travis heard excited shouts behind him. It was not far to the exit. He ducked his head, leaned forward, and pushed toward the inky black hole of the cave entrance as fast as he dared. They wouldn't dare shoot at him inside the cavern for fear of ricochets, he knew, but once outside, he'd be fair game. He had to hustle if he was going to outrun them. The blanket of night would help provide cover.

As he moved, he thumbed a mic on his radio and called out clear instructions to the army unit awaiting his commands. A joystick jockey somewhere safe and warm in the mountainous neighborhood was piloting an MQ-1C Gray Eagle drone by remote control. On Travis's command, the pilot would signal the drone to fire a bunker-busting AGM-114R Hellfire II missile at the cave.

The cave opening was just ahead. Breathing heavily, Travis pushed himself to the limit. Before he even reached the entrance he shouted into his radio, "Go! Go! Go!" He burst out into the starlight and immediately cut to the left, out of sight of the entrance. He heard the yells of the men behind him as they converged on the mouth of the cave, but their voices were quickly drowned out by the deafening shriek of the incoming rocket. The night lit up like the sun. A huge, fiery explosion erupted, and the world in Travis's vision tumbled end over end and finally went dark.

Travis ripped the virtual reality helmet off his head and turned to his teammates excitedly.

"Hoo-ah!" he yelled. "What a rush! What's the verdict? Did we score a hit?"

"Direct hit, captain," his warrant officer called out. "L-and-S ground station says images from the Gray Eagle confirm it."

Travis pumped his fist in the air as his unit cheered. The drone pilot at the army's logistics and support base had locked on the coordinates and had infrared pictures showing the blast site.

"Looks like we lost the avatar," Travis said, "but as long as we got that SOB Basir al-Samara that's what counts."

Travis knew that certain people, James included, would be pissed. The avatar was actually a tiny radio-controlled helicopter, but it was hardly a toy. James and his company had put hundreds of millions of dollars into R & D on the little gizmo, and Travis had just proved it was everything it was cracked up to be. First, he could control most of its functions with the virtual reality helmet. Turn his head, and the helicopter turned. Lean forward, and the little flying machine moved ahead; lean back, and it flew backward. Equipped with stereoscopic cameras, the device saw exactly what Travis would see if he were there in person. Better, Travis could shift to infrared night vision if needed. When Travis moved his eyes, not his head, tracking cameras in the VR goggles moved the helicopter's "eyes" in the same direction. Stereo microphones worked just like Travis's ears, but were even more sensitive.

All this was crammed into a package that could fit in the palm of his hand. The flying device was powered by a lithium-ion battery and backed up with solar cells so efficient they could generate electricity in starlight, so it had virtually limitless range. And, coolest of all, the olfactory detector that James's company had developed for video games meant that Travis could even "smell" whatever was in the little helicopter's vicinity. An olfactory sensor—essentially an electronic nose—constantly "sniffed" the air, sent the signals to a computer for analysis, and recreated the odors for Travis with a vast array of volatile oils, esters, terpenes, and other odorants. Travis knew that no one on the team would be happy to hear he'd lost one of the prototypes, especially given how much it cost. But the result had been worth it.

He was still buzzed with the excitement of how the mission had turned out when Warrant Officer Wilson, his second-in-command, signaled him with a wave. Some of his men clapped him on the shoulder with smiling faces as he walked over to see what Wilson wanted. As he approached, Wilson held out a handset wired to a radio transceiver.

"It's Major Townsend." Wilson mouthed the words.

Travis spoke into the handset. "That was fast, sir. Calling to congratulate us already?"

"No, captain, though I gather your mission was successful."

"Very successful, sir."

"Good for you. But we have a problem. You're being reassigned, effective immediately."

Travis felt a wave of disappointment break over him. He'd grown to like and, better still, trust his team. With the new technology he'd just put through the wringer, they could really begin to take the war on terror right to the terrorists. Root them out in their mountain hidey-holes. But duty called, apparently. And as freewheeling as his career in the army had been, allowing him to satisfy a lot of personal needs, its discipline had been good for him.

"Where to, sir?"

"Stateside," the major said. "You're going home, captain."

"What's the assignment?"

"Security detail."

Travis's heart sank.

After years of excitement on the front lines of the war, now I'm being asked to babysit some brass? To hell with that.

The major broke the silence. "It's James, Travis. We've intercepted what we believe is a credible threat. He and his family are in imminent danger. And you know what that would do to the program."

Travis felt his jaw clench. "I'll be on the first transport out, sir."

"You're the best person for the job. Oh, and captain? Congratulations on eliminating al-Samara."

"Thank you, sir."

"Good luck, Trav. I think you're going to need it."

CHAPTER 3

Now that she was awake, Tess sensed someone else in the room. It was hard to explain how she knew; she just did. At first it was a feeling, like something pressing in on her, something foreign taking up space in the familiar surroundings of her room. Then the presence took on more tangibles.

Sounds, for example. She knew every rustle and creak in the house, the hum of the refrigerator compressor, the distant rumble of the furnace and hiss of the air through the vents, the squeak of a floorboard in the hall or on the stairs to the ground floor, rain on the roof and the rattle of water in the drainpipes, the chirps and warbles of birds outside, and the fluttering of leaves in a soft breeze. From all that background noise she could pick out the sound of quiet breathing, the rustle of fabric.

Smells, too. Without even an audible sniff, she could taste the air around her, gathering in the faint scent of lavender, the stronger smells of caramelized bread and roasted coffee, as if someone had passed through the kitchen on the way to her room, and something else that reminded her of her young childhood—a buttery smell with a hint of lemon and vanilla that reminded her of the sugar cookies she'd made with her mother. And behind all that she caught a whiff of something sour, though not unpleasant. More like the smell of honest hard work. A little sweat and elbow grease.

Tess realized that the feeling was probably what had pulled her out of the nightmare in the first place.

She sat up and turned toward her closet. "Morning, Alice."

"Ah, you're awake," Alice said. "Good morning. I thought you might sleep forever. Isn't today your big day?"

"You know very well what day it is, Alice."

Tess heard her sigh.

"I suppose I do," Alice said. "Just a day like any other. Anyway, I've laid some things out here on your chair. Breakfast is ready whenever you are."

"I'll be down in a minute." Tess didn't hear sounds of movement. "I don't need any help. I've been doing this since I was three."

"And thank goodness for that," Alice said. "I have enough to do around here without worrying about getting you in and out of your clothes." Alice bustled toward the door, then paused. Tess opened her mouth, but before she could say anything, Alice said, "All right. I'm going. I'll be downstairs in the kitchen."

Tess let her go without another word. The bedroom door closed with a soft click. Tess was glad that Alice had made no reference to her nightmare, though she must have been in the room or close by when Tess had screamed. She resented the fact that Alice still treated her like a child sometimes.

I'm eighteen, for goodness' sake. An adult.

She swung her legs out of bed, got to her feet, and mentally pictured the layout of her room. With confident steps, she paced off the distance to the bathroom door, put out her hand, and touched the molding of the door frame. She could get ready in her sleep. It was the rest of the day she wasn't so sure about.

While she washed her face and brushed her teeth and hair, Tess thought about Alice. Short and slight, Alice was rather plain, though not unattractive. Tess didn't know how old she was, but the fact that Alice never wore makeup and almost always had her mousy brown hair wound up in a bun at the back of her head made her look older than she probably was. Tess knew she had a kind heart, but her manner was as severe as her appearance.

Alice had been part of the family for almost as long as Tess could remember—first as a nanny when they'd lived in California, and then as a full-fledged housekeeper after they'd moved to the Pacific Northwest. Alice had never been what Tess had considered warm and cuddly. Practical, maybe, or efficient—those words described her better. Tess had always gotten along with Alice, but they hadn't exactly been best buddies. Alice had been perfectly capable of pitching in when her mother had been too busy—taking Tess to gymnastics or piano lessons, helping with homework, that sort of thing. But Tess had never confided in Alice or snuggled up with her the way she had her mother.

Family—as if I even have such a thing anymore.

However much a misnomer, though, she supposed it was true. Alice was her family now. And what an odd, untraditional family it had become. Ironic, a housekeeper named Alice—like this was yet another episode of *The Brady Bunch*. The problem was that Alice wasn't her *real* family, not her real mother, but she'd taken over her mother's role. Tess could hardly stand it. Alice could never take her mother's place. No one could.

Tess counted off the steps to the chair next to her dresser, reached out, and touched the articles of clothing Alice had left there for her. She shimmied out of her pajamas and dressed carefully, minding where zippers and buttons and seams went. Reasonably certain that she hadn't done anything stupid like put the skirt on backward or button the blouse unevenly, she went back into the bathroom to brush her hair one last time and gather it into a ponytail. Next time, she'd try to talk Alice into letting her wear something simpler, like jeans and a sweatshirt. But Alice had insisted she look especially nice today.

The thought of what lay ahead made her nervous, and she clutched the edge of the sink for a moment, heart racing, her breath coming in shallow gasps. She felt the cool porcelain in her hands, the smooth, rounded corners of the basin somehow reassuring, solid.

Easy. You've been there before. No big deal.

But it was a big deal. First day of school was always a big deal.

She straightened and carefully walked through the doorway back into her room, taking small, slow steps. She was instantly aware of another presence, this time accompanied by the strong, sweet smell of sarsaparilla, reminding her of root beer floats.

"Tiger lilies," she said. One of her favorite flowers. "Good morning, Yoshi."

"Good morning. Yes, tiger lilies. So sorry for not knocking, missy. I'm thinking you all ready for school today."

She laughed. "You never knock, Yoshi."

"But you always decent when I come in, *hai*? And you always glad to see me."

"Yes, I'm always glad to see you," she agreed, though she couldn't remember the last time she'd actually laid eyes on him.

Yoshi, their gardener and handyman, was a more recent addition to the family. He'd come to work for her parents when they'd moved there. The house was enormous, and the grounds extensive enough that her parents had wanted the extra help. Her mother had loved flowers, but hadn't had the time she would have liked to tend the gardens and flowerbeds around the property. Yoshi took care of all of that. And, like the game Clue, the house actually had a conservatory with a small greenhouse attached. Her mother, with Yoshi's help, had been able to enjoy flowers year round.

If it hadn't been for Yoshi, Tess thought she might have lost her sanity in the past year. Unlike Alice, Yoshi had brought a fresh flower to her room and greeted her cheerfully every day after she'd gotten home from the hospital. Tess had arrived on a gurney with her pelvis broken in four places, three cracked ribs, a broken wrist, a broken jaw, a severe concussion, no eyesight—and her mother's reminder to fasten her seatbelt still ringing in her ears.

A fat lot of good seatbelts did my parents.

Despite her injuries, at least Tess had survived.

She'd rejected Yoshi's kindness at first, rudely pushing him away—just as she had anyone else who came close after the accident. She'd hated everyone, her pain and anger so consuming that there wasn't room in her mind or her heart for gratitude or even manners. If her jaw hadn't been wired shut, she would have yelled at all the people who cared for her, who fed, clothed, and bathed her. But the days and weeks of excruciating rehab were mind-numbingly boring. And Yoshi hadn't seemed to care how rude she was to him; he'd still shown up each morning with flowers and sunny words.

She'd noticed the differences in floral scents, and had asked Yoshi the name of each flower he brought her. Soon, she was able to name them by scent as soon as he entered the room. Not long after, Yoshi had brought other things for her to smell. Objects with strong scents at first: cinnamon sticks, oranges, garlic cloves, spring onions from the garden, bacon strips, chocolate, and more. She especially liked when he brought chocolate or mints—any type of candy, really.

Most of what he'd presented her on his early visits presented little challenge to either her sense of smell or her memory. She could visualize the things he brought from their scent. He'd quickly made a game of it, bringing her increasingly more challenging items to sniff out and identify. Things that required a little more thought. To make it interesting, he might present with her two or three items that smelled similar and prod her to tell him what they were. Leather shoes smelled different than a leather handbag, for example, and both smelled different than a leather-bound book. The shoes had an overtone of sweat and dirt. The book's leather smell included scents of dust and paper. A new basketball also smelled different than tennis balls. Both smelled of rubber, but the felt on the tennis balls gave them an odor distinct from the basketball.— knowledge she'd probably never use, only reminding her she'd never be able to play sports again.

Pretty soon, Yoshi had shown up with components of scents— essential oils, esters, terpenes, and aromatics. Many were positively nasty, reminding her of rotten eggs, decaying garbage, dead animals, or rotting fish. But most were pleasant—unless they reminded her of things that made her sad. Like hexanaldehyde, an alkyl aldehyde that smelled like cut grass, which brought back memories of playing with her father in their backyard in California as a toddler. He'd pretend to be a horse and let her ride on his back around the lawn after it had been mown. He'd even pretend to graze just like a horse. She knew she was too old for baby games, but she missed her father so much sometimes, it hurt.

Yoshi combined many of the ingredients, the way a perfumer or fragrance expert might, pushing her to refine her excellent nose. After a great deal of practice, she could smell an odor and pick out most of its notes or overtones.

"I have something for you," Yoshi said.

He held out his hand, palm up. Tess leaned forward and sniffed. She frowned and sniffed again.

"I don't smell anything," she said.

Yoshi laughed. "That because they not have any smell. Yoshi fool you."

He reached for her hand and pressed a smooth, flat stone into her palm. She closed her fingers over it, sensed its coolness, and felt her heart slow. Her thumb found an indentation in the stone, and she rubbed it slowly.

"What is it?" she said.

"A worry stone," he said. "Any time you feel life getting too hard, you rub. Feel better."

He took her other hand and pressed another stone into her palm. She turned it over in her fingers.

"What's this?" she said. "You think I'm so worried I need two?"

"Two stones," he said, "for two kinds of worries."

"How am I supposed to tell them apart?"

"You will know. They will tell you."

"How?"

"Be still. Just listen."

She frowned, but did as he said. The second stone felt the same, but different. It wasn't just the shape—slightly thicker at one end than the first stone, with an extra little dimple on one side—but something else. She held very still and tried to pay attention to the sensations coming from the stones. The first one had filled her with a sense of calm. But as soon as Yoshi had pressed the second stone into her hand, she realized she'd felt almost a tingle, some sort of energy, radiating up her arm.

She held out the first one. "What's this?"

"Pink quartz. Very powerful healing for the heart."

She thought about that for a moment. She wasn't sure there was anything in the world powerful enough to repair the hole in her heart. Not unless the stone she held could bring back her parents.

"And the other one?" she said.

"Blue obsidian. Protect you when you travel, and help you talk."

She laughed. "Some people don't think I need any help in that regard, Yoshi."

"Help you with schoolwork, maybe. And help you learn more Japanese."

"Oh, so like help learning languages?"

"And expressing what is in your mind. You feel it?"

She nodded. "Thank you. Would you put these in my bag?"

She handed them back to him, and as soon as he took them from her hands, she felt a little different, as though someone had hit a dimmer switch.

Maybe that's a bad analogy, considering my situation. In any event, she definitely felt a change in energy, and suddenly doubts crept back into her consciousness.

"Do I look all right, Yoshi?"

"Very pretty, missy."

"You wouldn't just say that to be nice, right?"

"Why say it if it not true?"

He made sense, but Tess suddenly found her nerves getting the better of her.

"Could you walk me downstairs, Yoshi?"

"*Hai.* You do me great honor, missy."

Yoshi took her hand, placed it on his arm, and guided her out of the room. She counted the steps down the hall, noting when Yoshi turned her gently and warned her that they were at the top of the stairs. She knew how many steps there were on the curved staircase—twenty-five. She put one hand on the banister to steady herself as Yoshi led her down. She used to slide down it when they'd first moved in. When she had still been a kid.

They reached the bottom and turned to walk through the foyer and down a long hallway toward the kitchen. The closer they got, the more nervous she became. She heard voices coming from up ahead. She could pick out Alice's voice. The other voice was male, vaguely familiar. She'd heard it recently. It suddenly dawned on her where, and panic welled up inside. Thoughts raced through her head, and feelings churned in the pit of her stomach.

So many questions . . .

They reached the kitchen door, judging from the way the sounds reached her ears, and Yoshi stopped. The conversation stopped, too.

"Ah, there you are," Alice said. "Guess who's here?"

Tess heard the scuff of chair legs before she could reply, and the male voice said, "Good morning."

It was all too much, too soon. More than Tess could handle. She whirled out of Yoshi's grasp, put her hands out in front of her, and fled back the way they'd come.

CHAPTER 4

I'd be the first to admit I'm no ladies man. I'm not a bad-looking guy. I'm a little over six foot three, somewhat lanky in frame, not beefy like a football player, but broad-shouldered like a swimmer. I've got all ten fingers and toes, a nose that's not grotesquely large, eyes the color of a hazy summer sky, brown hair that grows in twenty different directions, giving me an interminably sleepy look as if I've just gotten out of bed, and a wide smile that I probably offer too readily. Some might even say I'm handsome, but I wouldn't go that far.

In any case, I do okay around girls—young women—and even screw up the courage to ask them on dates now and then. I've been turned down some, but none of them has ever run away from me . . . until now.

Let me back up a little. My name is Oliver Moncrief. I know, what parent would saddle their kid with a name like Ollie? Parents named Moncrief, that's who. But before I was old enough to confront them about it, my parents were long gone. My mother, Rachel, died of cancer when I was a toddler, young enough that I don't have memories of what she looked like, only vague recollections of her presence. My father, Duncan, took off shortly afterward. Maybe he was brokenhearted, or perhaps the thought of raising a kid by himself was overwhelming. Whatever the reason, he left me with my mother's parents, and I haven't heard from him since.

Moncrief is a Scottish name, changed over the centuries from Moncreiffe, which means something like "hill-pasture tree" in the original Gaelic—a combination of the words "monadh" and "craoibbe," both of which are obviously unpronounceable in English. The original Moncreiffes were Scottish royalty of a sort, "lairds," or lords of extensive holdings of land and usually officers of the local Highlander clan. My father's side of the family split off from those Moncreiffes some time in the mid-1700s when my great-to-the-nth-power-grandfather, Alasdair, hightailed it to the New World after causing a scandal that everyone mentions in connection with the family history—with great sighs of consternation—but no one has explained to me in detail. Alasdair changed his name to Moncrief to prevent further shame from staining the family crest, and to stay a step or two ahead of the law. Turns out if he'd been caught and convicted in Scotland he would have been banished to America anyway. Apparently, Scottish courts thought being shipped to America was a punishment only slightly more merciful than death.

My first name pays homage to Oliver Cromwell, who was a buddy of Alasdair's great-great-grandfather Magnus Moncreiffe. The Brits, of course, later dug up Cromwell's body after he died of septicemia and executed him for treason. For good measure, they beheaded him, too, so you see how well that turned out. Magnus's cousin Thomas got back on the right side of English politics by taking a job as exchequer to King Charles II, the guy who dug up Cromwell as payback for ordering the execution of his own father, Charles I.

You probably think I've stepped back a little too far, and maybe you find all this history boring. I was never too good at history myself, but it's important to understand this stuff so you know where I'm coming from.

Okay, so by the end of the nineteenth century, while the now-thoroughly-American Moncriefs hadn't distinguished themselves as scholars, professionals, or the cream of polite society, Alasdair's great-great-grandson Fergus was smart enough to grab onto the coattails of another Scotsman by the name of Andrew Carnegie. You've probably heard of *him*, even if you're lousy at history. He made a fortune in the steel industry, among other businesses, and would have been worth hundreds of billions in today's dollars.

Whether by legal or illegal means—no one's quite sure—Fergus made a small fortune as a result of Carnegie's business savvy. A penny-pinching Scot to his core, Fergus managed to hang on to most of that money, even made it grow through sound investments. So a lot of his money was passed down through a couple of generations. And for some reason, each succeeding generation of my particular branch of the family consisted of one solitary male. My grandfather Donald and his wife Edith begat Duncan, my father, who begat me. Yep, I'm the last of the line—unless I have kids of my own someday.

I had a perfectly normal and happy childhood growing up with Nana and Pop-Pop, my mom's parents. Backyard, white picket fence, the whole small-town experience in a place you never heard of. I did well enough in school that I got into college. Actually, I did better than okay, but I don't like to brag. I finished high school in three years, but not because I'm a Mensa member. I have an eidetic memory, not exactly photographic—who'd want to remember everything in that kind of detail?—but darn close. While my grandparents weren't all that well-to-do, it so happened that a trust fund had been set up in my name to pay for my education. So when I turned eighteen, my then-elderly surrogate parents waved good-bye and told me I was on my own. I didn't mind. They'd done a good job; I was ready to leave the nest.

The deal with the trust was that as long as I stayed in school, the trustee, a lawyer by the name of Bigsby—nice guy—would pay the bills. I was supposed to get whatever was left when I turned thirty. The rationale, I suppose, was that I'd have some incentive to put my education to work before coming into vast sums of money. And, of course, I was heir to the Moncrief fortune, once my father dies, that is. If anyone can ever find him.

Unfortunately, my other grandparents, Donald and Edith, were a profligate pair, a couple of spendthrifts who lived on the twelfth hole of a golf course down in Florida living *la dolce vita*. I went to visit only once, during spring vacation when I was in fourth or fifth grade. The big house with the servants and the chauffeured Bentley and the extravagant parties impressed me, but my grandparents didn't. They were a couple of cold fish who tolerated me because I was a blood relation, and then only because they knew I wasn't staying and wouldn't disrupt their lifestyle. Donald smelled like scotch and stale cigars. Edith smelled like lavender and bad breath.

Right, I digress. The point is that I figured my best option was to stay in school as long as possible, since the trust paid all my bills as long as I was enrolled somewhere. The problem was that I kept getting degrees ahead of schedule. I earned a BA in English—my native language, good for easy As—from a major university in Seattle in two and a half years. I liked the climate and decided to stay. A master's degree was next. My focus was twentieth-century American literature. That took a year. I'd been working on a doctorate for the past six months, trying to write a thesis I'd called

"Tweets and Texts: A Comparison of 21st-Century American Literary Styles."

Not long ago—a few weeks to be accurate—I'd reached a critical juncture where I had to make some progress or reconsider my educational path and start all over as an undergraduate in, say, biochemistry or accounting. I was sitting in my favorite coffeehouse sipping a latte and contemplating my situation when I got a phone call that changed everything. It was from Leonard Bigsby, the lawyer. The gist of it went something like this:

Me: Hello?

Bigsby: Hey, kid. It's me, Leonard. Thought I'd give you a heads-up. I figure you've got two months.

Me: Two months till what?

Bigsby: Two months till the money runs out.

Me: What do you mean?

Bigsby: I mean the money's all gone. Well, almost gone. No more. Kaput.

Me: I thought as long as I stayed in school, the trust would pay for it.

Bigsby: Well, it would have. Except your grandparents embezzled half the funds before they croaked. So, the well's dry.

Me: What? You mean, like, there's nothing left? Not just the trust, the estate, too?

Bigsby: You got it, kid. Have a nice life.

Before I could think of a reply, the phone went dead. After several moments of shell-shocked silence and paralysis, I shook myself like a retriever coming out of water. I got up and scrounged around the coffeeshop for someone's abandoned newspaper, since I could now ill afford my own. Armed with a very thin section of want ads, I returned to my table and started looking for a job. Extensive knowledge of your own language isn't a qualification most employers care all that much about. Seems these days you can get a lot of jobs even if you don't speak English. But I found and circled several potential opportunities—security guard, day laborer, dishwasher, and one I was sure I'd be good at: personal assistant.

Most of the ads asked for a cover letter and résumé and listed a post office box number or an e-mail address. A couple of them listed phone numbers. I called those, getting turned down flat for one, being told another position was no longer available, and setting up an interview for a third. I saved the ad for personal assistant till last. When I dialed the number listed in the ad, a woman answered brusquely.

"Name and age."

"Oliver Moncrief. Twenty-one. Well, almost."

"Job experience?"

"None."

"None?" The woman sounded startled.

"Well, unless you count chores as a kid, like mowing the lawn, painting the fence, stuff like that."

"What do you do?"

"I'm a student."

"High school? College?"

"Graduate school. I'm working on my doctorate."

"At twenty? Isn't that a little young?"

"I took an Evelyn Wood speed-reading course." The attempt at humor was met with silence. I offered her a one-line explanation. "I've been in accelerated programs since elementary school."

"What are your qualifications?"

"Depends on what sort of personal assistance is required. I'm healthy, strong enough to carry groceries, read and write exceptionally well, type seventy-five words per minute, and know how to read a map. I'm smart enough to ask for directions when I'm lost, look presentable, and have been told I'm reasonably well mannered."

The line was silent for a moment then the woman said, "Do you have a valid driver's license?"

"Yes."

"Any criminal record, outstanding warrants, or convictions?"

"No."

"Be here in one hour." She gave me an address.

CHAPTER 5

One year earlier...
Travis barely had time to shave off his beard, change into a regulation combat uniform, and throw his gear into a duffel bag before a UH-60 Black Hawk helicopter came whirling through the night sky, homing in on their coordinates. It touched down fifty meters from their small encampment of huts abandoned by a local family that had been driven out by the Taliban. The downdraft from the powerful rotors kicked up dust and nearly blew the straw roofs off the mud huts. Travis quickly said his good-byes and shook hands with the other soldiers in the unit.

Travis and his men had been using the huts to blend in. As he hustled to the chopper, bent over against the rotors' backwash, he wondered what would happen to his teammates. They were all good men. He knew that they would have disbanded soon anyway, their mission essentially completed with that night's eradication of the al-Qaeda cell in the cave. All of them would soon be reassigned to other hunt-and-kill missions.

As well as they'd worked together as a team, Strategic Intelligence Collection & Containment didn't make a practice of keeping large units together for long. Unlike his time in Special Forces when he'd been part of a twelve-man Operational Detachment-A, or ODA, Travis usually worked alone or with just one other unit member, depending on the mission. They operated more effectively as individuals, could comingle with the general populace more easily alone. He preferred it that way, but found he'd enjoyed the camaraderie of the larger team more than he'd thought he would.

As soon as Travis climbed aboard, the chopper rose into the air, rotated 180 degrees, and quickly picked up speed, nose down. Within minutes, the chopper began flying high over the mountainous terrain, beating a path to the southwest at a speed of about 170 miles per hour. Travis peered into the darkness below and saw the brief muzzle flash of a rifle, probably from a sleepless Taliban member hoping to get a lucky hit. Travis wasn't worried.

After a few more minutes, he settled back in his seat and closed his eyes.

A little more than an hour later, the changing pressure in Travis's ears told him the chopper was descending. He opened his eyes and looked out the window. Scattered, twinkling lights from a large city asleep for the night spread out to one side. Travis saw that the chopper was still holding its original heading, flying into Kandahar Airfield, about ten miles outside the city. At one point in the not-too-distant past, more than five thousand military and civilian flights a day had operated out of the airfield, making it the busiest in the world. It appeared a little quieter now.

Travis's headset crackled to life. The chopper's copilot turned around to look at him.

"Captain Barrett?" the copilot said. "We're bringing you in as close as possible to your transport, but we're running a little behind schedule."

Travis nodded to let the pilot know he understood.

"You'll have to hustle, sir." The copilot flashed a grin. "Crew's pissed we're making them wait for you. Don't expect very good cabin service."

Travis smiled back and thumbed his mic. "After five months in the field, hot coffee would seem like first class."

True to the copilot's word, the chopper descended rapidly as it neared the airfield, buzzing low over the ground toward the end of a clay runway that ran parallel to the paved main runway. In the dark, Travis saw the silhouette of one of the big C-130 Hercules turboprop transport planes, airport lights illuminating a painted stripe on each of the spinning propellers. The pilot set the chopper down twenty yards away. As soon as it settled on its landing gear, Travis jumped out the open door, duffel slung over his shoulder. He ran toward the plane, the big open ramp in the rear beckoning him. Two soldiers standing in the opening waved him on.

The moment his feet hit the metal ramp, one of the crew hit a button and the ramp lifted off the ground. The other soldier spoke into a handheld mic and the big plane immediately began to roll down the runway. Travis dashed the rest of the way up the ramp, and all three of them scurried forward through the empty cargo hold to a row of webbed seats on the starboard side.

"Sit anywhere you want," a crew member yelled over the roar of the engines.

Travis nodded, stowed his duffel, and strapped himself into a seat. The plane accelerated down the runway and gradually lifted into the air, slowly climbing into the night sky. When they reached cruising altitude, a crewman unbuckled his seatbelt, dug into a cooler on the seat next to him, and fished out a bottle of water. He tossed it to Travis, who caught it and nodded gratefully.

Looks like I'm flying in economy.

He took a sip of water, closed his eyes, and let the drone of the engines slowly lull him to sleep.

Nine hours later, the big transport plane touched down in Wiesbaden, Germany. They'd been racing away from the sun, so it was still dark outside when they taxied in to the terminal. He thanked the crew, though they hadn't done much except watch him sleep, and deplaned out the port hatch. Stiff from the long flight, he tried to work out the kinks as he walked across the tarmac. Inside, he found a bank of vending machines and bought a cup of coffee that tasted terrible and a granola bar, which he consumed in three bites.

Personnel at an operations desk steered him to another part of the terminal for his next flight. No one manned the gate, and there was no transport plane on the tarmac outside the window, so Travis sat down and waited. When no one showed after fifteen minutes, Travis got up and paced impatiently. Catching a whiff of himself, he realized his uniform was getting a little ripe. He got some toiletries out of his duffel and went looking for a restroom. When he found one, he stripped to the waist and washed up as well as he could, donned a fresh T-shirt, and put on his uniform shirt again. After he brushed his teeth, he went back to the gate and reclaimed his seat.

Ten minutes later, a female enlistee in a blue Class B dress uniform approached him and stood at attention. She saluted as he rose to his feet.

"Captain Barrett?" she said.

Travis returned her salute. "At ease, corporal."

She relaxed. "Sorry you had to wait, sir. We've been fueling and servicing the aircraft. You're welcome to board now."

A tall brunette, she wore her hair pulled back and twisted in a bun below the uniform black beret. She led the way to a door that opened onto the tarmac. Travis followed, his mouth opening in disbelief when he saw that the transport wasn't another noisy cargo plane or big troop carrier, but a sleek C-37A, the military version of a Gulfstream V. USAPAT only sent one of its Army First Jet Detachment C-37s for top brass—nothing less than a full four-star general, and usually only for cabinet members.

"There's been some mistake," Travis said as the corporal climbed the folding stairs to the cabin door.

She stopped halfway up and turned. "No mistake, Captain Barrett. We need to ferry this plane back to Andrews, and we got a call that you needed a ride. No sense in wasting fuel."

Travis shook his head. "If you say so."

He climbed the staircase and ducked to enter the plane. Once inside, he had just enough headroom to stand upright.

The corporal motioned into the cabin. "Take any seat you like."

Travis looked at her nameplate. "Thanks, Corporal White."

He walked past a galley where a specialist was preparing something that smelled delicious. The corporal helped him stow his duffel, and he took a seat in a comfortable leather armchair. Before long, the plane rolled down the runway and leaped into the air.

Once they reached cruising altitude, Corporal White came into the cabin with a cup of coffee for Travis and made sure he was comfortable. They chatted for a few minutes, then she returned to the galley and finished preparing breakfast for Travis and the crew. After he ate, the corporal offered him a choice of movies to watch, which kept him occupied for a couple of hours. When the movie was over, he read for a while, then got up to stretch and walk around.

The specialist he'd seen in the galley, he learned, operated the plane's communications systems. During the course of the flight, he also met all three warrant officers who served as cockpit crew—a pilot, copilot, and flight engineer. He hadn't felt so pampered in a long time.

About an hour before landing, Corporal White served sandwiches to Travis and the crew, after which Travis settled back into the cushy chair and dozed off. He awoke when the corporal gently shook his shoulder and asked him to fasten his seatbelt for landing. Twenty minutes later, at only eight thirty in the morning local time, the sleek jet touched down at Andrews Air Force Base outside Washington, DC. It taxied in and stopped outside a hangar near the end of one of the runways. Travis thanked the crew profusely, retrieved his bag, and exited the plane.

A corporal in fatigues stood at the bottom of the stairs. He straightened and saluted as Travis descended.

"Captain Barrett, sir."

Travis saluted back. "At ease, soldier."

"I have transportation for you, sir." The corporal led the way to a jeep parked a few yards away. Travis threw his duffel in back and climbed in. The corporal started it up and accelerated quickly. Driving around the corner of the hangar, he headed for another large building behind it.

"When's my transport out?" Travis shouted over the wind rush.

"You have a little less than an hour, sir," the corporal said.

"Plenty of time."

He slowed the jeep and pulled up in front of a door that looked small in the side of the huge building. Then Travis noticed that the door was cut into a much larger door—one of a set of two on rolling tracks. Another hangar after all.

"What's this?" Travis said.

"Small detour, sir. Inside. I'll wait out here for you, sir."

Travis searched the soldier's face, but it was expressionless. He shrugged and got out, walked to the door, and opened it.

The interior of the cavernous building was dark. Travis stood just inside the door for a moment to let his eyes adjust to the gloom. He spotted a pool of light off to one side, nearly a hundred feet away, and walked toward it. The thud of his boots on the hard concrete floor echoed dully. A lone figure leaned against a workbench at the edge of the lighted circle. When Travis drew close enough to recognize the man, he stopped short in surprise and stiffened to attention, snapping a sharp salute.

"General Turnbull, sir. Good morning. I didn't expect to see you, sir."

Brigadier General Jack Turnbull returned Travis's salute. He was an inch or two shorter than Travis, but more imposing somehow. His brush-cut sandy hair was turning gray at the temples, revealing his true age of fifty-two, but he appeared to be in the same physical condition as Travis—broad-shouldered and muscular— despite being nearly twice his age.

"Good morning, captain." The general smiled, showing white, perfectly even teeth. "Now that we've got the formalities out of the way—how are you, Travis?"

"I'm good, sir. Tired, but fine. It's been a long flight. A couple of them."

"Glad to hear it. Come, sit down." The general motioned to a small table.

Travis took a seat, but the general remained standing, putting Travis on alert.

"I understand congratulations are in order," the general said. "That was good work last night. Intelligence analysts at this morning's briefings say taking out al-Samara may well have dealt a major blow to al-Q."

Travis sighed. "Thank you, sir. I hope so. Seems al-Q's more like a hydra than we bargained on. Ever time we cut off one of its heads, it grows two more."

"It won't always be like this, Trav. With your help, we are winning this war."

"Couldn't have done it without the team this time, general."

"Jack, please. We can stop being soldiers for five minutes."

Travis looked at him curiously. Brigadier General Jack Turnbull headed up the Strategic Intelligence Collection & Containment unit, and had taken Travis under his wing and into his confidence almost as soon as Travis had joined the unit. Travis had more immediate bosses, like Major Dunphy in Afghanistan, who'd given him his marching orders back to the States. But over the years he'd met with and gotten occasional calls from General Turnbull, checking in on him.

"Why am I here, Jack?" he said finally.

"Always on, aren't you, Trav? Can't rest for a second. Guess that's what makes you one of my most valuable assets." He paused. "Two reasons: first, to impress upon you the seriousness of this assignment—"

"I always take family seriously, sir," Travis interrupted, frowning.

Turnbull held up his hand. "Second, to suggest that this time we preempt the threat."

"What, like find out where the threat's coming from and neutralize it before it happens?"

"No, I mean carry out the threat before whoever's planning it does."

Travis stared at him, mouth agape. The idea was insane. "Are you joking, sir?"

"Hear me out," the general said.

CHAPTER 6

I stopped in the restroom to wash my hands and face and tamp down the most stubborn of the cowlicks, then hustled out.

By now you probably think I'm the worst kind of slacker—a trust-fund baby, spoiled rotten. I prefer to think of myself as having lacked direction, purpose. Maybe the call from Bigsby was just the thing I had needed, a swift kick in the pants to move me off what had been a stationary bike—lots of pedaling that had taken me nowhere.

I got on my real bike—I don't own a car since the trust fund only paid for education and basic living expenses—and pedaled back to the cramped efficiency apartment I lived in off campus. After changing into slacks, a dress shirt, and tie in record time, I locked up, got back on my bike, and rode several blocks to a bus stop close to campus. Fortunately, I didn't wait long before a bus arrived. I hefted the bike onto the rack in front and boarded, feeding most of my remaining cash into the fare box. If Bigsby wasn't pulling a late April Fools' joke, I'd have to stretch the few remaining funds I had until I actually started earning money.

The trip across the lake to one of the east side's more exclusive suburban enclaves took half an hour, which meant I had about twelve minutes to ride the remaining three miles and find the address. Eleven minutes later, I pulled up in front of an iron gate a little winded and slightly damp. An intercom and magnetic strip key box were affixed to a post on one side. I pushed the intercom button. A moment later a voice answered—the same woman who'd spoken to me on the phone.

"Who is it, please?"

"Oliver Moncrief," I said. "I have an appointment for an interview."

"Go straight to the main house," she said. "Park anywhere."

The main house?

With a click and a buzz, the massive gate rolled back, pulled on rollers by a chain. I walked the bike through, got on, and coasted down a long drive, first passing a tennis court and then what I supposed must be a guesthouse, though it looked as if it could accommodate two or three large families. Finally, a six-bay garage appeared just before the pavement ended in a large circle. At the top of the circle a porte cochere extended out over the drive from a structure that made the house my grandparents Donald and Edith had lived in down in Florida look like a shack.

I leaned the bike against a stone pillar flanking the steps up to the porch and went up to the front door, a monstrous slab of wood that looked as imposing as a bank vault door. Before I could push the doorbell, the door swung inward, revealing a petite, mousy-haired woman old enough to be my aunt. She looked more foreboding—and harder to get past—than the door. She looked me over, her eyes taking a hike from my tousled hair to the scuffed running shoes I'd worn instead of loafers in deference to practicality.

If ever someone could do a strip search by simply staring, she'd be the first. I was about to suggest the TSA might be very interested in talking to her about replacing their scanners at airport security when she offered a faint smile and put her hand out.

"Mr. Moncrief, won't you come in, please? My name is Alice. Alice Pemberton."

"Call me Oliver, please."

Anything but Ollie.

I shook her hand—she had a firm grip—and stepped inside a foyer that was two stories tall and tiled in Italian travertine marble. I recognized it thanks to an art history class—the travertine marble part, at least. The Italian part I deduced, since that's where a ton of the stuff comes from, and a guess that whoever built the house wouldn't settle for less than "the best." Don't ever let anyone tell you that you don't learn anything in college. A sweeping, curved staircase in warm cherry wood rose up to the floor above.

She looked past me, then turned to me with a puzzled look.

"Where is your car?" she said.

"I don't have one. I biked and bussed."

For a moment her brow furrowed in annoyance, but she shrugged it off and closed the door.

The entry opened out into a three-story great room with floor-to-ceiling windows that looked out onto the lake and the mountains beyond. Not easily impressed or taken to using words like *breathtaking*, even I have to admit the view made me forget to breathe for a moment. The room was tastefully furnished in modern pieces with clean lines, nothing garish or foo-foo. My entire living quarters could easily have fit into one of the room's sitting areas.

Alice led me down a long hallway filled with framed black-and-white photographs and colorful paintings and past a huge kitchen with so much stainless-steel-and-white cabinetry it looked like a hospital operating theater. Alice stopped at the doorway to a small room just beyond it and gestured inside.

"Please, have a seat."

The room was laid out like an office, with a desk, filing cabinets, a bookcase on one wall, and two chairs. I took the chair closest to the wall and perched on the edge of the seat as Alice rounded the desk and sat across from me.

"Did you bring a résumé with you?" she said.

"It didn't seem appropriate. I have nothing to put on one."

"You really have no work experience at all?"

"I worked in one of the campus dining rooms for a semester. I don't think I'm suited for a career in foodservice. But I was a TA in my master's degree program. It was a requirement."

"Teacher's assistant?" she sighed. "Well, that's something. Quite a lot, actually."

"I can give you names of several professors who can serve as references. Do you want to see my transcripts?"

"No, that's fine, Oliver. We will, of course, conduct a thorough background check before we offer you the position—if we decide to, that is. Since you can't tell me about your previous jobs, tell me about yourself. Are you from the area?"

I gave her the abbreviated version of my life, skipping all the family history, and answered a bevy of questions as honestly and enthusiastically as I could. She stumped me with one about what I want to be when I grow up. I think that's why I'd been a professional student for so long—not because I didn't want to grow up, but because I didn't know what I wanted to be. Alice looked at me for a very long minute before she nodded her head.

"Barring any criminal activity or other unsavory behavior turned up by the background check, I think you'll do," she said.

"I'm sorry, but I missed the part where you described the position," I said. "What, exactly, will I be doing?"

"I guess that's a fair question." She paused, as if trying to figure out what to say. "There's a young lady in this house who was ill for some time. She's a student, like you, and she's about to return to school for the first time in a year. She needs a personal assistant who can help her organize her schoolwork, take notes in class, serve as her secretary and type her papers, tutor her if necessary, and in general act as her escort and companion. You'll be responsible for getting her to and from school. We'll have to add you to the insurance policy as a driver and let you use one of our cars." She scribbled a note to herself. "And you'll take her wherever else she needs to go—errands, shopping, extracurricular activities, to visit friends, etcetera. Do those duties sound as though they're within your abilities, Oliver?"

"I think so, ma'am."

What she was describing sounded like a gofer to a spoiled little rich b___ (rhymes with "itch")—excuse me, *girl*. But slackers can't be choosers. And how hard could it be, really?

"Shouldn't I meet the person for whom I'll be working?" I said.

"That's not necessary. The decision isn't hers to make. It's mine." She paused "She's already observed most of this interview, anyway."

Alice half turned and waved up at the corner of the room. Like a wart, a small, dark Plexiglas dome protruded from the flat ceiling, no doubt concealing a video camera.

"Wow," was all I could think of to say. "So, you'll call me . . . ?"

"In a few days," Alice said. "When we've completed the background check."

"So, I guess that's it, then. I'll wait to hear from you."

Alice rose and came around the desk. "I think this will work out nicely." Her eyes trod all over me in hiking boots again. "Yes, I think you'll be just the ticket."

Two days later, Alice Pemberton called and offered me the job at a ridiculously low starting hourly wage. But she indicated that if things worked out, I'd be put on salary. She told me to come back to the house the next day at an hour when normally the only thing I see is the back of my eyelids.

I showed up at the appointed time, and Alice escorted me to the capacious kitchen. She sat me down in a breakfast nook and offered me a choice of eggs or pancakes. A large Latina woman in a white apron stood at the stove and nodded, a wide smile on her face, encouraging me to order. I asked for eggs, sunny-side up.

"You wan' choreee-zo with that?" the woman asked in heavily accented English.

"Sure," I said. "Why not?"

"This is Rosalita," Alice said. "Rosalita, meet Oliver."

Rosalita beamed even more and nodded, letting loose a stream of Spanish far too rapid for my limited linguistic skills to keep up. I smiled and nodded back, trying to be gracious.

As I sat down, it occurred to me that I knew very little about the person I'd been hired to assist except that she was female and a student. I didn't know if she was fat or thin, smart or dumb, a princess or a witch. I didn't even know what Alice's relationship was to the mystery woman. They could have been mother and daughter, but I got the distinct impression that Alice wasn't married and never had been.

"Miss Pemberton," I said. "Is it Miss or Missus?"

"Alice will be fine, since you may be with us for a while."

"Alice, then. I wondered if you could tell me more about the person I'll be assisting. It could help me prepare how I approach both her and the manner in which I assist her."

"I want you to keep a open mind, Oliver. Your client will tell you as much or as little as she wishes about herself."

She must have seen the look on my face because she added quickly, "Don't worry. I think you'll get along just fine. And given your educational background, you should have no problems with your duties."

Rosalita brought over a steaming plate of huevos rancheros on a warm tortilla, with a side of chorizo. She set it down in front of me and stood, waiting until I'd taken a bite, arms folded across her ample chest. Impressive biceps bulged from her short-sleeved white cook's blouse. She looked the part of Rosa, but I was having trouble with the "lita" part. Fortunately, I'm a big fan of Mexican food and spicy food in general. She looked momentarily disappointed when smoke didn't come out of my ears, but lit up when she saw sweat break out on my forehead and a smile on my burning lips.

"*¿Es bueno?*"

"*Muy bueno*," I said. "*Muchas gracias.*"

"*De nada.*"

She walked back to the stove, singing in a soft voice.

"Rosalita likes to have fun at our expense sometimes," Alice said, eyeing my red face. "You can ask for something different if that's not to your liking."

"It's good," I said. "Spicy. It'll wake me up faster than coffee."

Alice turned her head toward the door, and I caught the sound of footsteps approaching. I swiveled in my seat. A short, older Japanese man in khakis and a work shirt escorted a young woman on his arm. A girl, really. She couldn't have been more than eighteen, and she was drop-dead gorgeous. Long, black hair framed an oval face with a straight, upturned nose, wide mouth, and eyes the color of crystal-clear, azure water off a Bahamian beach.

"Ah, there you are," Alice said. "Guess who's here?"

"Good morning," I said, jumping to my feet.

With a small cry, the girl wrested free of her escort and fled back the way she'd come, arms waving in front of her as if feeling her way. I frowned, wondering if I had chorizo stuck in my teeth. What I'd seen slowly registered in my awestruck brain. The girl who'd just freaked out on me wasn't tripping on the way I looked.

"She's blind," I said to no one in particular.

"Very observant, Oliver," Alice said.

I faced her. "You hired me to be her guide dog?"

CHAPTER 7

Tess was horrified. She stumbled down the hallway, heard her flat heels hit the hard stone of the entry, and madly waved her hands in front of her until she found the wall that would lead her to the foot of the stairs. She raced up as fast as she dared, grasping the banister, slipping once and barking her shin on the edge of a stair. Sobbing, she reached the top and almost fell into the wall across the hall. Placing one hand in front of the other, she made her way down the hallway, counting doors as she went, tears running down her face. Finally, she reached the safety of her bedroom—a place where she knew every square inch. Even so, after a few faltering steps she put her hands out to feel for the soft duvet on her bed before throwing herself on top in frustration. In the distance, she heard Alice calling her from downstairs.

"Tess Barrett, you get down here for breakfast right now! You don't want to be late on your first day back!"

What difference could it make?

Tess was already a year late for school. The accident had caused her to miss the last few months of her junior year and most of her senior year. Technically, she *was* a senior. Once Alice had seen Tess accept Yoshi's gentle instruction, Alice had also stepped in as Tess's tutor, and had homeschooled her, riding Tess hard so that she passed equivalency tests for junior year and kept up with her classmates throughout senior year.

As much as she sometimes resented Alice, Tess had to grudgingly admit that Alice's cajoling and her unrelenting focus on Tess and her studies had given Tess the impetus she needed to keep going. Tess had found some of her former drive to excel. With Alice's help she'd even sent applications to several universities, including Brown, Stanford, Pepperdine, USC, and Cal Poly—where her parents had met. To her surprise, USC had turned her down, but she'd received her first acceptance letter from Brown. She hadn't heard from the others yet. Stanford was her first choice, but she liked Brown.

But a condition of attending college was proving that she could physically navigate school again in her condition. So, she was going back for the last trimester so she wouldn't miss the experiences of a high school senior, like the prom she hadn't attended junior year, and all the end-of-year senior traditions... So, fine. Now she'd be the same age as kids in her class instead of being the youngest. She'd been gone for a *year*. She dreaded the awkward looks, the stilted, forced conversations with the people who'd left her behind, both friends and enemies. And she was even more stressed about having to start over as the new kid again. She'd already done that, and had the scars to prove it.

Worse, she'd just made a fool of herself. This guy Alice had hired must think she was a complete basket case.

Soft footsteps padded into the room, followed by the faint scents of wisteria and green tea. Tess lifted her head and wiped her eyes with the back of her hand.

"Oh, god, Yoshi. I'm such a mess," she said.

"You frightened, missy," he said. "Is no shame in knowing fear, only shame in hiding from it. You must face your fear."

"You make it sound so easy. Try being blind for a while." The words tasted bitter in her mouth.

"We are all blind in our own fashion," he said softly.

"You? What are you afraid of?"

"Many things, missy. But I choose not to give in, not to show my fear. Now, come. We try again."

"Do I have to, Yoshi? Can't I go tomorrow? I just want to crawl back into bed."

"No, today a good day for school. And very handsome boy come all this way to take you there. You don't want to disappoint him, no?"

"He's taking me to school because we're paying him to. It's not like some huge sacrifice for this guy." She paused. "You think he's good-looking? He's not, like, a nerd, is he?"

"I not have a chance to know him yet, missy. But Alice not let just anyone have job."

Tess sighed. "Guess you're right. He can't be a complete loser."

He'd sounded nice, too, in his interview with Alice, Tess recalled. But that didn't mean she had to like him. Alice was forcing this on her—both going back to school and taking a chaperone with her. She sighed and let Yoshi take her hand, steadying herself as she climbed off the bed. She let him lead her downstairs once more. Halfway to the kitchen, she stopped and tugged at Yoshi's sleeve.

"Do I look okay?" she whispered.

A year earlier, she'd obsessed about her appearance. It had taken her an hour to apply makeup and do her hair before school. The cupboards in her bathroom had been full of cosmetics and skin care products. Her collection of lip gloss rivaled the displays at some department stores—drawers lined with scores of colors from dozens of brands. Now it didn't seem so important.

"You look fine," Yoshi reassured her.

"Okay, let's go."

Tess straightened and held her head high as Yoshi guided her the rest of the way to the kitchen.

"Ah, good," Alice said. "You're here. Don't dawdle now. Tell Rosa what you'd like for breakfast."

Tess turned toward the sound of a pan banging on the stove. "Something I can eat with my hands, Rosalita, *por favor*. A breakfast burrito, maybe?"

"Si, si. Un momento."

"Thank you."

Tess faced the spot where Alice's voice had come from and stuck her hand out a little to the left. She was angry with Alice for pushing her into this, but at least she could be polite.

"You must be Oliver," she said.

She heard the scrape of a chair on the floor and felt a rush of air as someone hurriedly stepped in front of her. She smelled soap and just a touch of something astringent. Not sweat, exactly, but perspiration, and definitely masculine. A warm hand clasped hers, dry, not moist, to her surprise.

"It's a pleasure to meet you," a male voice said. "I've heard practically nothing about you."

The voice had nice timbre, pitched somewhere between a tenor and a baritone. Deep, but still youthful. And apparently the man behind it had a sense of humor. She bit back a smile.

"You'll discover, if we don't scare you away, that we're full of secrets," she said. "I'm Tess, by the way. I imagine that's one of the secrets Alice managed to hide from you."

She heard him laugh, and the sound made her relax. It might be nice to have a guy around to talk to again. Besides Yoshi, that was. Someone closer to her own age. It had been a while—not since before the accident, she realized. But she remained cautious. She didn't know this guy.

A hand clasped her arm above the elbow.

"Would you like to sit down?" Oliver said.

"Yes, thank you."

She let him guide her to the table and heard a chair being pulled away from it. The hand applied just the slightest pressure on the inside of her arm, so she took a step to her left. Almost immediately she felt the edge of the chair gently nudge the backs of her knees. She lowered herself onto the seat, and the chair slid under her. Her father had done that for her mother. He'd opened doors for her mother, too, and her mother had had perfectly good vision. From the way she'd been seated Tess knew that Oliver must have been raised learning the same sorts of manners.

"So, Tess," Oliver said, sounding awkward, "Alice did tell me you're going back to school. College?"

Tess laughed nervously. "I wish. No, high school."

"Really? You look old enough. Oh, that didn't come out right, did it? I meant that you'd fit right in with all the other students on campus."

"No, I'm a senior, but . . ."

"You took some time off," Oliver finished for her.

"Yeah, I guess you might say that."

"So, are you ready to go back?"

"I don't know," Tess said. She squirmed in her chair. "Are you?"

"Ready to go back?" Oliver sounded surprised. "To high school? It will be like going back, won't it? Frankly, I kind of wish I'd seen the last of high school."

He sounded so mournful that Tess couldn't help a laugh this time. "What? You weren't one of the cool kids?"

"Nope. But I wasn't one of the geeks who got picked on, either. I guess I was pretty average."

"Average doesn't cut it in my school," Tess said, dread creeping into the edges of her consciousness again.

"You look like you're far from average, Tess."

Tess felt her face grow warm and wondered how much it showed. "What would you know? You don't even know me."

"I'm sorry," he said quietly. "You're right. For all I know you could be a dumb blonde. You're obviously not. Blonde, that is."

"No, *you* were right, Oliver," Alice said. "Tess is far from average—except when it comes to manners sometimes."

Tess's ears burned now, and she was sure she must have turned bright red from embarrassment and anger.

"*Aquí está tu burrito, señorita,*" Rosalita said, interrupting just in time.

Tess heard the soft thud of a plate being set on the table in front of her.

"*Gracias*, Rosa."

She reached for her napkin, found it with her fingers, and spread it on her lap. Then carefully feeling the outline of the plate with both hands, she moved her fingers in until they touched the burrito. She grasped it in both hands and brought it to her mouth. Alice and Rosa were used to seeing her make a mess of her meals, but she suddenly felt self-conscious in front of the stranger at the table. She realized she was too hungry to care and took a big bite. As usual, Rosa's cooking was amazing. She'd mixed scrambled eggs, chorizo, sautéed onion, fresh cilantro, diced jalapeño, *queso blanco*, and a touch of cumin and rolled them up in a warm, soft flour tortilla.

"*Mmmf,*" she said with her mouth full. "Did you get something to eat, Oliver? You should try this. It's delicious."

"Thanks, but Rosa already made me breakfast."

"Okay, Tess," Alice interrupted, "it's almost time to head for school. Finish your breakfast. You don't want to be late. Oliver, I've taken the liberty of preparing directions for you, and there's a GPS device in the car you'll be driving in case you take a wrong turn. Here's a class schedule with a map of the campus. Tess, I've got your bag ready with all the books and supplies your teachers say you need. Do you want to carry it, or shall I give it to Oliver?"

"OMG, Alice, it's the pink one, right? I think I better take it. I doubt it goes with whatever Oliver's wearing."

"I suppose you have a point. Oliver, you may want to bring of bag of your own next time so you can help with a few of those books. After all, Tess won't need them as much as you will."

"I don't—" Oliver said.

"Well, *I* certainly can't read them," Tess interrupted. "They're so you can follow along with the work I'm doing, and make sure I understand my assignments. You know, we 'dumb blondes' have trouble with that sort of thing."

CHAPTER 8

One year earlier...

"I'll give you a team," the general said.

Travis forced his mind to pay attention, still shocked by the enormity of what Turnbull had suggested.

"They'll have to be off the books, of course," the general continued, "but I'll make sure they're all former SF or SOG. We can't let any of this be traced back."

"SOG, sir? Can we trust those guys?"

The Special Operations Group was the CIA's covert military operations arm. Almost all of its operatives were former Army Special Forces soldiers. But Travis was convinced the CIA played head games with its people. After meeting a few of the guys from SOG in Afghanistan, he understood why its agents were called "spooks." They were like ghosts, but not just because they were invisible. They also were a little scary. Really intense, and not in a good way. It seemed they were in it only for the thrills, and had lost sight of the big picture—duty and country.

"Don't worry, I'll make sure everyone on your team is properly vetted," Turnbull said. "But it's important we don't take anyone currently active in the service. As of today, Travis, you're officially out of the army. Early retirement, sabbatical—I don't care what we call it, but if this is going to work, you can't be one of us anymore."

"What about resources? I'll need equipment as well as men."

"James has agreed to pay for security, so I imagine you'll have an unlimited budget even though it's coming out of his own pocket, not the company's."

Travis grimaced. Knowing James, the budget might be unlimited, but it would come with all sorts of questions and maybe even a few strings attached. He sighed.

"I understand the assignment, sir," he said, "and even if I'm no longer in the army you know I'll do whatever you order me to. But can I think about this idea of yours for a while before making a commitment?"

Turnbull nodded. "Of course, Travis. But don't take too long. We don't know how imminent this threat is. We could be talking weeks, but possibly only days."

"I'll give you an answer as soon as I can, sir."

The general inclined his head again. Without even looking at his watch, he said, "Better get moving, captain. You have a flight to catch. Sorry it isn't first class this time."

Turnbull stood and extended his hand. Travis met his grip, then stepped back and saluted. After the general acknowledged it with his own, Travis turned a crisp about-face and marched out of the hangar without looking back.

The flight from Andrews AFB outside Washington, DC, to Joint Base Lewis-McChord in Washington State gave Travis a lot of time to think. The general had been right—the flight was far from first class. He boarded a noisy C-17 Globemaster III, a transport jet even larger and faster than the turboprop he'd flown out of Afghanistan. Filled with a load of soldiers returning home from tours in Iraq, the plane was noisy in more ways than one. On almost every face Travis saw an expression of relief with a little incredulity thrown in, as if they couldn't believe they'd been lucky enough to walk away from the war alive and unscathed.

Support had filled the cargo bay with rows of seats, five abreast down the center of the plane and a row of jump seats on each side. The plane had no windows, and didn't offer an in-flight movie. The middle rows of seats looked moderately comfortable, but Travis had been assigned one of the jump seats. As soon as he sat down, he could tell that his butt would hurt within an hour. A master sergeant on one side faced him.

"Looks like we're stuck with other for the next five hours, sir," he said. He put out his hand. "Jones. Master Sergeant Hal Jones."

"Barrett," Travis said, shaking his hand. "These your soldiers?"

"Some of them. Got most of a company here. A few didn't make it."

"Where were you stationed?"

"Diyala Province, north of Baghdad."

"Stryker brigade?"

"Yes, sir. How about yourself?"

"I'm just hitching a ride, sergeant. I was in Afghanistan and got reassigned."

Travis made polite conversation with the sergeant for a while, but the enlisted officer quickly got the picture that Travis had a lot on his mind and desired a little solitude.

General Turnbull had given Travis the perfect opportunity to alter the course of events. If Travis could pull off this mission, it would literally be a game-changer. That's what it was, of course, all of it. A game. A bunch of overgrown kids—boys in men's bodies mostly, to be honest—in a map room somewhere, surrounded by computers, applying game theory to outmaneuver their opponents. They used people like Travis as pawns in the game, expendable pieces, moving them around the board at whim.

The real irony, Travis knew, was that the biggest gamer of them all, the game-theory genius, was a pacifist at heart. A man who abhorred war. James didn't understand war's necessity, didn't get why countries, religious factions, or ethnic groups couldn't solve their differences by playing an online video game. Sometimes you could bring those disparate groups to the table and hammer out an agreement. That wasn't the point. Travis knew that the aspirations and desires of individuals—greed, power, lust—usually outweighed the minor, or even major, differences of the groups they represented. And sometimes the cause was plain evil, pure and simple. Travis firmly believed evil existed in the world. He'd seen too many horrors not to.

Maybe, just maybe, though, this was Travis's chance to change the game. He'd have to be extremely careful. James wasn't stupid, and if he got even a whiff that something wasn't right, the whole thing could blow up in Travis's face. But if Travis played his cards right, he could take over the whole project, maybe even more, and flush out the threat at the same time. He'd love to see the look on James's face if he pulled it off. But if he succeeded, James would be out of the picture. Travis went through the pros and cons again.

He came to a decision.

He started to plan, making mental lists of what he'd need.

A few hours later, the big plane touched down at McChord AFB just south of Tacoma. He'd been traveling for more than twenty-six hours, but his watch said he'd left only about fourteen hours ago due to all the time zones he'd crossed. Waiting until all the other soldiers had deplaned, he shouldered his duffel and filed out after them.

Inside, he asked where he could find a car rental agency and was told there was one at the post exchange, or PX, over at Fort Lewis. Travis found it curious that army soldiers served on "posts," but sailors and airmen served on "bases." The combined army and air force operations at Fort Lewis and McChord AFB were also called a "base," though a joint one. He found a map of the base, pinpointed the building that housed the rental agency, went outside, and started walking.

A cold spring rain beat down on his head. Travis turned up the collar of his army combat uniform and tugged his green beret forward a little so the rain wouldn't drip in his eyes. He longed for his patrol cap. Travis hadn't walked more than a few hundred yards when a car pulled up next to him. He ignored it, but the passenger window rolled down and a voice called out.

"Captain Barrett!"

Travis turned to see the sergeant from the plane leaning out the window. A pretty blonde woman sat in the driver's seat.

"Hey, sergeant."

"Where you headed, captain?"

"Over to the PX to rent a car."

"Get in. We'll give you a ride."

"You just got home. I'm sure your wife has other plans."

The blonde leaned over the seat. "Not at all. It's the least we can do. It's on our way."

"Well, if you're sure it's no imposition."

Jones turned around and opened the back door. "You heard the lady, captain. Get in out of that rain."

Travis threw his duffel on the backseat and climbed in after it. He stared out the window on the way across the base, amazed by the activity, the constant motion and noise. Vehicles and planes traveled in every direction. The only movement in the mountains of Afghanistan had been goats and sheep, the occasional Taliban patrol on horseback in the distance, and sometimes a vehicle on the dirt road. Most of the locals were far too poor to own cars.

The sergeant's wife pulled up in front of a huge building and stopped. Travis got out and thanked them profusely for the ride.

They seemed almost embarrassed by his gratitude, so he reined in his emotions and turned away with a wave. Inside, he found the rental counter and filled out the paperwork for a compact. He wouldn't need much more than that to get around. He didn't plan on keeping it long. In a few days, he'd exchange it for something more utilitarian for his new "assignment." He got a map and directions along with his keys, and went out to find his car.

As he drove off the base, he wondered what it would be like to be a civilian again. On one hand, he'd had tremendous freedom in the army to perform his job as he saw fit. Though for the most part that had meant sleeping on dirt floors in huts without running water and cooking over an open fire for the past six years. The modernity all around him was a bit of a shock. The freeway was clogged with commuters driving personal vehicles, wasting gas and fouling the air. Everywhere he turned people were plugged into communications devices, talking or texting on cell phones, or networking on tablet computers. It was as if the world had passed him by.

Not that he hadn't had the world's best and coolest technology available to him in the Stans, courtesy of Uncle Sam and James's company. Communications, weaponry, navigation— all were made possible by the latest in hi-tech gear. They could see at night with infrared goggles, shoot at unseen targets with smart weapons, narrow down locations to one square foot with GPS devices, find and disarm IEDs with ground-penetrating radar, and listen in on the enemy with cell phone interception equipment and decryption software. James had made it possible for Travis to do his job without getting anywhere near the enemy. But here, back in the States, all that gadgetry seemed to isolate people more than connect them.

He drove north, past Sea-Tac airport, along the shore of Lake Washington, admiring the beautiful terrain. Water glittered on one side, forested hills rose up on the other toward mountains in the distance. He'd never been to that part of the world, but he could see why James had been convinced to move up there from California. While California held its own appeal, with wildly different topography and natural beauty throughout the state, Travis couldn't deny that Seattle was pretty, even in the rain.

After twenty minutes, he exited the freeway and meandered through a suburban neighborhood that felt almost rural. The area was hilly and heavily wooded, so the houses were hard to see from the road and unobtrusive. The curvy road wound between steep hillsides and deep ravines, both dense with towering trees and thick undergrowth, in spots blotting out the sun. He finally found the drive that led down toward the water. A house number engraved on a granite boulder at the edge of the drive matched the address he'd committed to memory.

Travis slowed and turned in, stopping momentarily. The property wasn't fenced and the drive had no gate, making the house below about as secure as a box of tissues. That would be among the first things Travis changed. He eased down the pitched drive, keeping his foot on the brake, passing a tennis court and a small guesthouse surrounded by trees on the way down toward the lake. He pulled up under the porte cochere at the front door to the main house. Leaving his duffel in the car, he went up the steps and rang the bell.

Travis waited nearly a minute. As he reached for the bell again, the door suddenly opened, revealing a beautiful young woman. Travis nearly bit his lip to keep from sucking in his breath with a startled gasp. His niece had grown so much since he'd last seen her that he'd almost mistaken her for his sister-in-law Sally.

The girl gave him a guarded smile. "Can I help you?"

"Is your dad home?" Travis said.

Before the girl could reply, a man's voice called out behind her, "Who is it, honey?"

"Someone for you, Dad."

The girl turned and swung the door open, and James stepped into view.

"Hello, big brother," Travis said.

James's mouth dropped open in surprise, then a big smile spread across his face.

"Tess," he said to the girl, "meet your Uncle Travis."

CHAPTER 9

The ride Alice gave me to chauffeur Tess to school was about as sweet as they get—a BMW 6 Series convertible in titanium silver. The drive wasn't as pleasant as it should have been in a piece of machinery like that since Tess was as sour as the car was sweet. She hated me. Well, she didn't know me well enough to hate me, but she hated the idea of me. And I had to admit that seeing-eye dog wasn't quite what I'd had in mind when I signed on for the position. But I'd only been on the job for an hour, so I figured I'd at least give it a chance. Besides, I still got chills thinking about the call from Bigsby. I needed the money.

Tess sat silently in the passenger seat. I thought she was staring out the window, but then I remembered that she couldn't see. It would take some getting used to; she didn't look blind. I mean, she didn't have that weird visor that was supposed to look like some hi-tech X-ray specs that the blind guy on *Star Trek* wore. What's his name—Geordi. She didn't wear shades to hide atrophied eyes like Stevie Wonder. In fact, she had some of the most gorgeous eyes I'd ever seen. Not that I was swayed by her looks.

I could get used to the silence, too. A mopey, quiet teenager seemed better than a rebellious, loud one. If I was going to spend a lot of time with her, though, it would help to be on speaking terms. I flipped on the charm switch.

"Okay," I said, "here's one for you. How many elephants will fit into a Mini?"

"What?" She turned her head.

"How many elephants will fit into a Mini?"

"I don't know."

"Four. Two in front, two in back."

"Oka-a-a-y."

"How many giraffes will fit into a Mini?"

"How many giraffes?"

"None. It's full of elephants."

Silence.

I tried again. "How do you know there are two elephants in your refrigerator?"

"I bet you're going to tell me," she said in a way that indicated she really didn't care.

"You can hear giggling when the light goes out," I said. I motored on without waiting for a reaction. "How do you know there are *three* elephants in your refrigerator?"

"I'll bite. How?"

"You can't close the door."

I heard a snort that could have been suppressed laughter and risked a glance at her. She'd turned her head, but I thought I saw the corner of her mouth curl up just a skosh.

"How do you know there are *four* elephants in your refrigerator?" I said.

She sighed. "Oh, please. Not more elephants."

"There's an empty Mini parked outside."

She exhibited no reaction, but I think it took all of her self-control to maintain a poker face.

"Okay," I said, "last one. How can you tell when an elephant's sitting behind you?"

"Duh! Like everybody doesn't know the answer to that one," she said, her tone about as acidic as espresso. "When you smell the peanuts on its breath."

"No, actually. I was going to say, 'When everyone ignores it.'"

"That's random."

"I was trying to be subtle."

"What does *that* mean?"

"The elephant in the room—or the car in this case—is the fact that you're blind. Want to tell me how it happened?"

"Not really." She folded her arms and leaned back in the seat.

"I'm sure I can find out from Alice."

"A car accident, okay?"

"You don't want to talk about it. How come?"

She sat up and said vehemently, "Because . . ." But before she finished the thought she shook her head and slumped back in the seat. "Just because."

"How long ago was this?"

"I said I'm not going to talk about it."

"Hey, just trying to make conversation as long as we're stuck with each other."

"I'm not stuck with you."

"Until Alice says otherwise, I think you are."

She was silent for a moment, apparently absorbing the truth of my statement.

"Is that how you see this situation? You're stuck with me?"

"Let me rephrase it. I'm stuck with this situation because I need a job. I don't live in a ritzy house with rich parents."

"My parents are dead!" She burst into tears.

I'm not sure which took me aback more, the shock of her admission or the crying. I was just glad she couldn't see me trying to wrestle my size-twelve foot out of my mouth. Judging from how hot my face felt, I was sure I turned a bright shade of vermillion.

"Tess, I'm sorry. I didn't know."

But with the amount of time I'd spent in school I should have been smart enough to figure it out—the interview with the housekeeper, no sign of parents in the house. Though they could have been the type who were too busy with their own lives to bother meeting the latest household hire. Maybe I'd been parentless myself long enough that the absence of hers hadn't registered. At least I'd had Nana and Pop-Pop. And now I'd made her cry twice in the first hour on the job.

Her sobbing eased. She pressed the heels of her hands against her eyes and screwed them in tight. I rummaged around in the center console, found a travel pack of tissues, and managed to pull one out. I reached over and tickled her hand with it, keeping my eyes on the road. She tugged it out of my fingers.

"I really am sorry," I said. "I'm usually not this big a jerk. Could we maybe start over?"

She sniffed. "A little late for that, isn't it?"

I didn't have an answer for her. I focused on driving for the next few minutes and pulled into the high school lot about eight minutes early. All the visitors' parking spaces were filled, so I pulled into the handicap space.

"We're here," I said.

I got Tess's pink book bag out of the backseat and went around to open the passenger door for her. She swung her legs out of the car and extended a hand. I took it, helped her stand, and handed her the bag. She slung it over her shoulder. I closed the car door, took her elbow, and walked her across the drive to the walkway leading to the front entrance. I dug into my pocket for her class schedule.

"Okay, so your first class is—"

"I know what it is. I've been in school, just not *at* school."

"Right. Wait, you mean you've been homeschooled? Who's your tutor? Alice?"

"Alice and Yoshi."

"And Alice has been teaching you in the same order as the school schedule? English history block with Prescott first? Curb."

"What?"

I stepped over the curb onto the walkway, but Tess stubbed her toe and would have done a face-plant on the concrete if I hadn't tightened my grip on her arm and pulled her upright. Her momentum swung her in a semicircle and she crashed into me. I grabbed her other arm and held her steady. When she realized she was all right and standing toe to toe with me instead of lying on the ground, she turned pink and her pretty face twisted up in fury. She wrested one arm loose, stepped back, and took a swing at me, landing a fist hard on my arm.

"Ow!"

"What the heck is wrong with you?" she cried.

"I said 'curb.'"

"That's it? No warning? Just 'curb' and I'm supposed to get it?"

"Well, yeah. You just pick up your feet. Why don't you use a cane or a stick, anyway?"

"Why don't *you* use one? Then maybe you could find your way over a curb without leading me right into it."

We'd turned a small crowd of heads, but since class was about to start curious onlookers gaped for only a moment and kept moving.

"I don't use a white cane," she said, "because they take a lot of practice, and I haven't had the time yet. And even if I could use one, I wouldn't last long before I got laughed out of high school. Bad enough I have you."

"Kids are that mean?"

"What are you? Have you never been to high school?"

I was glad she couldn't see my reddening face, and I mumbled a reply. "Well, yeah, but I skipped a lot of it."

"What do you mean? How did you get into college if you skipped high school?"

"It's not important. So, high school kids aren't so nice."

"They're worse."

"Okay, so we should have talked about this. Developed a system. When we're two steps away from an obstacle, I'll tell you what it is. Like 'curb,' or 'stairs.' If it's stairs, I'll tell you how many. If it's a door, I'll tell you to stop until I open it."

"What about a hill or a slope?"

"We can add things as we go."

"Okay, I guess." She didn't sound convinced.

"Look, this is new to both of us, so we're going to have some trial and error, but I'm not going to let anything happen to you. And I'm your assistant, so you call the shots. If it's not working for you or you're uncomfortable, tell me and we'll figure something else out. Okay?"

She bit her lower lip. "All right."

"Then let's go, or else you'll be late for class."

She let me take her arm again, and we managed to get to her classroom without incident. But the day had only started—plenty of time for things to go from bad to worse.

CHAPTER 10

"Who are you?"

Tess recognized Mr. Prescott's voice even though she hadn't been in his class since freshman year. But it was his scent that immediately clinched his identity. He had a reputation in school for "going natural" and not using deodorant. Tess had always done her best to ignore it and sit as far away from him as she could. But the sharp-sweet odor seemed stronger now than ever, and wasn't as innocuous as she'd once thought. He sounded close enough to touch, and for a moment she thought he was speaking to her. She opened her mouth to remind him of her name, but before she could speak, Oliver answered him.

"My name's Oliver Moncrief, sir. I'm Tess's personal assistant."

"You can't just roam the halls, Oliver. You'll need a visitor's pass from the office. Maybe they can see about getting you a permanent ID badge."

"I'll get one right after class, between periods."

"No, you'll get one now."

Tess heard a muffled snicker from a few feet away. Then she felt someone lean in close, and she caught a whiff of Oliver's shampoo.

"I'll be right back," he said in her ear. "Sit tight."

There wasn't much else she could do, so she faced forward and listened to the general rowdiness of students talking loudly as they shuffled through the room and took their seats, chairs scraping on the floor and books thudding onto desktops. Papers crinkled as students readied their books and notepads. Tess heard her name whispered, and caught fragments of conversation that made her flush with embarrassment. She heard scuffled footsteps close by.

"You're Tess Barrett," a girl's voice said, barely above a whisper. "I'm Tamara. Tamara Wilkinson. You probably don't remember me, but I was in your biology class last year."

"Hi," Tess said quietly.

She racked her brain and finally put a face to the name. Mousy girl a year behind her, really shy. Tess's friends had made fun of her, and though Tess herself hadn't joined in, she'd laughed at some of the mean comments. Until Tamara had saved her butt on a lab project they'd been assigned to as partners. It had been a DNA experiment, and while it should have been easy for Tess, she'd slacked off when studying the section. When it had come time to do the project, Tess hadn't been prepared, but Tamara had been. She was whip-smart.

"Sorry to hear about your accident," Tamara said.

"Thank you." Tess steeled herself for the inevitable comment about her blindness, dreading the days and weeks of pity ahead. But Tamara surprised her.

"I never thanked you for giving me all the credit for that bio lab."

"You did all the work—you deserved the credit."

"Well, not *all* the work. But thanks. Well, I better go. Mr. Prescott wants to start."

Tess stopped her. "Tamara?"

"Yes?"

"Thanks for saying hello."

"Sure. No problem."

Tamara Wilkinson didn't exactly run in the same circles Tess did, but Tess wasn't all that sure who her friends were anymore. The nothingness that now surrounded her was frightening, especially knowing that anyone could walk up to her and do or say anything they wanted. She was nearly helpless to defend herself. She could no longer afford to be choosy when it came to friendships. She would have to welcome all comers.

Maybe she could establish a rep as a kind of Switzerland of high school relationships. Remain neutral. Refuse to take sides or spread gossip. The idea excited her until she thought about how hard it would be to convince Adrienne and Emily of her sincerity.

Then again, we're seniors now. Maybe they'd matured.

"Let's get started, class," Mr. Prescott said. "I hope you all finished *The Great Gatsby* over the weekend. Before we discuss it, I want to remind you that papers are due Friday. No excuses. Okay, when we left off last week, Nick was . . ."

Tess tried as hard as she could to concentrate on what Mr. Prescott was saying, but her thoughts kept straying. First, she kept replaying the morning's sequence of events in her mind. She couldn't decide whether Oliver was as big a jerk as he'd suggested, or if she'd been partly to blame. After all, he'd been trying to make conversation, and it was only natural that he'd be curious about her sightlessness.

I could have been a little nicer, maybe.

The other direction her thoughts led filled her with uncertainty about this whole experiment. Going back to school might not have been such a good idea. She knew the people around her were whispering to each other about her. She could feel their stares burning holes through her, stripping her naked. She realized she wasn't ready to come back, but now she didn't have much choice.

Tittering came from the front of the room, and Tess suddenly realized that Prescott had stopped talking. She heard Oliver murmuring, "Excuse me, excuse me," his voice getting closer.

Then he was next to her.

"You're in my seat," Oliver whispered.

"Get your own seat," a boy said. "I'm not moving."

"Take a seat, please," Mr. Prescott called. "We're wasting time."

"I'll be in back," Oliver whispered in Tess's ear. "I'll come get you after class."

She squirmed in her chair as he fumbled through her book bag looking for a notebook and a pencil. She wished she could glare at whoever was sitting in the seat next to her. She turned her face and scowled, but received no indication that it had its intended effect.

"Tess?"

Tess jerked her head to face forward. "Sorry?"

"You're familiar with the material, aren't you, Tess?" Mr. Prescott said.

"What was the question?"

"Come on, people, stop daydreaming," Mr. Prescott said. "What was the question? Anybody? Jeff?"

"Why did Nick react the way he did to Gatsby's death?" Jeff called out.

Tess squirmed again, feeling her face get hot. "I'm not sure."

She was furious with herself. Alice had gotten her an audio version of the book, but she hadn't listened to it yet.

"Come prepared, Tess," Mr. Prescott said. "No excuses. Jeff, you want to answer that?"

Tess bit back her anger. She wasn't sure whether it was directed at Mr. Prescott for not acknowledging her obvious disadvantage, or at herself for not doing her homework. Alice had spoken to each of her teachers about what material their classes were covering to make sure Tess was caught up before she went back. Tess wouldn't let it happen again. She hoped Oliver was taking good notes.

"Sorry about that," Oliver said after class. "The guy was being a jerk. Next time I'll find a chair and sit next to your desk."

She reached down and found her book bag, shouldered it, and stood up. Oliver took her arm and guided her down the row between the desks. She could tell when they transitioned from classroom to hallway by the increased volume of noise as students rushed from one class to the next. The din, coming from all sides, was almost painful. Oliver's pace was quick. She had to hurry to keep up, and the motion as his gentle pressure on her arm led them in a zigzag pattern was almost dizzying. Occasionally, someone jostled her shoulder or bumped her hip as they passed, but Oliver seemed to avoid outright collisions adeptly.

"How come you don't read braille?" he said, close to her ear.

Again she was struck by his scent—not strong, not heavy with cologne or deodorant, not musky, just clean. She shook her head and concentrated on the question.

"How come you don't read Mandarin?" she said.

"How do you know I don't?"

"Do you?"

"No. I read French, sort of. You're saying it's like learning another language."

"Well, it is. The symbols look nothing like letters in the alphabet, so it's not like tracing A, B, C with your fingers. And you have to have really sensitive touch. I don't."

"Do *you* read Mandarin?"

"As a matter of fact, yes. A little. My mother is—was—Chinese. She moved here when she was very little, but her parents made her learn to read the language as well as speak it. She taught me some characters."

"Stairs."

"What? Oh."

Tess almost stumbled, but remembered Oliver's code in time to step down.

"Eight," Oliver said.

Tess counted the remaining seven and found herself on level ground again. She heard Oliver muttering to himself, "Three-oh-four, three-oh-four."

"Down the three-hundred wing, second door on the left," she said.

Oliver nudged her gently to the right, and a few seconds later she felt him slow down.

"You're right," he said. "How'd you know?"

"I go to school here, duh. I know my way around."

"Okay, okay," he whispered. "Pipe down a little. People are staring. I'll find us seats."

He steered her to a chair behind a table and sat down next to her. She heard him pull things out of her book bag. The rustle of paper told her he'd opened both a book and a theme pad—the sounds were different.

"You can remember where all the classrooms are?" Oliver whispered.

She shrugged. "I can see it in my head. I just can't see it with my eyes."

"But after a year?"

Before she could stop it, a tear spilled from the corner of one eye. Tess quickly swiped at it with her fingers, hoping Oliver hadn't noticed. She didn't know how to explain it to him—all the memories, as clear as day. And now nothing.

"Can I tell you something?" she said.

"Of course."

"Promise not to laugh?"

"Promise," he said. "It's not in my job description. Alice would fire me."

She smiled and relaxed a little. He had a point; if he *was* a jerk, Tess could tell Alice.

"It's weird," she said, "my memories are more vivid now than before the accident. You know how memories usually fade with time? You can't remember who said what, or the clothes someone wore. Even people's faces start to fade after a while. You forget what they look like. The opposite is happening to me. I can re-create whole scenes in my mind and tell you exactly what people said, where they stood, what they wore. It's a little scary."

"Allo!" a voice called. "Bonjour, Tess! Bienvenue. Qui est ton ami?"

"Good morning," Tess said. "Is that you, Mrs. Villeneuve?"

"En français, s'il te plaît."

"Bonjour. C'est vous, Madame Villeneuve?"

"*Oui*, Tess, *c'est moi.*"

Tess was about to introduce Oliver when she heard his chair scrape on the floor and she felt him rise.

"Bonjour, madame," he said. "Je m'appelle Oliver Moncrief. Je suis l'aide pour Tess."

"Welcome, Oliver," Mrs. Villeneuve said, switching to English. "Tess, it's good to see you back. Okay, class, say hello to Tess and Oliver, and let's get started."

Tess heard a chorus of hellos, most of which sounded bored or indifferent, but a few of which sounded enthusiastic. Most of these kids had been sophomores when she was in this class last year, she reminded herself. A few might know who she was, but most probably didn't.

I can do this. It will work out somehow.

CHAPTER 11

One year earlier...

"It's the only way, Jimmy, and you know it," Travis said.

His older brother flinched at the use of the nickname he'd outgrown at ten. Travis didn't care. James would always be "Jimmy" to him, like it or not.

James had picked the study for this conversation. Bookshelves lined two walls, reaching to an eighteen-foot ceiling. A rolling ladder on a track provided access to books on the higher shelves. Windows overlooking the lake covered most of a third wall, and a fire glowed in a hearth set into the fourth wall. Big, comfortable leather chairs formed groupings in the corners, making it easy to get lost in a good book. Travis and James sat on two large beige couches that faced each other across a low coffee table in front of the fireplace. James's wife, Sally, stood with her back to the fire, spreading her hands behind her toward the flames to warm them.

"It's not the only way," James said quietly. "But I agree it's probably the most expedient, given the circumstances."

"It seems so . . . final," Sally said. "Isn't there a compromise?"

Travis had hoped to get a decision from James and work out the details with him alone, but James had insisted on Sally's presence. Travis couldn't blame him. The situation involved the entire family. Sally had a right to take part in the decision and the planning.

"I'm afraid if we don't resolve the issue once and for all, these people will always be a threat," Travis said.

"If not them, it'll be someone else," James said.

"That's the point," Travis said. "You can't spend your lives looking over your shoulders. We need to neutralize the situation, take away the motivation to target you."

"You can take me out of the equation; they'll still come after the firm."

"Not if they don't see any value in it." Travis paused. "You *are* the company. The soul of it, anyway. If you're not there, what good is it to anyone?"

"You know how much I hate this."

Travis nodded. "I know. I had to beg you to play GI Joe games when we were kids. Cowboys and Indians, cops and robbers . . . You never saw the point. Hard to believe you went on to create some of the bestselling video game shoot-'em-ups of all time."

James stared moodily into the fire. "Anyone could replicate what I've done."

"Then why hasn't anyone?" Travis peered at him. "Lots of people may be playing with this technology, Jimmy, but you're the only one who can make it work."

James shook his head. "It's only a matter of time."

"How much time?"

"I don't know." James shrugged. "Months. Years. Someone could make an announcement tomorrow."

Travis ticked off points on his fingers. "No one else has figured out the miniaturization. No one else has figured out the power source. No one's tried to synthesize scent since Smell-O-Vision in the 1960s, and that was a huge bust. And no one can write code like you; no one's even close to providing the kind of VR experience I had yesterday."

James looked puzzled. "Why? What happened yesterday?"

Travis told him about the mission in Afghanistan and what had happened during the test of the prototype avatar, the miniature helicopter.

"You lost it?" James said when Travis finished. He looked incredulous.

"In a manner of speaking," Travis said. "That's all you care about?"

"You know how much that cost?" James was turning red.

"Calm down, honey," Sally said. "I'm sure Travis didn't mean to lose it."

"Well, more like destroyed—not lost," Travis said.

"Oh, that makes me feel a whole lot better," James said.

Travis could have cut the sarcasm in his voice with a knife.

"We had to take out the terrorist cell before they got away. We called in a missile strike. I got the avatar out, but those bunker-busters send out a heck of a shockwave."

James rubbed his chin. "Well, at least it won't end up in the wrong hands. It was the only one we had."

He watched the flames dance in the fireplace. Travis followed his gaze, but was diverted by the concerned look on Sally's face.

"How much time do we have?" she said.

"Not much," Travis said. "You need to get your affairs in order, quickly."

She nodded, but the worry lines etched in her forehead didn't ease.

James tore his gaze from the flickering light. "What if the threat you mentioned materializes before we're ready?"

"Good question," Travis said. "Your security sucks. You're pinned between a hill and the water, and you've got no protection from the road above. If I were you, I'd build a wall around the property and gate the entrance. And I'd install bullet-resistant windows on the side facing the lake. But we don't want to tip our hand, so I'm going to bring in a team in the meantime. Don't worry; I'll make sure they blend in. You won't even know they're here."

"You're going to bring bodyguards into the house?" Sally said. "Is that necessary, James? We have Yoshi and Alice."

Travis shook his head. "Nothing so obvious. I'm all you need inside, anyway. We have to prevent them from getting this far, if possible. No, they won't be anywhere near the house."

"They're good?" James said.

"Not as good as me," Travis said. "I'll get the best men I can."

The blood drained from Sally's face. "What about Tess?"

Travis nodded. "I thought of that. They could use her to get to you, so I'll put a detail on her as well. Same deal; I'll make sure they stay out of sight, but they'll be close enough to make sure nothing happens to her. Okay?"

"You promise?"

"I can't promise anything, Sally. But I'll do my best. You're my family, too, remember?"

"I know," she said. "It's just—"

Michael W. Sherer

"She's your daughter. I get it. I don't blame you for worrying, but I know what I'm doing."

She and James didn't look convinced.

"If this plan works," Travis said, "you won't have to worry ever again."

Sally sighed. "I doubt that, but okay."

James nodded. "Tell us what you need, Trav. I'll find a way to expense it outside the company so no one knows what it's for."

"I'll start a list."

Movement across the room caught Travis's eye. He glanced at the door and saw Tess enter hesitantly.

"Dad?" she said. "Mom? Everything okay?"

Sally met Tess halfway to the door and wrapped her arms around her. "Of course, sweetie. Everything's fine."

"What are you guys talking about?" Tess said.

"Nothing much, kitten," James said, putting a smile on his face. "Your Uncle Travis has been regaling us with stories about his heroics in Afghanistan."

Tess looked doubtful, and Travis worried that she may have heard more than she let on. The last thing he needed was a teenager blabbing to all her friends. As far as Tess was concerned, he needed to appear to be a visiting uncle on leave from the army—nothing more.

Travis laughed. "About the most heroic thing going on in our camp, Tess, was milking goats without getting kicked in the head."

Sally turned and looked at him appraisingly, gratitude in her eyes. She put an arm around her daughter's shoulders.

"Travis, you must be starved after that long trip," she said. "Tess, why don't you help me put together some snacks to hold us over until dinner?"

Tess rolled her eyes and shrugged. "Okay, if I have to."

Travis grinned, but quickly turned away before Tess could see. James saw it and threw him a stern look. That only made Travis smile wider.

When Sally and Tess left the room, James rose from the couch and paced in front of the fire. He stopped and considered Travis.

"You really think this time is for real?" James said.

Travis nodded. "They want what's in your head, Jimmy. If they can't have that, they want you dead."

72

"That seems a bit extreme, don't you think?"

"Extremes are what we fight to keep in balance. I've seen kids younger than Tess strap on explosives, walk into a crowded bazaar, and blow themselves up. Doesn't get more extreme than that."

"It's not that I don't appreciate what you do, little brother," James said. "I just wish we didn't need people like you. No offense."

Travis shrugged. "None taken. Somebody's got to do it. Somebody has to clean up the world's messes. It's not something I *like* doing. Well, not the killing part of it, anyway. It's just something I happen to be good at. You happen to be very good at what you do, too. Face it, the world needs both of us."

James hunched over morosely, elbows on his knees. "I suppose." His face brightened. "I'm glad you're back, anyway. We worried about you."

"Thanks."

"What do you say we go find the ladies and get something to drink to go along with those snacks?"

"Sounds good." Travis got to his feet. "Oh, there's one other thing before we go. Watch what you say from now on. With all this glass, it would be awfully easy for someone on the lake with a listening device to eavesdrop on conversations inside the house."

James looked startled, which didn't surprise Travis. For the head of a hi-tech company and someone as smart as he was, James seemed incredibly naive. It had always been that way—James the carefree, trusting soul who wanted nothing more than a good ride on his skateboard or time on the computer, and Travis, the street-smart adrenaline junkie with a nose for adventure and trouble. Even when James had been a hacker and had broken into some of the most secure networks in the country, he'd done it on a lark, just to see if he could, not maliciously or for monetary gain. Most of the time it had seemed as if Travis was the older of the two brothers.

"I can have my tech crew install jamming equipment," James said helpfully. "I never had it put in because this is our home, Trav. I never saw the need for it. I don't conduct business here. You know that."

"No, don't bother. That might alert them that we suspect something. I'll take care of it. Just be careful." Travis paused. "We're on our own, Jimmy. I'm officially out of the army. I can't use the army's resources, and they won't back us up if something goes wrong."

"You'll make it work, Trav. I trust you."

That's what Travis was afraid of.

CHAPTER 12

Somehow, we made it through the first couple of classes. I felt like a fish out of water. I'd been a student most of my life, but I didn't remember high school being that hard—academically or socially—maybe because I'd been so much younger. I think I'd managed to keep my head down and stay below everyone's radar in high school. I hadn't pissed anyone off, but I hadn't made many friends, either. It had made me difficult to pigeonhole. I hadn't fit into any clique. Or else I'd simply forgotten any traumatic events I may have experienced. But it wasn't like I had to do the actual work now, or suffer the slings and arrows of teen bullying or sarcasm. All I had to do was make sure Tess was in the right class, on time, and take notes for her. The rest wasn't my problem—or so I thought.

Even Tess seemed to be warming up to me somewhat. At least she wasn't giving me the cold shoulder and a lot of attitude. She coped pretty well, considering. She wasn't shy about asking questions if she didn't understand something, and she seemed to have no qualms about participating in class discussions. Kids stared at first and whispered, making both Tess and me a little self-conscious. But Tess held her own so well that they soon forgot she had a disability.

It was too good to last.

Fourth period, I walked her down to the farthest wing of the school and looked for the classroom number listed on her schedule. Art class with a J. Robertson, according to the sheet of paper in my hand. I had a funny feeling as soon as we walked in, though, that someone had made a big mistake. I suppose all the cameras resting on the tables, one in front of each student, might have tipped me off.

A woman I took to be J. Robertson looked up from a desk at the front of the room as we came in.

"Tess!"

At the sound of the woman's voice Tess faltered in midstep and stopped. A cloud of apprehension darkened her face.

J. Robertson stood up, rounded the corner of the desk, and came to a stop in front of us. She eyed me up and down, craning her neck to see the top of my head since she was about the size of a garden gnome.

"I think there's been some mix-up," she said. "Are you sure you're supposed to be here?"

Tess looked confused, and it was obvious she hadn't figured out who was speaking to her even though the voice sounded familiar. I might have been able to save the situation from deteriorating further if I'd acknowledged the error and backed Tess out of the room. But before I could jump in, Tess piped up.

"Why shouldn't I be here?"

J. Robertson apparently hadn't been schooled in social diplomacy; she had all the tact of a Palestinian peace envoy armed with a rocket-propelled grenade launcher.

"Well, because you can't see, dear," she said in a loud voice. "This is photography class, after all."

The classroom erupted in laughter. Tess turned one way then the other, the terror on her face reminiscent of a fawn cornered by wolves. Her eyes brimmed with tears.

"Oliver?" Her voice quavered.

I took her arm firmly, and put my other arm around her shoulder.

"We'll go to the office and find out what happened," I told J. Robertson over my shoulder as I turned Tess around.

Tess buried her face in her hands and sobbed as I walked her out. An electronic chime signaled the beginning of the class period. The empty hallway suddenly grew as quiet as a church. Tess's shoulders heaved. Since I didn't know what else to do, I tried to put my other arm around her. She shoved me away.

"Are you a complete moron?" she said. Tears streamed down her face.

So much for warming up to me.

"What did *I* do?"

"Why did you take me in there?" she cried. "That was so humiliating."

"How was I supposed to know? The schedule Alice gave me says it was an art class."

"I thought you were this smart college guy. Couldn't you figure it out?"

"Hey, look, as soon as I saw everybody with cameras I knew we weren't supposed to be there, but the teacher opened her big mouth before I could get you out."

"What's next? PE class? Make me play dodgeball?"

"I'm sorry. What do you want from me?"

She sniffled and swiped at the corners of her eyes with her fingers. I lifted the book bag off her shoulder, set it on the floor, and pawed through it, knowing there must be a tissue in it somewhere. I pressed one into her hand, and she used it to dab at the tear tracks striping her cheeks.

"I suppose you think I'm a total bitch," she said.

"It's a lot to handle in one day." I paused. "They shouldn't have laughed at you."

She heaved a shuddery sigh. "It wasn't just that. Mrs. Robertson can be a real pain sometimes, and totally clueless, but she's a good teacher."

"So what *was* that all about?"

"Are there photographs hanging in the downstairs hall at my house?"

"Sure. I noticed them right off when I came for my interview. Nice stuff."

The collection of large, framed, black-and-white photos featured artful shots of both people and landscapes. I'd assumed the people—a man and a woman photographed together and individually—were her parents.

"Those are mine," she said quietly. "I asked Alice to take them down, but she doesn't listen to me."

"Why would you want her to do that? They're terrific."

The lighting, shading, and composition had made me think they'd been taken by a pro.

Her lip quivered. "Because I can't take pictures anymore! Photography was one thing that I was really good at. I even thought about making a career of it."

"What, like fashion photography?"

"No, photojournalism. Now that's all gone! I can't believe Alice didn't switch me out of photography class. I don't know what I'm going to do now."

77

"Why don't we walk up to your counselor's office and see what classes are available?"

"Right," she said, "like there might be an opening in a drawing and painting class."

"Hey, if you need an art credit, maybe you can take ceramics or art history."

"You're right. I'm sorry."

"So, are you okay?'

She sighed. "Yeah, let's go."

After we explained the problem, Tess's counselor thumbed back and forth through the pages of fine arts courses in the curriculum catalog, poring over the descriptions for five fruitless minutes, muttering "*tsk-tsk*" and "oh, dear." I flipped through a copy lying on her desk and pointed to a music appreciation class.

"Will that meet the art credit requirement?" I said.

The counselor blinked and leaned forward to read the course description. "Certainly. It's a lead-in to music theory."

"Don't I get a say in this?" Tess said.

"Sure, why not?" I said. "Tess, are you okay with listening to classical music for the rest of the semester?"

"Anything," she said, "would be better than photography."

"We might have to juggle your schedule," the counselor said, turning to the computer. "No, you're in luck. One of Mr. Johnson's classes meets this period. You can go down there now and introduce yourselves while I take care of the paperwork."

So we walked all the way back to down to the far wing we'd come from and slipped into the back of Mr. Johnson's classroom. A tall man with ample girth leaned against the edge of a desk at the front of the room. He put a finger to his lips as we entered. He had a broad face and round ears that stuck out, giving him the overall appearance of a giant panda. He rocked gently in time to what sounded like strains of Berlioz's *Symphonie Fantastique*. Large-framed black glasses magnified pale blue eyes. They kept slipping down his nose. Each time, he put his finger on the bridge and pushed them up.

I walked Tess to an open seat directly in front of Johnson— the other students had crowded to the back of the room. I wondered which was more unpopular, Johnson or the style of music the kids were forced to listen to. The full sound of the orchestra and complexity of the music were a welcome respite from the monotonous beat of hip-hop that seemed ubiquitous most places I went. I didn't know about Tess, but I was going to enjoy this class.

After a few minutes, Mr. Johnson stopped the music and proceeded to explain the importance of the work in context, telling the class that it represented the beginning of the romantic period in classical music. I took notes. At the end of the class, I introduced Tess and myself and told Mr. Johnson about the mix-up in Tess's schedule. He said he was glad to have us—her—in class and looked forward to getting to know Tess. He said he would put together an outline of what he'd covered so far before the next class, and a list of works that Tess would be expected to know by the end of the year. Her face fell. Before she could start whining, I thanked him and steered her out of the room.

"Okay, Einstein," she said out in the hallway, "where to next?"

"Lunch," I said. "I'm starved."

I took her arm and followed the scent of cafeteria food. Classrooms of students spilled into the halls, creating pandemonium that made me dizzy. For a moment I thought Tess was lucky she couldn't see, but I quickly realized I wouldn't wish that on anyone. She was silent on the way to the commons. I didn't know if she had a lot on her mind or if she was still ticked off. If I'd been a gambling man, I'd have bet on the latter.

The clamor doubled in the commons, with more students using their mouths to yammer at each other than eat. A football sailed by, narrowly missing my head. An Asian kid at a nearby table dealt cards to the rest of the table and called for bets in Cantonese. Snippets of conversation from a table full of girls suggested they were comparing notes on the boys playing the impromptu game of football. A couple of geeky-looking guys with long hair sat side-by-side peering at their laptop screens. Everywhere I looked, forty-pound backpacks thunked onto tabletops or the floor, chairs scraped, and bodies moved: sitting, standing, walking, dancing.

I spotted some empty chairs on the far side and led Tess in that direction. She still wasn't talking. As I started to seat her, open-mouthed stares ringing the table made me pause.

"What?" I said.

A skinny kid gave me a one-eyed glance from under a fringe of bangs.

"Uh, I don't think you're supposed to be here," he said.

"Why not?"

"Like, we're *freshmen*." He sounded embarrassed.

Tess blanched, mortified once again.

"Yeah, thanks," I said. "I'm new here."

I steered Tess away from that section of the cafeteria.

"What other rules don't I know?" I grumbled in her ear.

"There are territories, boundaries you don't cross," she hissed. "Not that anyone couldn't sit with freshmen, but who would want to? Know what I mean?"

"Okay, so where do seniors sit?"

"Middle to far end of the upper level."

"Got it. Anybody in particular you'd rather steer clear of?"

She hesitated, then shrugged. "I suppose not."

Her mouth twisted in a grimace. There was something else she wasn't telling me, but I clamped my jaw shut. Spotting a couple of empty chairs a few tables away, I changed direction, pulling on her elbow. A table full of beefy guys gawked and snickered as we approached, nudging each other in the ribs and pointing our way. Subtle. A few of them shifted in their seats, faced the center of the table, and tipped their heads down as we got closer. Others continued to leer, leaning toward each other to mutter conspiratorially, no doubt sharing bad jokes.

A round-faced kid with a mop of brown hair in need of a cut and acne that marred what might have been decent looks openly stared with a smirk on his face. He leaned back in his chair, arm draped over the back.

I tipped my head. "Hey, how's it going?"

He grinned. "Good, man."

He looked relaxed, at ease, king of his little fiefdom, so I took my eye off him for a second, looking ahead to maneuver Tess through the tight space between tables and milling students. My mistake. I didn't see him move, so I couldn't swear to it, but it couldn't have happened any other way. I tripped over his foot and went down, sprawling on the floor, almost taking Tess with me.

CHAPTER 13

Tess tensed, the feeling of Oliver's hand gripping her arm now an irritation instead of a comfort. He seemed so clueless, as if he'd never set foot in a high school before. She'd found it difficult enough to navigate its perils when she'd been able to see. The thought of relying on him didn't comfort her. She cringed, wondering how many of the freshmen were laughing at her. Oliver's grip was unyielding; she had no choice but to follow his lead. Energy radiated off him in waves, shimmering in the space between them. Not anger, she sensed, but annoyance. She tried to pull away from it, but he held firm.

A smattering of sing-song syllables reached her ears over the general din. The Asian table, which shunned her because she was half white-bread American—even though a lot of white kids looked down on her because she was half Chinese. The "randoms" were next, followed by the cheerleaders and the jocks. Sure enough, a few steps later she heard the soft click of keyboard keys and the odd conversation of kids who didn't seem to fit into any of the other cliques. Almost drowning them out were the high-pitched squeals and excited chatter of the girls at the next table. Definitely cheerleaders.

Despite how bright she knew most of them were, the vapid conversations that floated to her ears reinforced the dumb cheerleader stereotype. With their combined brainpower they could rule the school, if not the world. She wondered why all they seemed capable of discussing was boys and makeup tips. She knew she shouldn't generalize. After all, Adrienne was a cheerleader, and she'd been Tess's best friend—once. Now, Tess wasn't so sure. Adrienne had come to visit Tess just one time during her year of recuperation. Tess hadn't been ready to talk to her—to anyone—and had turned her best friend away. Adrienne had never come back.

The cheerleaders' table went silent as she and Oliver passed, and Tess felt their laser stares excising holes in her flesh and her soul. The low-pitched laughter of the boys at the next table reverberated loudly in the absence of competing chatter from the girls. Tess straightened and aimed her sightless eyes forward, refusing to acknowledge the snub of the girls' silence.

"What a bitch," someone muttered as she passed.

"She's such a chonky," someone else said.

Tess bit her lip and choked back a sob.

They think I'm being rude? Do they think I'm supposed to automatically say hello to people I can't even see?

Tess felt Oliver's fingers tighten on her arm for a second, but he didn't say anything. She followed hesitantly as he took small steps, pulling her through the maze of chairs, tables, and moving students.

He suddenly tugged on her arm. Instinctively, she stopped and jerked upright to maintain her balance. His fingers left her arm altogether. From the floor in front of her came a soft thud. Gales of laughter erupted a few feet away.

"Talk about the blind leading the blind," a voice said.

Tess recognized it immediately, and the warmth flushing her face came as much from anger as embarrassment.

She whirled toward the source. "What did you do, Carl?"

"Carl who?" the voice said mockingly. "I'm not Carl."

"I'm blind, not deaf," Tess said. "I'd know your voice anywhere, Carl."

She heard scuffling at her feet, and felt Oliver's presence at her side, his subtle scent increasingly familiar and oddly comforting.

"No big deal," Oliver murmured in her ear. "Guy's a jerk, but no harm done."

"Who you callin' a jerk?" Carl said.

A chair scraped on the floor.

"Did he trip you?" Tess said to Oliver.

"The dweeb's a klutz, Barrett," Carl said, his voice closer now. "You'd have been better off with a dog. Oh, I forgot. You eat dogs, don't you?"

Laughter surrounded her once more.

"Shut up, Carl!" Tess said.

Oliver murmured in her ear again. "It's okay. I can handle this. Let's just go sit down."

"Not till you apologize for callin' me a jerk," Carl said.

"Excuse us, jerk," Oliver said. "Please."

"Hey, butthead, you can't—"

"What's going on?" another voice asked.

Tess caught a whiff of woodsy cologne and trembled involuntarily. She knew this voice, too, but she wished she'd been able to forget it in the months since the accident. Toby Cavanaugh.

"Nothing we can't handle," Oliver said.

"Yeah," Carl said, "nothing you can't handle without a blind girl's help."

"Carl!" Toby said. "Give it a rest."

"Yeah, whatever."

"You okay, Tess?" Toby said.

"I'm fine," she said, fighting to keep her voice from quavering. "It's Oliver you should be asking. After Carl tripped him . . ."

"Oliver, is it? I'm Toby. Everything cool?"

"Sure, everything's cool. We were just finding a place to sit."

"We can make room at our table. C'mon, sit over here."

"We—" Tess started to object, but Oliver spoke over her.

"Thanks, we'll take you up on that."

Oliver's hand cupped her elbow and steered her forward. Before she knew it, a chair was slipped under her and she was scooted up until her elbows gently bumped a table.

"Is everything all right, Toby?" a girl said.

Tess shuddered inside, but she plastered a smile on her face.

"Yeah, babe, it's all good," Toby said.

"Hello, Adrienne," Tess said quietly.

"Tess! I . . . I didn't . . ."

"You didn't think I'd recognize you? Because I can't see? I do know your voice, Addie. It's not like we weren't—oh, I don't know—friends once."

"We still are, aren't we?"

"I don't know, Adrienne. You tell me. I haven't seen you in, what, a year?"

"You haven't seen me because, well, you can't see, Tess."

Tess's ears burned. "You know what I mean. I haven't heard from you in that long, either. And I can still hear."

"Ladies, ladies," Oliver said. "No reason we can't all get along, is there? Tess, what do you want for lunch?"

"I'm not hungry," she muttered.

Oliver put his lips next to her ear and spoke softly. "We went to all the trouble of finding a table; you're having something to eat. Sandwich? Turkey and cheese?"

Tess reached up, found the back of his neck, and held him still.

"Don't leave me here with them," she whispered. "Please."

Oliver patted her hand and straightened, pulling away from her grasp. "I'll be right back," he said cheerfully.

"So," Adrienne said, "how are you, Tess?"

"Peachy. I nearly died. I can't see. How do you think I am?"

"Lay off, Tess," Toby said.

Tess could hardly believe her ears. "You're defending her?"

"She just asked how you're doing. No need to give her a hard time."

"Oh, my God, Toby!" Tess said. "Are you, like, seeing her? Are you and Addie together?"

She didn't want to know the answer. She jumped up, a sob escaping her lips, and stumbled away from the table. Arms flailing, she ran into someone.

"Hey! Watch it!"

She turned bounced off and ran into a chair. Fighting back tears, she felt her way past one obstacle after another, with no idea where she was going, only the desperate desire to get away.

"Tess!" Toby called. "Tess, stop!"

She forged ahead, jeers and laughter surrounding her frantic attempts to feel her way through the maze of bodies and furniture.

"Tess, please stop," Toby said, his voice now directly in front of her.

She whirled to one side. A hand latched onto her arm gently.

"I've got you," Oliver said into her ear.

She clutched at him, and a sob broke loose from her throat.

"Take me home! Please, Oliver!"

"Where are you going?" Toby said. "Tess?"

"I'm getting her out of here," Oliver said. "She's had enough."

She hung onto Oliver's arm as he led her to a door leading outside. The cool air on her face had never felt so good. The door slammed behind them, shutting out the lunchroom cacophony, all the snide comments and hoots of amusement that she knew were accompanied by stares of disgust and, worse, pity. She swiped at the wet tracks on her face.

"I can't leave you alone for ten seconds," Oliver muttered.

"What? This is *my* fault?"

He didn't answer for a moment, and she hoped he felt guilty for even suggesting she'd caused that awful lunchroom scene.

"High school sucks," Oliver said.

She couldn't have agreed more, but it went without saying.

"You've gotta get over it, Tess," Oliver went on. "I know this is your first day, and it's been rough on you. But every day is going to have its bumps. There will always be some inconsiderate ass that belittles you or insults you or makes fun of you."

"You're such a jerk. I can't believe you're saying this to me."

"That's my point. I'm not trying to make you feel bad, or put you down. I just think you're going to have to grow thicker skin if you want to get out of this place alive. You've got, what, three months? Less? Then you're off to college."

Tess wanted to pound him with her fists and scream at him, but she didn't. Part of her knew he was right. She didn't need Toby or Adrienne. She'd gotten along fine without them for a year.

"My books!" she said suddenly.

"I've got them right here," Oliver said.

"Thanks," she said, relief washing over her.

"You sure this is okay? Skipping out on your last class?"

"No, but I can't take any more. Please, Oliver?"

"Hey, I'm not the one going to high school here. Guess you'll have to figure out how to make it up."

"I'll take care of it," she said.

"No need to get touchy. I'm just saying, is all."

"Got it. Now can we please go home?"

"Your chariot awaits, my lady."

Oliver tugged gently on her arm, bringing her to a stop. A car alarm chirped next to her, and then the car door opened. Tess felt for the doorframe, faced out, and eased into the passenger seat. She swung her legs into the car. Oliver reached over her, set her bag on the floor at her feet, and shut the door.

Tess's cell phone beeped. She reached down, felt her bag for the right pocket and fished it out. Feeling carefully, she pressed some keys on the keyboard to activate the text-to-voice feature.

"You have one unread e-mail," intoned a voice, "from Dad."

Tess screamed.

CHAPTER 14

One year earlier...

Travis turned into the drive with a nod to the workman at the side of the road. The workman stood a few yards from a cable company truck, bent over an open manhole. A beefy man with a five-day-old beard, he looked up briefly as Travis passed, his expression impassive. Travis knew another man sat inside the vehicle. The one outside was Fred. The one in the truck was a short little fireplug named Barney, and Travis knew that anyone who cracked a joke about the pair's names faced the threat of a mouthful of fist.

They were both armed with .9mm semiautomatic pistols and had access to a veritable arsenal of assault rifles, rocket-propelled grenade launchers, flash-bangs, smoke bombs, and other weaponry in the truck. Travis had handpicked them from a list General Turnbull had provided. They'd all washed out of the armed services for one reason or another. On one hand, that presented potential trouble. They were mercenaries. They were loyal only to a paycheck. Which was why Travis had been so careful in selecting the team of six.

One of them—Red, a former Navy SEAL—had simply grown too old, by some standards, to continue serving in the field. He'd chosen to resign rather than become a desk jockey and try to climb the ranks. Fred and Barney—Special Forces soldiers who'd known each other in Afghanistan—had been bounced out for infractions, but none serious enough to give Travis too much pause. He'd figured after reviewing their files and talking with them that they hadn't gotten a fair shake. Neither had complained, however, simply chalked up their misfortune to being in the wrong place at the wrong time. Travis could live with mistakes. Striking an officer was one thing, but hitting an officer by accident in the middle of a barroom brawl was plain bad luck. Worse luck when the officer was a butthead who insisted on pressing charges.

At least none of them appeared to be a psychopath. The only one who worried him was Kenny, a former Army Ranger who'd been drummed out with an OTH—other than honorable—discharge for sleeping with a captain's wife. That was bad enough, but Kenny's file read like a fifth-grade troublemaker's jacket. Insubordination, fighting, harassment—Kenny definitely liked to mix it up, but when it came down to crunch time, every man in his unit had sworn that Kenny was their go-to guy. Fearless and a crack shot, Kenny had saved his unit more than once in Iraq, so Travis knew he had the goods. But he didn't trust Kenny, so he'd put him on yard duty to keep him close.

Travis rounded a curve in the drive and saw Kenny trimming the grass around a tree with a hand mower. Kenny had worked up a good sweat despite the cold, gray spring weather. It was good for the kid. He'd gotten a little flabby and could use the exercise. Travis saw Kenny spy the car from the corner of his eye, and knew Kenny had checked him out as soon as Travis's SUV had entered his field of vision. Travis saw Kenny glance in his direction once more as he drove past, just to make sure of the vehicle's occupant.

Luis, the only ex-marine in the group, raked a garden bed fifty yards away. There was a sad case. Kid had been decorated three times in Iraq. Someone in his unit had panicked one night on patrol and had shot an innocent civilian headed for home. Roused by the gunfire, a neighbor had burst out of the house next door, shouting and waving a kitchen knife. Feeling threatened, the nearest marine had shot him, too. Luis had tried to wave the others off, but a sort of madness overtook them all and they went through the house shooting everything that breathed to cover up their mistake. Everyone but Luis, that is. He'd kept his mouth shut, but word had eventually gotten out, and when the court-martial was over, Luis had been convicted of involuntary manslaughter even though he'd tried to stop the slaughter. Go figure.

Luis watched Travis with the same surreptitious gaze, the same wary expression as the others Travis had driven past. Travis grunted with satisfaction. They'd all proved to be alert. Travis feared that they might become complacent. Their biggest enemy was boredom. Hours and days of watchful anticipation could easily make them inattentive and careless. So far at least, they hadn't relaxed their vigilance.

Travis swung the SUV around in a tight circle at the end of the drive and backed it up to the far garage bay door. He wanted it nose-out in case they had to leave in a hurry. He'd returned the rental sedan and bought the big SUV—with James's money, of course. Travis couldn't take a chance on someone in the company wondering about all the sudden expenses for mostly military equipment, so James paid for it out of his own pocket. The SUV had a powerful engine, a lot more room, and a few extras like run-flat tires, bullet-resistant glass, and bulletproof ceramic plates lining the doors. He'd taken James's Range Rover in for the same modifications under the guise of an "oil change."

On his way to the house, Travis scanned the water. Two hundred yards offshore, a small fishing boat bobbed gently. A lone man in a slicker and a floppy hat sat in the stern, holding a fishing pole out over the lake. He didn't look like much of a deterrent, but Travis knew that Red could swim the entire distance to shore underwater, slip out without a sound, and kill a man a dozen different ways before he even knew Red was there. Age might have mellowed Red's temper, but it hadn't diminished his skills much.

Marcus, the sixth man and Travis's second-in-command, was at school shadowing Tess. Marcus had also been Special Forces, and was the only one in the bunch other than Red to have an honorable discharge. In fact, his record was spotless. He'd left the army to work private security in Iraq. The money was better.

Everyone in place and all was calm. Things were too normal. It wasn't just the transition from war zone in the 'Stans to the peace and quiet of civilian life that made the hairs on the back of Travis's neck stand up and his skin itch. This was more like the calm before the storm, the silence before the first shot was fired during an incursion. Travis had felt it many times before. A muscle at the corner of his eye twitched. Something was going to happen—soon. Travis just hoped he'd prepared adequately to handle whatever threat materialized. The key was planning and preparation, but Travis knew that even backups to backup plans could fall apart. The question was how well he could improvise if all else failed. Especially with three civilians in tow.

He locked the vehicle and walked to the front of the house. Off to one side, Yoshi pruned a rose bush. He nodded curtly as Travis went up the steps, then quickly shifted his glance to the two men working in the yard, eyes narrowing as he watched them work. Travis shrugged and opened the front door. James stood in the entryway, staring absently out a side window.

"You're home early," Travis said.

"What?" James turned. "Oh, yeah. Slow day."

"Everything all right at work?"

"Fine." James turned to the window again. "I feel trapped in my own home, Travis."

Travis followed his gaze to the two ex-military men posing as gardeners. "At least you have the nicest yard in the neighborhood."

"You know what I mean. I feel like someone's watching me all the time. I can't turn around without feeling like someone's there."

Outside, Yoshi rose and walked briskly toward Luis, gesturing with his hands. Luis looked up with a puzzled expression. Yoshi snatched the rake from Luis and took two careful swipes at the flowerbed, looked at Luis, and thrust the rake back into his hands.

Travis sighed. "No one's happy with the situation, least of all me. Despite those guys out there, you're still too unprotected."

"We've never needed protection before."

"Until we've identified and neutralized the threat the general alluded to, I don't think we have a choice."

"And you trust him?"

"Jack?" Travis had never given it a second thought. "Why wouldn't I?"

James shrugged. "You're the one who said a lot of people would do anything to get their hands on the technology."

"He already does. Well, did, until I let the prototype get blown up. What good would it do him to harm you or the family?"

James waved a hand irritably. "I don't know. I don't know what any of this is about. Maybe he wants to steal it and sell it to the Chinese."

"Not Jack. He's a patriot. He'd never sell out his country."

"If you say so." The furrows on James's forehead smoothed, his anger gone like a passing cloud. "Tess got her SAT scores back. She did great. Sally and I wanted to celebrate by taking her up to the pass for the afternoon and go boarding."

"When?"

"Tomorrow. Maybe the next day. Is that a problem?"

Travis rubbed his chin. "Actually, it might give us exactly the opportunity we need. I'm not sure I can pull it together that fast. Can you give me a few hours before you decide?"

"Sure. What do you have in mind?"

Travis was already headed for a computer. "I'll let you know when I figure it out," he said over his shoulder.

CHAPTER 15

"What?" I shouted. "What's wrong?"

I raced the rest of the way to the driver's side door and leaped inside, expecting to find a crazed slasher in the backseat threatening Tess with a twelve-inch butcher's knife. After the morning's screw-ups, topped off by Carl's stunt at lunch, I didn't think the day could get any worse. But there was nothing like a girl's scream to peg the needle on the fright-o-meter and send my adrenaline level soaring.

I found no knife-wielding psycho, only Tess holding a cell phone.

"What's the problem?" I said, calmly now, though my heart was still attempting a prison break by slamming against the bars of my ribcage.

"I got an e-mail," she said, dazed.

"Wait. How can you—?"

"I can't *read* them. Text-to-voice software. They're read to me."

"And you speak your reply?"

"I *can* touch-type, you know. But yes, it'll convert speech to text, too."

"So, what does it say?"

"I don't know."

"Then why the he—?" I stopped myself and took a deep breath. "Why did you scream?"

Her lower lip quivered, and a tear leaked from the corner of one eye and rolled slowly down her cheek.

She spoke so softly I could barely hear her. "It says it's from my dad."

"But you said he's . . ."

She nodded.

"Someone's sick idea of a prank. Don't let it get to you."

She swallowed hard. "But what if it's . . . ?"

"Really him? That would be tough, Tess. Not if what you told me is true. Don't know that anyone's pulled that trick for two thousand years. Unless it's a ghost."

"How can you joke about it?" She sobbed.

"I'm sorry, Tess. Really. Please don't cry."

She sniffed and toyed with the hands in her lap.

"Maybe you should find out what it says," I said.

"I can't."

"Why not? C'mon. You have to find out sometime. Besides, I want to know who sent it so I can kill the bastard."

She sniffed. "You'd do that? I mean, not kill somebody, but . . ."

"Well, it's probably not in my job description, but yeah."

"All right."

She pushed a button on the phone. A tinny, robotic voice said, "Seeing is believing, Tess. *Zho*, Dad."

"Oh, my god!" she cried.

Tears threatened to spill down her cheeks again, but she squeezed her eyes shut and dammed them up.

The sight of her crying, even almost crying, was my Kryptonite—it rendered me weak, indecisive, and nearly incapable of thought.

"What's '*zho*'?" I said.

She didn't hesitate. "Ex-oh, like hugs and kisses. He always signed his texts that way."

The text recognition software was smart enough to try to pronounce it, but apparently not smart enough to know *XO* wasn't a word.

"So, it really is from your dad?"

"Who else would it be from?"

"C'mon, Tess. How is that even possible? It's gotta be someone's idea of a joke."

"That's so mean! I *can't* see. Who would do that?"

I didn't have an answer for her, but I was willing to bet the building behind us held several candidates perfectly capable of such casual cruelty. Carl would have been at the top of my list, but I didn't know if he had the brains to plan an attack this devious or if he only took advantage of spontaneous opportunities. Like sticking out his foot when I got close.

"I'll take you home," I said.

I pushed the starter button. Only then did I notice the slip of paper stuck under the windshield wipers.

"Damn!" I muttered.

"What is it?"

"Nothing."

I opened the door, put one foot out, and reached around the door frame for the ticket.

"What are you doing?" Tess said.

"It's no big deal."

"Don't tell me you parked in the handicap space."

"Well, yeah. Why wouldn't I? I mean, doesn't blindness count as a handicap anymore?"

"Not without plates or a handicap card."

"Yeah, I know. I just figured . . . Never mind. I'll take you home."

Tess was quiet on the way back to the house. An e-mail from my father would have shut me up just as fast, even if I figured he was still alive out there somewhere.

I parked in the garage and walked Tess into the kitchen. Since she'd run out on lunch, I figured she might be hungry. Rosa was cooking something—dinner maybe. For such a small household, she seemed to spend a lot of time at the stove, but then I supposed some dishes and desserts took more time to make than others. Coming from a generation raised on microwave cooking, I expected meals in minutes, not hours. Judging from the smells— cumin, oregano, coriander, cinnamon, and more—Rosa's food was worth waiting for.

Rosa fussed over Tess and helped get her seated at the counter, then proceeded to shift gears and whip up lunch. Alice walked in from her office and raised an eyebrow.

"Oliver," she said, "a word, please."

I followed her into her office.

"You're home early," she said without sitting down. "What happened?"

I ran down the morning's events for her, doing my best to report factually and not embellish them with overt emotion, especially mine. I summed up with, "She had a rough go. I figured she'd had enough."

Alice managed to look down her nose at me, making me feel small even though I towered over her.

"All right," she said slowly. "Perhaps this once. I don't want you to coddle her, Oliver. She needs to regain her confidence."

"Yes, ma'am. I understand."

"How's her homework load?"

"Not bad. Pretty light."

"Well, after she's eaten you can help her with that. Depending on what time you finish, you can leave for the day or stay for dinner, if you wish."

"Thank you, Alice."

She rounded the desk and sat down, dismissing me. I turned for the door and nearly jumped out of my socks when Tess screamed—again.

CHAPTER 16

"*¡Ay, Dios mío!*" Rosa cried.

Footsteps clattered into the kitchen.

"What's wrong?" Alice said. "What's the matter?"

"*El fantasma de su padre,*" Rosa whispered. "*Dios mío.*"

"English, Rosa, please!" Alice said shortly. "Tess, what happened?"

Tess held up her phone and sobbed. "I got another e-mail message. From Dad."

"You must be mistaken, Tess," Alice said.

"I told her it's somebody's sick idea of a joke," Oliver said.

Tess swung her head wildly from voice to voice. "Stop it, all of you! You think I don't know an e-mail from my own father?"

She jumped up and fled from the room, arms flailing in front of her face to ward off onrushing walls. She cracked her knee against a stool, rapped her knuckles against a doorframe, and bruised a shoulder on a wall, but succeeded in getting away.

Behind her, Tess heard Alice say, "Oliver!" She stepped up her pace. Feeling her way down the hall, Tess grabbed the banister and bolted up the stairs.

"Tess!" Oliver called. "Wait!"

His footsteps pounded up after her, and she felt his hand on her arm before she reached the top. Oliver's breathing was heavy and ragged, and Tess took some small comfort in knowing she'd made him work to catch up.

"What do you want?" She wrenched her arm away and took another stair.

"Hold up. C'mon, Tess. Wait a minute. Look, I get it. I know what it's like."

"You couldn't possibly know what this is like."

"Yes, I do. My mom died when I was little, and my dad ran out on me. I don't know whether he's dead or alive. If I got an e-mail from him, I'd freak."

Tess digested that slowly, momentarily confounded. "You're probably just telling me that to make me feel sorry for you."

"No, I'm not. It's no big deal for me because it happened so long ago. For you, it's fresher, so it hurts more. I just wanted you to know I understand what you're going through."

Thoughts blazed through her mind, leaving trails of sparks.

No one could possibly understand what I'm going through.

She said nothing.

"It has to be a prank, Tess. Someone's messing with you."

"But why? What have I done to anyone?"

"I don't know. That kid Toby, maybe? Or Carl. He's a big enough asshole."

"Not smart enough. And I can't believe Toby would do something like that. Not to me."

"What about your friend? Adrienne? Not a lot of love lost between you two, I'm guessing."

Tess couldn't stop the tears that started running down her cheeks again.

Oliver groaned. "Jeez, not again. Everything's spinning, fading. I feel so weak. Kryptonite, I'm telling you. Got—to—shield—myself—from—"

Tess felt a tissue being pressed into her hand, and she laughed in spite of herself.

"Come on, let's get you something to eat. We'll figure this out."

"I'm not hungry."

"Okay, so let's go somewhere quiet and think this through."

"The library," she said.

"Which way?" Oliver said.

"I'll show you. Take my arm."

Tess turned. With one hand on the banister, she led Oliver down the stairs. She put her hand out and lightly touched the wall at the bottom of the stairs, but she could find the library easily without feeling her way or counting steps. When she reached the door, she stopped.

"This is it?" he said. "How did you do that?"

"I know my way around my own home."

She heard Oliver open the door. He guided her through the opening.

"Wow!" he said. "Nice."

"It's my favorite room."

She could picture it perfectly—the walls of shelves, two of which were bifurcated by a catwalk accessible from a spiral staircase. A pair of big, stuffed wing chairs flanked a leather couch in front of the fireplace. A reading table with four straight-backed chairs around it anchored the middle of the room under a hanging lampshade of green glass. It was exactly how a library in an old English manor should look. The rest of the house was contemporary, which may have been why she loved the library so much. It felt cozy, and much more inviting and warm than the other rooms, no matter how comfortable they were.

"My dad used to say this library was bigger than the library of Alexandria."

"Alexandria probably had nearly four hundred thousand scrolls."

"It took several scrolls to make a book," she said, "so it still didn't have that many books."

"How many do you have here? A few thousand?"

Tess nodded. "Around five thousand. But we sort of cheat. The Internet, you know."

She pointed in the direction of a study carrel in a corner. The nook was equipped with a computer and high-speed broadband connection.

"How do you do that?" Oliver said.

She turned to the sound of his voice. "Do what?"

"You pointed right at that computer."

"I told you, I know my way around the house."

"And that. What about that? You're looking right at me, Tess."

"I can't see you."

"But you're not looking at me the way a blind person would. You know, sort of unfocused and off to the side. You look at people when they speak."

"I don't know. There's nothing wrong with my eyes. I guess I'm still trying to see you talk. I just 'look' at the sound of your voice."

"If there's nothing wrong with your eyes, why can't you see?"

"They told me the accident probably caused a brain injury."

"I'm sorry." Oliver paused. "Is there . . . ? I mean, can they—?"

"No. There's nothing they can do. I don't want to talk about it." Tess swallowed hard. "I want to show you something."

She turned and took two steps before banging her hip into the back of a chair. Oliver's hand was on her arm in a flash.

"Let me help," he said. "Where to?"

She bit her lower lip and pulled her arm away. "I have to learn how to do this on my own."

Oliver didn't reply, so she put her hands out and felt her way around the table, oriented herself, and gingerly stepped to the bookshelf. Her hands worked out in both directions until they found the edge of a section. She moved books to the side and thrust her hand to the back of the shelf. Her fingers discovered the outline of a keypad. Tracing the keys lightly, she put her fingers in position and pressed in a ten-digit code from memory. She heard a satisfying click, and pulled. The entire shelf swung into the library, exposing an opening into a room beyond.

"Holy smoke!" Oliver said. "A secret panel? What's back there?"

"Come on," Tess said as she stepped through. "Help me. I haven't been in here in a while."

Oliver took her arm and walked her a few paces inside the room. They stopped. She imagined what he saw—a functional but still comfortable office. A large flat-screen monitor topped a teak desk. A couch ran part of the length of one wall.

"What is this?"

"My dad's private study," Tess said. "Specially designed and constructed to serve as a panic room if necessary. He used to come in here when he was working on a problem and didn't want to be disturbed."

"What sort of problem? What did he do?"

"Designed video games."

Tess wished she could watch him working at his desk, intense concentration on his face. Even though she was blind and he was gone, she could feel him in the room.

"They're not a prank," she said. "The e-mails. They're from him. From my dad."

"Tess," Oliver said, "maybe you should let your parents go."

She blinked back the tears welling up in her eyes. "How can you say that? Just forget they ever existed?"

"No, of course not. Love them. Cherish your memories of them. But let go, Tess. You'll go crazy, otherwise."

"He wanted me to know something. I'm sure of it. He's trying to tell me something."

"What did the e-mail say this time?" Oliver's voice was still soft, calm.

"'Don't believe everything you hear.'"

"That's it? You can't see, but 'seeing is believing.' You depend on hearing more than ever, but you're not supposed to believe everything you hear. Either that's the worst advice your dad ever gave you, or someone's punking you. Come on, Tess. What does that even mean?"

"I don't know!"

She wanted to scream and stamp her feet—or hit something. But it had slowly begun to dawn on her that this was her life now. Standing here in her father's study, she knew that if her parents *were* still alive, they'd both be telling her in their own ways to get over herself. To move on.

"But I know how we can find out," she said.

CHAPTER 17

One year earlier...

An op of this magnitude required time to plan carefully, and but Travis had had less than twenty-four hours. A shiver of excitement ran through him, and his stomach flip-flopped the way it always did before a mission. A hundred things could go wrong, but if everything went right, this op just might solve their problems.

He gazed out the darkened windows of the big snowcat, slowly panning in a wide arc. He had a surprisingly clear view of the terrain on almost all sides, but that meant he was visible, too—if someone knew where to look. The black highway snaked through the snowy pass below him, stretching nearly two miles in each direction before disappearing around the shoulders of mountains. The bright lights of the ski resort glowed on the other side of the highway. White ski trails climbed the side of the mountain above the resort, dotted with bright pools of light. Tiny black dots zigzagged down the mountain, dipping in and out of the pools.

He turned to the mountainside stretching away from the snowcat. The snow that had fallen steadily all day had nearly stopped. Cold air seeped into the cabin. Without the heater running, Travis could already see his breath. He rubbed his hands together. The conditions could not have been better. A wet, cold winter had dragged on into spring, resulting in one of the deepest snowpacks in years. Skiers and snowboarders would be happy to see the season extend to late May or early June.

He keyed his radio. "All units check in."

One by one, the men in the field responded, letting him know they were in position.

"Status, Red?" Travis said.

Red's reply crackled through his headset. "The package just reached the top. Headed down the chute now."

"Heads up, Fred," Travis said. "Could be the last run of the day. If so, you'll have to pick up the package at the bottom. Red, head out for the rendezvous. Everyone else—on your toes."

Marcus had objected to using first names in their radio communication, but they used mostly military-spec hardware, including tactical radio gear with encryption. The frequency they were on was a little-used military band that wouldn't interfere with the state highway department's radio equipment.

Travis turned to the man next to him. "Comfortable with the range, Luis?"

"I wouldn't mind being closer, captain, but I can hit the targets you gave me."

"Almost showtime."

"I'm ready."

Luis cradled an M3 MAAWS—medium antiarmor weapon system—on his lap. The recoilless rifle could launch a high-explosive round about eleven hundred meters. He fingered the large metal tube absently and glanced at Travis.

"Thanks," Luis said, "for giving me a spot on your team."

"No reason I shouldn't," Travis said, a little gruffly.

Luis looked about to say something else, but just nodded and said, "I'm going to set up."

He pulled on a pair of gloves and donned night-vision goggles over his ski hat, then opened the cabin door and jumped out into the snow. Travis lifted a pair of night-vision binoculars and did another sweep of the mountainside, the highway below, and finally the slopes at the base of the ski resort. His thigh muscle twitched. Waiting was always the hardest. All of them were accustomed to action, but he knew patience was key to success. He gloved up, grabbed an extra HE round for the MAAWS, and climbed down to the snow.

The radio buzzed to life, and Fred's voice said, "The package is down."

"For good?" Travis said.

"Wait for it," Fred said.

The seconds ticked by. Luis crouched in the snow several yards away with the MAAWS on his shoulder, looking back at him, waiting for his signal. Travis's heart hammered in his chest, but he felt calmer than he had a few moments ago.

"Boots are on the ground!" Fred said. "It's a go!"

"Roger that. Go! Go! Go!" Travis said.

He swung his binoculars left, to where the highway disappeared around a curve. He waited.

"Marcus, I don't see you," he said. "Are you in position?"

"Coming up on my mark right now. Setting up took longer than I thought."

Far below, headlights pulled onto the shoulder on the highway heading east, away from the ski slopes, and stopped with a bright flash of red. Emergency flashers reflected off the dark pavement and brightened the snow at the side of the road. Two minutes later, another pair of headlights rounded the curve toward the resort. With the binoculars, Travis could easily make out a semitrailer truck as it barreled down the road. Just before it drew even with the vehicle parked on the other side, the truck cab slewed left, and the whole rig went into a sliding skid. The trailer tipped up on one set of wheels and teetered before crashing on its side, taking the cab with it. The faint screech of metal on pavement as the rig slid along the highway floated up the mountainside. The truck skidded to a stop, effectively blocking the westbound lanes.

The driver's door popped up toward the dark, cloud-laden sky, and a figure climbed out. Travis breathed a sigh of relief, glad that Kenny hadn't been hurt in the wreck. The kid could drive as well as he'd said he could. Kenny clambered down from the rig and ran across the highway to the waiting car on the opposite shoulder.

The snow fell more thickly now, big wet flakes drifting down, partially obscuring the scene, like a fuzzy TV picture. Travis swung the binoculars to the frontage road. An SUV approached the main highway. A large snowplow followed in its wake and slowed when the SUV turned onto the main road. Travis could just make out Barney's small figure dropping safety cones across the highway entrance, then quickly swinging up into the snowplow cab with Fred. The plow slowly rumbled onto the highway behind the SUV. Travis gave Luis the high sign. The ex-marine double checked the laser rangefinder, sighted, and fired a shell.

More than half a mile away, deep snow muffled the explosion to a dull *whump*. A geyser of ghostly white plumed into the night air. Travis hustled over to Luis with the additional round, unloaded the spent shell, and loaded the new round in the breech. He stepped to the side as Luis adjusted the gun on his shoulder, found his range, and sighted his new target. Within seconds, he fired the second round. It landed with another huge concussion, closer this time. Both men ran for the snowcat and jumped aboard. Travis started it up and aimed it diagonally down the mountain's face.

They ran without lights, using night-vision goggles to steer their way through the trees across the snowfield. Ahead, the mountain seemed to shear off in two places and slide down into the valley below. The susurrant hiss of the avalanche grew to a roar they could hear above the growl of the snowcat's engine. Luis grabbed a pair of binoculars and steadied them as the snowcat bounced down the slope.

"It's going to catch them!" he shouted. "They're not slowing!"

Travis braked and lifted the binoculars around his neck. Far below, the SUV hurtled down the road. Its brake lights flashed several times, but it showed no signs of slowing. The river of wet snow ahead had nearly reached the road, and the SUV headed right into it. The second avalanche would thoroughly box it in from behind. Travis revved the engine, threw the snowcat in gear, and roared down the mountainside in the track of the second snowslide that Luis had triggered.

Travis drove down off the steep slope onto a snow-packed fire road that in summer was little more than a dirt track through the trees. It was smoother going and less precarious than traversing the mountainside, and they made good time to the bottom. Racing on the top of the slide, Travis followed what had moments before been the highway, aiming for the spot he'd last seen the SUV. Luis flipped a on a GPS tracking device and monitored the screen.

"Left!" Luis shouted over the engine. "That way! The avalanche rolled him off the road."

"Do you see him?"

"No, not yet. Keep going."

Travis churned on through the snow. Several hundred yards away, the other snowcat with Red at the controls angled down from the other side of the highway on a course that would intersect theirs.

"Slow down!" Luis said. "Over there! I see it!"

Travis spotted it, too—the SUV, half buried in snow, tipped up on two wheels, smashed almost beyond recognition—but intact, not crushed. He roared up next to it and leaped out of the snowcat before it came to a stop. Luis tumbled out right behind him as Red cruised up and stopped. Travis ran to the SUV and wiped snow off the driver's window, put his face to the glass, and peered inside the dark interior. He counted three bodies.

Travis had been in the middle of a war for nearly a decade, had seen the worst atrocities men could commit—boys barely old enough to shave strapping bombs to their chests and blowing themselves to bits in packed markets, men cutting off the heads of their enemies and using them for soccer practice. But he felt numb. These were people he knew. Innocent people, not soldiers.

Luis frantically dug snow away from the rear door. Red came up behind him and dug alongside until the door was clear. Luis yanked on the handle—locked. He pulled his sidearm from its holster and shattered the window with the butt of the gun. Bits of glass showered the girl lying unconscious on the backseat. Her face was bloodied and one leg was bent at an unnatural angle. Luis popped the lock and wrenched the door open. Stripping off a glove, he pressed his fingers against the girl's throat.

"This one's still alive!" he said.

CHAPTER 18

"A library with a secret room. Too cool."

Matt Tsang looked around the room, head bobbing in appreciation. Tall and thin, he moved with the grace of a puma. He carried himself with self-assurance uncharacteristic among those of his reputed ilk, but I acknowledged that Tess may have led me astray. He didn't look like a geek to me.

His gaze finally rested on her. "So, what gives?" He wore an impassive expression, but the fifty-meter dash his eyes took around the room again gave away his arrant curiosity.

"I—we need your help," Tess said.

"You said that on the phone."

The corners of her mouth twitched down. "Can you trace an e-mail back to the sender?"

He shrugged. "Sure. Easy."

Tess held out her phone.

Matt didn't move. "What's in it for me?"

"What? You're kidding. Like money, you mean?" Tess said.

He waved away the suggestion. "I don't want your money. But I wouldn't mind working at your dad's company."

Tess's nostrils flared. "In case you hadn't noticed, he's dead."

"Yeah, and I'm sorry about that. But doesn't your uncle run it now?"

"You don't give up, do you? Fine, I'll see what I can do."

Wordlessly, he stepped forward and took the phone from her hand.

"Okay if I use this computer?" he said as he rounded the desk.

Tess hesitated before saying, "Yes."

Matt played with the phone while the computer booted up. "I assume you mean the most recent e-mail. This one, from . . . your dad? Guess I get it now."

He typed and waited, typed and waited again for several minutes before glancing up.

"You're not going to like this," he said. "The sender's IP address is a computer at MondoHard, downtown."

106

"My dad's company?" Tess said. "Oh, my god. It really could be him."

"Don't get your hopes up, Tess," I said. "If your dad's alive, don't you think someone at work would recognize him? Maybe would have told you he wasn't dead?"

"Matt, can you tell where the computer is?" she said. "What office it's in?"

"Sure, if I hack into the IT department, there should be records of where they assigned the computer."

"I don't think you have to hack the system. I mean, you're sitting at my dad's computer."

He glanced at the desk and blinked. "Don't suppose you have a password."

"*Life of Pi,*" she said. "Unless he changed it. 'Life of three-dot-one-four-one-five-nine.'"

He keyed it in. "Hot damn. It works."

He concentrated on the monitor for several minutes. I watched tension and excitement grow on Tess's face, while feeling the skin between my eyebrows permanently furrow. Matt scribbled something on a scrap of paper and pushed away from the desk.

"Got it," he said. "Let's go."

"Whoa, fella," I said. "Who said anything about going somewhere?"

"Look, whatever's going on here, I'm in," he said. "Tess? What do you say?"

She fumbled with a silver chain at her throat. "He can help us, Oliver."

"Fine. We figure out who's messing with you, teach them some manners, and we're done."

"Okay. Welcome to the team, Matt."

"Just so you know, I'm not what you'd call a team player," he said.

I shook my head. "Great. It'll be a pleasure working with you. Either of you figured out how we're going to find this computer? You think they'll just let you walk in and look around?"

The room went dead silent. Tess chewed her lower lip. Matt shrugged like it wasn't his problem.

Tess's face brightened. "I've still got a key card my dad gave me—if I can find it. It should get us in."

Thirty minutes later, the three of us slipped through a side door of a new office building in the South Lake Union area of Seattle. Tess clutched my arm tightly. Tsang slouched along on her other side, hands in his jeans pockets. Most people were hard at work at their desks, but the few people we passed in the hallway were young and casually dressed, like us. We didn't look too out of place. That didn't make me any less nervous.

"Where is it?" I hissed.

"B-oh-four-north," Matt said. "Lower level, north side. Why are you whispering, anyway?"

"Because we're not supposed to be here."

"You'll just attract attention," he said. "Besides, if anyone asks, Tess is giving us a tour. After all, her uncle runs this place, right?"

"Makes a lot of sense, genius—blind girl giving us a tour."

"Shut up, both of you," Tess said. "Let's just find it."

She clutched my arm like a bird on a power line in a high wind. We ducked into the nearest stairwell. The door clanged hollowly behind us.

"Ten," I said automatically, patting Tess's hand to let her know we were about to descend.

She groped for the rail with her free hand and took the stairs in lockstep with me. When we reached a landing, I said, "Ten more," and steered her in a semicircle to the next flight. Matt pushed through the door at the bottom, ahead of us, and looked both ways before leading us left down a long hallway. Our footsteps echoed on the hard tile. The floor above had been carpeted. Matt stayed a few pace ahead of us, head swiveling like a Wimbledon spectator's as he searched for the right office.

"There! That's it."

He angled across the floor to a door like all the others we'd passed—except this one had a card reader mounted on the wall next to the jamb.

"Doesn't look like anyone's office." I stepped up to the door and knocked, but there was no answer. "Tess, we need your ID."

She fingered the lanyard around her neck and held out the ID card attached at the end. I guided her hand to the security pad. A green LED flashed, and the lock clicked. Matt pushed the door open and stepped through. We followed. Tess stopped inside and turned a slow pirouette.

"What?" I said. "What is it?"

"What is this place?" she said. "I smell computers, electronics. Lots of them, from the sound."

I sniffed the air, catching a whiff of hot plastic and rubber and a touch of ozone. A loud electric hum filled the room, along with the whirr of fan blades. Racks of computer equipment lined the large room like library stacks. The door behind us closed with a loud click that nearly made me jump.

"Servers," Matt said. "Tons of them. Awesome!"

"This isn't right," Tess said. "You mean the e-mails came from one of these servers? How will we find out who sent them?"

"Hang on a minute," Matt said.

A small computer station stood in a corner. He walked over and sat down in front of the monitor, slid a keyboard drawer open, and typed furiously for several seconds. I guided Tess closer and peered over Matt's shoulder. I couldn't make head or tails of what he was doing.

In a moment he looked up and said, "This is the computer that sent the e-mails."

Tess's face fell like a collapsing soufflé.

"You might want to try giving her good news next time," I told Matt.

"Hey, I thought that was good news," he said. "It means the e-mail isn't coming from some jerk messing with her head, right?"

"Anyone could have come in here and used this computer," I said. "Anyone with access."

"Whoever it was didn't have to physically come in here," Matt said. "Someone programmed this computer to send those e-mails. This terminal is online. If someone had the IP address, they could get in remotely, as long as the computer is on and connected to the Internet."

"Then we're right back where we started," Tess said. Her eyes glistened.

"Not quite," Matt said.

His fingers flew over the keys, and his brows knit in concentration.

"Damn. Almost had it. This guy is good." He shoved his chair back and looked up at us. "I thought I could back-trace this guy, but he covered his tracks really well. The good news is that there's another message here, ready to send. Want to know what it says?"

"Yes!" Tess and I answered in unison.

Matt rolled his chair back to the table and pressed his face to the monitor.

"Tick-tock," he read. "Watch the clocks. It's 10:05. I really need your help, Tess."

"It's him," she whispered. "It's really him."

"It may have been him," Matt said, "but the file date on this message is exactly a year ago."

"He sent it a year ago?" Tess said. She frowned. "How come I just got it?"

"He *wrote* it a year ago," Matt said. "The time stamps on the messages you got earlier are from today. Hard to tell whether he programmed this terminal to send the e-mails today, or if someone triggered them."

"Either way, it's him," Tess said.

"How can you tell?" I said.

"It's code," she said. "Nobody else could possibly know that."

"Uh-oh," Matt said softly.

"What do you mean, 'uh-oh'?" I said.

"Somebody's monitoring this computer. They can tell we're online. I'm guessing we'll have visitors in about two minutes."

"Then we damn well better be out of here in less than one," I said.

I grabbed Tess's arm and pulled her toward the door. Matt stayed where he was and typed furiously.

"Come on!" I said. "Let's go!"

"Be there in a second," he said.

"Oliver?"

"He's coming, Tess. But we've gotta go. Now!" I guided her through the doorway. "Matt!"

"Right behind you," he called.

I hustled Tess down the hall toward the stairwell. Matt came through the door behind us, footsteps racing toward us. I yanked open the door to the stairs and pushed Tess through.

"Up!" I said. "Ten."

"I remember!" she said, grabbing the railing and heading up.

Matt crashed through just as a voice down the hall by the elevators yelled, "Hey, you!"

"Go! Go!" Matt muttered, taking the stairs two at a time.

As the stairwell door closed I saw a security guard step off the elevator and break into a run. I raced up and took Tess's elbow. She stumbled and nearly fell on the landing. I caught her before she went down. She regained her footing and took the next flight two at a time. At the top we burst through the door into the hallway on the next floor.

"This way!" Matt said.

He hurried down the hall to a side exit. We raced across the parking lot to the waiting BMW, and moments later we blended into the rush of city traffic.

CHAPTER 19

Tess sat quietly in the car on the way back, not knowing whether to laugh or cry. She was certain her father had sent the e-mails.

But why, after all this time? Had he known that something would happen to him and Mom? Something as dreadful as the accident that had killed them? Or was it just some terrible joke? He wants my help, the message said. But does that mean he'd wanted my help a year ago? Or does he need my help now? How could he, if he's dead?

Images tumbled through her head as rapidly and fleetingly as snowflakes. Visions of both her parents in happy times. Her mother in the garden with Yoshi, a smile on her face as wide as the lake at the sight of one of his blooms. Her father on a skateboard in the park, his grin bigger than any kid's there, or hunched in front of his computer, fingers licking at the keys like hummingbirds. The memories swirled and melded with others—uglier recollections that refused to dissipate in strength over time. Things she'd said in the heat of a moment. Things she'd done in fits of rebellion or plain pique. Things she now wished she could take back, undo.

"Um, this is cool and all," Matt said from the backseat, "but I've got homework. Unless you need me. You know, to, like, break the code."

"I think I've got that," Tess said.

"Well, then, like, if you have any computers you need hacked."

"We're good, Matt. Thanks. I owe you. But don't make a big deal out of it, okay?"

"Yeah. No problem."

Matt fell silent. Tess figured she'd hurt his feelings, but she didn't care. It wasn't like *his* dad was trying to communicate from the grave. She shivered.

Several minutes later, Oliver asked Matt where he lived so they could drop him off. She only half listened to their conversation, her mind still filled with questions. The next thing she knew, they were home and Oliver was opening her door for her.

No sooner had they gotten inside the house than Alice's voice stopped them cold.

"Oliver, a word!"

"I know what you're going to say, Alice," Tess said. "It's my fault. I asked Oliver to drive me and Matt to the library."

"We have a perfectly good library here," Alice said.

"Not with the reference books we needed."

"What's this about?" Oliver said.

"I'm sorry I didn't make myself clear, Oliver," Alice responded quickly. "You're not to take Tess anywhere without letting me know first."

"Is that really necessary? I mean, she'll be with me."

"Trust me, Oliver, it's necessary. I'm sure you'll make a fine assistant for Tess, and an excellent chaperone in most instances. But since I'm responsible for her safety, I have to know where she is and who she's with at all times. Do you understand?"

"Stop treating me like a baby, Alice," Tess said. "You're not my mother."

"No," Alice said, her voice barely audible, "I'm not. I have an even harder job."

"What's that supposed to mean?"

"Never mind." Her tone was brisk now. "I assume you still have homework. And since you didn't eat lunch, I imagine you're hungry."

Tess realized, to her surprise, that her stomach was growling.

"You and Oliver can work in the library," Alice went on. "I'll send Rosa in with a snack. Oliver, do we have an understanding?"

"Yes, ma'am."

"Good." Alice's footsteps retreated down the hall toward the kitchen.

Tess hand-walked her way along the wall to the library door. She felt Oliver move beside her, smelled his scent, heard his breathing.

"Why didn't you stand up for me?" she said when they were inside.

"Why did you lie about where we were?" Oliver asked.

"Because Alice wouldn't approve. She can be such a bitch sometimes. So, what? You're worried about losing your job?"

"Yes, frankly. So is she."

"What do you mean?"

"That's why her job is harder than your mother's," he said. "She can lose it if she doesn't look after you. Be prosecuted, even, if something happened to you. She could lose everything. A parent is still a parent, even if they do a crappy job. They can't get fired—at least not easily."

"So you're on her side?"

"If it means keeping you safe."

She turned away from his voice and felt her way to the table, swearing under her breath when she barked her shin on a chair. She pulled it out and sat down heavily.

"What was that about a code?" Oliver said.

Tess sighed. "I think you were right. Someone's playing a joke on me—my dad. 'Tick-tock, watch the clocks,' is from one of my favorite books when I was a kid—*The Eleventh Hour*."

"I don't know it."

"It's on the shelf in the children's section. Look under *B* for Base, Graeme Base."

She heard Oliver move to the bookshelves.

"Got it," he called. His footsteps returned. "What's the code?"

"It's in the book. It's a puzzle book. Part of the solution is based on the time. In most of the pictures, there's a clock that tells what time it is. Look for a clock that says 10:05."

Pages rustled as Oliver thumbed through the book. Tess remembered bits and pieces of the beautiful illustrations. She was sorry she couldn't see and enjoy them all over again.

"Here it is," Oliver said. "The zebra and mouse are playing billiards. There's a grandfather clock by the door that says 10:05."

"Billiards? Wait, are there bookshelves in the room?"

"Yes. I guess it's sort of a library, like this."

"He's telling me there's something here, in this room," Tess said. A shiver of excitement ran through her. She pictured the room in her mind, trying to recall every detail. "Oliver, there should be a mantel clock above the fireplace. It's been broken forever. Is it still there?"

"I see it." His footsteps moved across the room. "I'll be . . . It's set at 10:05."

"That's it? Is there anything there?"

"Hang on," he called. "There's something taped to the bottom."

He crossed the room, pulled out the chair next to hers, sat down, and smoothed a piece of paper out on the table.

"Oh, boy," he said. "More code. Two letters, followed by a series of numbers separated by dashes. Looks like five numbers in each series."

"Give me an example."

"*U, A*, four, twenty-two, one-thirty-seven, sixteen, four. Wait, each line begins with either a *U* or an *L*."

Tess racked her brain.

What could the code have to do with the library?

"What else, Oliver? There has to be something else—some other common elements. Something that will tell us how to read the code."

"Give me a minute." He paused. "Okay, here's something. Second letters only run through K. First numbers run from one to eight. Second numbers don't run any higher than forty or so."

Tess rubbed her forehead. "They're locations, like a seating chart."

"How do you know?"

"My dad and I used to do this all the time, devise codes and ciphers for each other."

"So what's the key?"

Tess pictured the room.

He couldn't have known I'd end up blind, but he knew this was my favorite room in the house.

Silently, she counted her way around the room to test her theory. She nodded to herself.

"U is for 'upper'; L for 'lower,'" she said without hesitation. "Second set of letters is the bookshelf section. First set of numbers is the shelf. Then comes the book on the shelf, page number, line, and letter or word. Make sense?"

"That's brilliant," Oliver said.

"No, I told you—I've done this before."

Oliver pushed his chair back and walked way. Tess put her hand on the table. Her fingers brushed the sheet of paper.

"Oliver, you forgot the codes."

"Got 'em memorized," he called from the catwalk.

"The whole sheet? How's that possible?"

"I don't know. It just is."

"*¡Ay, caramba!*" Rosa's voice came from the doorway behind Tess. "Whatchu doing up there?"

"On a treasure hunt, Rosa," Oliver said.

"You come down and have some *sopaipillas* that Rosa make."

"In a minute, Rosa. Thanks."

A tray clattered on the table in front of Tess, and Rosa's voice sang in her ear.

"*Comer algo, señorita*. Eat. There is hot chocolate, too."

Rosa wrapped Tess's hands around a warm mug.

"Thank you, Rosa."

"*¿Qué es eso?*" Rosa said. The sheet of paper crinkled. "What is this?"

Tess put her hand out quickly and laid it on top of the paper. "Just a game Dad used to play with me."

"You are supposed to be doing the homeworks. You no work, I tell Alice."

"All right, all right, Rosa. Don't get all hot and bothered."

Rosa grumbled something in Spanish and left.

"How's it going, Oliver?" Tess called.

"Just fine. Think your dad could have come up with an easier way to send you a message?"

"Not his style. So, what's it say?"

"Patience, Tess. There's a lot of code to decipher. At least each series stands for a word, not a letter. That would have taken forever."

Oliver's voice moved from one part of the library to another as he spoke. Tess remembered the treasure hunts her father had devised when she'd been a little girl. They'd taken her through the entire house and lasted for hours. Her mother had been in on the planning for many of them, often lending her artistic ability to the cause, rendering beautiful sketches of where clues might be hidden, just like the Graeme Base book. Sometimes the sketches themselves were clues.

"Getting closer," Oliver said. "Almost done."

Tess sipped her hot chocolate. She realized she was gripping the mug so hard her fingers ached. She put it down, drew in a slow breath, and counted out five minutes before Oliver joined her.

"Well?" she said.

"Are you sure you want me to do this?"

"Just give me the message, Oliver."

"Okay, here goes. 'Tess, if you're reading this, I'm not there. It's up to you to save the world. Danger is everywhere. To help, focus first. Get the picture? We love you.'"

Tess's lower lip quivered. She fought to keep the tears at bay.

CHAPTER 20

Travis presented his "Visitor—No Escort Required" badge to the Metro entrance security personnel, along with his driver's license. He emptied his pockets and walked through the metal detector while a conveyor took his briefcase through the x-ray machine. A Pentagon Force Protection Agency guard waved him through. He collected his belongings on the other side and set off briskly down the corridor.

The Pentagon was a small city unto itself, with more than seventeen miles of corridors, restaurants, shops, and an athletic club—in addition to nearly four million square feet of office space. Travis knew it was at least a five-minute walk to his destination, a conference room on the third floor of the D Ring. He knew he had plenty of time, but he didn't waste any. The sooner he got in and out of this meeting, the better. He didn't like meetings, but this one had been unavoidable.

As he expected, General Turnbull was already seated at the table when Travis arrived.

"Ah, Travis," he said as Travis walked in. "There you are. Good to see you."

"You, too, Jack." Travis gripped the general's extended hand. "I wish it was under better circumstances."

"Me, too, son. I don't think I can do much more to keep this train on track."

Travis shrugged. "It's not your fault, sir. I'm head of the company now; it's my responsibility."

Turnbull shook his head slowly, his mouth a grim line. "I can't help but think that if I hadn't suggested—"

"That's not your fault, either." The words came out as sharp as the stabbing pain in his chest. "I executed the plan. Wishful thinking won't bring them back."

"You're right. We both knew the risks."

"It was the only way to keep it from falling into the wrong hands."

"But now it's not in our hands, either."

"Not yet, no."

The general was silent for a moment. "Do you want coffee? I can have some brought in."

"No, thanks. Had too much already this morning."

"Ah, gentlemen," said a voice from the doorway. "You're both here. Good."

A tall, lanky man with a silver mane stepped into the conference room, his piercing gray eyes taking them both in.

Turnbull stood. "Good morning, Senator."

"Jack, how are you? Travis, glad you could come."

Travis and the general shook hands with Senator Jeremy Latham, a member of the US Senate Appropriations Committee and chairman of the subcommittee on defense.

"So, Travis, what's the latest?" Latham said when they'd seated themselves. He smiled genially. "Good news, I hope?"

"No, I'm sorry to say. I spent the morning with one of our suppliers, trying to work out our differences. They're convinced it's a software problem on our side, and we're convinced their servos aren't designed to the same specs as those on the original prototype."

The senator's smile faded, his features taking on a vulpine cast. "It's been more than a year since you tested the prototype. I'd have thought you'd be able to reconstruct it by now and get the project back on track."

"Obviously I thought the same thing, sir, or I wouldn't have taken on the position."

"It seems a simple engineering problem to me."

"I wish it was that simple, sir," Travis said, "but my brother never made anything easy. No one knew he kept most of the design details in his head."

"Yes. Unfortunate that he's no longer with us."

The senator's eyes narrowed as though watching Travis for a reaction. Travis kept his face a bland mask.

"I miss him every day, senator."

"I'm sure you do. With or without James, we want to see this project succeed. The problem, Travis, is that we can't wait indefinitely. Time is money, and both are hard to come by these days on Capitol Hill. The subcommittee wants results. That's what we're paying for."

"What are you saying, Jeremy?" Turnbull said.

Latham faced the general. "You have until the end of May. If there's no working prototype by then, we're pulling the plug. No more funding."

"You can't do that, senator," Turnbull said.

"I can, and I will."

"We're getting closer, sir," Travis said. "We think we've got the stabilization problem licked. It's just a matter of time before we figure out how to reduce the weight enough to extend battery life within acceptable ranges."

"I'm glad, but that's not good enough," Latham said. "A working prototype, equal to the first one, or we shut it down."

"Have you forgotten that Travis here brought down a top al-Qaeda operative—along with an entire terrorist cell—with that prototype?"

"We need results, Jack, not talk. If MondoHard can't replicate those results, we're wasting taxpayers' money. Not to mention my time. I've got half a dozen other weapons systems from other defense contractors I could be bringing along. This one showed a lot of promise a year ago. But a year is a long time, gentlemen." Latham stood. "You've got six weeks. Good luck."

Travis watched him walk out, the weight of his words pressing him down. "That's it, then."

"Don't give up yet, son. You can still pull this off."

"I might have a working prototype by that deadline, but it'll never be as good as the one James built. We screwed up, Jack. We need James."

"I have faith in you, Travis. I know you won't let me down." Turnbull rose. "I've got another meeting. Keep me posted, will you?"

Travis sighed. "Of course, sir."

He remained seated after the general left, too discouraged to move. After a few moments, he chided himself. He'd never let a situation get the best of him before, not even when he'd been pinned down in the Afghan mountains by Taliban fighters without any hope of air or ground support. He could handle this. If nothing else, he'd use smoke and mirrors to buy time. There was too much money at stake—not to mention power for whoever wielded a weapon as potent as the little drone James had created.

His phone rang as he stood up. "Yes?"

"Cooper here," said the voice on the other end.

"What's the problem, Cyrus?"

"We've had a breach," said MondoHard's security chief.

"A hacker? Service attack?"

"No, a physical breach. An old security card was used to access the building and the server room."

Travis groaned. "Don't tell me someone sabotaged the servers."

"No, sir. Nothing was damaged. The intruders logged on to a terminal and accessed some files. That's the extent of it. They didn't install any software or plant any bugs."

"Thank goodness. Anything else? What did they want?"

"They removed a file. Near as we can tell, that's all they wanted."

"What was in it?"

"Not sure. They deleted it after downloading a copy. We reconstructed part of it; it was an e-mail. Looked harmless enough."

"Okay. Well, thanks for letting me know."

"One other thing," Cooper said. "The security ID card used to gain access belonged to your niece."

"Tess? Was she involved?"

"Yes. Security cameras show she had two unidentified males escorting her. Didn't look like they were coercing her in any way."

"I'll talk to her, Coop, as soon as I get back."

"Are you sure? This is pretty serious."

"I said I'll take care of it. I'll deal with it as soon as I get in."

"Whatever you say."

Travis hung up and sank back into the chair to think. Tess using the old ID card James had given her was worrisome.

It might be nothing—kids fooling around—or it might meanTess had finally grown curious. About the accident. About what James had really done at the video game company. Or even about me.

He wondered what file she'd been after.

But he worried even more about Coop.

Cyrus Cooper has access to far too much information. If I'm not careful, Cooper could learn the truth about everything.

CHAPTER 21

I braced myself for more tears. I had no trouble with being Tess's gofer, but I hadn't bargained on a waterlogged shoulder before the end of my first day.

"I miss them so much," Tess cried.

I put my hand on her arm. She shrugged me off.

"It's not fair!" she wailed.

"Whoa! Wait, your dad says he wants you to help save the world, and you're whining? I'd kill to have my father even ask me to go have coffee. What the hell's wrong with you?"

The tears never materialized. She looked through me in that disconcerting way of hers, mouth open in horror, and sniffled.

"I—" she hiccupped, "miss them."

"Of course you miss them. Nobody should lose her parents at your age. But they're gone. Get a grip. They're giving you a chance to do something to honor their memory. If I were you, I'd stop feeling sorry for myself and start living life again. They're not coming back, Tess. You have to move on."

"I can't believe Alice hired you," she whispered. "You're horrid. Mean, nasty—"

"Oh, get over yourself. How many people did she interview before she hired me?"

"What? I . . . I don't know what you mean."

"Oh, come on. Alice doesn't strike me as the impulsive sort. She's meticulous, and very careful when it comes to you. I bet she interviewed several people, and you nixed all of them. How many?"

"Five. But I—"

"Save it, Tess. Fact is, I like this job, and I'd like to keep it. I even like *you*, despite the fact that you almost cry at the drop of a hat. If you want to tell Alice what an awful ogre I am and ask her to fire me, go right ahead. But if you ask me, people around here need to stop coddling you and to start treating you like a normal person."

"You don't know the first thing about me, Oliver Moncrief," she said softly, "so you're the *last* person who should be giving me advice."

That was probably true, but she fell silent long enough that I thought she was taking it anyway, against her better judgment.

"What does it mean?" I said.

"The message? I don't know!"

"Think! You said you used to do this all the time."

"Give me a minute, will you? Stop pushing me."

"Somebody has to—"

"Stop it!" She wrinkled her nose. "He means my camera, okay? Just stop it."

"Your camera? Sure, that makes sense. Where is it?"

"I don't remember. Wait, yes I do. I left it at school. Last year. It must be locked up in the photography room, or in Mrs. Robertson's office."

"Let's go get it. I'll tell Alice where we're going."

"We've—I've got homework, Oliver. Which you need to help me with."

"What's more important? Homework, or saving the world?"

"Oh, come on. You can't believe that note's serious. It's a game. Everything was a game to my dad. That's what he did for a living."

The thought was as tough as a piece of gristle when I chomped down on it, so I discarded it.

"I'll tell Alice you forgot a textbook and we need to go back to school to get it."

"Oliver. Come *on*. I have to work."

I headed for the door. "I'll be right back. Don't move."

Closing my ears to more protestations, I left and found Alice in her office. I told her I had to take Tess back to school. She considered me from under knitted brows. When I assured her we'd be back in less than thirty minutes, she okayed the request.

Ten minutes later, I escorted Tess down the deserted corridors of the high school. Eerie silence filled the space, so boisterous and congested only hours before, as if a plague or some deadly predator had emptied the building of life. Tess murmured soft dissent, still grousing that she had homework and we shouldn't be there. Saving the world wasn't part of my job description, but I decided I hadn't been a very productive member of society up until then. I was beginning to think that maybe everything *does* happen for a reason. Maybe my financial troubles had come at an auspicious time.

The classroom where Mrs. Robertson taught photography was dark, long since abandoned by students and teachers alike. Robertson's office was locked, too.

"See, I told you we shouldn't be here," Tess said. "I can ask her tomorrow. Let's go."

"Hang on a minute," I said.

Upon closer inspection, the door appeared vulnerable. The gap between the door and the frame looked abnormally large, maybe from settling in an earthquake. I thought I might be able to work the latch open with the right tools. In addition to photography, the classroom hosted art classes of all types, including metalwork. A quick search yielded a utility knife and a long, thin strip of rigid steel that suited my purposes. I knelt in front of the door and worked the two pieces of metal against the latch, prying it open a millimeter with one and pinning it with the other.

"Keep an eye out, will you?" I said.

"Ha ha, very funny. What are you doing? Breaking in?"

"Not exactly. We're retrieving something that belongs to you."

"But the door's locked."

"That's funny. Apparently it wasn't latched tightly, since the door's open now."

I stood, swung the door wide, and took Tess's elbow.

"What kind of camera?" I said.

She told me the make and model. A locked cabinet on one wall beckoned as a logical place to keep valuable photography equipment. I wrestled briefly with the moral dilemma of committing a crime—breaking and entering—to achieve a greater good. Tess was right; we could wait until the next day to get the camera. But J. Robertson had pissed me off earlier by being so unfeeling. I stuck the rigid strip of steel into the gap between the cabinet doors and prepared to break them open, then had a better idea. I stepped over to Robertson's desk. One of the drawers relinquished a small silver key that fit the cabinet lock perfectly.

"Oh, heck," I said to the open cupboard.

"What's wrong?"

"There's a bunch of cameras in here."

"Some belong to the school. They're loaners for students who can't afford their own."

"Well, there are three that are the same kind as yours."

"Bet not. Mine's digital. The photography class studies film first, so the school's cameras shoot film. Anyway, mine has my initials etched on the base."

Sure enough, I found a digital SLR with a small *TB* engraved on the bottom. "Got it."

I gave the camera to Tess, locked the cabinet, and replaced the key where I'd found it. After collecting my burglar's tools, I steered Tess out of the office and closed the door behind us. I dropped off the tools, and we were back at the house ten minutes later.

Back in the library, everything was as we'd left it except someone had cleared the cocoa mugs and plate of *sopaipillas*. I tried to see what was on the camera, but the batteries were dead. Tess insisted on doing homework before I went looking for replacements, so we spent the next hour and a half going over her assignments. She breezed through her math problems, and I helped her with the French assignment. English and history were reading assignments, which meant she'd have to listen to CDs later. She'd missed chemistry after lunch. I pulled her assignment off the teacher's website and walked her through the chapter the class had started.

It was close to dinnertime when we finished. I accompanied her to the kitchen to see if Alice needed me for anything else, and brought the camera along. Tess felt her way to the big island and sat on a stool. I set the camera down on the counter next to her. Rosa stood in her customary spot at the stove. She glanced at us over her shoulder, her gaze resting momentarily on the camera. Alice must have heard us coming. She walked in just as I turned to look for her.

"All finished with homework?" she said.

"Yes, Alice," Tess said.

She rolled her eyes unconsciously. Though sightless, it had the same effect as if she could see. Alice's mouth tightened, and she nodded.

"She has reading assignments still," I said, "but she finished everything else."

"Good," Alice said. "Oliver, you're finished for the day, but you're welcome to stay for dinner."

"Thank you. First, though, I wondered if you might have some batteries."

Alice noticed the camera for the first time. "Where has that been, Tess? I haven't seen your camera for ages."

Tess hesitated only a moment, and said, "I thought I'd show Oliver some of my photos, but the batteries are dead."

"I'm sure I can find some that will work."

She disappeared into the garage.

Rosa faced us and, without a trace of an accent, said, "I'll take that camera, thank you."

Tess looked as surprised as I felt. She felt for the camera on the counter and gathered it in.

"It's my camera. You can't have it. What's gotten into you?"

"Just give it to me, you little bitch!"

Rosa picked up a big kitchen knife and took a step toward the island.

"Whoa, Rosa. What gives?" I took a step toward Tess and put my hands up, palms out.

She couldn't reach the camera across the island. She would have to come around. I positioned myself behind Tess, watching Rosa to see which way she'd move. The woman had gone loco.

Alice stepped back into the kitchen. She looked at us, then Rosa.

"What's going on here?"

"Stay out of this, Alice," Rosa said.

"Put the knife down," Alice told her.

She advanced warily. Rosa faced her on the balls of her feet with knees bent. The knife in her hand swayed gently back and forth, like a cobra head.

"I'm warning you, Alice. All I want is the camera. No one has to get hurt."

Alice cocked her head, taking in the shift in Rosa's character. She'd morphed from friendly immigrant kitchen help to cold-blooded, knife-wielding killer in the blink of an eye.

"What's going on?" Tess cried.

I moved up behind her and murmured in her ear. "Stand up. We may have to move."

Alice took another step. Rosa tensed, settling lower into a crouch, ready to spring.

"What on earth are you doing, Rosa?"

"Cut the crap! It's not 'Rosa.' Never was. Now move back before I cut you."

Alice shrugged and shifted her weight, then moved in like a cat, catching Rosa off guard. Rosa took a swing with the knife, but Alice ducked under it, smashed a palm into Rosa's nose, and stepped back out of reach. It happened so fast her hands were a blur. Blood trickled from Rosa's nose down her lip. She swiped at it and inspected the red stain on the back of her hand.

"Oliver, get Tess out of here," Alice said in a low voice. "I'll take care of this."

"Too late!" Rosa said as she made a wholly unpleasant sound more like a hyena's cackle than a laugh.

Two men dressed in black camo fatigues and face masks burst through the door from the garden, spread apart, and stopped several feet inside. They both carried ugly-looking machine pistols with long sound suppressors and short metal stocks.

"Don't move!" one of them said.

"What's happening?" Tess said.

"Shut up!" Rosa barked. "Now, since we seem to have the upper hand here, it's time you handed over the camera."

"Two men are pointing guns at you," I whispered to Tess.

"Guns?" she said. "Fine! You want it, take the camera!"

Tess shoved it hard. It slid across the granite countertop and crashed to the floor on the other side. Rosa bent to pick it up, and all hell broke loose. The little Japanese gardener I'd seen at breakfast suddenly appeared in the doorway behind the two men and flicked his wrist. One of them dropped his weapon and clutched at his throat—a sharp steel *shuriken* had embedded itself in his neck. Blood spurted between his fingers in a fine spray, dappling Tess's face. She shrieked. The other man twirled toward his falling partner, saw the gardener, and swung his weapon. With the stock unfolded, the gun was too unwieldy in the confined space. The small Asian stepped inside the gun's arc, landed three quick blows, and knocked the gun aside.

"Oliver!" Alice snapped. "Get her out of here! Go! Someplace safe! We'll take care of this."

I didn't need to be told three times. Yanking Tess by the collar, I wrapped an arm around her waist and half dragged her toward the garage. As we blew past, Alice had already waded in to block Rosa's path, ducking under the deadly swing of the knife blade.

CHAPTER 22

Tess shuddered, unable to get the ferrous stench of blood out of her nostrils. Her face was splattered with the sticky substance, and the thought that someone else's blood had sprayed her like the special effects in a horror flick turned her stomach. She squelched the impulse to vomit and focused on maintaining her balance as Oliver roughly pulled her through the garage. She heard the car door open and felt his hand press against the back of her head, forcing her to duck. She practically fell in. She fumbled with the seatbelt, but before she could latch it the car started with a roar and jerked forward with a squeal of tires on the concrete floor.

"Holy crap!" Oliver shouted. "Another one!"

A loud thump reverberated through the interior, and the car gave a hesitant shiver before accelerating again, pressing Tess into her seat.

"Another one *what*? Did we just hit something?" Tess gripped the edges of her seat with white-knuckled tension.

"Some*one*, not something. It's another one of those guys!"

"What guys, Oliver? What's going on?"

"Hell if I know! Your cook is a slasher, your gardener has Jackie Chan moves, and your housekeeper . . . My god, Tess, you should have seen Alice. She kicked Rosa's ass. Like that Bond chick—what's her name?—Michelle Yeoh. You're asking *me* what's going on?"

She felt the car swaying from side to side, and judging from the engine's growl, Oliver was pushing the car down the curvy road far faster than the speed limit. She held on.

"What are you talking about?" she said. "What happened in there?"

Nothing made sense, and her stomach grew queasy again from the twists and turns in the road as well as from the thoughts racing through her head.

"Rosa went psycho is what happened." Oliver said. "Alice should get her money back from whatever firm did the background check on *her*."

"But those other men . . . Who were they?"

"No clue. Mercenaries, maybe. Definitely ex-military. Heavily armed."

"And they were working for, or with, Rosa?"

Oliver briefly described what had happened. Tess fell silent as she tried to work it out.

"This is bad, Oliver," she said finally. "There's something on the camera. Rosa's obviously not who she seems, which means she's after something my dad was working on."

"An industrial spy? Gee, and she seemed so nice."

"Right. No, it might be even worse. My parents tried to keep it from me—to protect me, or whatever—but it wasn't hard to figure out my dad's company did work for the Department of Defense. Maybe this has something to do with it."

"The DoD? You're right—that's worse. They could be terrorists, from a foreign government. Jeez, we're in deep doo-doo here, Tess. How deep we'll never know without figuring out what was on the camera. And that's not likely unless Alice and Yoshi got it back."

"Don't be so sure," Tess said. She dug in her pocket and held up the camera's memory card.

"How . . . ? When did you pop that out?"

"When you handed it to me at school. I . . ." Her voice faltered. "I wasn't sure I wanted you to see my photos."

"Why, Tess? You're an amazing photographer."

She turned her head away so he couldn't see the tears filling her eyes. She bit her lip.

"Oh, yeah. You *were* an amazing photographer. It's because you can't see them, right?"

She didn't answer.

"Sorry. Stupid thing to say. I know, you're wondering how on earth I made it through college, let alone got an advanced degree with such a quick wits. Just think 'Mark Zuckerberg.'"

"Who?" she said.

"Facebook?"

"Oh. Right. No, actually, I was wondering whose blood is all over me."

"A member of the goon squad."

"Is he . . . ?"

"Dead? Yeah, I think so. Your gardener got him in the throat with a throwing star." Oliver paused. "Did you know he and Alice were, like, ninjas or something?"

She shook her head. "No way. Yoshi taught me some jujitsu when I was little. I liked it, so I joined a dojo. But Alice . . . ? This is crazy, Oliver. What are we going to do?"

"Lay low. Hope that Alice and Yoshi kicked ass and will call us when the coast is clear."

"Where are we going?"

"My place, I guess. I don't know where else to take you."

She didn't respond.

"Are you okay with that?" he said.

"I don't think we have much choice."

"Look, I know you don't have much of a reason to trust me after just one day—"

"And not exactly a stellar day, either."

"Yeah, okay. A pretty crappy day, but I promise I won't let anything happen to you."

"Too afraid of losing your job?"

He was silent for a moment, and Tess wondered why she'd let the remark out of her mouth.

"No," he said. "Screw the job. They waved guns at us, Tess. This is personal. No one should have to go through the kind of day you just did. I'll be damned if I'll let anyone do it again."

Warmth spread through her body, yet, oddly, Tess shivered. His words sounded more confident than she felt. Whoever wanted the memory card in her pocket wouldn't stop at just one attempt. They had to figure out what was on it and why her father had sent her in search of it. Suddenly, she felt Oliver's fingers gently caress her cheek, and her head jerked involuntarily. She held her breath. A moment later, he traced the line of her jaw with his finger and then cupped the back of her neck with his hand and massaged the tense muscles there. She sighed, melting into the seat.

No, this isn't right. I just met Oliver. And what about Toby?

A school of confused thoughts darted through her head, as if frightened by a predatory shark. She sat up suddenly and Oliver's hand fell away.

"Shouldn't we call the police?" she said. "Alice and Yoshi could be hurt. They might need help."

Wind rush and the steady growl of the engine filled the car. Tess feared she'd angered him, but when he replied his voice was thoughtful.

"What if they're after you, too, Tess? You're the one getting the messages."

"Isn't that all the more reason to call the police?"

"I don't know," he said slowly. "There'd be a lot of questions. And what if they didn't believe us? Alice said they'd take care of it. She said to take you someplace safe."

"Where safer than a police station?"

"I just don't think it's a good idea."

Tess fell silent again, trying to decide if Oliver's concern was genuine.

Why would he distrust the police?

She didn't have much choice but to go along. Alice seemed to think he was okay. Then again, Alice had also hired Rosa. And Tess and Alice hadn't exactly been seeing eye-to-eye recently.

As if I can see at all.

She shrugged and settled back in her seat.

The car slowed and danced to a syncopated rhythm of stop-and-go city traffic. Tess absorbed the sounds surrounding them—the low rumble of a diesel bus, hum of car engines, rush of tires on pavement, a honking horn, distant wail of a siren, and the muffled steady beat of someone's car stereo woofer nearby—all muted by their expensive car's soundproofing. Not long after, the car rolled to a stop and the engine shut off.

"Where are we?" Tess said.

"Not far from UW," Oliver said. "It's a short walk from here."

Oliver got out. A moment later, he opened her door and helped her out. He took her arm and walked her down the sidewalk and up some steps. His gentle tug pulled her to a stop, and she heard the sound of a key in a lock. The street sounds receded when the door shut behind them, replaced by hushed music coming through a wall and the clack-clack of her shoes on a hardwood floor. Oliver's footsteps gave off a soft squeak from what must have been athletic shoes. She tried to picture what he looked like, but quickly gave up in frustration. Smells of fried food, stale pizza, and something that reminded her of sweaty socks wafted past her nose. Oliver pulled her up short again and unlocked another door, then led her inside an even quieter space.

"Home sweet home. It's not much, but it's all I need."

He walked her around the small apartment, telling her what was where, letting her feel her way around. It wasn't much more than a rectangular box with a bed in one corner, a couch and coffee table across from a small television in the middle, and a kitchen at the far end with a table and chairs that doubled as a dining and study area. A sliding glass door in the kitchen led to a deck outside. She sat down at the kitchen table.

"Would you like something to drink?" Oliver said.

"Water, thanks, if that's okay."

A cupboard door squeaked and water ran in the sink. Oliver set a glass in front of her. She drank thirstily, and felt Oliver ease onto the chair beside her.

"Hold still," he said.

Before she could object, he dabbed her face with a warm, wet cloth. His touch was so gentle she wondered if the blood was even coming off. The thought made her shiver. The lovely sensation of the cloth against her skin and the gesture behind it stopped too soon.

"There," he said. "Much better."

She heard the soft hum of a fan and buzz of a hard drive as he booted up a laptop.

"Mind if I take a look at the memory card?" he said.

She fished it out of her pocket and held it out. "What good is it without the camera?"

Oliver took it from her fingers. "Universal card reader. I make a little money on the side putting together presentations for other students. It comes in handy."

"What, the money?"

"Very funny." He tapped the keys and clicked the mouse. "Nice photos, but nothing else here—No, wait. There's a file . . . Damn."

"What is it?"

"I don't know. I can't open it. I don't know what program to use."

"Try them all."

For a moment, the sound of keystrokes and mouse clicks filled the room.

"Nope. Nothing works. I think we need Matt again."

"Right now? Can't we just sit for a minute? I . . . I need to think this through."

"Yeah, I suppose. You must be starved. No lunch. Just a cup of cocoa this afternoon. Can I fix you something?"

"Like what?"

"Ramen? No? A sandwich, maybe? Turkey and cheese?"

"Sure. That'll be fine."

Oliver got up, and Tess heard him rustling around in the kitchen.

"I have to get rid of the car," Oliver said as he worked.

"Why? What do you mean?"

"Look, even if Alice and Yoshi took out Rosa and the bad guys at the house, there was at least one other guy outside who saw us get away. And whoever set Rosa up with that job meant to keep an eye on things, waiting for exactly something like this to happen. I don't know anything about you or your family, Tess. But whatever your dad wanted you to do, it's serious. And if it has anything to do with government stuff—military stuff—they can easily track us."

"You mean we aren't safe here?"

"I think we're okay for the time being. I'm new, so I don't think Rosa even knows my last name, let alone where I live. But they can trace the plates on the car."

"So what now?" she said.

Oliver set a plate in front of her. "Now you eat. I'll go dump the car somewhere in your neighborhood and find a way back here. Don't go anywhere, and don't answer the door for anyone but me. Okay?"

"Okay." Tess heard the tremor in her voice.

Oliver put a hand on her shoulder. "We'll figure this out. I promise."

Before she could think of a reply, she heard the soft click of the door closing.

CHAPTER 23

Travis sensed something wrong the moment he turned into the drive and saw the open gate. The one he'd had installed. The one that James should have put in when he'd built the house. The gate closed automatically once a vehicle passed through, unless something obstructed the electronic eye. It had happened before. A wet leaf had fallen on the infrared transmitter once, covering it. Another time a crow had tried to wrest the shiny reflector on the opposite side off its mount, bending the angle enough to disrupt the beam.

Travis stopped and got out of the SUV to check. He walked behind the gate pillar, where the LED beam was located. Bending down, he saw snipped wires dangling loose in the light from a streetlamp. The hairs on the back of his neck rose, and his pulse raced.

Tess!

Forcing himself to remain calm, he walked back to the SUV and climbed in. He leaned over, unlocked the glove compartment, and took out a pistol, the same HK USP Tactical .45 ACP semiautomatic he'd used in Afghanistan. He sat a moment before starting the engine, then decided to go straight in, act like nothing was amiss. He'd know soon enough if a frontal assault was a bad idea.

He drove down the slope slowly, gun ready in his lap, eyes searching the darkness for signs of ambush. But all was quiet. Pulling up in front of the house, he stopped. When no hail of bullets met his arrival, he put the SUV in gear and swung around the circle to the garage. Yoshi's pickup truck sat inside, as did the older sedan that Alice refused to give up. Even James and Sally's wrecked hulk that used to be a Range Rover sat in the far bay. He needed to fix it or junk it, but every time he thought about it, he hadn't the heart to get rid of it, nor the energy to repair it. Analogous, he knew, to the lives of the four people who still lived in the house.

The BMW, though, was gone. Which didn't mean anything by itself, but if Yoshi and Alice were in the house, he wondered why they hadn't closed the gate.

Unless...

His heart hammered the bars of the cage that held it. He made a point of slowing his breathing as his hearing became more acute and his field of vision narrowed. Adrenaline pushed his body into battle mode, and he eased out of the car, the pistol out ahead of him in a two-handed grip. He made no sound as he glided across the ground like a wraith.

At the door leading into the house, he crouched low and put one hand on the knob. It was unlocked. He turned it slowly, a fraction of an inch at a time, until it couldn't turn any farther. Drawing in a deep breath, he burst through the door, staying low, and rolled to one side as soon as he was clear. He came up on one knee, swinging the gun in an arc as he quickly panned the room. Yoshi and Alice sat across from one another in the breakfast nook, Yoshi bent over Alice's pale arm, which was stretched out on the table. Both the arm and the table were streaked red with blood. The pair looked up, startled, but didn't move or speak. On the floor, a man's legs stuck out from behind the island, black camo fatigues neatly tucked into combat boots.

"Any more?" Travis said.

Alice shook her head. Yoshi calmly went back to stitching up the laceration in Alice's forearm. Alice winced.

"Are you two all right?" Travis said, getting to his feet.

"Fine," Alice said. "Just a scratch."

"Tess...?" Travis let the question hang.

"I hired an assistant for her. Nice boy named Oliver. I told him to get her out of here and take her somewhere safe."

"Did he?"

She shook her head. "No idea. We think they made it okay."

"A boy? Are you sure?"

"Young man, then. He's smart, Travis. He'll figure it out. Tess, too."

"How many were there?"

"Three inside," Alice said. "Yoshi thinks he saw another outside, but he came in to help us before all hell broke loose. There may have been others. Judging from the firepower, though, I think they figured four would be enough. Three in here, and a lookout just in case."

"How'd they get in?"

Alice frowned. "Rosa. Hard to believe. She's been with us—"

"Since the accident," Travis finished for her.

"I'm sorry, Travis," she said. "It never should have happened. This is my fault."

"Not your fault," Yoshi said. "She fool us all. Important thing is you save Tess."

Travis looked around the kitchen. "Where's Rosa now?"

"She took off with the others. We fended them off long enough to give Tess and Oliver a good head start, but I dropped my focus, and Rosa cut me. Yoshi came to my aid, and they ran."

Travis walked over to the body on the floor and crouched next to it. He let out a low whistle when he saw the HK MP5K-PDW machine pistol.

"This is military spec hardware, not a street weapon." He rifled through the man's pockets, but found no wallet or ID. "Any idea what they were after?"

Alice nodded toward a camera on the table. "That. But the memory card's gone."

Travis frowned. "I've never seen that before. Is that Tess's?"

Alice nodded. "I have no idea where she got it. I haven't seen it in ages, not for a year at least." She paused, brows knitting. "Oliver took her to school before dinner to 'get a textbook.' She must have left the camera at school last year some time."

"Why was it so important she needed it now all of a sudden?"

Alice bit her lip and gazed into the darkness outside the window. Yoshi looked up from his work on her wound and stared at her.

"What is it?" Travis said.

"He need to know," Yoshi told Alice. "Better to tell him now."

Alice sighed and turned to Travis. "Tess thinks she's been getting e-mails from her father."

"James?" Travis felt his eyebrows climb up toward his scalp. "It's not possible."

"I know that, but she came home early from school very upset. Said she'd gotten an e-mail from Mr. Barrett. While she was sitting here waiting for Rosa to fix her something to eat, she screamed and said she'd gotten another one."

"You saw it?"

"No, I was in my office speaking with Oliver. But Oliver apparently did. He thought someone might be playing a prank on her. A while later, though, Oliver drove Tess and a school friend on some 'errand.'"

Travis knew what the errand had been. Cyrus Cooper had called him to tell him what Tess and her "escorts" had been up to. And if they'd traced the source of the e-mails to a computer at the office, that meant someone at the company had sent them.

"I wonder how Rosa knew what they were up to," Travis murmured.

"She took them a snack in the library," Alice said, "after they came back from their errand. She must have overheard or seen something."

Yoshi finished wrapping a bandage around Alice's arm. She pulled the sleeve of her cardigan down over it and rose from the table as if nothing had happened.

"I'm sorry about the mess, Travis," she said, all business. "We'll clean up as soon as we can. In the meantime, can I fix you something to eat? That must have been a long flight."

"Sit down, Alice," he said gently. "Please. I owe you and Yoshi a huge debt for protecting Tess. And after all those years in the army, I think I can manage to fend for myself in the kitchen. You're not to lift a finger until that arm heals. Now, would you like some tea?"

Somewhat cowed, she lowered herself into the chair and said, "Yes, thank you."

Yoshi got up, collecting blood-soaked towels, and went to the sink.

"I will make tea," he said. "Maybe you go call garbage collector." He glanced at the body on the floor and sniffed.

"That's a good idea, Yoshi. Excuse me a minute."

Travis set his gun on the counter and walked down the hall to a small study past the library. Even though he'd taken over the reins of James's company, he couldn't bring himself to use James's office in the house. The study suited him better anyway. Distrusting his cell phone and the house landline, he unlocked a drawer in the small desk and pulled out an encrypted satellite phone. Glancing at his watch, he saw it was close to ten in the evening on the East Coast—late, but not too late. He dialed a number by heart.

"There's been some trouble," he told the voice on the other end. "I don't know what it means yet, but we we've got one down in need of disposal. I'd rather not involve the locals. At least not for a while, until we know what we're dealing with. I know there has to be an official investigation, but any way we can keep this on the q.t. for now?"

"The line's clean, Travis. You can speak plainly. One down . . . Not one of ours, I take it. Anyone hurt?"

"Alice, but not badly. Jack, Tess is missing. I presume she's safe—some kid who's helping her with school got her out on Alice's orders—but they're both in the wind for the time being."

"Any idea what they're after?"

"James may have risen from the dead, general. Apparently, he's been sending Tess e-mails. Best we can figure out is that she was directed to retrieve a memory card on a camera."

"Could it be him? No, I know he didn't come back from the grave, Travis, but could he have set up some program to do this?"

"I wouldn't put it past him. I mean, look how far behind we are on the program because of the damn worm he used to infect the software for the prototype. Just when the tech geeks think they've got it licked, it morphs into something else."

"We can't afford more delays," Turnbull said. "Better figure this out quick, Travis."

"Until I talk to Tess, I'm not sure what I can do."

"Then find her."

"I'll call in the team. You know if any of them are out of pocket?"

"Not so far that they won't come when you call."

"You'll get someone on our garbage disposal problem?"

"It'll probably be a couple of hours, Trav, but I'm sure I can get a secure forensics team out of JBLM to take possession. Don't touch anything. I'll have them start an investigation but keep it off the books for now. That way, if anyone asks, you and the folks there will come out okay."

"Thanks, Jack."

Travis didn't see any need to tell him he'd already gone through the dead guy's pockets. After all, he hadn't really disturbed the scene.

"Good luck, son. Keep me posted."

CHAPTER 24

I'd never seen death up close before, other than roadkill, which doesn't count. Actually seeing someone die, violently, was different, unpleasant. For a brief moment I envied Tess, glad that what I'd seen wouldn't haunt her dreams for months the way it would mine. But shock had set in, distancing me from the event like a thick layer of fuzzy cotton, numbing me to its horror, its finality. I concentrated instead on keeping us alive, trying to figure out the right tack to take. I didn't like leaving Tess alone after what had happened, especially in a strange place, but I didn't see a way around it. The Beemer had to go, much as I enjoyed driving it.

Out on the street, I called Matt, told him what we'd found, and asked if he was willing to meet me. His nonchalance when he said he could was less than convincing. We agreed on the high school parking lot, and I told him to give me twenty minutes or so to get across the lake. The street bore the usual stream of traffic common at that time of evening around the U District. Knots of pedestrians clotted the sidewalks, students mostly, laughing and talking. Solo professionals on their way home from working late race-walked around them, heads down, eyes front. No suspicious characters lurked in doorways, but I executed three ungainly pirouettes on the way to the car to see if anyone had followed me.

Paranoia still skulked around my head when I reached the high school. I pulled in to the nearly empty lot, parked, and sat there a moment, checking for signs of a tail. When Matt stepped out of some shadows and rapped on my window, my heart tried to leap out of my chest.

"You trying to kill me?" I said as I climbed out.

"What's wrong with you?"

The funny smile he wore faded as I told him what had happened since we'd dropped him off earlier. By the end of it he looked a little green around the gills.

"You don't have to do this," I said.

"No, I'm in." He shrugged. "Nothing else to do."

A door banged open loudly. Voices floated across the parking lot. Several figures stepped through the rectangle of light at the far end of the gym and came through the darkness toward us. Baseball players leaving after a game.

"Woof, woof," called a voice as they approached. "If it isn't the seeing-eye dog."

Hoots of laughter followed as Carl and three friends walked into a pool of light.

"Trouble," Matt muttered.

"Where's your bitch?" Carl said to me. "Tsang, are you his bitch now?"

My hands balled into fists, but more laughter from Carl's buddies reminded me the odds were against me.

A tall blond kid I remembered from the jock table at lunch took a step. "Yeah, Tsang, you his *biatch*?"

"Shut up, Tad," Carl growled.

"You should learn some manners, Carl," I said.

"Who's going to teach me? You?"

"You want to go, just you and me?" I said evenly. "Come on, then, let's go. Or do you need your friends there to help you?"

He hesitated, unused to being challenged. A brief look of uncertainty crossed his face, but his friends were watching. His gaze darted, looking for a way to save face, and landed on the BMW behind me. His eyes lit up.

"Nah," he said. "You want manners? How's this? Give me the keys to your ride before we stomp your face into the pavement, *please*."

I hesitated, then tossed him the key fob. "Oh, what the hell. It's not my car."

Carl plucked the key out of the air and stared at it for a moment. His buddies hooted. I couldn't tell if he was disappointed he wouldn't get to rough us up or elated I'd just handed over an $80,000 car.

"Guess you're *my* bitch now, huh?" he said, eyes gleaming.

He strutted past me, key fob held high, buddies circling around him, clamoring for a ride. He shrugged them off, too selfish, apparently, to share ill-gotten gains, and climbed in the driver's seat. He started it up and backed out with a chirp of tires.

Throwing it in gear, he roared out of the lot. The others eyed us angrily, muttering, but slowly wandered off.

"What did you do that for?" Matt said.

"You liked the alternative more?"

"No, I mean . . . He just stole Tess's car."

"Let him have his jollies. We'll report it later. Have you got wheels?"

"Sure." He nodded toward an old, beat-up, compact car.

"Nice to see not all the kids here get a Mercedes when they turn sixteen. Let's go."

I directed him into the city, and a short time later I let us into my apartment. Matt headed straight for the laptop on the kitchen table.

"Oliver?" Tess said in a small voice.

"Yeah, we're back. Are you okay?"

"What took you so long?"

"We ran into Carl," I said. "It was no big deal. We didn't get into a fight or anything, but I sort of let him borrow the BMW."

"My mom's car? You let him take the car?"

"He won't go far with it. I'll get it back later."

"Uh, guys?" Matt said. "I can't help you much here."

"Why not?" I said, looking over his shoulder. "I thought you were the expert."

"I am. What you've got here is source code for a program of some sort."

"What does it do?"

"That's what I'm trying to tell you. It doesn't *do* anything. It's only *part* of a program."

"Great. Now what?"

"You didn't get any instructions?" Matt said. "Tess, have you checked your e-mail lately?"

"No, I usually get alerts on my phone. I haven't heard anything."

"Give me your address and password," he said. "I can get it faster."

She hesitated.

"Look," Matt said quickly, "Carl saw me with Oliver here, so my rep as an indie spirit with no allegiances is pretty much out the window at this point. And I could hack all your accounts anyway if I wanted to. Right now, I don't have time."

"You've got a point." She gave him the information.

"Okay," he said a moment later. "You've got a new e-mail from your dad. It says to upload the file to a web address. What do you think?"

"We've come this far," I said. "I think we do what it says. Tess?"

She nodded. Matt turned back to the laptop and played the keys like a concert pianist. He raised his right hand and hit "Enter" with a flourish. The smile on his face sank into a frown.

"What the—?" He typed something and peered at the screen.

"What's wrong?" I said.

"I uploaded the file," Matt said, "and it disappeared. Like, completely. Took the copy here on the laptop with it."

"You still have the original on the memory card, right?"

He shook his head. "Nope. Deleted that one, too."

"Can you download a copy from the site you just sent it to?"

Matt typed furiously again. "Damn, this guy's good, whoever he is. The website is gone already. And I checked the e-mail sender's IP address. It's not the same one he used to send the other e-mails."

"This didn't come from inside MondoHard?" I said.

"No. It was bounced halfway around the world and back. The guy could be next door and I wouldn't know it."

A phone rang, startling me. A female voice said in hitched, robotic tones, "Call from Tad Cooper."

Tess groped for her phone and connected the call.

Tad's voice came through loud and shrill. "Where is he? Where's your boyfriend?"

"Who?" Tess said "My what?"

"That son-of-a-bitch seeing-eye dog of yours!" Tad screamed. "Carl's *dead*! They shot him! In *your* car, bitch! He wasn't supposed to be there. They killed the wrong guy! Where is he?"

"Carl's dead?" Tess shook her head in shock.

We could hear Tad crying. "I'll kill him! You tell Oliver if I find him, I'll kill him! You hear me?"

The phone went dead, leaving the room quiet as a tomb. Whoever they were, these people were serious. My thoughts raced. I'd forgotten something. I couldn't put my finger on it. Then I had it.

"Oh, crap," I said. "Tess—your phone! Turn it off! They can track it just as easily as the license plates."

She quickly powered it down. Matt powered the laptop down, too. I hustled around the room and shut off the lights.

"Come on," I said. "We have to get out of here. Out the back, Matt."

I pointed to the sliding-glass door, and went to get Tess. Matt slid the door open silently and slipped out into the darkness. I grabbed my backpack and guided Tess out after him. He'd already swung a leg over the railing and jumped down to the grass yard four feet below. He set the laptop down as I led Tess to the railing. I told her what she had to do. She quickly swung one leg over, then the other and teetered on the edge, holding on to the railing.

"Ready," Matt said, holding his hands up.

Tess stepped into space and let go of the railing, falling right into Matt's arms. He set her down gently, and I vaulted over the railing after them, then stuffed the laptop in my backpack. Matt and I each took one of Tess's arms and walked her briskly out the back gate and down the alley to the street. As we rounded the corner, two men I didn't recognize strode up the walk to the front of the house down the block. I stopped and backpedaled, taking Tess and Matt with me. Too late.

"Hey you!" one of the men shouted.

"What's going on?" Tess said.

"Shit! They already found the apartment," I whispered. "We better split up. Matt, you better take off. I'm sorry we got you into this."

"Nobody twisted my arm, man. You guys cool?"

"Yeah, we're good," I said. "I've got a friend I think we can stay with."

"Later, then." He broke into a trot.

I hustled Tess to the corner, heading away from my apartment, and crossed the street.

"What are we doing?" she said.

"Getting the hell out of here," I muttered.

"Hey! Hey, you two!" A block behind, one of the men ran toward us.

"Run!"

I yanked Tess's arm and half dragged her up the street until she got her feet under her and nearly kept pace. The man gained on us, and the other one appeared behind him down the street. I cut left off the sidewalk onto a lawn, taking Tess with me. She managed to stay upright as we ran between two houses. I banged open a wooden gate into the backyard and kept going past a detached garage into the alley.

"Oliver!" Tess cried. "Slow down!"

"We have to keep moving!" I said. "Come on!"

I heard the gate bang open behind us and pulled Tess onto a walkway that led between two apartment buildings. Halfway through the passageway, I heard a funny thwack and whine, once, twice, and chips of stone exploded off the wall next to me, one grazing my cheek.

"Faster, Tess!" I pleaded.

I heard a muffled shout behind us, and the bullets stopped flying. We burst out onto the street and I pulled Tess away from the mouth of the passageway. A bus pulled up to the curb at the corner, and I tugged Tess's hand harder.

"Bus, Tess! We're getting on! Twenty feet. Almost there! Stop! Three steps. Up you go."

I shoved her up the steps and clambered on after her. She latched onto a handrail, chest heaving for breath.

"Let's go!" I told the driver.

"Is she—?"

"She's fine!" I said through gritted teeth, pulling change out of my pocket. "Just go!"

The driver closed the door and pulled away from the curb.

I grabbed Tess's hand and led her to a seat near the rear exit door. Nervously, I glanced out the window down the street, but there was no sign of the two men.

CHAPTER 25

Tess planted her feet. Oliver grabbed her hand and tugged, but she refused to budge.

"Come on, Tess," he said. "We have to move."

"I'm not moving! You can't make me."

On the bus, she'd barely caught her breath when Oliver had made her get off and start walking again. Now she was tired and not a little frightened.

"Tess, please! Let's go!"

Panic wrapped its arms around her, closing her throat and twisting her bra strap tight around her chest like a tourniquet, squeezing the breath out of her.

"I don't even know you! Why should I go anywhere with you?"

"Would you lower your voice? You're going to get us killed. Now, come on!"

"Not until you tell me what's going on. Where are we going? What are we doing?"

"I don't *know* what's happening. This is *your* life that's messed up, not mine."

"What do you mean?" she said, her voice sounding shrill in her ears. "I didn't have anything to do with this. I didn't ask for this."

"Tess, we can discuss it all you want. But can we please move?"

"Why should I?"

"Look, I know how this works. I've seen enough movies. Those two guys outside my place? The ones who were *shooting* at us? First, they go back and check out the apartment. They trash it looking for the memory card or anything else that might lead to us. Next, they get reinforcements and start hunting us down. And how hard can it be to find a guy leading a blind girl? So, can we please keep moving and get off the street?"

"Okay, okay. You don't have to yell."

He took her hand again.

"I'm not yelling. I'm imploring you. I want to keep breathing for as long as possible."

"For all I know, you made up that story about those guys shooting at us," she muttered.

Oliver squeezed her hand more tightly in response. She stumbled after him as he set a fast pace. Quiet at first, their way grew noisier with sounds of traffic as they walked along a commercial street for a while. Then it grew quiet again as they moved away from the thoroughfare and into a residential neighborhood. Her legs grew heavy, and her feet complained in the flats she'd put on after school. That seemed so long ago.

Has it really only been a few hours? The same day, even?

"How much farther?" she said.

"Not much," he said. " A few more blocks."

"Where are we?"

"Someplace safe, I hope."

She trudged along in silence, head whirling with questions.

Why now? Why did Dad wait a year to send me on this quest? What could be so important that he would risk my life in what was obviously dangerous business? Had he somehow foreseen his own death? And if so, how? If so ...

An even more horrible question popped into her head.

Was the accident that killed them and blinded me really an accident? Or had it been something else, something deliberate?

Tess shuddered.

"Okay, we're here," Oliver said softly. "Stay put a minute and let me check things out."

She pawed the air before latching onto him. "Where are you going?"

"Just up the walk to the door. I'll just be a few feet away. I won't let you out of my sight, I promise."

Reluctantly, she let his arm slip from her fingers. His footsteps moved away, the soft tread of sneakers on concrete giving way to a dull *thunk* on wooden steps. A bell bonged faintly from inside. A moment later, a door opened and she heard a man's voice. He and Oliver spoke in low tones. She only caught snippets of their conversation.

"No place else to go," Oliver said.

"Trouble ... go to the police," the man said.

"I don't trust them!" Oliver said, his voice a little louder. He lowered it, saying, "They'd take her home. It's too dangerous . . ."

So tired her bones ached, Tess tuned them out and thought of her own bed, soft and cozy. She pictured her room the way she remembered it from before the accident. The walls were pale blue, the color of a summer sky, the dresser and makeup table white. A bright yellow, floral print quilt lay on the bed, along with several throw pillows. The same fabric covered an easy chair in the corner near the window, where she used to curl up and read on rainy days.

Her cherished books still lined the bookshelves, along with the many trophies she'd brought home from her days on club teams in elementary and middle school—soccer and basketball, mostly. Her favorite was the one she'd earned for a first-place finish in snowboarding. She'd beaten out one other girl and five boys in the half-pipe during that competition. The boys had been so pissed, she'd never competed again—but she didn't have to. She knew she was good. Those days were long gone. She wouldn't be doing any aerials on a board anytime soon.

Oliver's voice intruded on her thoughts. "Hey, it's okay. We can stay."

She felt his hand in the small of her back, its light touch telling her which way to walk.

"Steps," he said. "Six."

She marched up without help. She felt a breath of warm air welling from the house, carrying scents of browned meat, fragrant spices, and a lingering trace of a cigarette. She sensed the presence of the man at the door and stood there, awkwardly.

The man took her hand warmly in his. "Eric. Eric Webster."

"Tess Barrett." Tess took her hand back, dropped it to her side, and squirmed. Her face flushed. Her parents would be disappointed she hadn't remembered her manners.

"Well, don't just stand there," the man said. "Come on in."

She stepped forward hesitantly, but Oliver was right there to guide her into the house.

"Excuse the mess," Eric said. "My father passed away not long ago. This was his house, and I've been trying to sort through his things."

"I'm sorry for your loss," Tess said. He didn't know what loss was, she decided.

"I finished dinner a while ago, but there's plenty left over if you're hungry."

"No, thank you," Tess said. "I already ate, but it smells delicious."

"Moroccan lamb stew," Eric said. "My favorite. Sit down and make yourself comfortable."

Oliver led her to an easy chair. She felt its contours, turned, and lowered herself into it. Music played softly in the background. Jazz. She recognized it as something her father used to listen to—Miles Davis.

"Oliver tells me you two are in some sort of trouble," Eric said.

"I didn't do anything wrong," Tess cried.

"Doesn't mean trouble won't find *you*," Eric said. "I know a thing or two about trouble. Want to talk about it?"

"Not really," Tess said. Her head hurt from all the thoughts and images crammed in there.

"Fair enough. But trouble sometimes ends up being a good thing."

Eric launched into a story about how being in trouble as a boy in Oakland, California, had led to him moving to Seattle to live with his grandmother. Good grades in high school and a love of writing had earned him a spot at Columbia University's School of Journalism. After graduating, he'd come home and gotten a law degree from UW. Though he'd practiced for a few years, alcohol and drugs had taken over his life, and he'd kicked around at a number of jobs, even working as a lumberjack at one point.

The more he talked the more curious Tess became. "How did you and Oliver meet?"

"Eric is my tennis instructor," Oliver said. "He's a pro at the Amy Yee Tennis Center."

"You teach tennis?" Tess said. "You gave up law? It seems such a waste."

"Tennis has been pretty good to me," Eric said. "It paid my way through Europe a few times, and provides a decent life for me now."

"Paid your way...You mean you *played* as a pro? In tournaments?"

Eric told them stories about his playing days and some of his travels. Brussels. Paris. London. He said he was even thinking of moving to Europe when he retired.

"You'd give up living here? But isn't this your home?" Tess said.

"It's true I grew up here. When my parents got divorced my father even came back to be closer to my grandmother. But roots are not always enough to keep someone bound to a place. Sometimes you have to get out of your comfort zone."

"Wouldn't you hate to leave your friends?"

"Arthur Ashe once said the hardest task in his life was being black in America. He said, 'Instinctively you are undervalued as a human being...too much time is expended showing to others your true value and worth.'"

"You're black?" Tess had never thought about the color of Eric's skin. "Gee, could've fooled me."

Eric laughed. "Guess it doesn't matter much to you. My grandmother was Native American. A Blackfoot. She faced prejudice every day of her life, but I think even she knew how much worse it can be for black people."

Tess wondered if she would have treated Eric differently if she'd known he was African American. She hoped not. Now that she'd been on the receiving end because she was different, she realized how cruel prejudice could be.

"Now I know why our principal keeps nagging us to be nice," she said.

This time Oliver laughed. "You're kidding."

"No, I'm not. He says we should treat each other the way we'd want to be treated."

"Good advice, if you ask me," Eric said.

The conversation quickly turned to other topics, and they talked for what seemed like hours. Eric had tons more stories, and Tess found him fascinating. Soon enough, though, she could barely keep her eyes open, and she stifled several yawns. For a while, the diversion had taken her mind off everything that had happened. Now exhaustion and fear began to overtake her again. Oliver must have noticed, because she heard him abruptly making excuses to

Eric about needing some rest. Eric offered Tess the spare bedroom and Oliver the couch.

Oliver came and took her hand. "Come on," he said in a low voice. "I'll show you where you're staying. Well, you know what I mean."

He walked her down a short hallway and helped her get settled. She wanted a hot shower, a clean nightshirt, and her own bed, but she was almost too tired to care.

"You going to be all right?" Oliver said.

"Yeah, I guess."

What other choice do I have?

"Well, goodnight."

She felt his hesitation, heard no movement. A thought struck her. "Should we check e-mail?"

"That's probably a good idea. I'll go get the laptop."

He was back a moment later, and she waited impatiently while he booted up the computer.

"Okay, I've got it," he said. "Two e-mails. One from Tad and one from, well, whoever's calling himself your father."

Tess bit back a retort.

I know the e-mails are coming from Dad!

Instead, she said, "Tad again? What's he want?"

Oliver was silent for a moment. "You don't want me to read this one."

"Why not? What is it?"

"Trust me, you don't want to hear it. He's ranting about Carl. He wants to know where you are—you're not going to respond."

"Fine. Read the other one."

"It says, 'It's 10:35.'"

"That's it?"

"No," Oliver drew out the word. "There's a file attached. I'm downloading it now."

A moment later, Tess heard the strains of a familiar song. An image of her parents singing it instantly came to mind, the memory bringing tears to her eyes before she could stop them.

"I'm . . . growing . . . weaker," Oliver said in a thready voice.

She laughed in spite of herself. "Oh, shut up, you. My parents would sing that whenever they wanted me to quit misbehaving."

"'Stop! In the Name of Love'?"

"The worst part was they danced to it like The Supremes used to." Badly, too, she remembered, which was funny the first few times, and embarrassing after that, but it had never failed to divert her from whatever she might have been doing.

"So, what's it mean?" Oliver said.

"I don't know. I suppose we'll have to get the book."

"Why? I can tell you exactly what's on that page. At 10:35, a bunch of the animals are playing blind man's buff. Sorry if that sounds insensitive, but that's what they're doing."

"You actually remember the page that clock is on? What else?"

Oliver described the scene in detail. When he finished, Tess was no closer to understanding what the e-mail was trying to tell them.

"Are you *sure* you can't remember anything that might connect with the song?" she said.

"No—wait, there's a radio up on a shelf. Nothing on it, though. There's a bingo card in the bottom corner."

"That's right—numbers that correspond to letters. But that's a clue to the mystery in the book. I don't think it'll help us here."

Oliver yawned. "Why don't we sleep on it? It's been a crazy day."

"I guess you're right. Well, goodnight."

Tess heard the soft click of the door closing. She lay down on top of the bed and curled into a fetal position. But sleep wouldn't come.

CHAPTER 26

I woke in the middle of the night, soaked in cold sweat, confused and disoriented. Through the window, a streetlight limned the unfamiliar shapes of Eric's living room furniture, and I slowly remembered our flight from the U District. The springs in the couch reached up through the padding and poked at me, but they weren't what had awakened me. It had been the troubling, and troublesome, thoughts about the responsibility squatting on my shoulders like an overweight organ grinder's monkey.

I'd taken a minimum-wage job with the possibility of advancement and performance bonuses, and ended up with a person's life in my hands. I was just getting used to the idea of being self-sufficient, and had been truly responsible for myself for only a few days. Worse, I discovered I actually cared about the snotty little Chiquita. I even liked her. But staying one step ahead of gun-toting mercenaries hadn't been part of the job description, and I laid there wondering if I owed Tess—or Alice—any allegiance. After all, I hadn't even been paid yet. Seemed like they were asking a lot for nothing.

My mind hummed with energy, flitting on rapidly beating wings from one tasty thought to another, alighting just long enough to sample the flavor before moving on. Intrigued by one, I hovered, lingering at several blossoms on the same bush.

I'd lied to Tess. By inadvertent omission—so maybe not a real lie. I'd since remembered that the border of the illustration I'd described to her contained a message written in Morse code. The windows were already turning gray from the encroaching dawn, so I swung my legs off the couch and reached for the laptop. It cast a blue glow across half the room as it booted up.

Had I ever joined the Boy Scouts, I'm sure Morse code would have been imprinted in my memory like most everything else. But I'd never been much of a joiner. I'd been one of those kids usually picked next to last for baseball teams or PE's dreaded dodgeball sessions. I pulled up the code online—combinations of dots and dashes representing the alphabet. It didn't take long to figure out the message in the book had nothing to do with the e-mail Tess had gotten. I sat back and thought. Someone had sent her an MP3 file—a song that held personal meaning for her.

Why? Exhorting her to "stop in the name of love?" Quit following clues? Warning us—her—it was too dangerous?

The tune echoed in my head, the chorus caught in an endless loop.

My aha moment smacked me in the face long after it should have—Tess probably would have figured it out far faster.

I grabbed a pencil and a scrap of paper from my backpack and started decoding the rhythm of the song. "Stop!" was obviously a dot. The Supremes also sang the words "in the" on short notes—so, dots again. "Naaame" had to be a dash, followed by "of love," two more dots. Discouragement soon set in when I realized how many ways the dots and dashes could be combined. Depending on phrasing, the notes of the song could stand for different letters. The notes of an *I* and a *T* together made a *U*, and an *M* and a *T* made a *G*. I played the song clip on low volume and listened to it several times in succession. Then I went to work again and wrote down possible series of letters. None of them made any sense. I listened to the clip one more time, trying to decide if notes were staccato dots or legato dashes. When I was satisfied I had the right string of letters, I realized that I could see them by light of day through the window and not the glow of the laptop screen.

Rustling sounds came from the back of the house, followed by the flush of a toilet and water running. Several minutes later Eric appeared and waved at me on his way to the kitchen. Pretty soon, a kettle in the kitchen whistled, and a moment or two later Eric brought me a mug of tea.

"You can stay as long as you need to," he said. "I have to get to work."

"I'm going to straighten this out," I said. "Today. We'll be out of your hair, I promise."

He shrugged. "No worries. Lock up when you leave."

"Okay. Thanks, Eric. See you around."

As soon as he left the house grew still again, traffic in the street the only sound except for the hum of the refrigerator.

I turned back to the letters in front of me. If they comprised a message, it had to be an anagram: *E, I, T, A, O, N, T, I, T, M.* I started moving the letters around to form words. The number of combinations that worked surprised me, but few made any sense. I picked up the mug of tea and discovered it had gone cold. A yawn nearly swallowed me whole. I'd been awake for hours—most of that time spent avoiding a decision.

I heard stirrings, and a small voice said, "Oliver?"

"Out here in the living room," I called. "Need help?"

"No, I'll find you. Just keep talking."

"Sure. Let's see. I'll start with 'Good morning, sleepyhead.' It's a beautiful day. Some showers, but right now the sun's broken through, and there are a few patches of blue up there. It's almost nine, so you're officially late for school. And—Ah, there you are."

Tess appeared at the end of the hall, straight black hair tousled, clothes rumpled. But she looked better than I did. She stopped and smoothed her hair demurely, suddenly self-conscious, as if reading my thoughts.

"Head straight for the sound of my voice. A little left . . . Almost there." I stood up and took her hand. "Couch is right behind you. Can I get you tea or coffee?"

She shook her head.

"How'd you sleep?" I said.

"Better than I thought I would. I laid awake for a while, but after that . . ." She lowered herself onto the couch. "Where's Eric?"

"Went to work."

"What have you been up to?"

"About that . . . I didn't describe everything in that illustration last night."

"Oliver! Why not?"

"Sorry. I forgot to mention the Morse code in the border."

"You didn't think that might be relevant?"

"I forgot, okay?"

She flinched. I rubbed the back of my neck, wishing I'd gotten more sleep.

"I didn't think you could do that," she said in a small voice.

"It's different." I thought about how to explain it. "Different types of memories are stored in different parts of the brain. We access them differently. I can pull up scenes, moments in time—

especially if they've made an emotional impact—and tell you with reasonable accuracy what people said, what they wore, where they stood, down to small details. That doesn't mean I don't forget things. I can be as absent-minded as the next guy."

"But you remember the code?"

"Every dot and dash. It doesn't help."

Her face fell. I was struck again by how normal she looked. A little dreamy, maybe, because her eyes couldn't focus, but unless she was feeling her way around a strange place, she didn't act like a blind person.

"I figured maybe we were supposed to use the Morse code to decipher a message in the song clip," I said.

Tess brightened and leaned forward. "What did it say? Did you find a message?"

"Nothing that makes sense. I'm sorry, Tess."

She frowned. "I don't understand. Was there something there or not?"

"Look, I went over the clip a million times. I came up with ten letters that don't spell anything in order. So maybe an anagram. There are all sorts of possibilities."

"Like what?"

"How about 'imitate not?' No? Doesn't work for you? Try, 'to me it ain't.'"

"Ain't what?"

"Yeah, that's what I thought. Okay, how about 'it ain't Moet?'"

She pouted. "That's terrible English. My dad wouldn't use 'ain't.'"

I sighed and steeled myself for what I was about to do. I couldn't avoid it any longer.

"I have to take you back, Tess."

"What? Why?" She bit her lip and sank into the cushions.

The anguish on her face stabbed me in the heart. I was glad she wasn't able to see my shame, my cowardice.

"I can't protect you out here," I said, "Whoever's after you has too many resources. They'll find us eventually."

"But Alice said . . . What if it's not safe?"

"Isn't your uncle ex-military? Can't he hire bodyguards?"

"I don't want to go through that again! Why can't you—?"

"I'm a student, Tess! I'm supposed to be your assistant, your guide dog. I'm not a bodyguard."

"What? It's not in your job description, so you're going to quit? What will happen to me?"

"Look, I think you ought to hand this whole thing over to your uncle. He's your guardian, right? Where's he been, anyway?"

"Traveling. On business. He's almost never home."

"He's the one who should be protecting you, not me."

"He couldn't keep my parents from getting killed."

"I thought that was an accident."

"So? All those men, all those guns . . . I don't want that again."

"What men?"

She told me about all the security Travis had brought in a year earlier, right before the accident. Men with guns to protect her father from an unexplained threat. Travis and her parents had kept the truth from her so she wouldn't be frightened, but she'd known something was wrong, had been aware of the presence of all the bodyguards. Not that they'd done any good in the end. They'd failed to protect her parents, and Tess, too.

"I still think it's for the best," I said when she finished. "At least they have a chance. We don't, not by ourselves."

Silence hung in the air like swamp gas with no dog to blame it on and neither one of us wanting to acknowledge it.

She caved first. "You mean *now*? Fine. I need a shower, clean clothes, lip gloss, a toothbrush, brush for my hair—"

"Shower's no problem," I interrupted. "But you'll have to wait on the other stuff."

I wondered how she managed, but wasn't brave enough to ask. She grumbled something unintelligible and made her way to the bathroom, refusing my offer of help.

An hour later, we sat on a bus headed toward downtown Seattle. Tess was nearly swallowed up by a sweatshirt I borrowed from Eric's closet. A baseball cap covered most of her hair. The brim pulled low made it difficult to see her eyes and disguised the fact that she was sightless. The baggy clothes made her look smaller, more childlike. I kept a paranoid eye out for anyone following us. Other than a toothless drunk who kept leering at Tess, no one paid much attention.

We changed buses downtown and caught one headed across the lake. I kept glancing at Tess on the way, but she was a closed cupboard, heart hidden from view. I wished she'd take it out and pin it to the front of her sweatshirt like a nametag: "Hello, my name is Angry." Something to give me an indication of where I stood with her. Then again, it didn't matter since I was about to quit.

"We're almost there," I said finally.

"I'm not talking to you." She folded her arms and turned away.

"Come on, Tess. You have to talk sometime."

She hesitated, then faced me. "So what's your plan? You going to call Alice and see if the coast is clear, or just brazen it out and walk in?"

She said it so coyly I wondered if she knew something I didn't.

"No, no plan," I said.

"For someone so smart, you're not too bright."

"I'll tell you what I'm *not* going to do," I said, rubbing the spot on my ego that had taken her hit. "I'm not going to walk right in, and I'm not going to check in with Alice. I don't trust anyone—not even you."

"Me? Why wouldn't you trust *me*? What did I ever do to you? I'm blind, Oliver, remember?"

"Precisely. You have no idea what's going on, so you don't know what might be important and what's irrelevant. You rely on me and others for visual cues. You know everything about your life, but I know practically nothing. Ergo, I can't trust you."

She pouted for a moment, then said, "What about Alice? She saved our lives."

"For all I know, she's behind all this. Come on, Tess, did you know your cook was an assassin? Or that your gardener's a ninja?"

She turned away again. I looked out the window.

"You were the one who said I should save the world," she said quietly.

"I didn't know someone would try to kill you. Kill *us*."

"So what are we going to do?"

I'm sure my silence answered her question. In avoidance, my mind went somewhere else.

"How about 'IT team on it'?" I said suddenly.

"Wait. What?"

"The anagram. Morse code?"

Her nose wrinkled. "IT team . . . ? That's it!"

My mouth opened in amazement. "You're kidding. I just threw that out there."

"When I was little and Dad's company was just getting started, he *was* the IT department. Whenever something didn't work right, Dad would say he'd get the IT team right on it. It was his little joke."

"How does that help us?"

She flounced on the seat. "How should I know? I just think that's the message, okay?"

"Don't have a hissy fit. If that's the message, then seems to me you need to figure out what he's referring to."

"What do you mean?"

"What isn't working right? What device did he have that didn't work properly? Something with memory."

She went quiet, and the blood drained from her face.

"What? What is it?"

"His iPod," she said. She choked back tears.

I didn't know what memory triggered the sudden sadness. I wanted to put my arm around her, but I couldn't.

"Do you still have it?" I asked. "Is it still around?"

She nodded. "It's in the Range Rover. In the garage."

The one her parents had been killed in. Total wreck.

"Why didn't you get rid of that car?"

"My uncle Travis wanted to keep it. I don't know why. He said he'd get it fixed someday. I think it just reminds him of what happened, what he couldn't prevent." She shivered. "I'm glad I can't see it. I'd hate to be reminded every day."

Tess sucked in a breath and held it, blinking rapidly. "I miss them, Oliver. I can't believe I'm saying that."

"Of course you do. They're your parents."

We rode in silence for a minute or two.

"I'll help you find the iPod," I said.

She kept her face pressed against the window. "Don't do me any favors."

"Hey, it might keep you alive. If you have something they want, they won't kill you unless they find out where it is."

"That's comforting."

I ignored her sarcasm. "We'll scope the place out. Get in if it looks safe and see if the iPod's still in the SUV. If everything's quiet, we'll check in with Alice and find out what the story is."

She didn't say anything for a while. She seemed to have as many moods as a caterpillar has legs, and they changed so fast I felt whiplashed.

A few miles from her house, we changed buses again, this time to a smaller van like the ones rental car companies use at airports. Five minutes later, the bus pulled to a stop a short walk from her drive. I helped her off, took her hand, and started walking. She tried to snatch her hand away, but I held on tight. Better that passersby got the impression we were boyfriend and girlfriend so they didn't look too closely.

The gate at the head of her drive stopped me cold. I hadn't thought about how we'd get in.

"Do you have a key card?" I said.

"I'm still not talking to you."

"Come on, Tess. Give me a break."

"Key card. Sure. In a purse in my room. Was that your plan? Use my key card to open the gate? Might as well announce our presence to the whole world. Uncle Travis put in video surveillance when he installed the wall and the gate."

"So you're mad at me. I'm trying to help here. You want to keep running? Sleep on a different couch every night? Always looking over your shoulder? Figuratively speaking, that is."

She shuddered. "Okay, okay. I'd rather sleep in my own bed."

"Any ideas?"

She sighed. "I know another way in. Take my hand."

She directed me to a neighboring drive—the blind leading the blind—and told me to turn in. We walked alongside a thick, tall hedge. She said there was a break in it, so I kept my eyes peeled. The growth was so dense that fifty yards farther I nearly missed the slight gap between the arbor vitae. I made her stop and wait while I stuck my head and shoulders through to see what lay on the other side. Barely visible under the overgrown brush was a winding path through the trees. I backed out and brushed off a spiderweb.

"Are you sure about this?" I said.

"We used to use it all the time. It leads to the tennis court."

"Doesn't look like it's been used in a while."

"So? You scared?"

"No. I just thought it might be rough going for you. It's pretty overgrown."

"I'll manage. I'm a big girl."

"No fence or wall. How come?"

She shrugged. "My dad thought the private drive on this side and the hedge were deterrent enough. He talked Uncle Travis out of spending the money it would have cost."

I took her hand and pulled her through the hedge. The branches caught in her hair and she nearly lost her footing trying to break free, but she clamped her jaw shut and didn't make a sound. I beat back the bush and tromped on the weeds as we went, clearing the path. Soon, the tennis court appeared through the trees. I murmured as much to Tess and proceeded more quietly.

"Before you get there," Tess whispered, "another path splits off down to the guesthouse."

I followed her directions and we ended up on a more groomed path through the trees toward the not-so-little guesthouse. The path came out at the back of the cottage and led around the side. From there it was a straight shot across the drive to the corner of the big garage on the side of the main house. I held Tess back and surveyed the grounds. There was no sign of life.

"Come on," I murmured, "but keep quiet."

I quickly towed her across the open space, aiming for the keypad mounted next to the far garage bay door.

"What's the code?" I said.

"One-oh-two-eight," she whispered. "Unless it changed."

I keyed in the numbers and the door rose, making an alarming amount of racket. I hoped we were far enough from the house not to be heard. We slipped inside, and I pushed the button to roll the door back down. Gloom reclaimed the interior as the descending door shut out the light. The wrecked SUV crouched in front of us, dark and menacing. A wounded beast. I wrenched open a battered door.

"Where is it?" I said.

"It should be on the center console," she said. "It was plugged in the last time we drove."

I looked on the center console, in the console compartment, and on the dash—no iPod. I squatted next to the door, leaned in, and peered under the passenger seat. Nothing was visible in the dimness, so I stuck my hand under and felt around, scraping a knuckle on a metal track. My fingers suddenly found the smooth contours of the media player and pulled it out.

"Got it!" I said. I placed it in Tess's hands.

Before she said a word, four of the doors rolled up. As they rose, men slid in underneath, shouting and pointing assault rifles and semiautomatic pistols at us.

"Stop right there! Don't move! Hands on your head!"

Both of us froze in fear.

CHAPTER 27

"Status?" Travis barked into his phone as he jumped up from his desk in the den and strode toward the door.

Nearly a year of setbacks on the project over which James died, I gave up my army career, my niece is missing and a potential target, and now this. Maybe it's not as bad as some of the shit storms I encountered in Afghanistan, but I don't know how it could get much worse.

"Intruders in the garage," Marcus's voice came back to him. "Teams are in position."

"Close in!" Travis said.

"Roger that. Everyone hear that? Go! Go!"

Travis heard muffled shouts as he raced down the hall, through the kitchen past a startled Alice, and into the garage on the heels of Marcus and Red. Flintstone and Rubble—Fred and Barney—steadily advanced from two open bay doors toward the far end of the garage. Over the tops of the other vehicles, he saw Luis and Kenny spread out from the garden door and head in the same direction. Two pairs of hands poked up in the air, their owners hidden from view. Travis hustled across the floor, squeezing past Marcus and Red. He didn't bother drawing his weapon. His team had enough firepower to put down a Taliban incursion at four-to-one odds. But this wasn't Waziristan.

Time to find out who breached security.

Travis rounded the end of Yoshi's truck and stopped short. His niece and a young man stood next to James's demolished Range Rover, hands held high, the barely perceptible trembling in their knees the only giveaway to their fear. The passenger door stood open.

Travis took a step forward. "Tess?"

She turned toward the sound of his voice. "Uncle Travis? What's happening?"

"Where the hell have you been? I've been worried sick about you."

"Alice told us to—"

"I know what Alice told you. But you should have checked in, at least. Let us know you were all right."

"Well, I'm not all right," she said, lowering her hands. "I've been chased and shot at, pushed around, and I had to sleep in my clothes last night. I'm tired and hungry, and I just want to go to bed."

She trembled and bit her lower lip to keep her emotions in check. Travis watched as the man—kid, more precisely—next to her shifted and dropped a hand toward her shoulders.

"Hold it right there, butthead!" Fred bellowed. He thrust the barrel of an HK416 assault rifle at him, freezing Oliver in midmotion.

"Who are you?" Travis said to him.

"Oliver Moncrief. I'm—"

"I know," Travis said, annoyed that he hadn't put it together more quickly. "What are you doing here?"

"Bringing Tess home, where she belongs." Oliver flushed. "Instead of berating her, you should be asking her what she needs. Where do you get off giving her a hard time? Where the hell have *you* been?"

Marcus took a step toward him. "Watch your mouth, son. You wouldn't want to piss off anyone here. Not with all this weaponry pointed at you."

Travis waved Marcus aside and saw a sour grimace cross his face. "The kid's right, Marcus. We weren't here—*I* wasn't here—to protect Tess."

"Yeah, well, we're here now," Red growled in his raspy bass.

"Sure are," Oliver said. "Seven against two. She's blind and I'm unarmed. Think you can handle it?"

"Can I pop the punk, boss?" Red said. A corner of his mouth turned up.

"Okay, stand down, everyone," Travis said. "Now she's back, we have someone to protect. We need to figure out where the threat came from and anticipate the next one. Marcus, five minutes, in my office. The rest of you, back to your posts. Tess, I'll see you inside. Oliver, bring her into the kitchen."

Oliver gave him a mock salute and took Tess by the arm.

The kid has a lot of cheek.

Travis thought he might pop him before any of the men got a chance. The men dispersed, heading out the way they'd come in. Travis turned and strode across the floor, then into the kitchen behind Marcus. Instead of following him down the hall, though, he detoured to Alice's office. He poked his head through the doorway and rapped a knuckle on the frame. She looked up from her desk and peered at him over half-frame reading glasses. A long-sleeved sweater covered her wounded arm, but a bulge along her forearm outlined the bandage underneath.

"Another deer?" she said.

"Nope. Prodigal niece and the assistant you hired."

She looked startled and frowned. "Why didn't they just come to the door? What were they doing in the garage?"

"They were looking for something. I'm about to find out what. Join us, please."

She rose and followed Travis into the kitchen. Tess sat facing them at the table in the breakfast nook. Oliver stood behind her, his stance relaxed but his eyes wary. Travis's estimation of him went up another tiny notch—after all, the kid had kept Tess alive the past eighteen hours—but he shrugged it off. It didn't make any difference now. Travis looked at Tess again. Her mouth puckered as if she'd eaten a lemon and her brows dove toward the center of her pert nose. She was pretty despite her sour mood, and Travis was suddenly struck by how much she'd matured in the past year. She was very nearly a woman.

Tess raised her chin. "Alice? Is that you?"

"Yes, Tess, it's me." She paused. "I'm fine. Thanks for asking."

Travis eased into the chair across from Tess. "Lucy, you got some 'splainin' to do."

"Why?" Tess shot back. "I didn't do anything wrong."

"What were you looking for in the Range Rover?"

"I was just showing Oliver—"

"Look, Tess," Travis interrupted, more gently this time, "Alice told me about the e-mails. And the camera. You clearly got another one that made you think there's something in the Rover. What was it?"

Tess squirmed in her seat.

Oliver stepped forward. "Sir, I think—"

Blind Rage

Travis motioned him to keep quiet. "You stay out of this. Tess?"

Tess dropped her hand under the table and shoved the iPod into her pocket. She extended her other arm across the table and opened her fingers. A thumb drive lay in her palm. Oliver's eyes widened. He stared at it. Travis plucked it from her hand.

"Thank you." He rose. "Don't move, either of you. I'll be right back. Alice, keep an eye on them, please."

Travis hurried down the hall to the small den. Marcus twisted in a chair as Travis entered. He started to rise. Travis waved him back into his seat as he rounded the desk and inserted the thumb drive in his laptop's USB port. He double-clicked on the icon when it appeared. The only files on the drive were a few photos and what looked like some of Tess's old homework assignments. His brow creased. He yanked the thumb drive out of the computer and tossed it to Marcus.

"Have someone check that," he said. "See if there's any deleted data that can be recovered."

"I'll get on it," Marcus said.

Travis rose and headed for the door. "I'll be back."

He used the walk back to the kitchen to steady his breathing and slow his pulse. His relationship with Tess would have been strained under the best of circumstances. She'd barely known him before he'd suddenly become a permanent fixture in her life. He was her uncle, not a parent or even a sibling, yet he'd been thrust into the role of caretaker and caregiver all at once. He didn't know how to be a parent. He'd been a soldier all his adult life, accustomed to the company of men and a solitary existence in the field. He'd been trained to take life, not nurture it, and the transition from soldier to civilian had been difficult. Raising a teenager was next to impossible, but raising a girl who'd been traumatized by the loss of her sight and her parents was something no one was equipped to handle. So he'd left most of the daily duties to Alice. A mistake, he saw now. He knew he would have to tread carefully if he wanted to maintain any sort of rapport with Tess, so he pushed his anger down beneath the surface.

"There's nothing on that drive but old junk," he said as he slid into his chair again.

"That's not my fault," Tess said.

"Empty your pockets."

"What? I gave you what you wanted."

"You heard me, Tess. Empty your pockets. I want to see all of it. I won't ask you again."

"You don't trust me? I'm not a child. You have no right to treat me this way." She dug into her jeans while she talked, despite the wounded indignation on her face. A tube of lip gloss and an iPod clattered onto the table. "There! Happy?"

"That's it? No wallet? No purse?"

"Are you crazy?" Tess yelled.

"We bolted," Oliver said. "We didn't have time to grab anything. I have her phone, by the way, which I told her *not* to use so she couldn't be traced. That's why she didn't check in."

Travis peered at them both and glanced at Alice. She nodded. He sighed.

"Somebody's playing a horrible practical joke on me," Tess said. "It's someone's idea of a sick game."

"This is no game, Tess!" Travis said. "They made an attempt on your life. Alice was attacked and hurt. People are dead, including one of your friends!"

"Carl was *not* my friend! He was just a big jerk!"

"He's *dead*!" Travis roared. "And you could have been killed! This is real life, Tess."

"This is *so* not close to real life, Uncle Travis, I can't begin to tell you," she said with such fierceness it surprised him. "The people I know don't have men with machine guns burst into their kitchens. My friends don't get chased down the street getting shot at. They don't have to run away from home to keep from getting killed. That may be real life in *your* world, but not here, not in mine. This had nothing to do with me."

Tears glistened in her eyes, and she clenched her jaw to hold them back.

"It has everything to do with you," Travis said. "You're involved, Tess, whether you like it or not. Someone made sure of that. I'm trying to help here. If you tell me what's going on, I can run interference, keep you safe."

"Like you did yesterday? Where *were* you?"

The tears flowed down her cheeks now, and Travis felt his own burn red with guilt.

"Tess, if I'd known you were in any danger, I never would have left on that business trip. I would have had the team in place before those men showed up."

"And what about Rosa, huh? She worked here for a *year*. And you didn't know? How are you supposed to protect me?"

Travis shook his head. "I know. I didn't do my job. That's going to change. But you have to help me, Tess. I can't keep you safe if I don't know what's going on. I need to know what they're after, what they want."

"I don't know!" she shrieked. "How should I know about any of this?"

Alice moved around the table and put a hand on Tess's shoulder. Travis couldn't remember when she'd ever expressed concern with that much emotion. She'd never been a very touchy-feely person. Travis had always respected her businesslike demeanor, but had found her difficult to *like* in a friendly way. She didn't warm up to people easily. Oliver hadn't moved, but Travis saw him strain to keep from going to Tess's side, consternation clearly etched on his face.

"Okay, okay," Travis said. "Calm down. We'll figure this out. Alice said they were after your camera. Where's the memory stick?"

Tess tipped her head back. "Oliver?"

Oliver hesitated, then stooped to rummage through a backpack on the floor next to him. He pulled out the memory card and leaned across the table to hand it to Travis.

"There's nothing on that, either," Tess said, "except photos. We checked."

Oliver glanced at her, then directed his gaze at Travis, his face expressionless. Travis turned the memory card over in his fingers.

"I'll have some tech guys check it out anyway," he said. "In the meantime, if you get any more e-mails like that, tell me immediately."

She dropped her chin and didn't respond.

"Tess? You understand? Don't make me hack your e-mail account."

"You wouldn't dare!"

"Try me."

So much for our relationship. If Tess didn't already hate me, threatening her privacy probably pushed her over the edge.

Travis didn't know what else to do.

"You're so mean," she cried.

Travis watched tears roll silently down her cheeks. The roiling they caused in his gut and the ache in his chest were far more painful than the shrapnel from a roadside IED explosion they'd dug out of his arm. Unlike that wound, he didn't know how to deal with the pain from this one.

He clenched his jaw and spoke through gritted teeth. "Oliver, you can go. We won't be needing your services anymore."

The kid stared at Travis blankly, like he was in shock.

"Are you sure that's a good idea?" Alice piped up quickly. "Tess can't drag the team with her everywhere she goes. And who will help her with homework? You don't have time. And I can't imagine anybody on the team relishing the idea."

"Forget it," Tess said. "He already quit."

"What do you mean, he quit?" Travis said.

Oliver stepped forward. "Sir, under the circumstances I felt that I wasn't very well-equipped to protect Tess. That's why I brought her home."

"Yes, but now that the security team is back in place," Alice said, "there's no reason you can't continue in your duties, Oliver. Don't you think so, Travis?"

Travis eyed the kid, his fingers drumming the tabletop. It would mean the team would have to protect two people, not just one. Travis wasn't convinced, but Oliver seemed bright enough.

"Okay," Travis said, "we'll keep you on and see how it goes. But when it comes to Tess's safety you do *exactly* what I tell you. Got it?"

"Yes, sir."

"Don't I have a say in this?" Tess said, her voice shrill. "He doesn't *want* to be with me."

"Oliver?" Travis said quietly.

"I never said that, sir. I like the job. I told her I didn't think I could protect her. There's more you haven't heard. Whoever's after Tess nearly caught us last night."

Little surprised Travis, but he'd assumed they'd gotten out cleanly, with no trouble once they'd left. He'd only worried about where they'd gone to ground, not whether they'd have to keep running.

I'm losing my edge—the instincts that had kept me alive in Afghanistan. *The kid, though, is resourceful, apparently.*

"Travis," Alice said, "if these people are as resourceful as we think, they'll identify Oliver eventually if they haven't already."

"You're right," Travis said. "We'll have to keep a close watch on both of them. Oliver, I'll want a full report later In the meantime, consider yourself still employed. And Tess, don't think I'm finished with you. We need to talk about your visit to MondoHard and the unauthorized use of your old key card." Tess froze, and Oliver shifted in his seat. "But not now. Tonight, when I get home from work."

Alice briskly walked around the table. "Well, now that's settled, I'll rustle up something for you two to eat since we no longer have a cook. You're late for school."

Tess groaned. "Do I have to go? Can't I at least take a shower and put on some clean clothes?"

"Of course," Alice said. "Run along, and make it quick. Breakfast will be ready by the time you get back."

Oliver looked from Alice to Tess and back, his face turning red. "Should I help?"

Travis glared at him. "Not under any circumstances, bud. Now yank those thoughts back into this kitchen before I change my mind about you."

Oliver jumped back a pace. "Yes, sir!" The corner of his mouth twitched.

Travis suspected Oliver was mocking him, but the little smile, if that's what it had been, was already gone. Tess got up and felt her way out of the kitchen and down the hall. Alice watched her go, and when Tess was out of earshot, she faced Travis.

"A little hard on her, weren't you?" she said.

"She needs a wake-up call," he said. "I thought we could breathe easy for a while, but the threat to James extends to her, too. You know that as well as I do, and her birthday isn't far off."

"Birthday? What happens then?" Oliver said, sliding into the chair Tess had just vacated.

"She becomes an adult," Travis said tersely.

Alice came over and set a glass of juice in front of Oliver.

"Tess's father owned the majority of the stock in his company," she explained. "Since both of her parents died, the shares have been held in trust for her. Travis is the trustee. When Tess turns twenty-one, *she* becomes the majority stockholder."

"Wow," Oliver said quietly. "Cool. So she's really rich."

"Not cool," Travis said. "Whoever wanted my brother out of the way may not want Tess to have control of the company, either."

"So why haven't any assassins tried to take *you* out?" Oliver said. "Maybe you're the evil uncle, vying for control."

Travis felt his face flush, and his fingers clenched into a fist.

Oliver suddenly grinned. "Just messing with you."

"Probably not a good idea until you get to know me better," Travis said, uncurling his fingers.

Oliver's smile faded quickly. "Why would they go after her now? Isn't she only eighteen? Which means she's already an adult, by the way."

Travis flushed with heat. "Don't push it." He paused as the import of what Oliver said slowly registered. "I don't know why they haven't attacked me, but my job is to protect her."

He turned to Alice. "I'll tell Kenny and Luis to take them to school. The cops are holding the BMW until they go over it for evidence, but I'll get it released as soon as possible so Oliver has a way to get Tess around. In the meantime, she doesn't go *anywhere* without one of the team."

Alice nodded. "She'll get used to it. You'll see."

Travis got to his feet. "I wish we didn't have to put a guard on her at all. I know it sucks, but she'll just have to deal with it. Anyway, I have to meet with Marcus briefly and get to work."

He hurried down the hall, just as worried now that Tess was present and accounted for as he'd been when he'd gotten home and discovered she was missing and on the run.

CHAPTER 28

Tess let the shower water cascade through her hair and run down her body. The scent of shampoo and soap filled the steamy enclosure. She let out a sigh. She felt safe here, cocooned in the water's warm embrace. She stood unmoving for several minutes, hands clasped over her collarbone, thoughts running through her head as fast as the water down the drain. She wondered what would happen if she never got out of the shower.

What could they do to me? I'd insist they bring my meals, a waterproof pillow for sleeping.

She rubbed her thumb across her wrinkled, waterlogged fingertips and giggled as she imagined what the rest of her might look like if she didn't get out—a big shar-pei. Reluctantly, she turned off the water, found her towel, and stepped out.

After drying off, she made her way to her dresser. She pulled open the top right drawer to find panties and a bra. The top left drawer held socks, sorted by color. She easily found jeans in the closet, then moved to the right and pulled a camisole top off a hanger. Choosing a sweater proved more difficult, but she found a cashmere V-neck that st was softer than anything else in her closet, so she knew it was the light blue one.

When she was dressed, she went back into the bathroom and brushed her hair and teeth. She couldn't apply makeup, so she didn't bother with anything except some pale lip gloss. Picking up the hairbrush again, she pulled her hair back and tied it into a ponytail. The rhythmic motions of her usual morning ritual calmed and relaxed her. She could hardly believe all that had happened in less than a day.

And Uncle Travis wants me to go to school? There's no way I'll be able to concentrate on schoolwork after what I've been through. It's not fair.

She sighed and set the brush down where she could find it again easily. Her mother had been a neatnik. *A place for everything, and everything in its place.* Tess heard her mother's voice in her head. It used to drive her nuts. What was wrong with a little mess now and again? Who cared if her clothes were draped over a chair or dumped on the floor instead of hung in the closet? But Tess had gradually come around to her mother's point of view during the past year. Organization made life simpler—at least her life, a blind person's life. She still disliked the work involved in keeping her belongings so orderly, but knowing where they were certainly helped.

Her mouth opened in horror.

Am I turning into my mother? God, I hope not.

Her face screwed up into a frown as she mimicked her mother's nagging. The thought of what she must look like turned her grimace upside down, and she giggled again. An image of her mother at work in the studio over the garage popped into Tess's head. The studio was the one place where her mother's rules had gone out the window, at least when she'd been immersed in a project. Tess saw her mother, head bent over a pad on her drawing table, hair mussed into a rat's nest, jeans and denim work shirt covered with splotches of color, oblivious to everything around her. No matter what the medium—oils, watercolors, charcoal, plaster, clay—her mother would manage to spread it everywhere. Sometimes it had seemed to cover every surface except the one that would ultimately reveal her inner vision. But, Tess remembered wryly, she'd always cleaned up at the end of her workday.

Tess strained to see her mother's face in that imaginary scene. No matter how she tried to position herself, her mother's face always seemed to be turned away, hidden. When at last Tess imagined seeing her face-on, her mother's features refused to coalesce, leaving Tess with only a fuzzy recollection. Tess's heart pounded and her chest tightened.

Is this what happens when people die? Their memories fade like old photographs until they're left as only indistinct images in sepia tones?

Tess squelched the panic that threatened to rise up in her throat.

I will not forget!

To be unable to "see" her memories would be as unbearable as losing her sight all over again. She didn't think she'd be able to live like that. At least normal people could fall back on photographs to remind them. She brushed away a tear, swallowed the lump in her throat, and found her way downstairs.

True to her word, Alice had made breakfast—pancakes—but Tess suspected they'd come out of the freezer. She chewed on one thoughtfully, smelling a hint of cardboard along with the syrup. Alice hadn't cooked in years, not since Helen had taken over those duties. When Helen had left, Rosa had taken over.

The witch with the knife. All that time Rosa had been pretending to be nice, pretending to like me, just so she could get her hands on . . . what? What sort of software program is stored on all these electronic devices?

Tess's hand involuntarily crept into her lap to check the slight bulge in her jeans, her fingers tracing the outline of the iPod her uncle had overlooked. Another thought pushed the memory aside.

"Alice?" Tess said. "Didn't *Helen* recommend Rosa for her job when she quit?"

Silence prevailed for a moment, then Alice said, "You're right, I believe she did."

"Doesn't that seem odd, considering how suddenly Helen left?"

"Who's Helen?" Oliver said.

Tess refused to answer. Uncle Travis may have rehired the big jerk, but that didn't mean Tess had to like it.

"She was the cook before Rosa," Alice said. "She resigned due to an illness in the family."

"That's what she told us," Tess said. "But what if it wasn't true?"

"I'll have Travis look into it," Alice said.

"Is he always such a hard-ass?" Oliver said. "He didn't even thank me for bringing Tess home—alive, I might add."

"I'm sure he appreciates—" Alice began.

Tess swallowed another bite of pancakes and interrupted her. "Yeah, why does he have to go all Rambo on me all the time? I'm so tired of all the guns around here. Aren't you afraid one of those guys is going to shoot you sometime? Just my luck, I'll be raiding the fridge some night and get shot."

"He's SICC, Tess." Alice said.

"What? Like, sick in the head?"

"No, as in *S-I-C-C.*"

Oliver's voice chimed in at the same time as hers. "What's that?"

"I shouldn't be telling you this," Alice said with a quick glance at the doorway, her voice barely above a whisper, "but given the circumstances, I suppose you're old enough to know. Travis was in a secret branch of the Army Special Forces—the Strategic Intelligence Collection and Containment unit."

"Intelligence? Like a spy?"

"More than that," Alice said. "The 'containment' part was essentially code for 'kill.' Your uncle was a trained assassin."

"Like Rosa and the men who tried to take my camera?"

"Well, not Rosa. She may have had some training, but her skills with a knife were better served chopping vegetables. She should have been able to kill me. But, yes, like the people who broke in and attacked us. Only your uncle was a whole lot better at his job than that team."

"Maybe he would have been if he'd been here." Tess tasted the bitterness in her words as they rolled over her tongue. "I can't count on him like I can you and Yoshi. I don't trust him."

"He's a good man, Tess," Alice said quietly. "Give him a chance."

"He's had a year of chances."

"That's not really fair, Tess," Alice said.

Tess didn't care. She was sick of Uncle Travis telling her what to do. He wasn't her father. "Well, it's not fair he's making me go to school, either."

"No, probably not," Alice said. "But since he is, you better get moving. Oliver, Kenny and Luis are waiting for you two out front. They'll drive you and check in with the administration to alert school security. Since they're armed, they won't be allowed on campus, so don't worry—they won't be following you around all day. They'll keep an eye on traffic in and out."

"And if we have problems?" Oliver said.

"They'll tell you what to do. Tess, don't forget a coat on your way out."

"I don't need one."

"Yes, you do. Oliver, make sure she has a coat before she goes out."

"Yes, ma'am. You ready, Tess?"

She felt Oliver's hand on her shoulder and started to pull away. She sighed to indicate there was no sense fighting a losing battle. She stood.

"I haven't even done my homework," she grumbled. "I'm going to be in so much trouble."

Oliver's laugh rang out. She scowled in his direction.

"Compared to the 'trouble' we had yesterday, that's nothing," he said. "I think you can handle it."

"You don't know my teachers." Tess shuddered.

She let Oliver guide her out of the kitchen and down the hall, and shrugged into the coat he held for her because she knew she'd never hear the end of it if she didn't. Outside, Oliver helped her into the backseat of an SUV. Kenny and Luis had it warmed up, for which she was grateful. The little warmth the sun had provided was gone, replaced by the cold drizzle more typical of spring around Seattle. She heard Oliver get in the seat next to her, and as soon as his seatbelt was buckled the vehicle began to accelerate smoothly.

"Ms. Barrett, I'm Luis," a voice in front of her said.

"How nice for you," Tess said.

Luis went on as if he hadn't heard. "I was here before. You know, last year. You probably don't remember me."

She thought she heard a note of regret in his voice, but she didn't stop to wonder why. She didn't care. "No, I don't. You people didn't exactly come out and introduce yourselves."

He still seemed unfazed. "I'm really sorry we frightened you this morning. If we'd known it was you, we wouldn't have rushed in like that, you know, with guns and shouting and all."

Tess stiffened. She hadn't expected an apology, but she still couldn't help resenting his presence—*their* presence. All of them.

"Shut up, Luis," Kenny said. "We were just doing our job back there."

"Our job is to protect this girl," Luis said, his tone indignant. More gently, he told Tess, "Let me have your phone, please. I'm going to program our cell numbers into it so you can reach us."

Tess dug into her pocket and held out her phone. A warm hand took it from hers.

"You've got VR on this phone, right?" Luis said. "Oh, yeah, here it is. Okay, so say my name on the count of three. One, two, three . . ."

"Luis," Tess said.

"Great," Luis said. "Now say 'Kenny.' Just a sec. Okay, one, two, three . . ."

"Kenny," Tess said.

Luis pressed the phone back into her hand. "Okay, you're set. Kenny and I are on speed dial. Just say either of our names, and you'll get one of us."

"What about me?" Oliver said.

"I was getting to you," Luis said. "Give me your phone."

Tess bounced and swayed with the car's movement in silence for several moments.

Luis spoke again. "I put our numbers on your speed dial. It's faster than voice recognition. So here's the deal: both of you, any hint of trouble, you call. You don't wait to see if there *might* be a threat. If someone you don't know approaches you for any reason, you call. If you get a substitute teacher in one of your classes, call."

"Aren't you being a little paranoid?" Tess said. "What could possibly happen at school?"

"Look, we'd rather be a lot closer to you for this kind of detail, but since we're not allowed, it'll take us longer to get to you if you have a problem. So you need to be alert."

"I'll take care of her," Oliver said softly.

Tess turned on him. "I don't *want* you to take care of me. I don't want *any* of you to take care of me. I just want to be normal!"

Her tantrum bounced off a wall of silence and echoed in her own ears. She turned her head away so none of them could see the heat shimmer off her cheeks.

"We're here," Kenny said as the SUV came to a gentle stop.

Tess immediately opened the door, grabbed the backpack off the seat next to her, and got out without waiting for Oliver. She homed in on a babble of voices off to her right.

"Tess, wait!" Oliver called. "Come on, wait up!"

She swiped the back of her hand across her eyes and kept going. She was sick of the whole thing. She wished she was anywhere else but here. She was sick of them telling her what to do, sick of school, sick of this game her father was playing with her.

How dare he? I'm not a kid anymore with dreams of becoming a forensic anthropologist or psychological profiler like some character on TV. Sure, it was fun to pretend I was following clues to unearth some ancient and priceless treasure, or solving some horrific crime. But this is real life, my life, and this treasure hunt Dad set us on has already gotten people killed.

She couldn't reconcile the thought of what he'd done with the man she'd known, and the horror of it nearly crushed her, blotting out all the good in her world.

She sniffled and suddenly stumbled, throwing her arms out as she pitched forward.

"Whoa!" Oliver grabbed her arm, slid a hand around her waist, and pulled her upright.

She struggled to free herself from his grasp. "Let me go!"

"Stop, Tess! Please. I'll let you go, I promise! But don't move!"

Somehow his words penetrated the anger and desperation that cloaked her like armor, and she went slack in his arms. True to his word, he released her.

"Now can I go?" she said.

"Sure," he said. "But just so you know, you're at the top of the steps down to the courtyard in front of the commons. Two flights, eight steps each."

Tess hesitated. "Like, right at the top?"

"Right at the top," he said. "Two feet away. One more step and you'd have gone over."

"Um, the railing . . . ?"

"Just to your left. A little farther. Almost. There."

Tess gripped the cold steel tightly to keep from shaking. She might have killed herself falling down the stairs if Oliver hadn't been there to stop her. She turned her head and swiped at her eyes.

Damn it, this is exactly what I hate about what happened. I can't even walk from the curb to school without someone's help. But it's about time I started trying.

She sighed and descended the stairs carefully.

At the bottom, she raised her elbow. "Oliver, would you help me? Please?"

"That's what you pay me for."

She didn't know whether to laugh or hit him. "Look, I don't *want* your help. I *want* to be able to do things on my own, find my way around by myself—be who I was before the accident. I've had enough. But I can't learn without help. So, I need you."

"Is that an apology I hear in there somewhere?"

"Apology? *You're* the one who should apologize."

He gripped her arm and steered her toward the voices. "Fine, I'm sorry. Whatever. I don't want to fight anymore. You tell me what you want, and I'll do it, okay?"

She fell silent, feeling awful.

"The commons is a zoo," he muttered. "Sure you want to go in this way?"

"Does it make any difference?"

"Must be the end of lunch. What's after that?"

"Chemistry," she said.

"Maybe we can just cut through and get to class early."

He pulled her to a stop and opened a door. The loud sound of hundreds of voices talking and laughing reached through the opening like a fist and pounded her ears. She stepped through, bolstered by Oliver's hand at the small of her back. She walked with confidence as he guided her with gentle pressure.

Suddenly, a voice screamed, "You freaking bitch! I'll kill you! You and your boy toy, too!"

CHAPTER 29

The commons fell as silent as a library after closing, and every neck craned, every head swiveled toward the source of the lunatic outburst—mine included. Carl's friend Tad barreled through the crowd, knocking people aside. He charged, head down, snorting, an enraged bull. When I realized he had us in his sights, adrenaline surged through my veins, kick-starting my heart.

As a kid, I'd never gone out of my way to avoid a fight, but I'd never picked one, either. By minding my own business, I'd managed to avoid involvement in schoolyard spats, and since I was always a year or two younger than my classmates, they viewed me as too easy a mark and not worth hassling. I'd never feared bullies, but rather had calculated how badly I might get hurt before allowing myself to get swept up in one altercation or another. As pissed as I was with my current situation—Tess's bad attitude, killers potentially still lurking out there somewhere, and an empty pocket that had forced me into indentured servitude—I was damned if some dumb high school jock was going to hurt Tess. I'd promised Kenny and Luis I'd take care of her.

I got a few steps out in front of Tess and leaned my shoulder into Tad as he rushed us, absorbing the brunt of the hit. Grabbing on as he bulled forward, I managed to twist aside and use his momentum to push him to the floor. A geyser of noise erupted into the commons as the cry of "Fight! Fight!" flowed through the hall like magma. Tad scrabbled to his feet before I regained my balance and came at me with a snarl and enough hatred in his eyes to poison a well.

"You killed him!" he shouted.

He took a swing. I didn't duck fast enough, and it caught me a glancing blow on the head. A small starburst of pain exploded in my skull. I got my hands up and hunched my shoulders.

"He *took* the car, dipstick," I said. "I didn't know. Tess didn't either."

He shook his head slowly. The chants around us grew louder, energizing him.

"*You* killed him," he said. "Whoever shot him wanted *you*. Or her. Maybe both of you."

"How do you know? Maybe he just pissed somebody off. Road rage. Carl was a jerk."

"Screw you!"

"Get him, Tad!" someone shouted.

His muscles rippled under his shirt, and I tensed, ready for his move. He came at me swinging, expecting me to back up under the onslaught. Instead, I ducked and moved forward under the arc of his arm. I slammed a palm up under his chin. His jaw clacked shut and his head snapped back. He clutched at me as he went down, nearly pulling me over with him. I jerked back, and my shirt ripped away from his grasp. He fell hard, banged his head on the hard floor, and lay there, dazed.

"Hey! Hey, break it up!"

A human mountain hustled over to see what the commotion was about. Students backed away to clear a path for him, boys cowing involuntarily as he passed. Muscles bulged under the fabric of his sweatshirt. He wore the sleeves pulled up, revealing black-inked tattoos on thick forearms the color of a mocha latte. Tad rolled onto one knee and got unsteadily to his feet. When I stepped between Tad and Tess, the giant put a hand the size of a catcher's mitt on my chest and pushed me back a step. I tipped my chin up to look at him. The overhead lights glinted off his shaved head.

"It wasn't me," I said. "He started it."

"Who are you?" the giant said.

Kenny suddenly appeared out of nowhere and wedged himself between me and the giant.

He thrust his face up close to the mountain's. "Who the hell are *you*?"

Luis circled around behind the giant, keeping an eye on Tad.

"John Kelly, school security," the giant said. "Who are you guys?"

"Bodyguards," Kenny said. "I'm Kenny. He's Luis." He jerked his head at Luis, causing Kelly to swivel his gaze.

The giant looked confused. "What? You two are guarding this kid?" He looked at me.

"Not me," I said, throwing a thumb over my shoulder. "Her. Tess Barrett. You okay, Tess?"

"I'm fine," she said. "How do you think Kenny and Luis got here so quick?"

I'd wondered about that. I threw a questioning look at Kenny.

"She called," he said. "We were in the office letting them know we're here."

"Thanks a lot, Tess," I said. "You didn't think I could handle a candy-ass punk like Tad? He's not too tough without his homeys."

"What did you call me?" Tad shouted.

He lunged forward, but Luis pinned his arms and held him back.

"Shut up, both of you!" Kelly's brow furrowed as he considered me. "Who are you, again?"

"I'm Oliver. Oliver Moncrief, Tess's assistant."

"He's a freaking killer, that's what!" Tad said, straining against Luis's hold. "Hadn't been for him, Carl would still be alive."

A voice behind me chimed in. "That's a serious accusation."

A man with a shock of black hair and a rounded belly that spilled over his belt ambled up to us. Greg Olton, assistant principal. I'd dealt with him the day before when Prescott, Tess's English teacher, had made me get a permanent pass.

"It's true," Tad said.

"We'll see," Olton said. "Back to class, Tad."

"But—"

Olton raised his hand. "I said *back to class*, before I cite you for fighting—an automatic suspension, I might remind you."

Luis let him go and Tad slunk away, head down, throwing me one last malevolent scowl as he passed by.

"Show's over," Olton said loudly, turning a slow pirouette. "Period's about to begin. Everybody get where you belong."

The milling crowd slowly dispersed, the disappointment on many faces reflecting the brevity of the fight.

Olton crooked a finger at me. "You, come with me."

"What for?" I said.

Olton pursed his lips as if it was a stupid question and turned to Kenny. "One of you can escort Miss Barrett to her next class. I want the other one off campus per our discussion. John, good work keeping a lid on things here. You can give me a rundown later."

I followed Olton out of the commons. Tess didn't say a word. Olton led me to his office, sat me down and left, making me wait. I figured he intended to make me squirm, but I didn't give him the satisfaction. He returned several minutes later with a uniformed police officer. I stood politely, but now I was worried. Olton didn't scare me, but the cop made me leery—for all the reasons I'd outlined to Tess the night before.

"You're Oliver?" the officer said. He didn't offer his hand.

I nodded and wiped my hand on my pants before sticking it in my pocket.

"I'm Detective Burns, the PD's SRO—school resource officer. Sit down." He sat next to me and pulled out a pen. "I understand you were accused of being involved in the death of a student. Can I get the correct spelling of your name, Oliver, along with your date of birth and address?"

I gave it to him and watched him write it all down on a pad of paper.

"You're not a student here, Oliver?"

"No, sir. I'm a personal assistant to a student who is, um, sight-impaired."

"The blind girl. Tess Barrett. You've had the job since yesterday?"

"Yes, sir."

"Anything to this accusation?"

"No, sir." I gave him the bare bones outline of what had happened in the parking lot the night before, leaving out the details of why Tess and I were on the run.

He looked at me without expression. "Why didn't you report the car stolen?"

I shrugged. "I figured he'd bring it back once he'd had his fun. And if I reported it he would have said I just gave him the keys."

"About that. Why'd you just hand them over?"

"Seemed the easiest way. There were four of them. I could have let them beat the crap out of me, but what would have been the point?"

"Miss Barrett wasn't with you?" One of his eyebrows rose.

"No. I drove here to meet a classmate of hers who was going to help her with homework. When Carl 'borrowed' Tess's car, we took her friend's car instead."

"And this friend will corroborate your story?"

I nodded. "I don't see why not, since it's the truth. His name is Matt. Matt Tsang."

"And you have no idea who killed Carl Gant?"

My palms started to sweat. "No, sir. Like you said, I've only known Tess for a day. How would I know who killed one of her classmates?"

He considered me for a moment then looked up at Olton, who'd been sitting quietly.

"Could be a misunderstanding," Burns said. "I'll make arrangements to speak with the boy who made the accusation, but I see no reason to detain Oliver any longer. All right with you?"

"What do we know about this person?" Olton nodded his head toward me.

"I spoke with Miss Barrett's housekeeper who said she ran a thorough background check on him. He has no record."

I raised my hand. "Excuse me. I'm right here. Whatever you want to know, you can ask me. I've got no secrets." I regretted the words as soon as they left my mouth.

"Everybody's got secrets," Burns said without a smile. He stood. I half expected him to challenge my statement, but he faced Olton. "I'll see where they are on the investigation and get back to you, Greg. I think you can let Oliver return to his duties."

Olton waved at me. "Go on. Get out of here."

I didn't need a second invitation. Someone was bound to tell Olton or the cop about Carl tripping me in the commons. The cop might think that gave me motive and haul me in for more questions. No, thank you.

I found Tess's chemistry classroom without too much trouble and slipped inside. The teacher gave me a stern look as I headed toward an empty seat at the back of the room, but didn't miss a word as she explained a problem on the board. She might as well have been speaking Greek. Helping Tess with this class would be a challenge. Kenny seemed relieved to be relieved, bouncing up out of his chair the moment he saw me. I switched directions and headed for the seat he'd just vacated. He got an even sterner look from the teacher on the way out.

Tess ignored me and focused on the class work. I took a few notes, but mostly concentrated on the formulas the teacher put up on the board and how she arrived at answers. The bell rang, sending students scrambling for the door in a mad dash. I stood and collected Tess's things.

"Tess Barrett?" the teacher called.

Tess raised her hand.

Her teacher walked over, stood in front of our table, and looked me up and down before addressing Tess. "Tess, I'm concerned you may not be able to handle this course with your disability. It's tough enough when you can work out problems with paper and pencil. You'll have to do all the work in your head. Lab work is another problem."

"I can handle it, Mrs. Jessup," Tess said. "I passed the midterm by studying at home. I'll do even better hearing explanations firsthand."

Jessup looked skeptical. "You weren't here yesterday. You have a lot of catching up to do."

"I'm fine. I'm sorry about yesterday. First day back was overwhelming, so I went home after lunch. But I'm okay. Really. I can do this."

Jessup looked at me. "You're her assistant? You can't do the work for her, you know."

"I don't understand it anyway," I said. "English major."

She nodded, as if that explained everything. "What will you do if she needs help?"

"If I can't explain what I see you do in class, we'll find a classmate who can."

"Matt Tsang," Tess said quickly. "He's offered to tutor me if I need help."

Jessup nodded. "Okay. Matt knows his stuff. But I'm not cutting you any slack. If you can keep up, fine. If not, we'll talk again."

Jessup walked back to her desk without waiting for a reply. I stood up and slung Tess's backpack over one shoulder.

"You ready?" I said.

Tess sighed and got out of her chair. "You really don't understand chemistry?"

"Rudimentary concepts." I paused. "Just because I don't understand it doesn't mean I can't do it."

"How's that possible?"

"Parrots talk," I said. "Doesn't mean they know what they're saying. Come on, let's go."

Toby Cavanaugh and a group of friends stood in a semicircle in the hallway outside the door, waiting for us. The girl Tess had called Adrienne at lunch the previous day hung on Toby's arm like a fashion accessory. Two other couples completed the group, the guys tall, athletic, and good-looking like Toby, the girls perfect, unblemished proxies for teen-magazine models.

"Tess, I've been looking for you," Toby said.

Tess jerked her head up. "Toby. Adrienne? Is that you?"

"Yes," the cheerleader said, nose wrinkling. "It's me."

"Thought I smelled you," Tess said. "What do you want, Toby?"

Toby colored, unsure how to defend Adrienne's honor. He took the cowardly, and smart, way out—by doing nothing.

"Look, Tess," he said, "we want you to be straight with us."

"We?" she said. "Who's 'we?' Are there more of you?"

She turned her head side to side. A couple of them squirmed in discomfort. I knew the feeling; she had the uncanny knack of making people forget she was blind. No one else in the group spoke up.

"A couple of guys from the team," Toby said finally. "It doesn't matter. We just want to know—did you set Carl up or not?"

"Set him up? What do you mean?"

"After what happened in the commons yesterday, we just thought—"

"Listen, asshole," I said, stepping toe to toe with him, "Tess had nothing to do with what happened to Carl. And FYI, neither did I. Carl and his buddies were all primed to thump on me to get the keys to Tess's car, and I figured it just wasn't worth it, so I gave them to him. But neither one of us had any idea he'd get killed. You ask me, it wouldn't be a surprise if we find out he just pissed someone off bad enough to shoot him. You ought to pick your friends better."

Toby shifted his weight and looked around before answering. "Friend or not, he was a teammate. And nobody deserves that, not even Carl."

"So what are you saying, Toby?" Tess said. "You'd rather have seen *me* get shot? Or Oliver? Is that why you're here?"

"No, I . . . I—we just thought there might be more to the story than what we've heard." Toby fidgeted with his belt buckle. "It just seems strange, doesn't it? I mean, I know Carl could be a pain, but he wasn't *that* stupid. I just can't believe someone went after him like that."

Adrienne stroked Toby's arm and straightened a little, eyeing Tess. "Are you sure you didn't, like, say something to your uncle about the car? Wasn't he, like, some spy or something? Maybe he put a hit out on Carl."

"That's an even dumber idea than me shooting Carl," Tess said. "And no, I didn't tell Uncle Travis. Toby, I can't believe you would think I had something to do with this."

"You haven't exactly been the same old Tess this past year."

"How would you know? I'd say your attention has been elsewhere."

"Hey, that's not fair! You didn't—"

"No, Toby," she said, *"you're* the one who changed. What do you care, anyway?"

"I just want to see you get out in front of this, whatever it is."

"He doesn't want to see you get hurt," one of the guys said.

Adrienne glanced up at Toby, in shock. "You *care* about her? You *do*! Oh, my God, Toby!"

Toby flushed. "It's not like that, Adrienne. Come on, you know me better than that."

"I don't think I know you at all," Adrienne said, lower lip trembling. "Do you *like* her?"

"No! I mean, not like that." He glanced at Tess. "Sorry, Tess."

"Whatever." Tess shrugged. "You and Adrienne deserve each other. I hope you're happy."

"We *are* happy!" Adrienne turned and quickly kissed Toby on the cheek.

She could vamp all she wanted, but it wouldn't make Tess jealous if Tess couldn't see it.

"Come on, Tess," I said. "We're done here. These people aren't worth your time."

I took her elbow and shouldered my way through the gauntlet. Toby lifted his shoulder and let it fall. He stepped to one side, looking almost apologetic. He and his friends may have been on the same baseball team as Carl, Tad, and others from the night before, but they gave off a completely different vibe. They didn't seem the kind to go around bracing people. It made me wonder if someone had put them up to it. I felt Toby's eyes on my back on the way down the hall.

He called out after us, "We'll be watching you, Tess."

CHAPTER 30

Travis wheeled the Range Rover into the reserved parking space on P-1 and got out. The sign affixed to the wall in front of the SUV's grill made him pause on the way to the elevator. It conveniently read "Barrett," so he'd never had to change it. But he knew it had marked James Barrett's spot, not his. Travis had never been prone to bouts of insecurity where James was concerned. James had been brilliant, Travis knew he was merely clever. But Travis had had his own role to play. He'd been the more physical of the two. James had ridden circles around him on a skateboard, but Travis had been faster, stronger—a better athlete in every other sport.

They'd never really competed with each other, partly because of the difference in their ages. But looking at the sign meant for his brother, Travis wondered if he was cut out for the roles he'd assumed now that James was gone: CEO of a major software company, parent of a teenager, civilian. Travis reminded himself that it still wasn't a competition. James wasn't around, to begin with, and Travis wasn't trying to play any of the parts as well as James would have. He was doing things his own way. He always had, even in the army. That's why he'd been a perfect fit for the SICC unit. His superiors hadn't cared how the missions had been completed so long as the job got done.

He took an elevator from the garage directly to the sixth floor and walked down the corridor to the executive suite. Robyn Alia, James's assistant—now his—met him with a big smile outside the door to his office. A petite brunette a few years younger than him, Robyn kept the office running smoothly, organizing his schedule and handling all of his correspondence. She had an innate sense of how to prioritize everything, including blowing off a board meeting to take a simple phone call that might result in billions in new business or prevent the loss of an existing contract. She also had an uncanny knack for reading people as quickly and easily as search engine tags—from their general personality type to their mood on a particular day. Her intelligence analysis had been key to the successful outcome of countless meetings, saving Travis and the company time, money, and embarrassment on many occasions.

"Good morning, Mr. Barrett," she said as he approached. "How was your trip?"

"How many times have I asked you to call me Travis?" he said. "James may have been 'Mr. Barrett,' but I'm just plain Travis. Please, Robyn."

She flushed. He knew she addressed him formally to ensure there was no question about their relationship. But it seemed old-fashioned to him. The global business environment had become very casual, particularly at companies like MondoHard. Most of the employees had never owned a tie let alone a suit, and the use of first names was a matter of course. The only place he knew of that still insisted on using formal titles was the *Wall Street Journal*, though he didn't doubt there must be other places—old-money private clubs, embassies, and Britain's royal family, maybe— where titles were part of everyday speech.

He realized that he had more selfish reasons for pushing Robyn to use his first name. He wanted their relationship to be something more than boss and employee. He knew almost nothing about her personal life other than what he'd gleaned from her personnel file. She drew an indelible-if-unseen line between the job and her after-hours activities. As much as he'd wanted to suggest lunch or a drink after work, between the demands of the job and the invisible barrier she'd erected, he'd never summoned the courage. The irony, considering his two Purple Hearts, a Bronze Star, and a Silver Star, brought a wry smile to his lips.

"The trip was not what you'd call a success," he said. "Latham wants to pull the plug on our DoD contract."

Robyn's smile faded. "Sorry to hear it. What can I do?"

"Am I jammed up today?"

"No, actually your day is pretty light."

Travis glanced at his watch. "What's left of it. I need to see Williams right away. And could you check on when Cyrus is free this afternoon?"

"I'll get on it right away."

"Oh, and Robyn? Sorry I'm late. Some things came up at home. I should have checked in."

"Problems with Tess again?"

"You might say that." Travis wished he could tell her everything.

"Nothing to worry about," she said. "You didn't miss anything."

Travis nodded and entered the huge office reserved for the company president. Furnished in glass and stainless steel with ash wood highlights, the room was almost stark in its simplicity. A large, glass-topped desk was centered against a wall of floor-to-ceiling windows. A small conference table took up one side of the room. A small sitting area next to a bookcase occupied the other. Travis had altered nothing, but not because of any superstition or maudlin effort to preserve it as a shrine to James. He found it utilitarian, and had collected no personal knickknacks or photos of his own to decorate it with—not that he had any.

That's what ten years in a war zone would do for you. Until a year ago, the army had been his family. He'd had no permanent address except an APO and an e-mail account he rarely checked. His friends had been the men he'd served with, most of whom had moved on to other assignments, either undercover or in other parts of the world. The transience of his nomadic life had suited him then, but now he felt an unfamiliar restlessness, a desire for some permanence, some stability, a place to put down roots. He shrugged it off and sat at the desk to check his voicemail and return the calls he'd missed while in DC.

Fifteen minutes later, Williams knocked softly and entered without waiting for a response. Tall and gaunt, his long, thin nose under bushy eyebrows gave him the aquiline appearance of a raptor searching for prey.

"You wanted to see me?" he said.

"Where are we on the project?" Travis said.

Williams took a deep breath. "Close."

"How close? Days? Weeks?"

Williams shrugged. "Can't say. Every time we think we've got this thing figured out, it morphs. It's the most adaptable worm I've ever seen. Attack it, and it builds new defenses. Delete it, and it replicates somewhere else."

"But you *can* beat it, right Bill?"

"We *think* we can learn to live with it. Neutralize it so it doesn't screw things up. Kind of like a dormant bug. We've been testing different 'inoculations' to see if we can't immunize the system against it."

"We don't have much time," Travis said.

"We're doing everything we can."

"Better figure out how to do it fast, or we won't have a project anymore."

"That bad?"

Travis nodded. "Damn James anyway."

"You don't know it was James," Williams said.

"Who else could it have been?"

"You know as well as I do, Travis, how many people want to see us fail."

"No one else could create a worm like that. And who else knew the system software well enough? Or had access?"

Williams scratched his head. "Why would he sabotage his own work?"

Travis sighed. "I never knew reasons for half the things my brother did. Just fix it, okay?"

"Of course."

Williams turned for the door, but Travis stopped him. "Bill, who's our best coder?"

Williams faced him, brows furrowed. "We've got several excellent programmers."

"I'm not talking about code monkeys. I mean someone who knows it *all*, someone who sees the big picture."

"I'd probably say Dave Bradley," Williams said, rubbing the back of his neck. "Probably the best systems designer we've got."

Travis waved dismissively. "Too cautious. Come on, Bill. There must be someone who at least comes close to James's level."

Williams gazed past him at something out the window for a moment. "There is a kid in the gaming division who shows some promise. But I don't think he's ready for a project like this."

"Who is he?"

"Derek Hamblin. But I'm telling you, Travis, he's not your guy. Not for this."

"Maybe not, but let me take a look at his file first."

"It's your call. Is that all?"

"Yeah, that's it. Fix this, Bill. We've come too far to let the Senate Appropriations subcommittee shut us down."

"We'll do our best."

Travis reached for his keyboard as soon as Williams closed the door and typed a password to access the HR files. He pulled up Hamblin's information and scanned it, quickly deciding the kid was worth meeting. He closed the file, straightened his desk, and went to see Cyrus.

He found Cooper in his office, a windowless room behind the reception area on the ground floor. To get there, he first walked through a large space filled with closed-circuit television monitors, computer terminals, and radio equipment. Two uniformed security guards routinely scanned the activity on the monitors. One of them nodded to him in passing, his bored expression fleetingly relieved. He turned his attention back to the pixelated screens.

Cooper looked up from his desk when Travis entered, his underslung jaw and permanent scowl giving him the appearance of a bulldog. He was hunched over some paperwork, his powerful, simian arms covering much of the desktop, his thick neck disappearing into broad shoulders. His short, gray hair stuck straight up like the bristles of a stainless-steel brush. Pale blue eyes that looked as if they'd been bleached out like denim jeans bored through Travis as if he was a nervous supplier or dishonest employee.

Cyrus was a brutal man who'd gone from high school nose tackle straight into the Marines. Travis knew Cooper had seen action as a grunt in Grenada and later in Desert Storm, the first war in Iraq, before resigning his commission in the early nineties as a second lieutenant. From there he'd gone to Bosnia and fought as a mercenary before getting into the security business. Travis also knew there'd been rumors Cooper had illegally profited from the Iraq war, but he'd never been proved of wrongdoing. He was good at what he did, but Travis had never been sure of how far his boundaries extended.

Cyrus grunted. "You're back. Thought you'd be in yesterday."

"Got in yesterday afternoon, but some things came up at home," Travis said. "You may want to tighten things up here."

"They're tight. They're always tight. Why? That little incident yesterday with your niece?"

"Well . . ."

"Well nothing. We could have stopped her. Braced her and shaken her up—the two chuckleheads with her, too. But she *does* have a valid key card. And, as you've pointed out, technically she's a majority stockholder in this company, which means *she's* my boss, not you. Excuse me, not you, *sir.*"

"Enough with the sarcasm, Cyrus. I never said you didn't handle the situation properly."

"Did you talk to her?"

"Not yet. But she knows I know. I told her we'd talk about it when I get home tonight. No, what I meant was we may have a bigger problem."

He told Cooper about the attack on Tess, Alice, Yoshi, and Oliver. Cooper listened without expression until Travis had finished.

"You want me to put a detail on your house?" Cooper said.

Travis brushed the words out of the air. "I've already taken care of security at the house. I'm more concerned that whoever ordered the attack might try to breach security here. They're after something specific, Cyrus."

"Let me get this straight. Your niece thinks she's getting e-mails from James? And the attackers want whatever it was that he's instructing her to get?"

Travis nodded. "Near as I can tell. I may know more tonight after I talk to her."

"It doesn't make sense. Whatever it is she thinks she's finding for your brother—or his ghost—it obviously isn't here. I don't think we have anything to worry about."

"Humor me. Make sure we're buttoned up. I've got enough problems with the folks in Washington. I don't need Senator Latham breathing down my neck over a break-in or lapse in security, too."

"Fine," Cooper said gruffly. "I'll take care of it."

"Thanks, Cyrus. I'll let you know if I get anything else out of Tess. But you know teens."

"Yeah, actually, I do. My boy Tad is a senior this year. He was pretty upset last night. I guess one of his friends got killed. I didn't want to bring this up, but in light of what happened yesterday, I think I better." Cooper paused. "Tad says Tess had something to do with it. This kid, Carl, was driving her car?"

Travis clenched his jaw. "All I know is what Tess and this new assistant of hers, Oliver, told me. They say Carl threatened to beat up Oliver if he didn't hand over the keys. My guess is that whoever attacked the house yesterday went after the car thinking Tess was in it. But it's a police investigation now, Cyrus. It's out of our hands."

Cooper drummed thick fingers on the desk. "What do you know about this Oliver person?"

"Alice ran a standard background check. He's clean."

"We'll run another. Hers might've missed something."

Travis shrugged. "Suit yourself. I think it's a waste of time."

"Look, I understand she's your niece, Barrett, but even you have to admit something's not right. So, like it or not, I'm putting some eyes on her."

"I've got people on her twenty-four/seven," Travis objected, even though he knew Cooper was right. Tess was definitely acting squirrelly.

Cooper laced his fingers behind his head and leaned back. "Well, then, between yours and mine, I'd say we have her covered."

"Hope you have it covered in your budget, Cyrus."

"I know how to run my department."

Travis raised his hands. "Whatever you say. I have to get back to work."

"Anything else?"

"Yeah, there is one other thing. Rosa, the cook . . . Our old one, Helen, recommended her when she left. See if you can find Helen. I want to talk to her."

Cooper leaned forward and placed his hands on his desk. "Yes, *sir.*"

Travis ignored the slight inflection Cooper placed on the last word. He knew Cooper thought his former branch of the armed services—the Marines—was superior to the Army, where Travis had served. And he felt Cyrus may have had some personal grudge with Travis—his assumption of the top spot without ever having worked at the company, for example. Or maybe they just didn't like each other. In any case, Travis knew he'd have to pick his battles with Cooper, and now was not the time. He met Cooper's gaze until the older man finally looked away, then turned for the door.

A dozen things demanded his attention in his office, but he muzzled the nagging voice in his head and took the stairs up two flights. Wending his way through a warren of cubicles, he came to another windowless office and entered without knocking. The large space was dim, lit only by two desk lamps and several computer screens. The air was stale and overly warm, and underlying the strong odor of hot wiring and electronic components was a note of high school gym locker.

Three kids not much older than Tess, all male, crowded around a large video monitor. They all wore the uniform of the day—T-shirts and jeans—and all were badly in need of haircuts. Pale skin, turned blue by the light from the screen and mottled with sparse patches of fuzzy facial hair, signaled how little sunlight they saw. One of them sat in front of the monitor, the other two hunched over on either side, all of them intent on the action on screen—flashes of light as vehicles and buildings exploded, geysers of blood as foes were dispatched with every weapon imaginable. Travis recognized the video game as one of the more popular releases in recent years. It wasn't one of MondoHard's— and definitely wasn't James's.

Several moments passed before one of the onlookers took notice of Travis, the excitement on his face quickly devolving into a serious expression as he turned. His companion glanced at him and did a double take at Travis.

The first one nudged the game player and nodded at Travis. "Hey, what's up?"

Travis nodded. "Derek Hamblin?"

The kid in the chair spun around and looked at Travis from under a tangled sheaf of dark hair. One eyebrow was accented with a silver ring. He slouched in the chair, gray vest over a black T-shirt open in front to reveal a line-art drawing of Kurt Cobain. His black jeans were frayed and torn, but Travis figured the kid had bought them that way instead of wearing them out. Five Chinese characters were tattooed on one forearm in black ink.

"I'm Derek," he said. "Help you with something?"

The two still standing looked at each other. Some unspoken signal passed between them, and they headed for the door.

"Hey, man," one said to Derek. "Catch you later. We're going to get a bite. Want anything?"

"Nah, I'm good," Derek said with a small wave.

Travis took another step forward as the two on their way out parted and went around him. His gaze took another hike from Derek's grungy sneakers to his unwashed hair. Derek was everything Travis wasn't—rude, insubordinate, undisciplined, surly, and lacking in any social graces.

Which means he's probably a dead ringer for James at about the same age. Just what I'm was looking for—if I'm careful.

"You know who I am?" Travis said.

Derek shrugged. "Not really."

"I run this company."

"Well, yeah, I knew that much. I thought maybe you were getting existential on me."

Travis jerked his chin toward the monitor. "Is that what you do all day? Play video games on company time?"

Derek glanced over his shoulder at the frozen screen. "Pretty much. Gotta know what the competition is doing before you can come up with something that'll blow people away."

"Ah." Travis fingered the memory stick in his pocket. "You good?"

"What? At playing? Designing? Or coding? Take your pick—I'm the best."

Travis raised an eyebrow. "Big words."

"You want a list of secure sites I've hacked? I'm talking about NSA-level, supposedly impregnable websites. Code? Is that what you're talking about? The last two titles this company put out? Both mine. Yeah, I'm good."

Travis nodded and held out the memory stick. "A file got deleted. Can you recreate it?"

Derek snorted. "Even *you* could probably do that. There's a ton of recovery software on the web. You don't need me for that."

"I'm not finished," Travis said. "First, I don't think you're going to find it that simple to restore the file. But I also want you to see if you can figure out how it was deleted—and where it went."

Hamblin stared at him curiously, and Travis knew he had him hooked.

"What's in this file?" he said.

Travis shrugged. "I don't know. If you can recreate it, that might be your next job. There could be others after that."

Hamblin rubbed his chin and stared at the floor for a moment. Finally his gaze rose and landed on Travis's face. "Why me?"

"Your rep, first of all. A few other people have noticed your work." Travis watched the effect his words had. Hamblin almost glowed, but quickly wiped the small smile from his lips so it wouldn't look like he was gloating. "Frankly, I need someone I can trust. Someone not vested in his or her work on the defense side of the business. Can I trust you, Derek?"

Hamblin chewed on the question for a while and seemed to like the taste. He nodded.

"Sure, why not?" he said. Worry darkened his face. "You're not talking about anything illegal, are you? I mean, it's not like I'm a wuss. I may have skirted the law myself on occasion. It's just—"

"No," Travis said, "nothing illegal. But you can't tell anyone. Not even your best buds. And this doesn't take the place of your normal responsibilities. You'll have to figure out a way to do this on the side, without your friends finding out."

He shrugged. "They're not really what you'd call friends."

"Okay, then. Seems we have an agreement."

Expectancy brightened his expression. "Will I, like, get anything extra for this?"

Travis felt the smile on his face harden to a brittle grimace. "You'll get the satisfaction of knowing you did the right thing."

Hamblin rubbed the back of his neck and reached for the memory stick. "I guess that's okay."

Travis squeezed his outstretched hand into a fist. "Good choice—partner."

Hamblin reached out and hesitantly hammered the top of Travis's meaty hand with his own fist.

CHAPTER 31

"That certainly went well," Tess muttered to herself.

"What?" Oliver said.

She hadn't really intended him to hear, but it didn't make much difference. "Second day of school. And I was there for only one period."

"Uh, yeah, I know," Oliver said. "I was there, too."

"You weren't humiliated in front of all the people who are supposed to be your friends."

"And you didn't almost get your ass kicked by a crazy person. Or get called into the principal's office. Sorry, assistant principal. Or get questioned by the cops. Why? Because I was there to do all that for you, Miss I-Have-to-Be-Perfect-or-No-One-Will-Like-Me."

"It's not *your* school," she said, heat rising in her face. "You don't have to go there for the next three months and deal with these people."

"Well, as a matter of fact, I have to do *exactly* that. Get it through your thick head, Tess, I'm in this with you. So whatever happens to you happens to me."

"It's not the same! Don't you understand?"

"Oh, I get it all right. I get that you're a spoiled, self-centered, whiny brat who's more concerned about her image than her life or the lives of those around her."

"You are so *mean*! I hate you!"

"Keep it down back there, you two," Kenny said. "I need to focus on the road."

She turned away and felt the moving vehicle rock her gently. She blinked back tears, determined not to give Oliver the satisfaction of seeing her cry—again.

"Bad day?" Luis said, his voice close, as if he'd turned around.

"The worst!" Tess said. "Everyone thinks I had something to do with Carl getting killed. Even Toby."

"Toby?" Oliver said. "Oh, now I understand. You like him, don't you?"

"No, I don't."

"Adrienne sure seems to think so. What's the deal with you and him?"

"I don't *care* about Adrienne." Tess heard her voice rise, but she couldn't help it. "She's such a bitch! She—"

"Shut up!" Kenny shouted. "God, you two sound like you're married. I can't concentrate."

Tess pressed herself against the door to get away from Kenny's anger.

"Hey, man," Luis said. "Chill! They're just kids. Sorry about that, Miss Barrett. If you could try to keep it down a little, it would help, but Kenny needs to learn some manners."

Silence fell inside the vehicle, thick and foreboding as dense fog. A pang of something like guilt ran through Tess, stirred by a fleeting memory that was gone before she could see what it was. Her heart beat so loudly she was sure the rest of them must have been able to hear it, too.

"Sorry," Kenny said gruffly. "Just trying to do my job, you know? Protect you."

"That's okay," Tess mumbled.

"No, it isn't," Kenny said. "I should be able to concentrate even if there are bombs going off around us. It won't happen again."

The fog in the SUV seemed to lift, and some of the tension in Tess's shoulders eased.

A moment later Oliver said in a low voice, "She *what?*"

"She who?" Tess said, confused. "You mean Adrienne? She stole Toby."

"You and Toby were dating? What happened?"

Tess turned toward the sound of his voice and pointed at her face. "This happened."

"The accident?"

She nodded and swallowed hard, fighting tears again.

What is wrong with me? It's not like it happened yesterday. Toby hasn't been part of my life for a year.

"The accident." She said. "After that, we stopped seeing each other. Literally."

"His loss."

She didn't reply. People always said something like that, as if it would somehow make things better.

Yes, it was Toby's loss, but mine as well.

"Why'd you break up?" Oliver said.

"I don't want to talk about it." Tess folded her arms and turned away, pressing her forehead against the cold glass.

The silence returned, almost comforting this time. It was several minutes before the vehicle came to a stop and Luis announced that they'd arrived at the house. Tess let herself out. She hadn't heard the garage door open, so she assumed Kenny had stopped in the circle outside the front door. Without waiting for Oliver, she made her way instinctively toward the door, tentatively extending each foot in front of the other until she encountered a step. She felt for the railing and used it to guide herself up the remaining steps to the door.

"Not again," Oliver said behind her with a groan. "Come on, Tess, wait up."

She ignored him and pushed through the big door, stripping off her coat as soon as she was inside. She left it on the floor and hurried toward the kitchen. On familiar ground, she moved faster, leaving Oliver farther behind. By the time she reached the kitchen, the house had grown quiet.

"Alice?" she said.

No response. Distantly, she heard the front door close.

"Tess?" Oliver called. "Where are you?"

She didn't answer.

Let him figure it out. If I can get around without eyesight, he can find his own way to the kitchen.

The stillness returned, not even broken by Oliver's footsteps or the sound of the SUV outside.

"Alice?" she said again, softly this time, already knowing there would be no answer.

Nervous now, she took a step and stretched out her hand in search of the center island. She heard the soft tread of a footstep behind her. Before she could turn, an arm snaked around her throat. Adrenaline flooded her system, jump-starting her heart and jolting her muscles into action. Instinctively, she latched onto the arm with both hands and turned, thrusting her hip out. She rolled her shoulders, nearly doubling over, and felt the weight of the person behind her shift onto her hip and off again as her motion propelled the body up and over.

The body thudded on the floor in front of her. Still holding the person's arm, her hands slid up until she felt a wrist. She grasped it, fingers quickly finding pressure points. She pressed down hard and bent the hand back, dropping onto one knee. She heard a *whoosh* of breath as her knee landed on the person's chest, and she forced the hand back even farther, angry and frightened enough to break it if she had to.

"Who are you?" she screamed. "What do you want?"

Someone gently tapped her wrist. "*Aieee*, missy! Enough!"

"Yoshi?" she said. As soon as she said it, she recognized the earthy scent of loam and mulch mixed with vanilla and green tea that was uniquely Yoshi's.

"*Hai*, missy. You remember."

"Holy crap, Tess! Do you know what you just did?" Oliver's voice this time.

"What? Oh, Yoshi, I'm so sorry." Confused, Tess struggled to keep her emotions in check as her heart pounded. A strong hand grasped her upper arm and helped her up.

"That was awesome," Oliver said. "Where'd you learn to do that?"

"I don't know . . . What do you mean? Do what?"

"She remember the jujitsu I teach her," Yoshi said, on his feet now, his voice level with her ears. "We spend many long hours practicing out in the garden when she was a little girl."

"Not that little, Yoshi," Tess said. "And don't forget, I went to a dojo during middle school when you were too busy to teach."

"Ah-so, not too busy. Just thinking you should learn from different sensei."

"But why did you do that? Why did you pretend to choke me like that? Unless you're one of *them* . . ."

"No, no," he said hurriedly. "I not like those bad men. I want you to remember, to know you are not so helpless as you feel."

"My god, Tess. I wish you could have seen yourself," Oliver said. "You were amazing."

She flushed. It *had* felt good, even if Yoshi had nearly scared her to death.

"What about stones?" Yoshi said. "You use stones I give you?"

"What stones?" She frowned. "Oh, right, the ones you gave me before school yesterday. I think I put them in my backpack."

"You be good to use them, missy."

"What kind of stones?" Oliver said. "What do they do?"

"Some people call them worry stones," Yoshi said. "But they have special powers. You see. And now you see you still know jujitsu, we practice every day after school."

Tess groaned. "Not *every* day. Besides, how do you know I can really do it? If I can't see you coming, I won't know what to do."

"You see me coming that time? I not think so. You practice. Every day."

"Maybe." She drew the word out. "I'll think about it, Yoshi."

"You not think too hard, missy or you hurt your head."

"Ha, ha! Very funny. Get a little closer and maybe I'll show you how much jujitsu I *really* remember. Then we'll see who's laughing."

"Ah-so, welcome back, missy. Now excuse, please. I work."

Yoshi shuffled out almost as silently as he'd come in.

"Is he gone?" Tess said.

"Yes. Why?"

"We need to get to work, too."

"I'll get your book bag."

"I'm not talking about homework." She reached in her pocket and took out the iPod they'd retrieved from the Range Rover. "We need to see what's on this."

"Are you sure you want to do that? Instead of homework, I mean."

Her heartbeat had just started to slow from the initial fright and exertion of her encounter with Yoshi. Now it sped up again.

"Better than thinking about having no friends." She reached out and felt for the island, found a stool, and sat down. "You'll have to do this for me."

Oliver sat next to her and gently lifted the iPod from her grasp. "What am I looking for?"

"I don't know. The most recent song? We might have to hook it up to a computer and see what files are on it."

Tess chewed a fingernail in the ensuing silence. She forced herself to pull it out of her mouth and placed her palm flat on the counter. She concentrated on the feel of the smooth, cool stone under her hand. She could see its colors in her mind—black with streaks of hunter green and flecked with bright crystal facets beneath the surface that reflected silver or gold, depending on the light. She pressed hard, willing her fingers to tell her which colors they touched.

"That was pretty cool how you pulled one over on your uncle," Oliver said after a moment. "You know, with the thumb drive. You sure you should have done that?"

"Look, if Uncle Travis was supposed to get whatever we're looking for, then my dad would have sent the e-mails to *him*, not me. So if my dad didn't trust him, why should I?"

"We still don't know for sure it's your dad. Could be someone is getting you to steal something that *belonged* to your dad."

"I thought you wanted me to do this," she said. "Besides, who else would have known about the puzzle book?"

"Your uncle?"

"He was in Afghanistan most of the time I was growing up."

"Alice?"

Tess chewed on that notion for a moment. Alice had never been warm and cuddly, but she'd always been there, helpful and efficient. While Alice was no substitute for her mother, Tess didn't know what she would have done without her for the past year.

"I don't think so," she said. "Why would she save us from Rosa, then? She's been with us since I was little. I just don't see it."

"Hey, I'm just trying to look at this thing from all angles. What we don't know *could* hurt us, you know." He paused, but before she could say anything, he went on. "Okay, I've looked through all the music files, and there's nothing very new. But in the video files, there's one that's a lot more recent than the rest."

"Come on! What is it?"

"It's a clip of you snowboarding."

A chill ran through her like cold IV fluid. It brought back memories of her long stay in the hospital—and something else, too. She heard her father's voice as clear as blue sky in August yell, "Atta girl! Nice air!" Her mother's whoop of encouragement echoed a moment later through the speaker, the sound tinny and so much smaller than life. The embarrassment she'd felt at the time had lit up her face like a torch, but the shame she felt now burned white-hot and deep inside.

She managed no more than a whispered croak from her constricted throat. "It's from the last time I saw them."

"This was taken the day of the accident? Never mind. Dumb question. I'm sorry, Tess."

As much as she dreaded it, Tess forced herself to remember that day.

What had been so special about that day that Dad would now want me to pull something relevant, something important, from a video clip? Everything, of course.

It had started out as a celebration of her SAT scores. A surprisingly crisp and clear spring day. As much as she hated to admit it, she'd had fun, too, with her parents. She'd thought that without her friends the trip would be a drag, but it had been the opposite—a relaxing respite from the grind of schoolwork and the drama of junior year. She hadn't even allowed herself to be flustered by her father's lame jokes or her mother's attempts to baby her—until her father had brought out the iPod to shoot her coming down a run. She'd suddenly become self-conscious, as if the other kids on the mountain would think she was showing off for the camera. As a result, she'd almost missed a big mogul entirely. But she'd managed to catch it at the last second and twist into a nice corked cab 360. That had been on their last run. Afterward, of course, the day could not have gotten worse.

She ran through the scene again in her mind, pulling up images that her eyes could no longer see. She watched her father get out ahead of her on the long run, carving sweet turns and occasionally catching some air. She and her mother had followed, Tess the faster of the two. Her father had disappeared around a bend, and by the time Tess had reached his spot, he'd stopped far down the slope and was getting ready to video her run. Other than her discomfort, though, she couldn't think of anything else out of the ordinary.

"What do you see?" she said.

"You snowboarding. That's it."

"Go through it again. See if there's anything strange. Other boarders or skiers. Voices."

She waited while Oliver played the clip again. It was short, less than a minute. She heard nothing different the second time through.

"Nothing," Oliver said when it ended. "It's nothing special. I mean, I'm sure it was a special moment for you, for your folks . . ."

Oliver's embarrassed barely registered as she puzzled. "There must be something. Or else it must be another file."

"That's the most recent. There's nothing else on here that isn't at least a few months older."

"Are you sure?"

"I'm not a complete idiot, Tess. I think I can figure out how to work this thing."

"Okay, okay. I just . . . There has to be something there!"

"Well, if there is, it's really well hidden." Oliver sounded peeved.

"Of course it is," Tess said, pressing a hand to her forehead. "Why didn't I think of it before?"

"What? What is it?"

Busy digging in her pocket for her phone, Tess didn't answer. She pushed the voice recognition button on the side. After the prompt, she said, "Call Matt."

"It's a hidden file," she said to Oliver while Matt's phone rang. "It has to be."

"Yo," Matt's voice said over the speaker, "Better be someone I know. If not, hang up. If so, you know what to do." After a pause, Matt's voicemail beeped.

"Matt, this is Tess. Call me. I need to—"

"Tess, it's me," Matt said, breathing hard. "Sorry, I was driving."

"Can you come over? We really need you."

"I can't, Tess. I'm on my way to work. Can it wait till later?"

Tess's shoulders slumped. "I suppose."

"Is it something I can help with over the phone? I've got a few minutes now."

"Maybe. We've got my dad's iPod. The last file on it is a video clip. I think there might be something hidden in it somehow."

"An embedded file? Sure. That's fairly easy. There's software on the web that can help you find it and isolate it. Is this another one of those mystery files?"

"I think so," Tess said. "Can you tell Oliver what to do?"

"Sure," Matt said. "But before you do anything with it, e-mail me the video so we have a copy. Remember what happened last time?"

"Right. Okay, we'll send it now. And here's Oliver."

Michael W. Sherer

She held out the phone, and Oliver took it from her.

"Okay, Matt," he said. "What am I looking for?"

Oliver had taken the call off speaker, and for the next few minutes Tess heard nothing but "uh-huh" and "got it" from him. She wondered what sort of hoops Matt was making him jump through.

Finally, he said, "Did you get the e-mail? The video clip? Okay, then I'm going to run this program . . . No, I copied the clip to my laptop. I'll run it on that . . . Yeah, hang on a sec."

"Oliver . . . ?" Tess said.

"Working on it. Here it goes. Yes! Another file, embedded in the video. Matt, you'll want to look at this when you have a chance. More code . . . Okay, we'll talk to you later. Thanks."

"He hung up?" Tess said.

"Had to go to work," Oliver said. "But we got it, Tess. Another piece of the program. Have you checked your e-mail lately?"

Tess pressed the voice activation button on her phone and said, "E-mail." The phone responded in that robotic voice, "You have one unread e-mail."

"Open e-mail," Tess commanded.

"E-mail, sent today at 10:48, from Dad. Bitly slash seven-eight-four-Q-X."

"Bitly . . . ?" Oliver said. "What's that?"

"It's a link to a web address," Tess said. "Here we go again. Guess you better upload the file and see what happens."

She waited while Oliver pecked the keys on his laptop.

"There it goes," he said. "And, yes, it's really gone. Took the file on the laptop with it, but I still have the original video clip."

Tess frowned. "He made a mistake. That's not like him."

"No, *someone* made a mistake. Which suggests it might not be your dad. I mean, come on, Tess, you can't really believe he's still alive."

A man's voice came from across the room. "Believe who's alive?"

Tess heard footsteps on the tile floor and caught the strong scent of men's cologne, something with notes of coconut, hazelnut, and caramel. She recognized it, but couldn't remember where she'd encountered it or who'd worn it. A second whiff triggered a memory from middle school. She must have been in seventh grade. Bert Shirovsky had sat next to her in earth science. Big for his age, when so many girls were so much more developed than boys, he'd cornered her in the hall one day and had tried to kiss her. She might not have minded, except for the major crush she had on Toby Cavanaugh—and the fact that Bert's breath had smelled like Yoshi's compost bin out in the greenhouse. She'd managed to slip out from under his grasp and had shied away whenever the strong scent of his deodorant appeared close by.

"No one," Tess said, thinking furiously.

"We were just talking about the boy who was killed last night," Oliver said quietly. "Tess is having a hard time accepting the fact that he's dead. I don't blame her."

"Ah, yes," the man said. "It must be very upsetting. My sympathies, Miss Barrett. This is Marcus, by the way. Marcus Jackson. I'm head of the security team."

"My *uncle* is head of the security team," Tess said.

"When he's not here, I'm in charge."

His tone told Tess not to push it. She remembered Marcus, a tall black man who'd trained with Uncle Travis in the Special Forces. She'd tried to ignore all the men Travis had brought in to protect them before the accident, but he'd been an unavoidable presence.

"I have strict orders from Travis—from your uncle—to keep tabs on you at all times," Marcus said. "You should have let me know you were home from school."

Tess's voice rose. "How was I supposed to know—?"

"You didn't," Marcus said bluntly. "I'm informing you now. Please keep me advised of your whereabouts."

"You could have just asked Kenny or Luis," she complained.

"I could have, but I need to hear it directly from you." His voice was cold. "Those are my orders."

"You might as well lock me up. Then you'll know where I am all the time," she grumbled.

"It might come to that," Marcus said.

Tess blinked back tears as his footsteps receded.

CHAPTER 32

I watched Jackson's broad back retreat, sinewy muscles rippling beneath his cashmere turtleneck like a panther's. The creamy color of the pullover complemented his skin tone, like foam on a cappuccino. Black silk trousers and Italian leather loafers completed the ensemble. He moved athletically, with the graceful stride of a wide receiver or a point guard. But he had more bulk, more like a tight end or a power forward. Something about his demeanor, his less-than-sympathetic exchange with Tess despite his words of condolence, made me distrust him. Luis and Kenny had feigned friendliness, at least. Jackson had all the charm of a cobra.

"He's gone," I said when Marcus disappeared down the hall.

She shuddered. "They're all so mean. Why can't they just leave me alone?"

"You know why. We—well, you—have something someone wants."

"These files." She shook her head. "But we don't even know what they are. Why did you cover for me, anyway?"

"I don't trust him," I said. "I don't trust any of them, not even your uncle. Especially not your uncle."

"You can't be serious. Why not?"

"You don't trust him. Why should I? I don't *know* these people, Tess. Think about it. Who has the most to gain from getting you out of the way? The most to lose if someone screws up the business? We're probably talking a lot of money here. Maybe enough to turn your uncle over to the dark side. He may have been in Afghanistan when you were growing up, but he's been back now, what, a year? Plenty of time to figure out how to take control of the company."

"He already *has* control of the company. He knows I don't want anything to do with it." She waved her arms in frustration. "Besides, we don't even know what's going on."

"The men who came after us last night? They weren't looking for help with homework or your advice on what to wear to the prom. This program, whatever it is, is big. Important enough to kill for."

I paused, attention drawn to the video clip frozen midframe on my laptop screen. My mind triple-jumped to another topic. "You don't really think you're dad's still alive, do you?"

Tess swallowed hard. "No, I guess not. But he could have set all this in motion before the accident."

"If he did, then maybe he wants you to have a copy of this file for some reason. Maybe that's why we were able to copy this. Maybe he wants you to figure out what the program is, what it's for."

She snorted. "I've never done any programming. I don't understand it. Dad always tried to show me how, but I just didn't get it."

"Yeah, but you know people who do understand it. Mark might be able to piece enough of it together to figure out what it does." I remembered something else as well. "We didn't copy the file on the camera's memory card before we uploaded it. Something may have been hidden in that file, too. Damn, that might have made it easier for Matt."

Her head drooped and swung from side to side. "I guess I better figure out my homework before trying to decipher some weird computer code, or I'm in deep trouble."

"Good point. Sorry. I'll help you get started. You want to work here or in the library?"

"Library."

I gathered up books, backpack, and laptop and got her settled in the library. She managed to focus for about an hour, knocking off math and chemistry assignments fairly easily and finishing most of her French homework. Just as she started to get antsy, twirling a strand of hair with two fingers and fidgeting in her chair, Alice walked in and headed straight for our table.

"I picked up a rental car for you," she said, handing me a set of car keys. "Are you two hungry?"

"Not really," Tess piped up before I could admit I was famished. "Can we take a break? I need to get out for a little while. A half hour or so, that's all. Take me for a drive, Oliver, please? I promise I'll finish up the rest of my homework as soon as we get back."

I looked at Alice with raised eyebrows.

She glanced down at the books and papers on the table. "How's she doing?"

"A lot of reading for the American studies/literature block," I said, "but otherwise she's pretty much caught up."

Alice nodded. "Fine. Go for a drive. But don't stay out long."

"What about Marcus?" Tess said. "He wants to know my every waking move, and I just can't deal with him right now."

"I'll handle Marcus," Alice said. "But don't leave until I've spoken with him. You know he has to put a detail on you."

"What? Like, *follow* us?" Tess rolled her eyes, a gesture at once completely natural and yet somehow disturbing.

"It's for your own protection, Tess. I'll tell Marcus to make sure they're discreet. You'll never know they're there."

"I'll know," Tess said. "I just won't be able to see them."

I would have complimented her on at least having a sense of humor about it, except that she didn't look at all happy.

"Come on," I said, "let's get you out of here."

Five minutes later we rolled out of the drive and past the gate, a black SUV with Kenny and Luis on board not far behind. Tess wriggled into the seat next to me, getting comfortable.

"Smells funny," she said. "It's not as nice as my mom's car. You miss it, don't you?"

"Your mom's car? Sure. It's cool." The nondescript gray rental sedan made me miss the BMW more than I thought I would. I'd never been attached to material things all that much, never cared too much about what sort of clothes I wore or car I drove. But I had to admit that, having experienced the performance and creature comfort of the BMW, anything less paled in comparison.

"You really never drove one before?"

"A Beemer? No, why?"

"I don't know. I thought you were a trust-fund baby. Figured you had lots of nice things growing up."

"Not really. Nana and Pop-Pop didn't have a lot of money. I mean, they weren't poor or anything. They had a nice house. Nothing fancy, but big enough for the three of us, a yard to play in. Nice neighborhood, but nothing like yours. Nice neighbors, at least. Anyway, the trust fund only paid for education, not cars.

What about you? Ever ridden in a beater like this? Something the peasants drive?"

"Hey, I never said you were a peasant. As a matter of fact when I was little, my dad drove an ancient Saab he bought when he was in college. And my mom drove a beat-up Honda. It wasn't until Dad's company took off and we moved up here that my parents got nicer cars."

"Nicer cars, nicer house . . . I'd say they did all right."

"They earned it," she said quietly. "They worked really hard for it, and what good did it do them? They're not here to enjoy it, are they?"

I had no glib answer for that. We drove in silence for a while under low, gray clouds that scudded across the sky in search of a suitable place to dump a load of raindrops.

"I want to see Helen," Tess said suddenly.

"Helen. As in your former cook?"

"Yes, Helen. Doesn't it bug you that after years with us she suddenly quit?"

"I didn't know her. Was she happy working for you? For your parents?"

"Of course she was happy. Why wouldn't she have been?"

"I don't know. Depends on how she was treated. It's one thing to have a steady job with reasonable hours and nice employers. It's another to neglect your own family to cook from morning till night for some rich folks that treat you like dirt."

"We did *not* treat Helen like dirt. She *was* like family. I know my parents paid her well, and no, they didn't work her to death. She always seemed happy to me."

"Got along okay with Alice?"

Tess shrugged. "Sure."

"So where does she live?"

"Down in Renton somewhere. I'll get the address."

She pulled out her phone and asked it to map the address for Helen Corday, then handed the phone to me. I glanced at it and handed it back.

"Need to keep my eyes on the road," I said. "Will it work like a GPS device? You know, give me directions?"

She spoke some commands into the phone and it immediately spoke back, giving us the first turn. In a few minutes I was on the freeway and headed south toward Renton. Breaks in the trees flashing by on one side revealed glimpses of Lake Washington, gray under the clouds. Tess was quiet the whole way, the monotone instructions from her phone my only company. I kept checking the rearview mirror, but couldn't tell if Kenny and Luis were still behind us or not.

Soon we were back on a city thoroughfare. The route took us close to downtown Renton, winding around the bottom of the lake and back up into the hills surrounding it. We turned off the main arterial onto a side street into a neighborhood of older, small homes. A few blocks farther, we found the address listed for Helen—a single-story Cape Cod cottage with weathered shingle siding. I pulled up to the curb across the street from the house and shut off the engine. A car passed by and turned at the corner, leaving the street quiet and still.

"What do you see?" Tess asked, fingers splayed on the dash as if to keep from being thrown through the windshield.

"Not much." I described the house to her.

"She's probably not even home," Tess said. "I bet she's at work."

"Are you nervous about seeing her?"

"I don't know what to say. I mean, I don't want to accuse her."

"Just ask her."

I got out, circled the front of the car, and helped Tess out. She gripped my arm tightly as we crossed the street. There was no sign of Luis and Kenny.

I rang the doorbell and took a step back from the door. Curtains in the front window were drawn tight, and the house looked dark and empty. Scraggly rhododendrons on either side of the stoop clawed their way up the side of the house, looking for a grip on the gutters. Dandelions speckled the yard, poking up from grass that was badly in need of cutting. I leaned forward and stabbed the bell with a finger again.

Tess tugged on my arm. "Come on, let's go. No one's home."

"Hang on a second. I thought I heard something."

I pushed the bell a third time, and when the chime faded away, I heard soft footsteps approaching the door. It opened a crack and a woman peered through the opening, face etched with worry, gray wisps of hair trailing down her cheeks. Brown eyes ringed with dark circles widened in surprise at the sight of Tess, and the worry changed to fear. She opened the door another inch, then her eyes darted one way and another as she took in the street behind us.

"Helen?" Tess said. "Is that you?"

A soft groan escaped the woman behind the door. "Go away, child. You shouldn't have come."

"Helen, please," Tess said. "Let us in. We need to talk to you."

Helen sighed. "About what? It's all been said."

"No, it hasn't. Please, there's so much I have to tell you, so much I want to know."

"I can't help you. Go away."

Helen's face receded into the gloom, but before she could close the door, I stuck my foot in the crack. She leaned forward, her eyes narrowed.

"Look," I said, "you can let us inside for five minutes and answer a few simple questions, or we can stand here banging on your door for the next five minutes. I'm sure the neighbors would love that—not to mention any passersby."

Helen shivered, the same look of fright painting her face a ghostly shade. "Fine, come in. But I'm telling you, I can't help you."

She swung the door wide and reached out with bloodless, skeletal hands that clutched at Tess's sleeve and pulled her in. She motioned me inside impatiently and shut the door behind me, checking the street once more before latching it tightly.

"Can't help, or won't?" I said.

She peered at me in the dim light. Without answering, she waved a bony hand in front of Tess's face and got no reaction.

"It's true," Helen whispered. "You *are* blind." She gulped and took Tess by the hand. "Well, fine, come on in then. Sit down. Ask your questions."

She led the way into a living room cluttered with bric-a-brac and old furniture. A faded chintz couch sagged along one wall, behind a scarred coffee table topped with magazines, a bowl of dusty potpourri, and several knickknacks. A worn easy chair faced a small television, the small table next to it littered with newspapers. Perched on top of the pile were a remote and a pair of half-frame cheaters with a loop of chain dangling from the earpieces, as well as a chipped mug. A small dining area took up the far half of the room, an open door leading to a kitchen beyond.

Helen steered Tess to the couch and got her seated. Without looking at me, she perched in the easy chair. I sat next to Tess.

"So what's this all about, then?" Helen said, wringing her hands. "Why the sudden interest in old Helen after all this time?"

Tess's eyes grew big. "My parents were killed, Helen. And you can see what happened to me. I'm sorry it's taken me so long to come find you, but I've had other things to deal with. Why did you leave us, anyway?"

"Had other fish to fry," Helen mumbled. "My husband was sick. Had to be here to take care of him. Got a night job on an office cleaning crew so I could be with George during the day."

"I didn't know," Tess said, hanging her head.

"I'm sure there's a lot you don't know," Helen said. "I knew you had your own troubles. Didn't want to burden you with mine."

"You recommended Rosa to Alice," I said. "How did you know her?"

Helen leaned forward and peered at me again. "And just who are you, exactly?"

"Oliver," Tess said. "He's my assistant, and I want to know the answer to that, too."

"I didn't know her," Helen said. "I heard about her from someone. I don't remember who."

"Rosa's gone," Tess said.

Helen looked at her sharply, but her face quickly softened into a bland mask. "Sorry she didn't work out. What's it to me? You and Alice going to blame me for recommending her?"

"Not at all," Tess said. "We just want to know who told you to suggest her."

Helen drew herself up in the chair, but it still dwarfed her. "No one. I heard she was a good cook, so I passed on her name. Didn't want to leave Alice in the lurch, that's all."

"Rosa tried to kill Alice. And Tess." I gauged her reaction. Her mouth tightened, and fear crept back into her eyes. "Look, Helen, Rosa's gone. Alice and Yoshi chased her off, along with a couple of goons. But whoever sent them won't stop there. Tess is in danger. We need to know *who* told you to quit and let Rosa have your job."

She shook her head, jaw clamped tight.

Tess tipped her head to one side, reading into Helen's silence.

"Helen? Please. Why would you lie? Do you hate me so much you want to see me dead?"

Helen blanched again. "I don't hate you, child. I just can't tell."

"They threatened you," I said.

Helen nodded. "Me, my family."

"We have to stop them," I said. "I won't let them do to Tess what they did to her parents. You have to help us, Helen. Who threatened you?"

A tear leaked from the corner of her eye. "They said they'd kill us all. George first, then my daughter Harriett, and me last if I didn't do what they said."

I looked around. "Where is your husband, ma'am?"

Sadness washed over her. "He died. Bad heart. I told you, he was sick."

"I'm so sorry," Tess said. "You must feel awful. Was it recent?"

"Must've been six months ago. Hard to say—the days just blend into each other."

"You've been alone all this time?" Tess cried. "That's terrible."

Helen shrugged. "It's not so bad. You get used to it. Gave me a chance to think. After taking care of you folks all those years, and then George, I hardly had time to myself. Been catching up on some reading."

I heard a noise from the kitchen, like the creak of a floorboard, but when I glanced through the open door I saw nothing. Helen didn't seem to take notice.

Tess's face brightened. "You should come home with us. Now that Rosa's gone, we need you, Helen."

"Oh, I couldn't," Helen said. Color rose in her cheeks. "Don't need no charity, now. I'm doing just fine."

"No, really," Tess said. "We *do* need you. You cook so much better than Alice."

"Don't let her hear you say that, child. Goodness, she'll ground you till you're gray."

"I'm sorry about your husband, too," I said softly, trying to bring the conversation back on point. "But if he's gone, then maybe it's time to undo the lie. We need a name, Helen."

She stiffened, then slowly settled deeper into the chair as she considered what I said.

"It might just be time," she said. "Lord knows Harriett has no use for me anymore. Stood by her when she went through a bad patch with her husband, but they're divorced now, and she hardly speaks to me."

She heaved a sigh and stared at me. I leaned forward expectantly, elbows on my knees. Her mouth opened, but what came out was a loud *pop-pop-pop* like firecrackers going off, and a red flower bloomed on Helen's chest, quickly staining the front of her dress a deep claret. Without thinking, I dove sideways for the floor, hooking an arm around Tess's shoulders as I went and bringing her with me. Tess cried in fright and pain as we crashed hard. The bang of a slamming door made me twist and look back toward the kitchen—just in time to see a dark shape flash past the window and disappear.

I scrambled to my feet and pulled Tess up off the floor. "Come on," I growled. "We have to get out of here."

"What's going on?" she trilled. "What happened?"

I practically dragged her to the front door. "Someone just shot Helen. She's dead. We've gotta go. Come on!"

She got her feet under her and hurried up the walk to the street alongside me. I craned my neck one way and the other to try and spot the intruder, expecting the same quick fusillade of bullets to find both Tess and me any second. Across the street, Luis tumbled out of the SUV and hurried toward us.

"Is she hurt?" he said.

"No, thank God." I said.

He took Tess's other arm and we hustled her toward the SUV. She stumbled along without protest, eyes glazed with shock.

"What happened?" he said. "I thought I heard shots."

"Helen's dead!" Tess said as we pushed her into the backseat.

"Who's Helen?" Luis said.

"Former cook," I told him. "She used to work for the Barretts. We came to ask her some questions." I leaned in and helped buckle Tess's seatbelt, then noticed that the vehicle was empty. I turned and faced Luis. "Where's Kenny?"

He lifted his shoulders and let them drop. "I don't know. We got here, parked, waited a minute. He said he was going to check on you two. Headed up the street."

"Hey!" a voice called. "What's up?" Kenny jogged up the sidewalk from the corner.

"Where you been, man?" Luis said.

Kenny looked confused. "Taking a walk. Why?"

"The girl almost got herself killed, that's why," Luis said. "Come on, let's move out."

"What about the police?" I said. "We need to report this."

Luis shook his head. "No cops, man. Come on, let's go before someone sees us."

I hurried to the rental car and got in, looking around to see if any curious eyes were watching from behind living room curtains. The street was deathly quiet. I climbed in and started the car, thoughts racing furiously, wondering if I'd just left Tess in even graver danger than she'd been in a few minutes earlier.

CHAPTER 33

All the bodies squeezed into the den that Travis used as his home office spoke at once, trying to talk over each other. He couldn't decide if the pandemonium was more like a Chinese fire drill or a clown car. He'd come home only moments earlier to find them all knotted around one of the SUVs in the courtyard like conspiracy theorists around a water cooler, looking both suspicious and guilty at the same time. His own antennae quivering, he'd herded them into the house to find out what was wrong. Now he faced them all from behind his desk and raised a hand. The squabbling continued unabated.

"Ten-hut!" he barked.

Luis and Kenny faced him and snapped to attention immediately. Tess and Oliver came around more slowly, their heated conversation diminishing in volume and belligerence until they both looked at him questioningly. The boy looked pale, shaken, and Travis couldn't remember when he'd seen Tess so frightened.

"What the hell is going on?" he said.

For a time, no one spoke. The four eyed each other nervously.

Luis stepped forward. "These two were involved in a shooting."

"Not involved," Tess said quickly. "It wasn't like we went out and shot someone. We just happened to have been there when—"

Travis cut her off. "Been *where*? Where the hell were you? You were supposed to be here, doing homework."

"She needed a break," Oliver said. "Some fresh air. We went for a drive."

"And ended up at a shooting?"

"Alice okayed it," Oliver said, color coming to his cheeks.

"You keep making it sound like we're Bonnie and Clyde or something," Tess said, her voice rising. "We didn't shoot anybody, okay? We *witnessed* a shooting. Well, Oliver did. I didn't see a *damn* thing."

Travis held up his hand again to stop her before the tears brimming in her eyes spilled down her cheeks. "Watch your mouth, young lady. I get it. Tell me what happened, from the beginning."

As Tess ran through the afternoon's events Travis felt his pulse rise and his breathing grow shallow. He'd spent a year trying to relate to Tess as she kept mostly to her room, trying to coax her back to living at least a semblance of the life she'd had before the accident. Now, after just two days back in the real world, he could no longer seem to protect her.

I'm a trained assassin, a career soldier, and I can't keep my own niece out of harm's way.

"Why on earth did you decide go talk to that woman?" Travis said when she finished.

"Because it didn't make sense," Tess said. "When we found out Rosa was—"

"No, I know all that," Travis said. "I meant why did you go *alone*? Why didn't you talk to me first?"

"Do I have to ask permission to do everything around here?" Tess cried.

"You do now!" Travis said, heat creeping up from under his collar. "I already talked to Cyrus Cooper about her. I was going to have him investigate her. You never should have tried to talk to her alone."

"You didn't even know her," Tess shouted. "She was part of *my* family, not yours. You have no right telling me who I can and can't talk to. You are *not* my parent."

Travis stared at her, teeth clenched, while she got the anger out of her system. He wished he had a valve somewhere he could open to let off some of his own steam.

Finally silent, Tess stood motionless except for the tremor in her knees.

"Are you finished?" he said. She tossed her hair. He went on quietly. "I'm asking you to check with me or Alice or Marcus before you go anywhere. It's to make sure you're not putting yourself in danger. Obviously, there's a threat out there to you, to all of us. It's my job as your guardian—*not* your parent—to guard you, to keep you safe. I can't do that if I don't know where you are."

He turned to Luis and Kenny. "And where the hell were you two in all this?"

Luis pinked and glanced at his feet. "I . . . We . . . We were parked across the street. We had an eye on the house, and nothing seemed out of the ordinary. The street was quiet. We saw the woman let the kids in the house. Figured she knew them. I thought everything was cool."

Luis snuck a look at Kenny before turning his eyes back to Travis again. Kenny stayed ramrod straight, eyes ahead, no expression on his face.

"That how you remember it?" Travis asked him.

"No, sir. I left my post to walk up the street and get some air."

"You left your . . . What the hell were you thinking?"

"What Luis already told you, sir. We saw the woman invite the kids in, so we figured they were safe for the time being. I thought as long as I didn't go too far, I could spare a few minutes while they were inside. You didn't tell us you were going to have the woman investigated."

"Doesn't matter. Your orders were to protect her. And Oliver. Consider your pay docked. Screw up again, and you're gone. Got it?" He waited for Kenny's nod. "You saw nothing?" Travis squinted at him with narrowed eyes.

Kenny put his hands out, palms up. "Not a thing, I swear. Just those two coming out of the house like it was haunted."

"You didn't hear shots fired?"

"No, sir. Nothing I could clearly identify as gunfire."

Travis turned to Oliver. "I want every detail you can remember. Take your time."

Oliver let his gaze drift up toward the ceiling as if seeing a movie projected there, and immediately began describing the scene—the contents of the room, their positions relative to each other, the woman's demeanor. Travis listened without interruption, and was surprised at the level of detail. Most eyewitnesses to a crime, particularly a sudden and violent one, tended to focus on one or two things, forgetting or even unaware of other details. Their testimony was notoriously unreliable, yet juries still often believed more strongly in eyewitness accounts than other forensic evidence.

"And you never got a look at the shooter's face?" Travis said when Oliver finished.

Oliver shook his head. "It happened so fast. He was out the back door before I had a chance to look."

"The gunfire . . . You're sure it was three shots?"

"Yeah, definitely three. Not like *bang, bang, bang*. More like *brat-tat-tat*. Fast."

"And you say you could hear okay afterward?" Travis pressed.

Oliver nodded. "Sure. A little ringing in my ears, but the shots weren't as loud as I thought they'd be in that small space. Like firecrackers—Black Cats. I thought a shot would be more like an M-80."

Travis glanced at Luis and Kenny and saw his same realization reflected in their eyes.

"Assault rifle," Travis said. "On semiautomatic. A three-round burst. Suppressed, too, from what Oliver described." The two soldiers nodded in agreement. "That means military hardware, most likely. Someone didn't want her talking. Which means she had something to say."

"I told you," Tess blurted. "She was about to give us the name of the person who forced her to quit. Someone scared her into recommending Rosa for the job. And now she's dead! It isn't fair!"

Travis heaved a sigh. "No, it isn't fair. Neither is this, but you're just going to have to live with it: You're grounded. You go nowhere but here or school."

"Why?" Tess cried. "I didn't do anything!"

"You nearly got yourself killed!" Travis roared. "Again!"

"But Alice said I could—"

"Enough! I don't care what Alice said. You're grounded, and that's it."

"I hate you!" Tess shouted. "I wish you'd never come back! My parents would be alive if you hadn't come back. I hate you!"

She whirled and stumbled for the door, waving her arms to feel her way. Travis wordlessly watched her go, pulse racing.

Does she know something? Could she have somehow learned that I was there on the mountain the day her parents got in the accident? Has she found out the part I played in that accident?

He didn't see how, but . . .

Travis sighed again, then turned to Oliver. "I don't think it's a good idea for you to go home tonight. Not until we're sure you and Tess aren't being targeted."

Oliver's eyes widened. "But I thought you said . . . "

"I don't have any doubt Tess is in danger, which means you are, too, since you're with her most of the time." Travis rubbed a hand across his mouth. "Someone clearly wanted to get to the Corday woman to keep her from talking. If they had wanted to kill you and Tess, you'd be dead. Anyway, you can sleep in the guesthouse with the guys tonight. Now, go help Tess."

Travis waited until Oliver was gone before addressing the two former soldiers still at attention.

"Stand down, you two. Kenny, go find Marcus and round up the rest of the crew. We need to talk. Luis, stay here. I want to get your take on what happened."

Kenny gave Travis a curt nod and hustled out.

"Where was he, Luis?" Travis said softly.

Luis craned his neck to make sure Kenny was gone before turning back to Travis. "I don't know, boss. Honest. I saw him take off up the block, and I don't think he cut back across the street, but I had my eyes on the house. He could have circled around and gone in the back."

Travis looked down at the desk and drummed his fingers for a moment. "Yeah, but where'd he get a weapon?"

Luis shrugged. "I have a hard time believing it was him, boss. But he wasn't with me when it went down, and that bothers me." He paused. "I'm really sorry. I screwed up. I shouldn't have let Kenny go, and we should have reconnoitered and checked the perimeter of the house. If we had, we would have stopped the shooter before he got inside."

"Or if it *was* Kenny, you'd be dead, too." Travis looked grim. "Apology accepted. Stay on your toes next time."

Travis looked over Luis's shoulder as Marcus came through the door with a grim look on his face. The others began to crowd in behind him as he spoke.

"I gave her a direct order to see me before she went anywhere," Marcus said. "You better have a word with Pemberton. She's to blame for this. She didn't have the authority to—"

"Chill, Marcus," Travis said. "It's okay. I'll speak to her. I'm not blaming you—or anyone—for this. And I've told Tess in no uncertain terms that she's grounded. She goes nowhere but school."

He looked around the room, suddenly made almost claustrophobic by the addition of five large men—seven including Luis and Travis. They shifted uncomfortably on their feet since there weren't enough places to sit. The sudden influx of testosterone charged the room with tension, squeezing out the air and making it hard to breathe. The constriction around his chest, the smell of sweat and male pheromones, was as familiar to Travis as the sound of his own voice.

"Okay, I'll keep this brief," Travis said. "You all probably heard that someone hit a witness that Tess was trying to get information from. We need to tighten things up."

"I don't get it," Red growled. "How did the shooter know your niece was going to see this woman?"

Red's tousled hair and wrinkled cheek suggested Kenny had woken him for the meeting. Travis knew Red had pulled guard duty on the graveyard shift for the past week and felt badly for him, but it couldn't be helped.

"I'm not sure," Travis said. "But since the rental car they drove is new, I'm guessing someone is watching this house, or at least who's coming and going. From now on, whoever's on shift needs to check the perimeter and see if there's any suspicious activity outside the grounds."

He turned to Marcus. "We need to get more cameras around the grounds. When are they going to fix the one up at the gate? If we'd had a video feed today, maybe we could have seen who followed the kids."

Marcus gave a little shrug. "I'll call the security company again and tell them to put a rush on it. They're scheduled to come and fix the gate tomorrow. I can add cameras to their list then."

"Okay, work out new security details as far as who gets patrol and who shadows the kids at school. Let's plug the holes, gentlemen. I don't like being screwed with. Anything else?"

They looked at each other and shook their heads, then shuffled toward the door and squeezed through in single file. Travis waited until they'd gone before rounding the desk and softly closing the door. He sat down again and pulled an encrypted cell phone from a desk drawer, then dialed a familiar number.

"We've got problems," he said when Jack Turnbull answered at the other end.

"What kind of problems?" Turnbull said.

Travis brought the general up to speed on all that had happened since they'd last spoken, finishing with a quick recap of the day's events.

"Sounds like someone's tying up loose ends," Turnbull said.

"It's worse than that, general. It could mean we still have a leak—maybe even someone still on the inside. Even after we got rid of Rosa. And I still think I should have prevented that from happening in the first place."

"You were all in shock at the time," the general said. "And you weren't responsible for that hire."

"I still should have insisted on screening her."

"You couldn't have known." He paused. "So where do you think the leak is coming from?"

"That's the problem, Jack. At this point, it could be anywhere. I don't trust anyone anymore. It could be that someone set up surveillance on the house and got lucky when the kids went out for a drive. But I'm worried. The only person I told about the Corday woman was Cyrus."

"Cooper? The company's head of security?"

"Yes, and if he's involved somehow, then this thing is far bigger than even *I* thought."

"Don't jump to conclusions, Travis. Could be Cooper told someone. I'd hate to think your entire company is at risk. Cooper's got access to everything, doesn't he?"

"Pretty much. I don't want to think it, either. I can't imagine what would motivate him. I mean, the guy earned a chest full of medals during his career, right? You'd think that would make him bleed red, white, and blue."

"Ye-e-s," Turnbull said slowly. "Don't forget, though, he resigned his commission after Desert Storm under somewhat suspicious circumstances."

"Illegally profiting from the war or something? That was never proven." Travis paused, but heard only silence. "James trusted him, and he's paid well enough. Can't be about money."

"I'll look into it, see what I can find out about him, but I think you're right, Trav. Seems doubtful Cooper would be your leak. Any other possibilities?"

Travis rubbed his forehead. "Too many. In the meantime, I've had to put Tess under house arrest, and she hates me."

What sounded like a chuckle came over the line. "Welcome to teen parenting."

Travis groaned. "It's like owning a cat. Hot, cold. Sweet, bitchy. Warm and gentle, mean as a pit viper. I hate cats."

"You'll live. Remember, what doesn't kill you . . . "

"Doesn't have enough ammo to finish you off?"

Turnbull chuckled again. "No, it makes you stronger." He paused, and when he spoke again, the semblance of a smile was gone from his voice. "Find the leak, Travis. We're running out of time."

CHAPTER 34

Tess tried to concentrate on the voice playing through her headphones narrating *The Great Gatsby*, but she failed miserably. Instead of a scene conjured by Fitzgerald's words, she kept imagining the scene in Helen Corday's house, the horror of it closing in on her like fog. She could still smell the dust and hint of mildew, the souring garbage emanating from the kitchen, a sniff of lavender from Helen's perfume—that couldn't quite mask the stale body odor of a person who hadn't bathed in a while. All signs of Helen's state of mind. Helen had been fastidious when she'd worked for the Barrett family, not bordering on OCD, but careful to clean as she prepped and cooked, using sanitizers to scrub cutting boards after she'd worked with raw meat or poultry.

In her mind, Tess replayed the events that had preceded the odd muffled sound like firecrackers in a barrel. Sounds she hadn't been able to identify at the time—until Oliver had told her what they were. She'd first noticed Helen's fear, almost palpable in the close confines of the little cottage. It had grown as she and Oliver had pressed for answers. And then a faint, cold breeze had stirred the air, bringing with it the scents of wet earth and vegetation, and a hint of something tropical that she couldn't quite grasp among all the other smells. Only moments later, she'd heard the sounds and Oliver had tackled her to the floor. In an instant, all those scents had been overwhelmed by the acrid, sulfuric stink of burned gunpowder and the ferrous smell of blood—like a rusted bike chain.

The odors drifting past her nose now were nothing like those. She barely detected Oliver's scent; she felt his silent presence more than smelled it. He'd stubbornly refused to say anything since Uncle Travis had dismissed them to do homework, and she wondered if he, like she, was in shock. She still fumed every time she thought of what Uncle Travis had done.

It's so unfair! And how could he even think I'd be capable of doing homework after what just happened?

But she didn't know who she wanted to strangle more, Uncle Travis or Oliver.

They're both useless.

She shut her eyes, as if that action would blank out the images in her head, and wished she could turn back time. Her parents hadn't been perfect—she remembered that the last thing they'd done before the accident was prohibit her from going to prom with Toby—but anything would be better than the two men who had invaded her life. The thought of her parents triggered the tear factory she seemed to have become of late, and she squeezed her eyes shut even tighter to prevent the tears from welling up.

Through the headphones, she heard her cell phone *bong*, alerting her to incoming e-mail. She sighed and pulled the headphones off, hanging them around her neck while she instructed the phone to read her e-mail.

"You have one e-mail, from Dad," the phone's artificial voice intoned.

"Great. Here we go again." Tess sucked in a breath and spoke into the phone. "Read e-mail."

"It's 10:49." The phone went silent.

"Oliver?" Tess said. "Did you hear?"

"I'm sorry," he said. "I thought someone just said my name."

"Come on, Oliver. What do you want?"

"Oh, I don't know. Maybe a thank-you for saving your life."

"It's Helen's life you should be thinking about," she said. "My god, don't you care that people all around us are dying?"

"Heck, yeah, I care. You think I pulled you to the floor to protect myself?"

"Jeez, it wasn't *that* big a deal. You heard everyone say that whoever shot Helen only meant to keep her from talking. You nearly broke a couple of ribs."

But she knew it *was* a big deal. She knew that she'd been mere inches and seconds from death. She knew that, had she actually witnessed what had happened to Helen, she would be sick with panic right now. For the first time since the accident she was glad that she couldn't see. What an irony—to be grateful for something that had so completely ruined the rest of her life.

"Better than you getting killed," Oliver said. "Sorry if I seem testy, but I'm not used to people getting shot around me, let alone right in front of me. Makes me nervous. Keeping you safe makes me nervous."

"Then don't," she said. Everyone seemed to want something from her. "After all, it's not part of your job description."

The room went silent. When Oliver finally spoke, his voice was quiet. "Yes, I heard the e-mail. You want to know what's in the book. Fine. If memory serves, some of the animals are in a passageway with stone columns on either side. The cat's front and center. Behind them the alligator, tiger, elephant, and swan are playing tennis. You can see the zebra and rhinoceros sitting in a tower in the distance. The page has an Egyptian feel to it. Hieroglyphs cover the stone columns and some of the page's border."

Tess frowned. "Okay, I remember. The hieroglyphics are a coded message of some sort. Can you decipher it?"

"Sure, but the illustration is only about the puzzle in the book, Tess. All right, give me a second and let me get some paper and a pencil."

He rustled through her backpack and got what he needed, then the library went quiet again except for the scratching of pencil on paper.

"I'm telling you, Tess, this doesn't help. It's all about the book. You know, stuff like, 'tick, tock,' and 'put no trust in hidden codes.' Oh, hell, maybe it's all a big joke. Everything we've gotten up to now has been b.s. Someone's leading us on a wild goose chase."

Tess shook her head violently. "No! I refuse to believe that. There must be something we're missing. Check the e-mail for me." She held out her phone.

Oliver took it from her hand. "Okay, so I was wrong. There are some hieroglyphs here."

"What do they say?" Tess felt a mixture of excitement and dread.

"Hang on while I decipher it. It says, 'Call me.'"

"That's it? Call me?" She paused and thought. "Okay, sure. Give me the phone, please."

Oliver placed the phone in her hand. She found the right button, and said, "Call Dad."

Nothing happened for a moment. Then, from somewhere not too far away came the muffled sound of punk rock music.

"That's my dad's ring tone!" Tess said. "'London Calling.' The Clash. His idea of a joke."

"Sounds like it's coming from his office," Oliver said.

Tess got to her feet and headed toward the sound, hands out in front of her to find the swinging bookcase that led to the hidden room. She felt Oliver's breath hot on her neck. She pushed on the bookcase, squeezed through the opening, and headed straight for the desk. The ringtone was louder now. She homed in on the sound and groped across the surface of the desk.

"To your left," Oliver said. "A little to your left."

Her fingers closed around a smooth, rectangular object, and she picked it up.

"Maybe this is it," she said. "Maybe this is the last thing we need to do."

"I hope so," Oliver said.

"What if it's not? I can't keep doing this if it means more people will die."

"I don't think you have a choice, Tess."

She shuddered and held it out. "You take it. See what's on it."

Oliver's hand closed over both the phone and her hand, and he led her out of her father's office and back into the library. He helped her back to her seat.

"This could take a while," he said. "Get back to your reading, and I'll let you know if I find anything."

Reluctantly, she slipped the headphones back over her ears and once again tried to focus on the words being read to her. Slowly, the story pulled her in, making her forget, for a moment, her own troubles. She didn't know how much time passed before Oliver laid a hand on her arm, but it must have been nearly half an hour. She removed the headphones.

"There's nothing here," he said.

"There must be," she said.

"I went through all the contacts, all the photos, every nook and cranny on that phone," Oliver said patiently. "I ran a search on all the photos, looking for embedded files. I didn't find a thing."

"It's not possible. Why would he want me to find his phone if there's nothing on it? It doesn't make sense."

"Nothing that's happened since I got here makes any sense, Tess. There's nothing normal about this situation."

"What do you mean? *I'm* perfectly normal."

"No, you're not. You're blind. Your parents are dead. You live with an evil uncle in a huge palace surrounded by guards. This is beginning to sound like a fairy tale."

"What? And you're my prince?" She snorted. "Dream on."

"You have to admit, it doesn't sound like the life most kids lead."

"I suppose." She chewed the inside of her lip. "I thought fairy tales were supposed to have happy endings."

"Well, sure, but that's after you fight off dragons, recover from poisoned apples, escape from a dungeon, and all the rest."

Tess smiled. "Girls sure have to work hard to find happiness."

"Nah, only princesses," Oliver said.

"Well, you definitely have one there," another voice said.

"Are you spying on us, Uncle Travis?" Tess said.

"Whoa, calm down. I know you're angry, but there's no reason to take that tone with me. I just came to tell you that Alice has dinner ready. We'd like you to join us if you're at a stopping point."

"We'll be there in a minute," Oliver said quietly.

Tess bit her tongue to keep from making some smart remark, though she couldn't think of anything that didn't sound lame. She waited for the sound of her uncle's departure, but heard footfalls approaching them instead.

"Is that a new phone?" Travis said.

Tess's heart caught in her throat until she realized she'd done nothing wrong. "No, it's Dad's. I found it in his office. I wanted to show Oliver some photos on it, but they aren't here."

She hadn't told him the truth, but it wasn't exactly a lie, either. And she was tired of letting her uncle know everything about her. She deserved to be able to keep a few things to herself, especially where her parents were concerned.

Travis may be a war hero, but he can't hold a candle to either of my parents. He just doesn't understand.

"Sorry to hear it," Travis said, bringing her thoughts back. "I hope you find them somewhere. See you in a few minutes?"

She nodded. "We'll be right there."

This time he left, and she breathed an inward sigh of relief.

Tess fidgeted uncomfortably throughout dinner. Neither Uncle Travis or Alice were very good at conversation, though Oliver made attempts to engage them—and her—by asking about their family and other topics he thought might be of interest to at least someone. But she found it too painful to talk much about her absent parents, didn't care about sports, wasn't up on the latest current events, and didn't feel much like talking. He managed to elicit a series of monosyllabic answers to most of his questions, and the only other sound was that of chewing. She was relieved when the sound of forks clattering on china signaled the end of dinner, and she asked to be excused to finish her homework.

Oliver stayed to help clear the table and wash dishes, so she made her own way back to the library and settled in to work. He joined her about half an hour later and sat quietly while she listened to the rest of her English assignment. Then he helped her with the history portion of her American studies and literature block. After an hour of going over the material with him, she yawned widely.

"I can't study anymore," she said. "I'm fried."

"You're essentially finished anyway. I'll pack up your books."

"Aren't you tired?"

"Yeah, I guess I am. Too much excitement."

She shivered. "Not exactly what I had in mind when I woke up this morning."

"Yeah, well, me neither. But a good night's sleep should help."

She yawned again. "I hope so. Goodnight, Oliver."

"Goodnight. See you in the morning."

She made her way upstairs to her room and stumbled through her bedtime ritual on autopilot, washing her face and brushing her teeth without really being aware of it. She found some comfy flannel pajama bottoms and a fleece sweatshirt and tumbled into bed. She was asleep in seconds.

Sometime during the night, the familiar dream came back to her. Everything about it was the same—her last snowboarding run with her parents, their decision regarding prom, her hissy fit on the way to the car, getting on the road . . . But this time, for the first time, it changed. Instead of closing her eyes and dozing off, she continued the argument with her dad about what music to play. His gentle teasing turned to annoyance when Tess's insistence on something other than Kenny G turned strident. He told her to wait a moment until he could take his eyes off the road, but she leaned forward between the seats and grabbed for his iPod. Her mother flinched in surprise, and her father turned to see what was wrong. Distracted, he swatted Tess's hand away. She flounced back into her seat, and that was when she saw the moving wall of snow outside.

Her mother gripped her father's arm, and Tess felt the tension in her fingers and heard the susurrant roar of the avalanche as it descended the mountain above them. With growing horror, Tess watched the wall of snow ripple down the mountain like a tsunami, snapping trees on its way like toothpicks.

"Hang on!" her father yelled.

Tess clutched the door handle and heard herself scream . . .

She flung her arm out and pulled herself toward wakefulness, scrabbling away from the nightmare. When she finally heard her own ragged breathing and felt the thumping of her heart in her chest, she knew she was back in the present despite the blackness and silence of a house asleep. Why she still thought that she would open her eyes one day and be able to see, she didn't know. She shook off the tendrils of the dream and wiped her damp forehead with the sleeve of her sweatshirt. Strands of hair stuck to her neck and cheeks. She pulled it back out of her face.

Her heart continued to race as she thought about the nightmare.

Was that what had really happened? Was I partly to blame for my parents' death? Have I blocked it out until now?

Pangs of guilt stabbed at her—a thousand tiny knives pricking her soul, and it bled sorrow and pain. For a moment, she wondered if she could die from that feeling, from this death of a thousand cuts. She shook herself and slipped out of bed. She knew she was being foolish, but she couldn't rid herself of the feelings.

She found her backpack and rummaged through it until her fingers found the smooth, cool surface of the two stones that Yoshi had given to her. Clutching one in each hand, she climbed back into bed and pulled the covers up to her chin. She set one of the stones next to her hip. With both hands, she slowly explored the contours of the other. Cool to the touch, it seemed to send a small electric charge coursing up her arms. The faint stirrings of an idea formed in the back of her mind, but she couldn't quite grasp it and pull it out where she could see it.

She sighed, set the stone down on the nightstand, and picked up the other one. This stone felt warm compared to the first, and as her fingers gently stroked its surface, that warmth spread through her limbs and into her chest. She relaxed and snuggled farther under the covers, the dream almost completely forgotten. Her eyelids fluttered closed and she drifted back into sleep.

CHAPTER 35

I couldn't sleep. The security team had staked out all the beds in the three-bedroom guest "cottage," and I'd been relegated to a pullout couch in the living room. The main house probably had six bedrooms or more, but I imagined that, in addition to reminding me I was an employee and not a guest, Travis didn't want me any nearer to his niece than I already was. But it wasn't just the thin, uncomfortable mattress that kept me awake. I kept seeing the blood welling out of Helen's chest like a time-lapse photo of a blooming rose. A three-shot burst, military style.

I didn't know why I hadn't just walked away from the whole mess. It was obviously above my pay grade, and the stakes were entirely too high. But Tess intrigued me, and apparently she still had something the bad guys, whoever they were, wanted. I had nowhere else to go, no other job prospects, and no other means of support if I quit. So I accepted the fact that I was all in, whether I liked bullets flying around me or not.

I got up, retrieved my laptop, and took it into the kitchen. I poured myself a glass of juice from the refrigerator and took it to the table while the laptop booted up, and got online. I couldn't understand what it was like to be blind, but I could learn more about Tess's blindness. She'd said that physically there was nothing wrong with her eyes. Her pupils still reacted to light, dilating or constricting as conditions changed, due to reflex. She tracked sounds with her eyes, which gave the uncanny impression that she could still see. The only thing her eyes couldn't do, since no image registered in her brain, was focus. Eventually, the muscles that controlled the thickening and thinning of the lens would atrophy.

Her vision loss, called "cortical blindness" had been caused not by damage to her eyes, but to the occipital lobe in her brain, the visual processing center. The more I learned, though, the more I questions I had. The research I turned up suggested that loss of eyesight due to traumatic brain injury, in the occipital lobe anyway, should also result in loss of visual memory and visual dreams as well. But Tess had said that, for a time at least, her memories had become more vivid than ever, and she was still haunted by intense dreams. I wondered if her blindness might be only temporary. I found information on "transient cortical blindness," but the cases I found were typically caused by temporary lack of oxygen in the occipital region of the brain, such as during a medical procedure.

If her blindness was truly caused by lesions in her brain, I wondered whether she might be able to regain her sight if those injuries healed over time. Or perhaps surgery at some point might be able to repair the lesions. It didn't seem likely. But, unless she had a rare case of cortical blindness, she shouldn't be able to "see" memories or dreams. Which led to one other possible conclusion: she had "hysterical" blindness. The clinical literature now called it a "conversion disorder," but hysterical blindness was often brought on by trauma, and had psychological, not physical, roots.

In other words, being blind might be all in Tess's head. That didn't mean she was faking it—she really couldn't see—but it meant that she could easily regain her sight if she got over whatever head trip had caused her to blot out reality.

The upshot was a lot of ten-cent words that didn't tell me much of anything except that Tess might have this condition or that disorder, may or may not be blind, and might or might not be curable. I yawned mightily, pushed back from the table, and knuckled my eyes, dry and gritty from staring at the screen. If I kept this up I might go blind, too.

The back door of the cottage opened quietly and one of the two Bedrock residents—the big guy, Fred—let himself in. Dressed in black slacks and a black windbreaker, he was nearly invisible against the dark doorway, except for his face. A large semiautomatic pistol was holstered prominently on his hip. He shut the door quietly and nodded when he saw me.

"Can't sleep?" he said in a stage whisper.

I shook my head.

"Happens," he said. "Been a few times I was too scared to close my eyes because of what I might see. You'll get over it. Like watching a horror movie, you know? After a while you put it behind you and forget about it."

"I hope so," I said.

He stood there awkwardly for a moment. "Well, I'm going to try to catch some shut-eye. Back on shift in four hours."

"Goodnight," I said.

He disappeared down the hall. I got up and turned out the kitchen light, then crawled back under the blanket on the couch and settled in for a restless night.

The windows had lightened when I woke again for the last time, but the sky outside was still the color of ash. Somewhere close by, drops of water steadily *plonked* into a metal downspout. I laid still for a while, letting random thoughts ping-pong through my head, but finally swung my legs out from under the covers and got up. Trying not to wake anyone, I padded to the bathroom and stepped into the shower. After getting clean, I quickly rinsed off and got dressed.

Outside, the clouds had sunk of their own weight almost to the ground, leaving the treetops and roof of the house wreathed in mist. The heavy air was laden with so much moisture I wished I had gills to breathe. As I headed down to the main house for breakfast, I noticed an open garage bay door and changed direction. Cutting through the garage would be the fastest way to the kitchen. I stepped through the opening into the gloom and heard a scraping sound in the far bay. Curious, I skirted around the back of Yoshi's truck, sneakers making no sound on the smooth concrete floor.

A pair of legs stuck out from beneath the wrecked Range Rover parked in the last bay. I was about to call out and ask if the person needed help when I noticed that the legs were encased in a nicely tailored pair of slacks, the feet shod with expensive-looking loafers—Marcus. Good thing Yoshi kept the garage floor immaculately clean. Whether because I was reminded of how unpleasant he'd been to Tess the previous afternoon or because some other instinct warned me away, I closed my mouth and turned away. I didn't want my day to start off in a conversation with Marcus.

The kitchen greeted me with bright cheeriness and the smells of bacon and coffee, which made my stomach growl. Alice must have cooked earlier and gone on to other tasks because Tess was alone, seated at the table in the nook, sleepily pouring milk into a bowl of cereal. The tip of her finger was hooked over the lip of the bowl, and when the milk in the bowl rose high enough to touch it, she tipped the milk carton upright on the table. Clever girl. She stuck her finger in her mouth and sucked the milk off, pulling it out between pursed lips with a pop.

"Good morning, sunshine. You're up early. Sleep well?"

She turned toward the sound of my voice and made a halfhearted attempt at a smile.

"I feel like a zombie," she said. "I hardly got any sleep."

"Me neither. We'll be a real pair at school today."

She groaned, bent over her bowl, and shoveled a spoonful of cereal into her mouth.

"Hey," I said, shifting my weight. I remembered she couldn't see the color creep into my cheeks, but that didn't seem to settle the butterflies in my stomach. "I wanted to apologize for being such a dick yesterday. I mean, seeing Helen get shot like that really got to me, but that's no excuse for bad manners."

"That's okay," Tess said. "I guess I was probably kind of a witch myself."

"Nah, you were fine. Considering I tackled you and all."

She spooned more cereal into her mouth instead of replying, so I figured the subject was closed. I grabbed a plate from a cupboard and served myself bacon and toast from the serving platters next to the stove. I poured myself a cup of coffee and sat down at the table across from Tess with my breakfast.

"I was thinking." I swallowed a bite of toast. "Maybe the clue we got yesterday was designed to throw us off. I mean, finding that phone was too easy, you know?"

She raised her head and chewed slowly.

"Remember what the first couple of e-mails said?" I went on. "'Seeing is believing' and 'Don't believe everything you hear.' Maybe that's the point. We're not supposed to believe the ringing phone in your dad's office is the answer to the clue."

She took another bite and ruminated.

"He used another phone for work," she said at last. "He made me promise not to call him at that number unless it was an emergency."

"Do you remember it?"

Her face screwed up as she tried to recall. The muscles in her face suddenly relaxed, and her hand groped the table instead, eventually landing on her own phone.

"I have it programmed," she said. "I never called it. I always left him texts or voicemails on his personal phone. He always got back to me eventually."

She activated the speakerphone feature and spoke a command. The line connected and the phone on the other end rang three times before a male voice answered.

"Hello?"

Tess turned her face toward me in shock. I motioned her to say something and realized she couldn't see me. I reached for the hand holding the phone and lifted it toward her mouth. She resisted, then snapped out of her trance.

"Who's this?" she demanded.

"Who's calling, please?" the voice said.

"I asked you first," Tess said. "Who is this? Why do you have my father's phone?"

After a moment of hesitation the voice said, "I think you must have the wrong number," and hung up.

Tess held the phone out. "Do you believe that? Someone stole my dad's phone."

"Come on, Tess. He hasn't used it for more than a year. His account was probably canceled and the number assigned to someone else."

Her nose wrinkled. "Why would they cancel his phone? They didn't cancel his personal number."

"I don't know. Maybe the company wanted to save some money. It's no big deal. We'll figure out what the clue meant some other way."

She put a finger in the corner of her mouth and nibbled the nail. "I know that voice, Oliver." Her eyes widened. "Tad. It was Tad."

I frowned. "How did he get your dad's phone?"

"I don't know." She bit her lip and blinked. "But that was Tad's voice, I'm telling you."

"Okay," I said softly, "we'll check it out." I thought for a moment, munching on a strip of bacon. "We need to figure out some way to get him alone. He'll never say anything if he's with his posse. Any ideas?"

Tess fell silent, but I could see the wheels turning in her head.

"Last year," she said, "when Tad got his license, his parents gave him a car—a nice one. He trashed it. Got drunk one night and totaled it. His dad was so mad, he told Tad he could walk until he earned enough money to buy his own car. So he walked or got rides from guys like Carl. I bet he hasn't bought a car yet, and with Carl . . . well, you know, Tad's probably walking again."

I glanced at my watch. "You know where he lives?"

She nodded. "I can tell you how to get there."

I wolfed down the last strip of bacon and bite of toast, and washed it down with a gulp of coffee. Rising from the table I said, "Are you ready?"

She'd already picked up her bag from the floor next to her chair and put her phone in it. She stood.

"We need to get my books," she said.

She put out her hand. I took it and placed it on my arm. She walked faster and with more confidence when I escorted her, I noticed, though she knew the house well enough to navigate on her own. As soon as we were in the hallway outside the kitchen, she turned her head and called over her shoulder.

"Alice, we're on our way to school. I want to be early. Could you please tell Marcus? I don't want to have to go find him."

Alice's voice floated out of her office. "I'll take care of it."

On the way out, I grabbed Tess's backpack from the library where we'd left it. Fred was back on patrol, and when we emerged through the front door, he nodded at me and got on a cell phone. By the time we'd gotten in the rental sedan, Fred's partner Barney had hoofed it over from the guesthouse and joined Fred in the SUV parked in the circle. They pulled out right behind us. I eyed the rearview mirror nervously. I wasn't thrilled to have eyewitnesses to what Tess and I were planning. But I had a feeling that Flintstone and Rubble wouldn't hassle us.

We drifted out onto the road, the gray car a ghost in the swirling mist. The SUV quickly disappeared in the fog behind us, the only sign of its presence two round, bright patches in the murk—its headlights. They must have been able to see spots of pink where our taillights rouged the gloom, because the lights maintained their distance.

Tess told me that Tad lived off the same main road she did, but about a mile closer to school. If he walked to school, he'd have to be on the road by now in order to get there on time. I drove slowly so we didn't overtake anything too quickly. Nonetheless, the dark figure of a pedestrian alongside the road loomed out of the fog so fast that we passed it before I pulled the car over to the shoulder and braked to a stop. I jumped out and walked back past the trunk before the figure materialized out of the mist. Behind me, I heard Tess open her door and take tentative steps.

Stooped, with eyes downcast, Tad trudged toward me, weighed down by a backpack loaded with books. The glow of the car's taillights caught his attention, and he raised his head, eyes moving from me to Tess and back.

He straightened and stopped. "What? You giving up your ride for me or something?"

"We just have a couple of questions," I said.

Twin cones of light swung to the side of the road and straightened, illuminating him from behind. He glanced over his shoulder. When the headlights didn't move and no one emerged, he faced me again and trudged forward.

"Hey, we want some answers," I said.

"Blow me," he said as he passed by.

I grabbed his arm and swung him into the side of the car. He folded over the trunk, and I quickly stepped next to him, grabbed the back of his neck, and bounced his face off the sheet metal. He squealed in protest. One hand flew to his nose and he used the other to try to lever himself off the trunk. I shoved his head down again, this time rapping his knuckles against the car. In turn, his nose was mashed into his palm. He screeched in pain. I grabbed his collar and pulled him up.

"Okay, okay! Stop!" he yelled. "No more."

"Not so tough without the homeboys around, huh?" I said.

I spun him around and bent him back over the trunk lid with an arm across his chest. Tears sprang to his eyes and he gently felt around his nose with a thumb and three fingers. Tess placed her hands on the far side of the trunk and felt her way around the back end of the car. I snuck a glance behind us, but there was no movement in the fog, just the steady beam of the SUV's lights weakly burrowing into the mist.

"My dad's phone," Tess said. "How'd you get it?"

Tad's face went blank. "What the hell are you talking about?"

"I called you. This morning." Tess's voice grew shrill. "You answered my father's work phone. How'd you get it?"

"You are one crazy bitch," Tad said. He sniffed and spat on the pavement. "I didn't take anyone's phone, and I sure as hell didn't talk to *you* this morning. You must be high on something."

I bent him back farther and pulled an arm back, fingers closed into a fist. His eyes grew wide.

"Jeez, wait! I'm telling you straight! I don't know what the hell you're talking about."

Tess sighed. "Let him go, Oliver."

I grabbed a fistful of fleece vest, hauled him upright, and gave him a shove in the direction he'd been walking. He stumbled a few steps. When he regained his balance, he straightened and turned, his mouth twisted into a snarl.

"You're both dead meat," he said. "I don't care how long it takes—you'll both pay for this."

"Yeah, yeah," I said. "I'm shaking. Get out of here."

I took a step toward him. He startled, turned, and hustled away, glancing once over his shoulder to see if I was following.

Tess had already found her way back to the passenger door and got in, slamming the door. I climbed in the driver's seat. She faced forward as if staring out the windshield.

"I was sure it was Tad's voice," she murmured. "He doesn't know anything, does he?"

"Not from what I saw." I started the car and pulled out into the street. When I passed Tad, he glowered and gave us the finger. Lights flashed in the rearview mirror as the SUV pulled onto the road behind us. The fog thinned enough for a moment to see Tad stare at the SUV as it passed him.

"I know who it was . . ." Tess said quietly. "Tad's father."

I glanced at her. "You sure you want to go down this road again so soon?"

Her nostrils flared. "It makes sense. They sound almost exactly alike. And I could see why Mr. Cooper might have my dad's phone—he's head of security at MondoHard."

I looked for a flaw in her reasoning but didn't find one. "Okay, so the question is how you can get it back."

She chewed on a fingernail for a moment.

"Uncle Travis," she said.

CHAPTER 36

Travis swiped his key card and ducked into the stairwell. Besides needing the exercise climbing the stairs provided, he wanted to keep a low profile. The elevator was too busy this time of day. Then again, anyone who wanted to trace his movements could monitor the security cameras all over the building, or simply track his key card swipes. No sense getting paranoid about it. He took the stairs two at a time, wondering why no one else took advantage of the easy workout. A few flights up, his heart rate had increased to about 110 beats per minute and his breath came fast and raw in his throat. Too fast. He hadn't been working out enough. His pulse should still be below a hundred, but it dropped quickly as he eased through a door into the hallway and slowed his pace. He checked his watch. Still early by office standards, but later than he usually made it in.

Pushing his way through a door, he entered the large office shared by some of the game coders. As usual, the ambient light was dim, most of the illumination in the room coming from the glow of large monitors scattered around the room. The air was already warm from the heat of several computer towers, though Travis knew these guys spent most of their day accessing the servers over fiber-optic Ethernet cable. The office was empty save for Derek, who sat at his station, fingers flying over his keyboard. Travis let a hint of a smile pass his lips, pleased to have guessed right about the kid. He walked up behind Derek and put a hand on his shoulder. Derek jumped in his seat and jerked his head around.

"You!" He clutched his chest. "Jeez, man, don't sneak up on people like that."

"Good focus," Travis said, "but you always want to keep part of your brain on alert."

"Yeah, and how do you do that?"

Travis shrugged. "Practice." For an instant, he thought of all the nights in Afghanistan that he'd slept with one eye open, hearing attuned to the slightest sounds. It didn't make for very sound sleep, but it had saved his life on more than one occasion.

Michael W. Sherer

Derek swiveled the chair to face him. "What's up?"

"You tell me."

Derek reached behind him and grabbed a memory stick off his desk, fingers idly toying with it as he held it up.

"This is one fascinating little piece of work. I was able to recreate most of the missing file. It's source code for some kind of program. Whoever wrote it is a freaking genius."

"Why? What is it?"

"Hell if I know, man. I'd need to see a lot more code to begin to guess. But part of this is a logic tree that boggles the mind. Whatever runs this program is likely to be as close to AI as anything I've seen."

"Artificial intelligence?"

Derek's head bobbed up and down, and his eyes glowed with excitement. "Dang straight. The coder wants something to think, analyze some sort of situation and make a decision based on input—*sensory* input."

"You mean like visual and aural cues?" Travis said, his chest tightening. He kept his voice calm and hoped he looked nonchalant.

"Yeah, and I get the impression it could analyze even more data than that. Maybe temperature, humidity, spatial make-up, like the contours of the surroundings and air quality."

Travis chewed the inside of his lip. "But you don't know what the program actually does?"

Derek's brows knit. "Well, no, not really. Like I said, I'd need to see a lot more code."

Travis let out a breath, then reached for another chair. He pulled it close, spun it around, and plunked down in the seat, rolling it so close to Derek's their knees nearly touched. Derek had traded one black T-shirt for another, this one imprinted with a graphic of the Ramones. His black jeans were clean, too, which led Travis to the conclusion that the artfully tousled hair and trimmed facial stubble were deliberate. He gestured at the memory stick still in Derek's hand.

"You think this guy is good, huh? How'd you like to see if you're just as good?"

Derek smiled. "I know I am. Well, I could be, given half the chance. Why?"

246

"You know what we do on the other side of the building?"

"Government contract work. Department of Defense, mostly."

Travis nodded. "One of the projects we've been working on for a long time got screwed up. Software glitch. We haven't been able to fix it."

"A worm," Derek said. His smile faltered. "Unless that's urban legend."

"No, it's the real deal. Want to take a crack at it?"

"Hell, yes!" As fast as he leaned forward, Derek changed his eager expression to nonchalance and slouched deeper into his chair.

"Good. I'll send you the background and the program so you can get started. You sure you have time for this?"

His brows flew up then drifted down like a fresh sheet onto a bed into a single line over his frown. "You mean this is the same deal as the memory stick—OMOT? On my own time?"

Travis nodded. "Sorry, but yes. I'll find a way to make it up to you eventually. Stock options, maybe. In the meantime, I shouldn't have to tell you—"

Derek quickly put a finger to his lips. "Yeah, mum's the word. I got it."

Travis inspected his face like a dermatologist looking for melanoma. "It's no joke, kid. Unless you haven't been paying attention, lives are at stake."

Derek stared back, trying too hard to look indignant. He conceded a nod. "I said I get it."

Travis held his eyes a second longer, then got up to leave. He took out a pen, tore a scrap of paper off a pad on Derek's desk, and scribbled on it.

"One more thing," he said, holding the paper in front of Derek's gaze. "I want you to hack my niece's e-mail account and retrieve copies of all the e-mails she's sent and received in the past week. Can you do that?"

Derek's mouth hung open. "Well, yeah, but are you sure you . . . ?"

Travis nodded. "It's important. And she can't find out she's been hacked."

Derek scratched the back of his head. "I don't know, man. That seems like crossing a line to me."

"Believe me," he told Derek, "when it comes to protecting the people close to me, we're not even close to the line yet. If I didn't think it would save her life, I wouldn't ask. Can you handle that?"

Derek drew in a breath and let it out slowly. "Yeah, I guess."

"Good. I'll be in touch."

Satisfied they were on the same page, Travis stepped out into the hall and checked both directions before quickly striding to the fire door and pushing through the door into the stairwell. He went back down to the first floor and wriggled his way through the tide of employees streaming toward the bank of elevators. He nodded at the few faces he recognized and murmured a "good morning" to each. He waved his key card in front of the reader next to the door behind the reception desk and slipped through. A few short steps took him to the security office. He scanned his card again and heard the faint click of the lock. He opened the door and stepped inside.

One of the guards sitting in front of the monitors briefly turned his head and noted his entrance with bored eyes, a stifled yawn, and a short nod before turning his attention back to the screens. The staff was long overdue for a simulation drill. Fire, B&E, earthquake, terrorist attack—Travis made sure Cooper mixed it up and ran each one as if it was a real emergency, not a drill. Travis insisted on staging them as realistically as possible, even using actors, stunt people, and movie props and makeup. But now was not the time.

He crossed the room quickly, knocked on Cooper's door, and walked in without waiting for a reply. Cooper looked up, startled. Travis didn't give him time to recover.

"You have James's business phone." Travis made it a statement, not a question. "I'd like it back, please."

A cloud of confusion scudded across Cooper's face before he grunted assent. He leaned over, opened a drawer in his desk, and took out a cell phone. He held it out.

"Why do you have it, Cyrus?"

"It's protocol," Cooper said without hesitation. "You know that, Travis. Whenever anyone leaves this company, in whatever fashion—a better job offer, termination, even death—we immediately retrieve all electronic devices assigned to that person and comb through the contents before destroying the memory. Computers, phones, tablets—doesn't matter."

Travis could detect no prevarication there, but he wondered if Cooper's answer wasn't a little too slick, offered a tad too quickly.

"How did you get it?"

Cooper tipped his head slightly before answering. "My men went through the Range Rover after the crash, before it was towed back to the house. I thought you were aware of this. Why all the questions now?"

Travis shrugged and lightened his expression with an easy smile. "Sorry. Tess called me and said some of her favorite photos are on that phone. I must have forgotten that a team went through James's things back then. Shock, I guess."

"I suppose," Cyrus said. "James's death hit us all pretty hard at the time. Well, you're certainly welcome to take it. We've had plenty of time to look through it."

Travis stepped to the desk and took the phone out of Cooper's outstretched hand.

"Thanks, Cyrus. Sorry to have barged in like this. Seems to be one of those days."

"Take a deep breath. Start over."

"Right. Well, thanks again." Travis turned for the door.

"One more piece of advice before you go, Travis. Cut back on the caffeine. You seem wound a little tight."

Cooper smiled at him, but Travis saw no mirth behind it. He forced a smile of his own and left, annoyed with himself for letting his emotions go unchecked. Cooper should not have been able to read him so easily.

Back in his office, he went through the motions—returning phone calls, attending a couple of meetings, reviewing contract terms for a couple of vendors, and reading through a marketing plan for a proposed new video game. But he found he couldn't concentrate. He was caught more than once with his mind elsewhere, putting a crimp in the contract negotiations for a while and forcing the marketing team to go over portions of their presentation twice.

The distractedness disturbed him. He'd never found it difficult to focus before. It was one of the reasons he'd been so good at his job in Afghanistan. His focus was so intense that he was hypersensitive to sights and sounds and smells around him, able to analyze, interpret, and act on that sensory input in fractions of a second. His innate skills had not only kept him alive all those years, but had made him one of the army's most effective antiterrorist weapons, its best assassin. He wasn't proud of the number of men he'd killed. Some of them, the ones that haunted his dreams occasionally, had been mere boys. But he was proud of how many people he'd saved as a result. Even most of those "boys" had been programmed to kill, to sacrifice themselves for their cause—as long as they could take several people with them.

This new feeling of inertia was like being encased in one of those padded sumo wrestler costumes, and as close as he'd ever felt to being helpless. He didn't know if it was because the rules of civilian life were so different than those he'd known most of his adult life, or because *he* was different.

All the hard edges honed to razor sharpness by combat and living under the radar had been dulled, softened by his new roles as guardian, surrogate parent, boss. Even his budding friendships with some of his teammates, and especially with Robyn, had awakened in him emotions long suppressed. The job in Afghanistan had been almost exclusively black and white, the gray shaded well enough usually to be easily discernible. Now he saw so many colors that he sometimes couldn't see the composition of the picture itself, let alone tell the good guys from the bad guys. This life was more dangerous, fraught with more ambiguity, than his life as a soldier. He had to find a way to adapt.

The problem was Tess. He'd never felt so responsible before, never carried so much weight on his shoulders—not even when he'd had to decide when and how to take a life. That was nothing compared to protecting a life, to keeping someone from harm, even from the smallest slights from mean kids at school. He couldn't do it. He couldn't protect Tess, not from everything. But he knew he had to try.

He gave up trying to work at around four o'clock, and stopped at Robyn's desk on his way out. She stopped typing and tipped her head up expectantly.

"Taking off?" she said.

"I think I've made enough of a mess for one day."

She gave him an encouraging smile. "We all have days like that. And it wasn't so bad. We got a lot accomplished."

He sighed. "I think you would have gotten more done without me."

Robyn shook her head. "We couldn't possibly do without you, sir." She blushed. "I mean, Travis."

Travis felt his own face get warm. "Thank you for saying so. You're just being kind, but I promise I'll have more focus tomorrow."

"Tess again?"

"Among other things. But it's not your problem. I'll see you then."

Her smile broadened; it lit up his world. He felt better despite the memory of all that had gone wrong with the day.

Less than half an hour later, he pulled into the garage at home. It still felt strange to call it that. It was no more his home than the huts they'd "borrowed" in Afghanistan for missions. A temporary place to lay his head, filled with other people's things, reminders of their past lives. He had none of that, not even snapshots of the men he'd served with, fought with, killed for. He had a closet full of clothes in a guest bedroom in his brother's house. As he let himself into the kitchen, Travis wondered if he would ever feel truly at home anywhere.

Alice stood at the stove, cooking. The smell of onions, garlic, and spices made Travis's stomach growl. He realized he hadn't eaten lunch.

"Smells great," he said. "What is it?"

Alice turned and wiped her forehead with the back of her hand. "Nothing fancy. The boys haven't had a decent meal since they got here, I suspect. They've been ordering takeout all the time."

"You'd be surprised at how many of them can cook."

She shrugged. "Anyway, I'm making a big pot of spaghetti sauce. They can take most of it over to the guesthouse and leave the rest here for us."

"Good idea. Thanks, Alice."

She held his gaze. "We need a cook. Especially with all these mouths to feed."

He hesitated, then nodded. "We'll be more careful this time."

"I'll put the word out tomorrow. Maybe even post something online tonight."

"Fine. Where's Tess?"

"In the library, studying."

"How did her day go?"

Alice frowned. "Fine, I suppose. I haven't heard a peep out of her." She paused. "You know, she confides even less in me than she does you, Travis. She's a teenager. What do you expect?"

Travis shifted his weight. "I don't know. That's the problem. I don't know what I'm supposed to do."

"Just let her know you're there for her no matter what."

"She'll never believe that. Not coming from me."

"She has a hard time believing that from anyone, Travis. She lost her parents. She doesn't know who to trust."

Travis studied the stone tile in front of his feet and saw an entire mountain range in miniature in the waves of ridges weathered across its surface. When he finally looked up, Alice had turned back to the pot on the stove, her arm a piston that slowly drove a spoon in circles through the sauce inside.

"How do you think this kid is working out?" he said.

"Oliver?" She didn't turn. "I think he's just what she needs, but she doesn't know it yet. She's getting used to having him around, and I think he's gaining her trust."

Travis considered her words silently.

I'm the one who should be earning her trust, but maybe I missed my chance. It has been a year, and what have I done in that time to make her think I'm even sympathetic? Venture an occasional attempt at conversation when we've been together for meals?

He'd been consumed by the task of learning James's company inside and out, figuring out the best way to keep it afloat without its genius founder. He'd had no time for coddling a blind teenager.

No, that's not true; I haven't made time to help my niece, my own flesh and blood, recover from a terrible loss. Two, in fact. Perhaps it isn't too late to rectify my mistake. At least I can try.

He left Alice at the stove and quickly strode down the long hall to the library. Tess and Oliver sat next to each other at the rectangular oak study table, Oliver's chair turned at an angle toward her, his head bent over an open textbook. Oliver looked up when Travis stepped through the doorway, and Tess cocked her head in that curious way that indicated she was homing in on the location of the sound of his footsteps.

"Hello, sir," Oliver said.

Travis nodded as he approached. "Oliver, could you please give us a minute?"

Wordlessly, Oliver rose and rounded the end of the table, brushing past Travis on his way to the door. Travis waited until he heard the click of the door closing, then stepped toward the table.

"Hey, there, how are you doing?" he said softly. "It's me, Uncle Travis," he added lamely.

Tess rolled her eyes. "Duh. I'm okay. Why?"

"No reason. Just thought I'd check up on you. I know things have been rough for you lately. Especially being there yesterday when that woman was shot."

"Helen," Tess said. "Her name was Helen. You knew her, Uncle Travis. She wasn't 'that woman.' What's wrong with you?"

Travis felt his shoulders bunch. He was handling this all wrong. "I'm sorry, Tess. You're right. I did know her. Not very well, I'm afraid, since I'd been here only a few weeks when she left. But, yes, I knew who she was. I shouldn't have referred to her that way."

He paused, but she sat in stony silence, arms folded across her chest. He forged ahead. "Look, Tess, I'm sorry about a lot of things. I haven't been here for you since the accident. I've been so worried about your dad's company and your future that I forgot about paying attention to your present, what's going on for you here and now. I'm going to change that. I know I can't replace what you've lost, but I want you to know that I really *am* here for you. I'm not trying to make your life miserable. I'm only trying to protect you."

Tess pressed her hands on the table and leaned forward. "By making me feel like a prisoner wherever I go?"

"That's not my intent, but until we know what's going on, until we find out who's behind the attacks on you, Alice, and Yoshi—and the one on Helen—you're in real danger. And if anything happened to you, Tess, I'd never forgive myself. Besides, your father would kill me."

She fell back in her seat, hands still on the table. "Like that's gonna happen."

"Don't be so sure."

Her expression turned quizzical, but he moved on quickly before she could pursue the thought.

"I brought you something." He leaned over the table and put James's cell phone next to her hand so it touched her fingers. "It's your dad's phone. You were right, Mr. Cooper had it."

Her fingers wrapped around its smooth surface and she squinted up at him. "Why?"

"It's a security precaution. Cyrus forgot he had it." He paused. "Look, I know you miss him and your mom. But you've got to stop obsessing over him, Tess. He's gone. No amount of wishful thinking will bring him back. I know you think he's been e-mailing you, but it's just not possible. I'm worried about you. I know how hard this is for you, but you've got to accept that they're gone and move on."

She didn't say anything. Travis straightened and looked around for words or some sort of direction on where to take the conversation next.

"You and Oliver getting along okay?" he said.

Tess shrugged. "He's okay. At least he's smart. Smart enough to help with homework."

"Good. I'm glad." Travis glanced around the room again, but even with the vast number of books shelved on the walls for inspiration, he was at a loss for what to say. "Dinner in a little while. I saw Alice in the kitchen. Smells really good."

"Pasta. I know," Tess said.

"I have a few calls to make first, so I'll see you there. And remember, Tess, if you need anything, anything at all, just tell me."

She flashed a wry smile. "I need Oliver to help me finish here."

"You got it."

Oliver was leaning against the wall across the hall, arms folded and ankles crossed, when Travis emerged. He gave Travis a curious look, but said nothing when Travis nodded. He simply pushed off the wall and headed back into the library.

Travis stopped in his office first. He needed to meet with Marcus and get a report on the day's activities, and he wanted to get out of his suit and into comfortable clothes before dinner. But there was something that couldn't wait. He unlocked the bottom drawer of his desk, pulled out the encrypted phone, and dialed.

"It's me," he said when the general answered. "It's worse than I thought."

"Talk to me, son," Turnbull said.

Travis told him about James's phone and his conversation with Cooper.

"Well, that sounds right," Turnbull said when Travis finished. "He followed protocol."

"But he lied," Travis said, "and I can't figure out why."

"About what?"

"How he got the phone. He said a team picked it up before the Range Rover was towed back from the mountains. It's a crock. My guys stayed with that vehicle from the moment we found it after the avalanche."

"Are you sure? That was a long time ago, Travis."

"Positive, sir. You know what this means." He paused, reluctant to voice the thought. "There's someone else on the inside. It's the only way Cyrus could have gotten the phone."

CHAPTER 37

After dinner, Travis told me he thought it would be safe for me to go back to my apartment. Just in case, he had Red follow me in one of the big SUVs. They let me take the rental car—better than taking the bus. I found a place to park on the street about a block away from my apartment. Red waited in the street with the engine running, then drove me around the corner to my building. He double-parked and told me to stay in the car. He opened his door and swung one massive leg out. Before he got out, he turned his head toward me and held out his hand.

"Give me your keys."

"What for?"

"So I can check your apartment, kid. What do you think, I'm moving in?"

I dug in my pocket and handed him the keys. He hit the flashers and ducked his head to get out. I craned my neck to watch him saunter down to the end of the block behind me and turn the corner. Headlights of cars slowly passing in the street glinted off the wet pavement. City sounds—the rush of traffic on a nearby arterial, the growl of a bus pulling away from a light, a distant siren—drifted in, muted by the closed windows. I pressed my fingers on the cold glass and felt it vibrate to the beat of the bass from a passing car's subwoofer.

My eyes flicked involuntarily toward any type of movement—a couple strolling, a man out walking his dog, tree branches waving in a puff of breeze. A long five minutes later that set my teeth on edge, Red popped back into view through the windshield, strolling up the block with his hands in his pockets. He glanced casually from side to side as if taking in the sights, softly whistling some unidentifiable tune to himself. He didn't look in the direction of the SUV, and when he pulled abreast, he turned and skipped up the walk to the door of my building. He shoved the key in the lock, swung the door wide, and disappeared inside.

I hopped out and darted up the walk behind him, dashing up the steps just in time to get a hand on the door before it swung shut and locked. I pushed it open wide enough to peer down the hall through the crack. At the far end, Red bent over with the key in one hand and peered at the door. I slipped through the front door and tiptoed down the hall silently. Red pocketed the key, pulled a large handgun out of the back of his waistband, and put his hand on the door. The sight of the splintered jamb next to the knob told me why he hadn't bothered with the key. He cracked the door an inch. One of the floorboards creaked as I put my weight on it. Red turned his head and gaped at me.

"What the hell are you doing here, kid?" he whispered. "I told you to wait in the vehicle."

"Got bored," I whispered back.

"Well stay the hell behind me, okay?"

I nodded and crouched behind his bulk, peering over his shoulder as he opened the door. He pushed through the doorway with me on his heels, gun hand extended, panning the room in a smooth, fast arc.

The place was trashed, the few belongings I had so scattered that it looked like a hoarder lived there. Whoever had done it was long gone, but Red stepped over to the small bathroom and swung the door open with the barrel of the gun to double check. It, too, was empty, but the contents of the medicine cabinet and the cupboard beneath the sink littered the floor.

Red ambled into the middle of the room, his large frame filling it, and tucked the pistol back into his waistband. He righted the table and picked the TV up off the floor.

"You don't have to do that," I said. "I can clean up this mess."

"It's okay, kid. I don't mind. And it's a hell of a lot more interesting than standing around in the dark waiting for something that ain't likely gonna happen."

"You don't think they'll come after Tess again?" I crouched and stacked an armful of books.

"They'd be pretty stupid to try an assault on the house again with no one on the inside, like that cook." He joined me down near the floor, most of the remaining books within the arc of a simian arm. He scooped up half of them. "That doesn't mean they won't try somewhere else if they think she has what they want."

"What do they want?"

He shrugged. "Not even Travis knows the answer to that one. But I bet he's got some guesses."

I picked up the stack of books, tipped it sideways, and put it on a shelf. I'd rearrange them later, or maybe not at all.

"Something to do with the company? MondoHard? A project?"

Red nodded as he stood with a stack twice the size of mine in his arms. He squeezed each end with a meaty hand as if playing an accordion, and turned the stack sideways the way I had. He set the books gently on a shelf and stepped back to admire his work.

"Not just any project," he said. "The same one he's been working on for the past year. The one he tested for his brother when he was still in Afghanistan."

"Some top-secret weapon?" I said lightly.

His eyes bored into me, Blu-ray lasers reading me like a DVD. My smile vanished.

"Yeah, something like that. The prototype helped him take out a terrorist cell."

I felt my eyebrows bump into my hairline. "Seriously? Wow, I didn't know. So what's his deal, anyway? He's always so tense. I've never seen him lighten up, crack a smile."

He turned and hefted the mattress back onto the bed frame. "He takes his responsibilities seriously. That's not an easy situation he walked into. This isn't exactly what he signed up for."

"You knew him before?"

"Before the accident? Not long, but yeah. I was part of the team assigned to protect the family. We all were—every last one of us. I was surprised to get the call after what happened a year ago, but Travis is loyal that way. I was a Navy SEAL, and I don't think I've met a better man than Travis Barrett. That's saying a lot."

I chewed on that for several minutes while I picked up slashed couch cushions and shoved stuffing back into them.

"What happened, anyway?"

He stopped what he was doing and straightened. "Don't know for sure. The Barretts got caught in an avalanche, but Travis said he thought his brother could have avoided it. If James had braked, he might have missed it. Travis said it looked as if he gunned it instead, drove right into it. I thought somebody might have messed with the brakes. I told Travis to check, but I don't know that he ever did. Maybe a cursory look, but it seemed like it didn't matter one way or the other. He figured he'd failed at the one thing that meant as much to him as his career in the Special Forces—protecting his family. They were all he had. Now it's down to his niece. And I know it eats him alive every day to think that he could have done something to prevent her from going blind."

"I think she's afraid of him," I said quietly. "If he cares that much, you might let him know he should cut her some slack. Maybe just act human around her."

"Not my place," he said. A beat later he added, "But I'll mention it if I get a chance."

Red ran out of steam, and for the moment I'd run out of questions. He'd given me plenty to think about—not least of which was why Marcus might have been underneath the Range Rover that morning.

We finished picking up most of the mess, and Red turned to go. He pointed to the broken door. "You should get this fixed."

I sighed. "Landlord won't be happy. He'll make me pay. Deadbolt still works, at least."

"Send the bill to Travis." He saw my surprise. "I'm not kidding. He should pay for it, not you. You were keeping Tess safe. Props, by the way. Travis briefed us on what you did."

"Thanks." I shifted my weight. "I mean, it wasn't much. I just got her the heck out."

"While you were under fire. Not too many people could keep their cool in that situation."

Now I felt a flush rising up my neck. "Yeah, well . . . " I didn't know what to say.

He smacked me lightly on the shoulder with his fist, a meat tenderizer softening up a roast before throwing it in the oven. I willed myself not to rub it.

"Hang in there, kid. You're okay."

A smile spread across his broad face, squinching his face under the bushy red brows until his freckles melted together. And then he was gone, leaving me standing there like a tornado victim, numbed and violated.

The rational side of my brain said the men who had searched my apartment wouldn't be back. I propped a chair against the door anyway and managed some restless sleep before waking for good sometime near dawn. I showered, dressed, and drove back across the lake to Tess's house ahead of the morning commuters.

She said little at breakfast and seemed out of sorts. I stayed out of range and let her sulk. When it came time to leave for school, she hemmed and hawed with excuses about why she couldn't and shouldn't have to go. Alice made it clear she didn't have a choice, so she reluctantly let me lead her out to the car. Kenny and Luis were on tap to shadow us. Once I finally herded Tess into the car, we convoyed to school.

I broke the silence first. "Rough night? You look tired."

"I didn't sleep."

"Me neither. Scared?"

"No, I'm not scared."

"I am. When I got back to the apartment last night it was thrashed. I kept wondering if they'd come back."

She looked surprised. "You mean those men the other night? The ones who chased us?"

"Yeah. They searched my place. What a mess."

She fell silent for a moment.

"Red helped me straighten up," I said. "It wasn't too bad. Hey, it's just stuff."

"I kept thinking about Helen and how that could have been us," she said in a small voice. "And yesterday almost felt normal, like nothing happened. I keep waiting for the other shoe to drop. You know?"

"Yeah, I do."

We said nothing the rest of the way, each lost in thought.

The first sign that her premonition might come true came about twenty minutes into Prescott's class. He pitched an assortment of questions to get a discussion started, and finally lobbed a softball at Tess that she should have been able to field in her sleep. When she couldn't come up with any answer, let alone the right one, he jumped all over her for not being prepared. Naturally, she took it out on me after class, chewing me out for not giving her the correct assignment. It wouldn't have done any good to argue even though I knew I'd told her which pages to read, so I clamped my mouth shut.

The real trouble started after third period. Just before the class ended, one of the runners—kids who volunteer a free period to help in the office—came and pulled me out of class.

"What's it about?" I said. No one other than my employers knew where I was, and they could easily have texted me.

The kid shrugged. "You'll have to ask Mr. Olton."

The assistant principal, my favorite administrator in the whole world.

I sighed. "Tess, can you get to your next class? I'll meet you there."

"Sure, fine, leave me here. I should have no trouble finding my way. After all, I'm only blind."

I thought her first sentence had a sharp enough edge to cut to the bone. The rest was overkill. The runner kid turned away, a mixture of pity and fear on his face as he watched me wither. I grabbed his sleeve as he moved for the door.

"Hey, wait. What's your name?"

"David."

"Yeah, okay. David, escort Miss Barrett here to her next class, will you, please?"

"I have to get to my own class. I don't have time."

"Yes, you do," I said. "She's a fast walker."

"Okay, okay, I'll take her. Come on, come on, let's go."

"Give me a break, will you?" Tess said. "Oliver, take my book bag."

"Please?"

"Oh, for . . . Yes, please take my book bag."

"I'll see you in a bit."

I hustled out and broke into a jog down the hall, weaving and darting through the masses of students milling from one class to the next. I figured Tess would be all right for a few minutes with an escort, but I niggled the little seed of worry that the summons from Olton had planted in my head. Out of breath by the time I got to the office, I had to pull up in front of the secretary's desk and take a couple of deep breaths before I could talk.

"Mr. Olton wants to see me?"

The secretary looked up and waved to an empty chair behind me. "He has someone with him at the moment. I'll let him know you're here as soon as he's finished."

I sat on the edge of the chair and looked around, trying not to let my impatience show. I let three minutes go by, then two more before I focused on the secretary. She felt me staring at her and checked her watch before glancing at Olton's closed door. She turned back to her work without looking at me. Another five minutes went by before Olton's doors opened and a teacher walked out. The secretary looked at me and nodded toward Olton. I rose and walked to his door, catching him just before he sat down at his desk.

"You wanted to see me?" I said.

His face went blank. "I think you're mistaken."

"A kid named David came and pulled me out of class just before the end of third period. He told me you wanted to see me. I've been sitting out there for ten minutes."

"There's been some mistake," he said. "I didn't send for you."

"Then sorry for the interruption." I turned and scratched my head on the way out of the office. Had the kid, David, made a mistake? Or was someone playing a joke? If so, who? No one knew me well enough—or disliked me that much, I hoped—to pull a prank on me.

Tess.

With the halls now empty, I fairly flew over the polished concrete floor to the classroom we had left at the end of third period. I passed it at a dead run and rounded the corner at the end of the hall, taking the route Tess and David most likely would have taken to her next class. The building was laid out like a grid, her fourth-period class in the third hallway down. Voices grew louder as I drew closer. Low, deep voices of boys jeering, laughing, the high voice of a girl crying, pleading. I ran faster.

I took a short flight of stairs three at a time and rounded the corner into the three-hundred wing. Four of them hemmed Tess in a circle, playing a mean game of blind man's buff. I recognized Tad and two others from the baseball team. The fourth roughly shoved her across the circle to another jock, laughing as she stumbled and bit back a cry. Those facing me looked up as I ran toward them, making the others turn in surprise. The ball player holding her by the shoulders grinned and shoved her back across the circle to Tad, but he was staring at me. Tess bounced off him and fell to the floor between him and another player who bent down to hoist her up. With four-to-one odds they probably expected me to stop and reconsider. I didn't.

I barreled into the one bent over Tess and knocked him ass over teakettle, as my Nana used to say. He flew into another one, catching him below the knees and bowling him over. I backed up quickly, my eyes on Tad, until I felt Tess right behind me.

"Tess, get up!" I said. "It's Oliver. I'm right in front of you."

"Oliver," she sobbed. "Where have you been?"

Still in shock, Tad looked at the others to see if they were going to help him, or if he was on his own.

"No time for that," I told Tess. "Pull yourself up and hang onto me. Do it now."

She patted my leg, grabbed a handful of fabric, and got to her feet. Tad eyed me warily and took a tentative step closer.

"This is a private party," he said with a sneer. "You weren't invited."

"I kind of figured that," I said as Tess got a grip on my waist. I could hear her crying. I murmured to her, "Hang on tight and go with me, Tess."

"Where you going?" Tad called, taking another step.

I kept my weight forward, ready for him to make a move, but I backed away from him, pushing Tess behind me toward a classroom door.

"You had your fun, Tad. Time to go."

The player I'd knocked over was back on his feet and now shuffled nervously over to his backpack on the floor next to the wall.

"Come on, Tad," he said. "We're late as it is. Let's get out of here."

"I want to see if lover boy here dances as good as his girlfriend," Tad said.

The other two circled in closer, apparently more interested in helping Tad than getting to class. I moved back some more.

"You want a go with me, that's fine," I said. "Anytime. What you did was chicken shit, and next time you think of getting near Tess, I'll mess you up, Tad. I mean it."

"Come on, let's get him," he growled, moving in.

I backed Tess up to the door with a bump, turned, and opened it, shoving her inside as Tad swarmed over my back, his two buddies not far behind.

"A little help here!" I yelled into the classroom. I caught a glimpse of a room full of startled faces before the door shut.

Tad wrapped one arm around my throat and pounded my head and shoulder with his fist. I staggered away from the door, grasped his forearm, and threw him over my hip onto the floor. By then the other two waded in, throwing punches. I got my arms up in front of my face and the first few blows bounced off harmlessly. But a fist to my midriff doubled me over, and I gasped for air and cringed, waiting for another to finish me off. The sound of the door opening saved me.

"What's going on here?" a voice demanded.

Footsteps pounded down the hall, signaling retreat. My mouth worked like a fish out of water. I felt a hand on my shoulder.

"Are you all right?"

Air rushed into my lungs and I put my hands on my knees, taking several more deep breaths before I could say, "Yeah, thanks."

"What happened?" The concerned face of a teacher peered at me.

I waved in the direction Tad and his buddies had fled. "They hassled Tess. I broke it up."

"You should report this to the office."

"Thanks, but we're late for class. Maybe later."

"Well, if you're sure you're all right."

"Fine, really."

I followed him back into the classroom and took Tess's arm.

"Excitement's over, people!" the teacher called out. "Settle down."

"Come on, let's go," I murmured to Tess. I led her out while the teacher tried to get the class under control.

She was racked with sobs, and her shoulders shook as I put an arm around her. She shrugged it off.

"How could you do that?" she cried. "You left me!"

"I'm sorry, Tess, really. It was a trick. They called me to the office to get me away from you."

"You never should have left me alone. You're supposed to work for me."

"What was I supposed to do? They said Olton wanted to see me. I couldn't say no to the vice principal."

Tears streamed down her face. "You could have waited. Or taken me with you. *I'm* your responsibility. It's your *job*."

"I got it, Tess. It'll never happen again, I promise."

I retrieved her book bag from the far side of the hall, walked to her side, and tried to take her arm. She shook my hand off.

"It'll never happen because I'm going to make sure Alice *fires* you. You're terrible! You let them humiliate me."

"I came back, didn't I? Why didn't you hit your panic button? Fred and Barney would have gotten here pretty quick."

"I couldn't get to my phone! Why do you think?" She clutched my arm. "Oh, just take me to class. Now I'm in trouble for being late."

"I'll explain it," I said. I glanced back at the room number of the classroom we'd just vacated. "I'll get the teacher in that classroom to vouch for us. It'll be okay, Tess."

"No, it won't. I'll never trust you again."

Her words flew in close and jabbed with venomous barbs. We walked in silence until the sting wore off a little.

"Are you okay?" I said quietly. "Did they hurt you?" I couldn't imagine how terrified she must have been.

She sniffed. "I'm fine. Nothing that some ice and ibuprofen won't help."

"I really am sorry, Tess."

"So you keep saying."

I gave up and shut my mouth.

CHAPTER 38

Reluctantly, Tess let Oliver lead her to the commons. She still didn't want anyone to see her. Even though she'd had a class period to calm down, she knew she must look a mess—eyes puffy and red from crying, face streaked and dirty, hair flying every which way. But she couldn't do much about it. Oliver had turned out to be useless as a bodyguard, and she doubted he'd be any better at hair and makeup. Not that she would let him within ten feet of a girls' restroom. Her stomach growled. Despite the indignities she'd undergone, she felt hungry. There was nothing to do but let Oliver take her to lunch.

"What would you like to eat?" Oliver asked her as they walked into the commons.

The sheer volume of noise in the, commons amazed her. She hadn't given it a second thought the year before, but now . . . Without her sight, the clamor seemed to hit her ears with that much more force, like walking into the sun after being in a dark room had assaulted the eyes.

At least I don't have to worry about that anymore.

"A turkey sandwich, please. Jack cheese, avocado, and lettuce," she said.

He guided her to the sandwich station and they stood in line, taking one step closer each time someone ahead of them got his or her order. They didn't have to wait long before Oliver ordered two sandwiches. When they were ready, Oliver put a paper sack into her hand to carry and took her arm. He leaned in close, his breath warm on her cheek. She smelled a hint of cinnamon.

"Where would you like to sit?" he said.

"Well, not with Tad and his friends," she said. She clamped her jaw.

After a few moments, Oliver said, "You have to talk to me sometime, Tess."

"No, I don't. You work for *me*. All I have to do is tell you what to do."

"Fine, then tell me where you want to sit."

"Oh, for heaven's sake, Oliver. I don't care."

He fell silent after that, guiding her with a hand on her elbow and the lightest touch in the small of her back. He gently pulled her to a stop, and she heard the scraping of a chair on the floor. The hard edge of a chair nudged the backs of her knees, and she lowered herself into the seat. She felt for the table in front of her, and pulled herself closer. Oliver pulled out the chair next to her and sat down. All around them, students carried on loud conversations.

"Hey, you guys mind if I sit here?" a voice said over the din.

"Matt!" Tess said. "Of course not! How are you?"

Another chair scraped against the floor.

"I've been looking for you guys everywhere." Matt said. "What's going on?"

"What *isn't* going on?" Oliver muttered.

Tess fished in her pocket and pulled out a smartphone. She held it up.

"My dad's," she said. "Want to see if there's something on it?"

"Yeah, sure." Matt tried to be nonchalant, but Tess heard the excitement in his voice. He took the phone out of her hand.

"When were you going to tell me about this?" Oliver said in a low voice next to her ear.

"Like I've had a chance today to tell you about it."

Oliver sucked in a breath.

"Uncle Travis gave it to me last night," she went on, a little more gently this time. "You'd already left." She paused, but he didn't say anything.

Well, it's too bad if his feelings are hurt.

She faced where she'd last heard Matt's voice. "So, Matt, what do you think?"

"Oh, there's definitely an embedded file here," he said. "Give me a minute to pull it up. It's very clever. There's a text file here named 'TB' that's about the last thing saved, but buried in the text is a JPEG. A picture of you, Tess, with some dude—"

"Let me see that," Oliver said. "Do you always carry your laptop around with you?"

"Pretty much," Matt said.

"Oh," Oliver said. "It's Travis."

Tess thought hard. "That must have been taken the night he came back from Afghanistan."

"Yeah, well, there's source code embedded in the photo. I got it. I assume you're supposed to upload this to a link somewhere. Mind if I check your e-mail, Tess?"

She sighed. "Sure, why not?"

The events of the past few days swirled through her head, a dizzying array of violent and confusing experiences that had led to nothing but more trouble.

"Wait, Matt," she said. "Don't send it yet. I can't do this anymore. I want to stop. Can you, like, send a message *with* the file?"

"Sure, I can tag something on it before I upload it."

"Tell them I want to stop. This is it."

Tess heard the tapping of keys on the laptop.

"Done," Matt said.

Tess's phone *bonged* once, almost immediately. Startled, she took it out and keyed voice activation.

"He says you can't," Matt said before she could even retrieve her message.

"People are getting killed," Tess said, her voice turning shrill. "I can't keep doing this."

Matt's hands flew over the keys, and they clacked in syncopated rhythm. The sound stopped for a moment.

"He says what you're doing is too important. 'World-changing,' he says. If you stop, even more people will die."

"I can't," she whispered. "Tell him, Oliver."

"You can do this, Tess," Oliver whispered fiercely. "It's the only way they'll leave you alone."

"Maybe," she said. "But I'm through. He can't make me do it."

"What the heck is this?" Matt said suddenly.

"What?" Oliver said. "Show me."

"It's some kind of code, I think," Matt said.

"Hieroglyphs," Oliver confirmed. "Hang on, I can translate. It'll be easier if I have paper and pencil."

He rustled through the book bag, and soon scratched out a message letter by letter.

"You're not going to like this, Tess. It says your e-mail account is being watched. He wants you to do one more task. It could save thousands of lives."

Tess heard more scratching.

"It says he'll be in touch," Oliver said. "That's it."

"That's it? I have to do something else?"

Tess's phone chirped, signaling an incoming text message. She issued a voice command to retrieve the text, but nothing happened.

"There's something wrong with my phone," she said.

Oliver took the phone from her. "It's a picture message, not text. More hieroglyphs. Wait."

She heard the pencil scratch more letters on the paper.

"He wants you to open a new e-mail account. Don't let anyone know. Well, anyone but us, I guess."

"I can do that," Matt piped up. "Who do you wanna be? Lisbeth Salander? How about Jane Smith?"

Tess made a face.

"What? You can't be Tess Barrett."

"Fine." The name of a fictional girl spy popped into her head. "I'll be Cammie Morgan."

Matt typed. "Taken. How about Morgan Cammie?"

"Whatever." Tess was sick of the whole thing.

It's not a game anymore. It never was.

"Okay, you're set. Morgan Cammie at Gmail. Password?"

"How about 'not having fun'?" she said.

"Works for me. Okay, uploading the new address to the link. There it goes. Okay, so tell me—who else got killed?"

Matt's question sounded so matter-of-fact that Tess shrieked in frustration. The voices babbling around her went silent for an instant, and she felt a dozen stares bore into her from all sides. Just as quickly, the jabber returned to normal.

"Don't you understand?" she cried.

"What? What did I say?" Matt sounded bewildered.

Tess couldn't bear to say any more about Helen. In low tones, Oliver told Matt what had happened after school on Tuesday. Matt let out a low whistle.

"I didn't know," he said when Oliver finished. "I'm really sorry, Tess."

Tess pushed her sandwich away without saying anything. She'd lost her appetite.

"Tess, I'm going to throw this trash away," Oliver said. "I'll be right back. Matt, will you stay with her a minute?"

"Sure. Is that all right with you, Tess?"

She nodded and slumped in her seat. Oliver got up and left, his scent lingering for an instant.

"Man, this is some crazy stuff happening," Matt said. "Say, what did you do to Tad? He's looking over here like he wants to kill you. No, now it's cool. He's on his phone. He stopped staring. No, wait. He's looking over again."

"Matt, shut up!" Tess said. "I don't care about Tad. He's a jerk."

"Who's a jerk?" a voice said behind her. Someone slid into Oliver's seat. "Matt, give us a minute, will you?"

"Yeah, sure," Matt said. "See you, Tess."

Tess placed the voice as soon as she got a whiff of a familiar scent. "Toby, what do you want?"

He leaned in the way Oliver had. It had excited her once, made her weak in the knees. Now she felt strangely uncomfortable. She stiffened.

"What are you playing at, Tess?" he murmured.

"What do you mean?" She drew away.

"I heard my dad talking on the phone with Chief Clifford last night. Sounds like you're mixed up in a murder. I'm not talking about Carl, either. What's going on?"

Tess gasped and put her fist to her mouth. She knew Toby's father was on the city council and was friends with the police chief, but she couldn't figure out how either of them could have heard about Helen.

How did my name come up? Luis and Kenny got us away from Helen's house so quickly, no one could have seen me.

"You must be crazy," she said. "You think I killed someone?"

"Calm down, Tess. I didn't say that. I heard them talking about a murder, and your name came up in the conversation, that's all. I thought you might have been involved somehow. Like, maybe you were a witness." He paused. "I'm worried about you, Tess. You've been acting so strangely since you came back."

"What? Because I don't hang on your every word anymore? Because I don't follow you around like a puppy dog?"

"No, I didn't mean it like that. I . . . you're just different."

"Of course I'm different, Toby. I used to be able to see."

"That's not what I meant. You—"

"I know what you meant." She bit back her anger. "I'm a year older. I've been through a lot in the past year, Toby. Yes, I've changed. So have you. It's called growing up. You're sweet to still care, now that you and Adrienne are together. But I'm okay, Toby. And don't worry. I'm not mixed up in any murder. You must have misunderstood."

"Maybe." He sounded doubtful. "But I—"

Oliver interrupted him. "Everything all right, Tess?"

"Fine. Toby just stopped to say hi."

"I was just leaving," Toby said. The air beside her moved. "Call me, Tess, if you ever need anything."

"A little late for that, but I'll keep it in mind."

Oliver settled into the chair. "What was that all about?" he murmured.

"No big deal," she said. "Why? Jealous?"

He snorted. "Come on, let's get you to class."

That night, Tess flew through her homework as soon as Oliver got her home after school. The sooner she was rid of him, the sooner she felt she'd be able to breathe. The anger that simmered below the surface surprised her in its intensity. It was about trust, she realized. She couldn't trust any of the men in her life. Her father had essentially abandoned her. That was unfair of her, she knew; the accident wasn't his fault. But he was gone nonetheless. Uncle Travis treated her like a prisoner, which was far worse than when he'd simply ignored her. Toby had dumped her for a girl Tess had thought was her closest friend. Tad was obviously psycho, and now Oliver kept disappearing when she needed him most.

None of the women in her life were trustworthy, either. Her mom . . . Tears sprang to her eyes. She blinked and pushed the thought out of her head. Adrienne, her former BFF, obviously was a traitor and a witch. Alice was cold and distant, and though Tess liked her an awful lot—maybe even loved her like one would love a doting aunt or a grandmother—she found it hard to confide in Alice. And Rosa was gone, thank God, but she had been even more Looney Tunes than Tad.

Which left Tess pretty much on her own. Or so she thought, until Yoshi came to collect her for jujitsu practice. Alice came with him to check on her homework, and when Tess told her she'd finished, Alice sent Oliver home. Yoshi waited in the front hall while Tess went upstairs to change. When she came down in her *gi,* or uniform, Yoshi took her arm and escorted her to the gym in the other wing of the house.

Not long before, she'd dreaded this walk. She used to think it was cool that the house was so big it included the gym. It had a weight and exercise room, a half-size basketball court, sauna, hot tub, and changing rooms. After the accident, though, it had become her personal torture chamber—where she'd done all her physical therapy. She'd hated it then, had hated the fact that her parents had been wealthy enough to afford a facility like it in their home, something only a handful of other families had. But as she'd slowly recovered from all her other injuries, she'd come to appreciate the fact that she didn't have to go out in public to get the therapy she needed.

She heard the clank of metal on metal before they reached the gym. Someone from the security team lifting weights, she guessed. Travis would have okayed their use of the facility to keep them from going nuts with boredom. Yoshi led her past the weights and exercise equipment to an open area in the exercise room. Thick mats covered the floor. For the next hour he pushed her hard, reviewing the things she already knew and teaching her new techniques: arm locks, wrist locks—and how to break out of them—hip and shoulder throws, and several types of escapes.

She'd been a blue belt before the accident, finding the mental discipline needed for the martial art a nice complement to the freestyle snowboarding she enjoyed. Now, despite how quickly she was able to remember many of the techniques, Tess found herself slamming into the mat time after time. Without her sight to orient her, she could only guess when she was about to land, making it difficult to break her fall. She was soon frustrated and sore. But Yoshi didn't cut her any slack. He made her perform each technique over and over until he grudgingly indicated his satisfaction or she became so frustrated that she simply moved on to something else before she exploded. When Yoshi finally let her stop for the day, she was exhausted, drenched with sweat, and ached in every part of her body.

"Why so scared today, missy?" Yoshi asked as they headed back to the main part of the house.

"Because I can't see what I'm doing," she said, exasperated.

"How many times today I tell you to *feel* the movement, flow with your opponent and use his momentum and weight against him."

She sighed. "Only a couple dozen."

"Yes, but how many times I tell you same thing before the accident?"

She thought about it and finally got the point. "Maybe a few million?"

"Ah-so, now you truly see. Yes, to kick your opponent from a distance you must see him to know where he is. But when he is close, when he attacks, you know. You can strike, disable, change the direction of his attack, fend him off. All because you feel what he is doing."

"It's just so different than what I'm used to."

"No, not different. Just a different way to sense it. Your body knows what to do. I see that your muscles still remember. Just let go with your mind."

"I'll try, Yoshi."

"Tomorrow." Yoshi sounded as relieved as she felt.

Tess laughed. Maybe she'd given him a workout, too.

As she and Yoshi approached the front hall, the sound of voices arguing in made her heart beat faster. Alice was speaking with a strange man at the front door.

"No. I'm sorry, but you'll have to speak to the family attorney," Alice said.

"What's going on?" Tess said.

"Nothing you have to worry about," Alice said. "Go on up and take a shower."

"Miss Barrett!" the man called from the doorway. "Miss Barrett, it's Detective Pete Erickson. I have questions for you."

"I told you," Alice said firmly, "she can't speak with you."

"Alice . . ." Tess said, frightened, "why do the police want to talk to me?"

"It's about your former cook, Miss Barrett," Erickson said loudly. "Helen Corday? She's been murdered. We got a tip that you may know something about it."

"That's enough, detective!" Alice said. "She's eighteen, which means she can talk to you without her guardian present if she wants. But she's blind, which means she relies on his protection, and he's not here. Even if he was, you'd still have to speak to the family attorney. Now please leave."

"I understand," the detective said. "I'll get in touch with Mr. Barrett and make an appointment to talk to his niece."

"You do that," Alice said.

"Oh, by the way," Erickson said, "is Oliver Moncrief here?"

"Oh, my god," Tess said. "Not Oliver, too?"

"Shush, Tess," Alice said. "Oliver's not here, detective."

"Do you know where I can find him?"

"I certainly wouldn't know where he spends his time off," Alice said. "Perhaps you should try him at home."

"We'll do that, ma'am. Thank you for your time. Oh, and Miss Barrett? We'll be talking with you soon. Real soon."

The sound of the door closing somehow didn't make Tess feel any safer.

CHAPTER 39

Travis sat on the bench in the bus stop shelter and waited, tapping his foot. Misty, cold showers that had persisted overnight and for most of the day had finally given way to some broken clouds. Blue sky appeared in fits and starts, and bright sunlight even poked through in spots, dappling the pavement. A rude breeze peeked under ladies' skirts as they passed by, bullied litter on the street, and ruffled branches of nearby trees. Travis zipped up his windbreaker and stood up when he saw Derek headed up the street.

"I got your text," Derek said as he got close. "What's up?"

"I didn't think it was a good idea to meet at the office," Travis said. "Too many prying eyes. Let's walk."

Derek fell in beside Travis and matched his stride. Travis sensed the kid's excitement, but something else, too. Wariness.

"What have you got?" Travis said.

"On what?"

"The worm. Any progress?"

"Jeez, man, you just gave that to me yesterday. You think I can work miracles? You did say this stuff is extracurricular. I actually *work* for your company, you know. We don't just sit around and play video games all day."

Travis allowed himself a small smile. He had a feeling Derek wouldn't have been able to keep from working on anything he threw at him. Part of it was Derek's desire to please a superior, to get a little recognition. But it was mostly ego. Travis knew Derek couldn't resist the challenge. Derek thought—no, *knew*—he was good, better than anyone else at programming. To match wits with a master who had stymied MondoHard's best coders was exactly the opportunity Derek had been waiting for. Travis had seen that kind of brilliance, that enormous-but-quiet ego before. He'd lived with it, grown up with it.

James.

"Okay, so I took a look at what you sent me." Derek said. "I gotta admit that whoever wrote it was brilliant. The fact that it can morph and adapt to whatever you try to use to kill it or excise it is amazing. I'm pretty sure I understand how he's managed to protect it. It's kind of like genetic modification. From the sample I got, I can see that once the worm got in, it divided itself into little snippets of code, pieces that attached themselves at random in the infected program. Finding the snippets is hard enough because they're so small they look innocuous. But if you do find one and delete it, it replicates itself somewhere else."

Travis glanced at him. Derek's eyes glowed, his cheeks had spots of color, and he was breathing fast—partly because Travis set a quick pace and Derek was talking and walking at the same time. This stuff got Derek excited, like it had James. Travis knew he'd made the right choice. But he remained reserved. He didn't want to get ahead of himself.

"Can you eradicate it?" Travis said.

Derek frowned. "I don't know. I doubt it. But I'm pretty sure I can neutralize it. I'm getting a feel for how it works. If I can anticipate what it will do then I can get ahead of it, prevent it from adapting or morphing. Same thing with how it interferes with the program itself. If I can figure out how to anticipate where it will attack next by looking at where the snippets, its DNA, are hiding, then I can stop it from carrying out attacks on program functions."

"You really think you can accomplish what no one in the company has managed to figure out in a year of working on it?"

Derek nodded. "It won't be easy, but yes."

"How?"

"Because I *get* this guy. I know how this guy thinks. Your coders have been trying to attack the problem without understanding what the problem is. Kind of like treating the symptoms without diagnosing the disease. Whoever wrote this is sick."

"Like psycho?"

Derek grinned. "No, I mean, like, crazy good."

"And you're better? This worm infects at random. How are you going to beat that?"

"That's my point. It's *not* random. It looks like it's depositing DNA and gumming up the works randomly, but it doesn't act indiscriminately. It only infects portions of code that are parts of commands. It's not like some dog that takes a dump wherever it feels like. It's more like a dog that's trained to do its business on selected lawns, but in an unpredictable sequence."

"And how does that help?"

"It means this guy used an algorithm. I just have to figure it out, then I'll be able to predict where the worm will do its business next."

Travis digested the news. It sounded good, but the kid still had to deliver.

"How long?"

"Jeez, keep your pants on," Derek grumbled. He shrugged. "I don't know. Maybe a few days. Could be a few weeks. You've already had a year. Give me a break."

Travis turned into a small park and headed for a bench in a patch of sunshine. He sat down and motioned to the empty bench beside him. Derek glanced around, then eased onto the bench.

"That's good work, Derek. I'm glad you're on this project."

Derek's eyes narrowed. "Am I?"

Travis sighed and contemplated a pigeon pecking the ground next to the bench. "It's complicated. The fact is, I don't know who to trust anymore, Derek. That's why I came to you. You've got nothing invested here except a paycheck. So, right now this is all unofficial, as you've gathered. But if everything works out, I'll go on record about the help you've provided and make sure you get a promotion and a raise. Just go with me on this, will you?"

Derek looked at his shoes, then studied him and nodded. "Yeah, sure."

"Good. Okay, so tell me what you found in my niece's e-mails."

Derek hesitated. "You sure you want to do this? Seems like an invasion of privacy to me."

"She's my ward, Derek. I'm not happy about it, either, but it's my job to protect her. I can't do that if she keeps secrets from me."

Derek shoved some dirt around under the bench with the toe of his sneaker. "Okay, look, I'll tell you what I found out, but if anyone asks—especially your niece—I'll deny I ever did anything you asked me to."

"Fair enough."

"That file you gave me? The one on the memory stick? She uploaded that to the web. The guy who asked her to do it has been e-mailing her for the past few days."

"Has she uploaded anything else?"

Derek nodded. "Three files so far. All erased as soon as they finished uploading. And the sites disappeared shortly after the files were received. Whoever this is, he's careful. Covering his tracks. I couldn't find a trace of the sites or where they originated. Not that it would tell us anything anyway. You can open a site on a server in Uzbekistan and do business in Cedar Rapids."

Travis rubbed his chin. "And the files were erased? Any chance of recovery?"

"Some," Derek said. "Kind of like the memory stick. There's a ghost of a file, but it's fragmented. And the files are on a laptop. Not your niece's. I had to hack it and try to retrieve the files while it was connected to the Internet. Not easy, but I managed to retrieve what's there."

"And . . . ?" Travis leaned forward, rested his elbows on his knees, and looked at Derek.

Derek studied the pattern his sneakers had made in the dirt. "Looks like more of the same code that was on the memory stick."

"You know what it is yet?"

"It looks like some sort of kill command."

"For shutting down an electronic device?"

"Yeah, but not just shutting it down. This will probably fry its circuits. How'd you know?"

Travis sat back and took a deep breath. "I had a hunch. Can you recreate the missing code?"

Derek shook his head. "I could take a guess, but I might be way off base. Besides, there's not nearly enough here, given the kind of logic tree this thing follows. You're missing a big chunk."

"Another file . . . "

Derek gave him a nod. "That would be my guess."

"Well, we just keep watching her e-mails."

Derek looked like he was about to admit he broke Travis's favorite coffee cup. "There's a problem," he said slowly. "I told you this guy is smart. He must have figured you'd monitor the girl's e-mails. He told her to set up a new account."

Travis swore softly. "This is worse than I thought."

He ran through all the permutations in his mind, but he couldn't come up with a plan for handling this.

"What are you going to do?" Derek said.

"I'm not sure. Keep a close eye on Tess, I guess."

Derek shifted on the bench and rubbed his hands on his thighs. "Is that it?"

Travis considered him. "For today. Go on, take off. I'll check in with you tomorrow."

"Thanks." Derek got up and shuffled away, head down.

Travis pulled out his phone and dialed Jack Turnbull's number as he watched Derek leave. As it started to ring, he reconsidered. His statement to Derek hadn't been off the mark—he really *didn't* know who to trust. Derek turned off the path from the park and onto the sidewalk. When he suddenly picked up his pace, Travis made up his mind, closed the phone, and followed.

CHAPTER 40

Happy to have been dismissed for the day, I drove into Seattle in the rental car. I spent most of it wondering why getting along with Tess sometimes seemed so difficult. Then again, maybe she was right; I should think of it more as an employee-employer relationship. We didn't have to be friends. I simply had to do what I was told. "Go along to get along," Pop-Pop used to say. He might have been referring to diplomacy in the workplace, but when he said it I think he really had been talking about how he'd survived more than fifty years of marriage. Either way, it was good advice.

After I found a place to park and walked the block or so to my apartment, I felt uneasy about actually entering. I wasn't afraid to go in without Red's bulk to back me up. But the thought that a person or persons unknown had busted in and messed up the place, had gone through every inch of my life, still creeped me out. I felt violated.

Instead, I walked aimlessly, wandering my neighborhood, always good for people watching and usually a good laugh or two at the things they did. Since I lived close to the university, pedestrians littered the sidewalks and street traffic was heavy most times of the day. It was noisy, bustling, a little frenetic, and always interesting. But the creep factor of the previous few days had made me a little paranoid. It didn't take me a long time to notice a sort of Goth-looking guy in black jeans, tee, and windbreaker dogging me. Thing was, around the U District there were lots of guys that looked like that. What stood out about this one, though, was the fact that he didn't seem to be doing anything.

The first time I noticed him I'd turned around to watch a couple of really pretty coeds walk past. Down the block, the guy practically had dived for the pavement and fumbled around on the sidewalk as if he'd lost a contact lens. The activity wasn't all that suspicious, but it had drawn my attention. The next time I saw him, I stopped in front of a shop window to look at the display. I got an itchy feeling between my shoulder blades. In the reflection on the glass, I saw him standing across the street, staring at me. I turned to walk up the street, and as soon as I glanced in his direction, he looked away.

I made a point of turning left at the next corner. Once out of sight, I picked up the pace and hustled up the street. At the next corner, I turned left again and looked down the block. Sure enough, the guy was nearly running to close the gap. I stopped, counted to five, and walked back around the corner the way I'd come. When the guy saw me headed straight toward him, his eyes widened in surprise and he ducked into a video store.

I followed him in. He moved to the back of the store and stared up at the video boxes on a high shelf. I headed straight for him and was about to open my mouth when he turned around, as if he hadn't found what he wanted.

As he walked by he murmured, "They're watching us."

A river of ice flowed up my spine. I took a deep breath and thought about it. I scanned the shelves and casually turned, pretending to look for a specific title. The store specialized in hard-to-find movies on video and DVD, and it stocked thousands of titles. I meandered through an aisle, flipping through some of the cases, pulling one out here and there to read the cover notes. Slowly, I made my way around the store until I was a yard or two away from where the guy still browsed. I pulled a video off a shelf and held it out toward him.

"Seen this?" I said.

He looked up, saw the video, and shook his head.

"Who's watching?" I murmured.

"Couldn't tell you," he said aloud. In a lower voice, he said, "Meet me later. We'll talk."

"Where?"

He named a sandwich shop a few blocks away. "One hour," he muttered. He shrugged, then in a louder voice said, "Sorry I can't help." He wandered off.

I put the video back on the shelf and browsed a different aisle. Out of the corner of my eye, I saw him leave the store. I picked out an old black-and-white comedy from the 1940s, walked it up to the counter, and paid the rental fee. When I left the store, the guy was nowhere in sight. Nor did I see any sign of anyone watching me. But the thought that someone was out there crawled over my skin like an invisible spider.

I killed most of the hour in a bookstore not far away, checking the street occasionally to see if I could spot who might be following me. Either Goth Guy had been yanking my chain or my watcher was very good. Nothing appeared out of the ordinary.

At the appointed time, I walked over to the restaurant. Inside, two employees wearing bored expressions, tan short-sleeved shirts, and baseball caps embroidered with company logos lounged behind the counter. The shop was empty, which seemed odd given the time. I figured I must have gotten there first, and I wondered if the mystery man would even show. Then I spotted him sitting on a stool in back, at a high counter facing the wall. Realizing I was famished, I went up to the counter and ordered something to eat. The order came up quickly, and I took it back to where the guy sat.

"This seat taken?" I waved my sandwich at the stool next to his.

He looked up, glanced around the restaurant, and shook his head. "You can drop the act."

"Look, I don't know you or what you want, but *you* followed *me*. No need for sarcasm. You got something to say, spit it out. If not, I'll take my sandwich home. I don't need this crap."

I turned away, but he grabbed my arm and stopped me. "Sorry. This is weird. Sit down."

He was about my age, maybe a little older, and I wondered if he meant for the closely trimmed beard to make him look older.

"This is new to me," he said.

"Stalking people?"

He reddened. "Okay, yeah, I checked you out. But it's not like you think."

"All right, you know who I am. Let's start with who you are, then."

"Sorry. Derek. Derek Hamblin." He paused. "I work at MondoHard."

I waited. I had a million questions, but silence was often a better way to prompt someone who had something to say into talking.

He sighed. "There's a guy who's been sending you e-mails. Well, not you, but Tess Barrett. He sent me one, too."

I didn't see *that* coming.

"Why? Do you know Tess? What's he want?"

He raised his hand. "It's a long story. I don't think we have time for the whole thing. They'll wonder why it's taking you so long to eat a sandwich. So I'll give you the bare bones. The head of the company, Travis Barrett—well, you know who he is—Barrett came to me to check out a flash drive. I guess he got it from his niece. Tess."

"Why you?"

"Because I'm good. You know, with computers and stuff." He waved his hand. "I retrieved part of a program from the memory stick. Source code. Interesting stuff. I think it's designed to give a device the ability to think."

I blinked. Computers weren't my forté, but I ended up with a lot of extraneous crap stored in my head because of they way it's wired—my eidetic memory. "Artificial intelligence?"

He nodded. "That's only part of it. Next day, he wants me to work on a project that's stymied the company's best coders for a year. The software for one of the big defense contracts they're working on somehow got infected by a worm. He asked me to take a look at it and see if I could figure out how it works because no one's been able to eradicate it. It adapts, changes."

He closed his eyes, erased an imaginary blackboard again, and started over. "Doesn't matter. Next thing Barrett did was ask me to hack Tess's e-mail account and find out what she's been sending and receiving. Like, okay, so she's still a kid, but that's a little over the top. That's a real invasion of privacy. So, I'm not sure I should trust Barrett, but he's the president of the company so I can't really say no. On the other hand, I don't know who I can trust. You with me so far?"

I nodded. I still had a million questions, and some of it didn't make sense because he was skipping over a lot of details, but I got the gist.

"What about the e-mail you got?" I said.

Derek nodded. "I was getting to that. So this morning, I get this e-mail from someone I don't know that says he knows who I am and what I've been asked to do. He says I need to help Tess. Well, it's pretty obvious it came from the same guy who was sending her e-mails, too. But I don't know this person, so I try to back-trace the e-mail. But he's bounced it from server to server around the world so there's no way I can track it.

"So I think about it. I wondered why someone would involve Tess—and you—in something this big, something obviously this dangerous, unless it was legitimate. Unless he really needs the help and it truly is a matter of life and death like it said in the e-mails to Tess."

I chewed on what he said along with a bite of my sandwich. I swallowed and said, "So, who's sending them?"

He shook his head. "I don't know. But I can tell you this much. Whoever it is knows as much about game theory as James Barrett did, and knows his video games inside out."

I frowned. "Game theory?"

He tipped his head. "It's kind of like a form of psychology. You form games in such a way that players must make intelligent, rational decisions based on strategies of either conflict or cooperation. It's a way of seeing how people behave to get what they want from others. All kinds of people use it, including the military. That's why the DoD came to MondoHard in the first place. They wanted James Barrett."

"You can tell this from some e-mails?"

He nodded. "Look at what he's gotten you to do. Look at what he's gotten *me* to do."

"Why are you telling me all this?"

He looked away for a moment, formulating his thoughts. "I read more than graphic novels, okay? The accident that killed James Barrett and his wife was big news. Everybody knows Tess Barrett was blinded in the crash, even dweebs like me. It wasn't hard to check you out. You're listed as a TA on your UW advisor's web page, along with your thesis topic. Pretty easy to backtrack from there and get your history. Whatever I can't find in the public domain I can get anyway, since I can hack just about any network out there.

"I had to ask myself, if push came to shove, who would I believe? My money's on the blind girl and the squeaky-clean grad student. Someone wants me to help you. Since you're at a distinct disadvantage, well . . . " He shrugged.

"What if we're *all* being played? I mean, if this guy's as good at game theory as you say . . . "

He grinned. "I say we play both sides against the middle. Let everybody else figure it out."

I didn't see the humor in it. "I count at least three people dead, two of them killed right in front of me. This is no game."

His smile disappeared. "No, right. I mean, of course this is serious. That's why I want to help. I could lose my job just for talking to you."

"Yeah, and Tess and I could lose our lives."

He dropped his gaze, cowed under my stare. I backed off and mused, taking some of my irritation out on my sandwich.

"Look, man," he said finally, "I didn't know anybody had been killed over this. I'm sorry. But that's all the more reason you need my help."

I swallowed and took a deep breath. "Okay, what next?"

He reached into his pocket, took out a cell phone, and glanced around the restaurant before handing it to me.

"This is a burner, a throwaway. Two people have the number, me and our mystery man."

I took it. Derek's gaze remained on the phone until I slipped it into my pocket.

He let out the breath he'd been holding. "Okay, he wants me to tell you it's 10:50, whatever that means. And he sent me this."

He handed me a slip of paper with a series of odd marks that looked like squares and right angles set in different positions.

His eyes searched my face. "You know what it means?"

I shook my head.

"Well, I did my part." He stood. "Guess it's up to you now."

"Wait. Who's following me?"

"Does it matter? Look, it's better if they don't know you know. So don't go looking over your shoulder all the time."

"So that's it?"

He shrugged. "Until I find out differently."

He paused, but there was nothing more to say. I watched him walk out and then turned my attention back to what was left of my sandwich. I scanned the marks on the slip of paper while I ate, and called up my memory of the page in Tess's book, *The Eleventh Hour*, with a clock face whose hands read 10:50. When I took the last bite of sandwich, I wadded up the wrapping paper and napkin and dumped it in a nearby trash can. Then I walked up to the counter and asked to borrow a pencil. I went back to my seat and sketched out what I recalled from the page in the book. In five minutes I had deciphered the message.

It read, "Dig deep inside yourself."

I frowned. Riddles within enigmas. This guy was driving me nuts.

I nearly jumped out of my skin when the throwaway phone Derek had given me vibrated against my thigh. I fished in my pocket, yanked it out, and dropped it on the counter as if it had burned my fingers. The screen said, "1 MSG." I opened it and read.

Tess needs you. Help her do this.

CHAPTER 41

For a moment, Tess froze in terror, awakened from a sound sleep by the scent of something familiar, something that signaled danger. She struggled into wakefulness, knowing despite her fear that she was safe at home. She pushed herself upright in bed. Out of habit she screwed her knuckles into her eye sockets and rubbed the sleep out of them. She still couldn't see, but she felt more awake. And now she sensed someone's presence in her room. She cocked her head, listening intently, hearing the rustle of fabric as the person moved, the soft thud of someone's tread on the carpeted floor.

"Ah-so, good morning, missy."

"Yoshi," she said, relief flooding through her. "You nearly scared me to death."

"You must have had bad dream. Nothing scary here. I bring you nice coconut orchid today. Brighten up your morning."

"Thank you. Is it pretty? I wish I could see it."

"Very beautiful. Bright red. One petal white with red spots, like tongue of child with measles." He chuckled.

Tess tried to imagine the flower in her mind. But the image failed to appear. The scent kept nagging at her, forcing the picture out of her head. Finally, she recognized what bothered her. The smell reminded her of the whiff of scent she'd picked up at Helen's just before the shots that killed her and the confusion that followed.

Strange.

She yawned and stretched, wondering why her muscles felt so sore. Then she remembered: from her practice with Yoshi the day before. The rest of the day's events came rushing back, too.

"Yoshi?" she said. "Can I ask you something?"

"*Hai*, missy."

"I don't know what to do. Someone keeps pushing me to do things. But it seems every time I do, someone gets hurt. I think I might be going crazy. I don't know who to trust anymore."

"You can trust Uncle Travis."

"I *hate* Uncle Travis. He grounded me. Look at me, Yoshi! I'm a prisoner."

"He care about you, is all. He try to protect you. He is a good man, an honorable man."

"Why?" she grumbled. "Just because he was in the army?"

"No, because of what he try to do with his life. Always about serving others, not himself."

"He's got himself a pretty nice life here. He just walked into it. Didn't do a thing for it. My parents built all this, not Uncle Travis. They worked hard and earned it. What did he do?"

"Maybe, if not for you, he would choose to be somewhere else. Maybe this not the life he want, just the one he accept because he is needed here."

She felt a pang reverberate through her like the peals of a gong. Swinging her legs out from under the covers, she flounced onto the floor.

"Oh, that's just great. So he doesn't even *want* to be here. That makes me feel special."

"He want to be here. He just sad that he *must* be here because of what happened. You do not see it, but the pain you feel because of the hole your parents left when they died he feels, too. You lost your parents. He lost his brother and sister-in-law. You not the only one in this house who has suffered."

She wanted to dismiss what he said, but it slowly dawned on her that he was right.

Even Yoshi and Alice must miss my parents. Not as much as I do, surely, but they must feel the loss, too.

She'd never considered what Uncle Travis had lost until Yoshi had voiced it. But the fear that had first awakened her still lingered, making it hard to shake off her grumpiness.

"Well, maybe Uncle Travis is doing what he has to," she said. "But I can't even talk to Oliver. Not after what he did to me yesterday."

She shook her head and walked to her dresser, putting her hands out to keep from stubbing her toe against it. Orienting herself with the feel of its contours, she opened a drawer and took out a pair of jeans.

"So," Yoshi said softly, "did you have a question for me?"

She whirled toward the sound of his voice. "What should I *do*, Yoshi?"

"Trust your heart. It will know what to do when the time comes."

"I don't know what my heart wants. I don't know what *I* want."

"Use the stones," Yoshi said. "They will help you see things more clearly."

She sighed. Hard to see things more clearly when she couldn't see at all. "What time is it?"

"Nearly seven."

"Oh, my god. Shoo! Get out, Yoshi. I have to get ready."

"*Hai*, missy."

Tess could hear the smile in his voice and wished she could throw a pillow at him. He teased her relentlessly. But his advice was worth it. His soft footsteps headed across the room, and the door closed with a click. Tess found the rest of an outfit and went into the bathroom to take a quick shower.

Twenty minutes later, she slid into a chair at the table in the kitchen for breakfast. Alice brought her a bagel, yogurt, and juice. She'd just started eating when Oliver came in, said good morning, and sat down next to her. She stiffened, the memory of being roughly shoved around Tad's circle of friends still fresh. He leaned in close, strong scents of his shampoo and soap indicating he'd just showered, too.

"We need to talk," he murmured. "After breakfast."

After breakfast was just fine with her. After lunch would be even better. Best would be if he never talked to her again, but at least breakfast would be pleasant this way. She listened to him make small talk with Alice about his studies and her childhood. Tess found herself interested in spite of herself. She'd never heard Alice discuss her personal life, and was surprised by her revelation that she'd been a bit of a wild child. Tess couldn't imagine Alice as a girl, let alone one who terrorized the neighbors by riding her tricycle through flower beds.

Breakfast ended far too quickly for Tess. She could have listened to Alice's stories all morning. She felt jealous that Alice had opened up to Oliver, had shared things that Tess never knew in all the time Alice had been with the family. But all Oliver had done was to ask Alice some questions, show a little interest. Whatever Tess didn't know about Alice was her own fault. She'd asked Alice a million questions when she'd been little, but had taken her presence for granted over the years and had never bothered to really get to know her. She swallowed the self-pity that welled up inside.

No sense feeling sorry for myself. It's not too late if I truly want to get to know Alice better.

Alice excused herself to return phone calls from some contractors who were preparing bids on repair and maintenance work around the house.

"I know you're still upset," Oliver said as soon as she was gone, "but I need to tell you about what happened yesterday."

"You left me alone," Tess said. "That's what happened."

"No, I mean later. When I went home." He told her about his meeting with Derek, about how they had somebody inside MondoHard now who could help them.

"I can't help anymore," Tess said when he finished. "I'm not getting anyone else killed."

"What about what the e-mail said?" Oliver pressed. "What about all the people who might die if we don't help?"

"What about me, Oliver? What if these people keep coming after me? What about *my* life?" Tess bit back tears.

"Then get out of here. I'll take you wherever you want to go."

"Oh, please. Where would I go? What would I do? I have no money—it's all tied up in trust accounts that Travis manages. How would we live? You said yourself you need this job to pay your rent." She paused. "Besides, Travis would find me no matter where we go. You don't know him, Oliver. He spent nearly ten years hunting down terrorists. What chance would we have?"

"Okay, so maybe that's not a good idea. I told Derek as much. You've got protection here."

Oliver fell silent for a moment.

"I have to get ready for school," Tess said. "Will you help me get my books?"

"Sure." He helped her up from the table. "Look, Tess, I know this is hard, but think of it another way. If you give this person what he wants, then they'll all leave you alone."

She sighed. "Find and upload the last file, you mean, whatever it is."

"Yes."

She stood still, her outward calm belying the storm that raged inside her, tossing her from one side of the argument to the other like a leaf in a gale.

"What did he say this time?" she asked.

"'Dig deep inside yourself.'"

"What does that mean?" Tess said.

She couldn't stop the tears. She'd tried so hard to do the right thing. Had held it together while people around her were dying. Had gone further, braved more, endured more than any normal person would in her situation.

But I'm not normal, am I? Not by a long shot. I can't even see.

CHAPTER 42

Travis hurried down the hall toward the kitchen, hoping to quickly grab a bite of something to eat. He was running late. After a night of fitful sleep on a mattress he still found too soft after years of sleeping on packed dirt floors, he'd awakened early, tired and out of sorts. Unable to fall back asleep, he'd showered, dressed, and gone to his study to make some calls to the East Coast, where the morning was already well under way. He hated the politics of the job most, and wondered how James had been able to stand the sucking up, putting on a polite smile and saying "thank you" while someone reamed you. Members of Congress complained that the company's projects were too expensive. Shareholders complained that the company wasn't charging enough or making enough profit. He felt like a hotshot fighting a wildfire with a water pistol.

He heard voices as he approached the kitchen, and was about to walk in when something about their tone made him pause. He stopped short and listened. He made out Oliver and Tess speaking in murmurs, as if they didn't want to be overheard. That right there was enough to make his ears prick up. When Tess mentioned him by name, she got his undivided attention. Hardly daring to breathe, he silently moved closer, straining to hear.

Jesus, they're talking about leaving, getting out, running away. No, wait. Tess's pessimistic logic is holding sway.

Travis nearly sighed with relief. Until what came next sucked the breath out of him like a gut punch.

The last file! They're looking for the last file.

It was all coming to a head with astonishing speed, and once again Travis was reminded of a wildfire burning out of control.

Tess's cry of frustration brought him back to his senses, and he quickly turned and hurried back the way he'd come. Breakfast was out of the question now. He ducked into the living room and pulled out his phone. Moving toward the windows so he wouldn't be overheard, Travis looked out over the lake, placid this early in the morning. On the horizon beyond the far shore lay a jagged line of mountain peaks still covered with snow.

"Hello?" a voice answered.

"Meet me," Travis said. "Same place. Twenty minutes. Got it?"

"Sure, but—"

Travis hung up. He didn't have time to argue. As he walked out of the living room, he nearly ran into Oliver and Tess coming down the hall.

"Good morning, you two," he said. "Off to school?"

"Good morning, sir," Oliver said.

"Morning, Uncle Travis," Tess mumbled.

Travis watched the color rise up her neck into her face, a sign of her guilty conscience, not embarrassment. Travis would have loved to challenge her just to see her squirm, but couldn't spare a moment. Besides, she wasn't going anywhere. She'd already opposed the idea of making a break for it.

"Have a good day," Travis said. "I'll see you later." Already focused on what he had to do now, he didn't hear their replies.

Twenty-two minutes later, Travis walked into the park not far from his office and headed straight for the bench where Derek Hamblin already waited. Derek paced in a small circle, his movements jerky, hurried.

He's nervous. Good. That will keep him off balance.

As he crossed the grass, Travis thought about how to approach him. He considered going straight at him, but decided to bide his time and see what Derek would reveal.

"Update, please," Travis said when he reached the bench.

Derek's brows knit. "Jeez, man, we just met fourteen hours ago. What update?"

Travis stared at him.

"Okay, okay," Derek said. "I'm making progress on the worm. I took another look at it last night, and I'm close to figuring out the algorithm the coder used. Once I get that, I'll start building a bot that will follow the worm around and zap the DNA it deposits."

"That's good work, Derek." Travis's praise was sincere.

Derek straightened as he filled with pride.

"Thanks. It shouldn't be long now."

"Great," Travis said. "Is that it?"

Derek shifted his weight from one leg to the other and ran his fingers through his hair. "Well, yeah. I mean, I worked most of the night. Didn't have time for much else."

Travis studied him and said softly, "Security spotted you last night up in the U District."

Derek's eyes widened, but he recovered quickly. "Duh. I live in that neighborhood."

"You need to be more careful, Derek. Don't forget that what you're doing is against company policy and probably illegal."

"Wait a minute. What's illegal? You asked me to help work on that software."

"Hacking e-mail accounts and personal laptops?"

"Now, hold on. I did that for you. And now you're going to bust my chops? Besides, it wasn't me that security was following. It was—"

Travis nodded. "I know who it was."

Derek eyed him suspiciously, then the light dawned. "*You* had me followed."

"See, here's the thing, Derek. Yes, *I* followed you. But I didn't have security follow you or Oliver. Don't act so surprised. I saw you 'bump into' him. I figure you guys met up later. But that means somebody else put the tail on one of you. Might not even have been company guys."

"You mean some third party's involved here?"

Travis nodded. "What do you think I've been trying to tell you? Somebody wants those files—badly. We need to know what's on them, and we need to make sure that whoever Tess is sending them to is one of the good guys." He paused and scanned the park. "What do you know, Derek? Why meet with Oliver?"

Derek glanced at his shoes, then thrust his chin out. "I got an e-mail from James."

Travis jerked involuntarily. "My brother?"

"Well, okay, some guy. Same guy that's been e-mailing Tess."

"Why do you think it was James?" Travis pressed.

"The way he's been playing Tess and Oliver. He knows game theory. Plus he knows Tess, knows how to push her buttons. And if he's the guy who wrote the code in those files, then it has to be James. The stuff is brilliant—just the kind of stuff he'd come up with."

Travis rubbed his chin. "You know that's impossible, right? You heard about the accident, the avalanche that wiped out the family car and blinded my niece."

Derek shrugged and stuffed his hands in his pockets. "I don't know, man. All I can tell you is if it isn't your brother, it's someone who knows him inside out. Someone who knows your family history."

Travis pondered for a moment. If the men who had followed Oliver and/or Derek the night before were MondoHard security, then it was possible Cyrus was up to something. But Travis wouldn't put it past General Turnbull to put someone in the field, either, just to keep an eye on things.

Maybe because he has an ulterior motive. He's been pressing me pretty hard to get the prototype back up and running ever since the accident. And Jack was the one who had proposed it in the first place.

Travis brought his attention back to Derek.

"Oliver told you what this was all about?" Travis said.

Derek nodded.

"I don't blame you for playing both sides against the middle," Travis said.

"Didn't look as though I had a choice," Derek said.

"No, I guess not. I'm not surprised that whoever roped Tess in got to you, too. If I found you, it would only have been a matter of time before someone else discovered your talents as well."

Travis drew in a deep breath and let it out slowly. "I'm not James's enemy, Derek. Never was. I only have his best interests at heart, and that includes the safety of my niece, above all. She's my *family*. Do you get that? I might be their only hope here. I asked you to trust me. You want to do what this guy says, that's fine. But don't cut me out, okay? I'm trying to help."

Derek rocked back and forth, thinking it through. "Okay," he said finally. "I'll tell you whatever I find out. But whatever you do, it better be soon. They'll kill Tess to stop this if they can't get their hands on the files. And she's got the clue to the last file. I gave it to Oliver last night."

"That's what I was afraid of," Travis said.

CHAPTER 43

The BMW sat in the circle out front, sparkling clean and looking like new. Alice told me it had been returned the previous afternoon. The police were finished with it, and the windshield had already been replaced. Tess noticed its return as soon as I opened the door for her. Maybe the sound of the door latch or the smell of the leather interior wafting out clued her in. Her breath caught. Before getting in she ran her hand along the smooth roofline above the door, as if stroking an errant pet. Fred and Barney stood next to one of the ever-present SUVs, waiting until we were ready to go before climbing in. They followed us up the long drive and out onto the road.

I glanced at Tess. She caressed the corner of her seat absently.

"This stupid car is all I have left of her," she said suddenly. "My mom, you know?"

I couldn't find a suitable reply.

"Photos are worthless," she went on. "Every once in a while I'll smell something that reminds me of her—fresh dirt in the garden, or what I think is her perfume. But, of course, that's impossible, since she's not here and no one else in the house wears it. Not even me. I couldn't bear it."

I saw an opening and took it. "Look, Tess, I could tell you that you still carry your mom in your heart, but we both know that's a crock. It's not the same as having her here. But if she were here, I think she would definitely want you to get on with your life. And I also think she'd want you to see this situation through."

"I'm not figuring out that last clue. I'm done." Her voice rose as she spoke. "I don't know who I was kidding. I don't care who the e-mails are from—I'm not getting anyone else killed!"

None of what had happened since I'd met Tess even remotely fit into my sense of who I was. I'd gone from grad student to seeing-eye dog to action figure in four days. I wasn't sure if any of the roles suited me, but I wasn't complaining. Her incessant whining grated on my nerves, though.

"Does that include yourself?" I said. "Because I'm pretty sure that if you don't finish this, they'll make sure you can't. They'll kill you, Tess."

"I'm not doing it!" she shrilled. "I don't have to do what you say. You do what *I* tell you!"

I gritted my teeth. "Fine. If that's the way you want it. See if I care."

The problem was, I *did* care, and I didn't know what to do about it. I spent the rest of the drive to school trying to figure out what, exactly, my relationship with this strange girl was. More important, I wondered what I wanted it to be.

The rest of the morning unfolded so disagreeably I found myself wishing more than once for a do over. I couldn't seem to do anything right. Tess found fault with everything from the seats I picked in class to the way I held her arm in the hall between periods. Her mind definitely wasn't on schoolwork. Half the time she failed to notice when a teacher called on her. And she couldn't answer most of the questions they asked. Lunch was no better. I tried to find seats out of the way, but we still attracted attention—along with catcalls and some mean-spirited comments. The humiliation wore her down, and she took her anger and frustration out on me. I grew thicker skin and kept my mouth shut.

At the end of sixth period, Mrs. Jessup, the chemistry teacher, asked Tess to stay a moment after class. She noted again that since she had joined the class late in the semester, she needed to catch up to the other students. She outlined a plan that would allow Tess to complete the labs the class had already covered so she'd be ready for the final exam when it rolled around. Tess wasn't happy about the extra work, and as we left the room she let me know.

"When am I going to have time for all those labs?" she said.

"Come on, Tess. You're the one who said you could handle it. I'm the one who has to do all work. All you have to do is write the reports based on my observations."

"But I shouldn't have to—"

"Hey, Tess!"

Both of our heads jerked toward the sound of Toby's voice. He was slouching against a wall, hands in his pockets. The halls were deathly quiet since the day's seventh, and last, period had already started.

"Toby?" Tess said. "What are you doing here?"

He pushed off the wall and ambled toward us. "Waiting for you. Why haven't you gone to the police, Tess?"

The question startled her—and me—and I saw a cloud of fear darken her face. "Police? About what? Why should I go to the police?"

"If you've got nothing to hide, why won't you talk to them?"

"I already told them everything I know about Carl," she said, a note of panic creeping into her voice.

I fixed Toby with a stare and said quietly, "Why don't you leave her alone?"

"This is between me and Tess," he said. "I want to know what you're hiding, Tess. Why can't you do the right thing?"

"We're leaving," I said. I took Tess's elbow and steered her toward the commons, but Toby stepped in front of us and blocked our way.

"Look," I said, "you need to back off. She already told the cops what she knows."

"No, she didn't," he shot back. "Not about the woman's murder down in Renton. She used to work for your family, didn't she? You know something, don't you, Tess?"

The color drained from Tess's face. "How do you know about that?"

"I told you. I heard my father talking to Chief Clifford. Tad told me that the woman was your cook. Seems a little much to be a coincidence. What's going on, Tess? I want to know."

No one was supposed to know that Tess and I had witnessed Helen's murder. Something didn't feel right. Toby was stalling, delaying us for some reason. I glanced over my shoulder. Down at the far end of the empty hallway, Tad pushed open the exit door. Two men in black commando gear rushed inside. My ears filled with the low thump of my heart pushing adrenaline through my veins.

I faced Toby. "You, too? Those aren't cops!"

He stared down the hall, brows knit in confusion.

I grabbed Tess with one hand and fished in my pocket for my phone with the other. "Tess, we have to run."

"What's going on?" she cried.

"Run!" I growled. "We've got trouble!"

Toby pulled himself together when he saw us moving around him into the open hallway, and halfheartedly tried to block our path again. I shouldered him aside and speed-dialed Fred's number on my phone.

"Let's go, let's go!" I said, pulling Tess down the hall. She got her feet under her and picked up the pace, but when I looked back the men behind us had quickly gained ground, Tad on their heels. Toby stood in the middle of the hallway, facing them with his hands up as if to stop them.

"Wait! Wait!" he called.

They bowled over him, knocking him to the floor. But when I glanced back again, one of them had gotten tangled up and had gone down in a heap with Toby. The other one kept on coming, steadily closing the gap, his pounding footsteps echoing loudly off the walls.

"Faster, Tess!" I said. "He's catching up!"

"Who?" She sounded terrified. "Who's catching up?"

"Just keep moving!" I said.

I willed her legs to pump faster, the sound of our pursuer's footsteps closing in. Only a few steps later, a hand grabbed my sleeve and yanked hard, pulling me off stride. I lost my balance and slammed into the wall. Pain rocketed through my shoulder. A blur of black whipped past and swarmed over Tess from behind. She shrieked in fear. Instinctively, her hands went up to the massive forearm curled around her neck. She planted one foot and pulled down on the man's arm, bending at the waist the same time. I regained my balance and pushed off the wall as Tess's attacker went up and over her hip. He wasn't expecting it, and he went down hard. I raced past Tess and slammed the toe of my shoe into the side of his head, aiming for some imaginary goalposts. The kick rolled him over to one side of the hall.

"Come on!" I shouted, grabbing Tess by the arm.

She came without a word, kicking into high gear without any prodding. There were almost always people hanging out in the commons. If only we could get that far, the men wouldn't dare attack Tess with people around. I heard footsteps behind us again.

"Stairs!" I shouted. "Ten!"

Tess slowed and stumbled. I pulled her up and she grabbed for the railing. When she found it, she tried to take the steps two at a time and tripped. I caught her and half dragged her up the remaining steps. Once more, we took off running, and a few paces later Fred and Barney rounded a corner from the commons and ran toward us. Fred's longer legs put him out front.

"Behind us," I gasped. "Two, at least."

Fred nodded and barreled down the stairs.

"We got this," Barney yelled as he followed. "Get out of here!"

We didn't need to be told twice. Thirty seconds later we raced out the main entrance and into the parking lot. I steered Tess toward the car and pulled the key fob out of my pocket. A push of a button unlocked the car with a chirp. Tess focused on the sound and hurried toward it. I stayed with her and hustled her to the passenger door, leaning in front of her to open it. While she scrambled in, I raced around the car and got behind the wheel. Without bothering with a seatbelt, I started it up, backed out with a squeal of rubber on asphalt, and peeled out of the lot on smoking tires.

"Which way?" I yelled.

"Just drive!" she screeched. "Anywhere! And stop shouting at me."

I yanked the wheel to the right at the end of the drive, out onto the street, and gave the car some gas. Movement in the lower parking lot caught my eye as I headed down the slope from campus. An SUV accelerated across the lot toward the street, moving way too fast. I realized that it was going to try to cut us off. Heart hammering in my chest, I jumped on the throttle. I could feel that the BMW had plenty in reserve so I backed off just a little, wondering if I could time it right. The other driver glanced up at me, and I could see he was thinking the same thing.

"Oliver?" Tess said in a small voice.

"Hang on tight!" I said through clenched teeth.

We sped toward the entrance to the lower parking lot, the SUV on a collision course. I jammed the accelerator to the floor. The engine howled, and the car leaped ahead.

"What are you doing?" she shrieked as she was pressed into her seat.

I tensed and gripped the wheel tightly, my bloodless hands skeletal. Fear hunched in my gut, heavy and brooding. I cringed as we flashed by the lot entrance, waiting for the inevitable blow and screech of rending metal. The SUV loomed in Tess's window and then vanished as we slid past. A squeal of brakes filled the air. Behind us, the SUV skidded out of control across the street and smashed into the ditch on the far side. I turned my eyes back to the road in front, heart pounding and blood roaring in my ears.

Barely slowing, I turned at the corner on protesting tires and raced through residential streets until we came to an arterial leading to the freeway. I got on heading east and melded into the flow of traffic, checking the rearview mirror every few seconds for signs of pursuit.

CHAPTER 44

Travis's phone vibrated. He eased it out of his pocket and held it in his lap under the table. A quick glance told him all he needed to know. The text on the screen said: *911.* He excused himself quietly and got to his feet. Most people remained focused on the speaker at the head of the conference table, but one or two glanced at him as he left the room. He noted which faces looked simply curious and which looked peeved. It couldn't be helped.

Those who are miffed by my exit can go take a leap. I have a company to run.

In this case, however, he knew the emergency came from home. He dialed the number as he left the room.

"Talk to me," he said when the number connected.

"They rabbitted," Fred said.

"You let them get away from you?" Travis saw the startled reaction of an employee down the hall, and lowered his voice as he headed for the elevators. "What the hell happened?"

"It's not what you think," Fred said in clipped tones. "A team got inside the school and tried to take them. They hit the panic button and made a run for it. We intercepted them and told them to go. Figured they'd be safer outside while we secured the scene."

"And?" Travis paced in front of the elevators. Changing his mind, he headed for the stairs, moving quickly now.

"The two of them had already done a pretty good job of it. Put one of the assault team down with a serious concussion. Another wanted to start a firefight in the middle of a hallway, so we took him out quickly. Spotted their vehicle on the way out, smashed up in a ditch, so we figure probably two more. No sign of them. They probably cut and ran."

"Damn! You left them there?"

"Didn't have much choice," Fred said. "It was either that or answer the cops' questions for the next two or three days. Figured you might need us, so we boogied. It was a good shoot, Travis. A couple of kids saw us in the hallway. The guy threw a couple rounds at us, then tried to take one of the kids hostage. Barney put a single round in his head. We rattled the kids, told them to keep their mouths shut. Gave 'em some b.s. about national security. But we won't be able to avoid law enforcement for long."

"Where are you now?" Travis huffed as he took the stairs down two at a time.

"On the way back to the house. We've alerted Marcus. He's mobilizing the troops."

"Okay, I'm on my way." Travis thought for a moment as he raced down another flight of steps. "Make sure my gear is loaded. I'll change when I get there. You have a lock on the car?"

"Yeah, we've got them. They're heading out of the city."

"Okay. I'll call the school and the authorities on the way and give them a heads-up about the attack. I'll stall, let them know we have an ongoing situation, and say we'll report in later. I'll see you in twenty."

"Right."

Travis hung up and banged through the door into the parking garage. He sprinted for the Range Rover and wheeled out of the building in a matter of seconds. He navigated the city streets as fast as he dared, keeping an eye out for SPD patrol cars, and reached the freeway minutes later without incident. With fewer distractions on the highway, he used the Range Rover's Bluetooth feature and called Derek first. Tersely, he outlined what had happened and told Derek to be on standby in case there was any activity in Tess's e-mail account, or in the event Oliver contacted him. That accomplished, Travis called the school to let them know he'd been apprised of the situation there and would alert the authorities.

By the time Travis calmed the principal down and got off the phone, he was pulling into the drive at the house. He held off calling the police chief. He wanted to be on the road before he alerted law enforcement. Once the police got involved, Travis and his team would be sidelined, relegated to watching, and Travis wasn't about to take a backseat to anyone, especially local cops, when it came to Tess's safety. His men had more training, more combat experience, and had more insight into the type of adversary they faced than some patrol officers with a few weeks' SWAT training. Nothing against cops. Travis respected the job they did. But not for this.

Both the SUVs were parked in the circle, ready to go when Travis pulled up. Luis was closing the tailgate of the one in the rear. The other men stood at the ready by the doors, which meant both vehicles were loaded and ready to go. Travis jumped out and hustled up to passenger side of the lead vehicle, nodding at Fred across the hood. He turned and looked back at the other SUV. Marcus, Kenny, and Luis climbed in and waited. Travis got in his vehicle and twisted to face Red and Barney in the backseat as their small convoy got underway. Barney wordlessly handed him a neatly folded pile of tactical black camouflage clothing. Travis shimmied out of his dress slacks, shirt, and tie, and changed into the combat gear.

He swiveled to look at Red. "You all set?"

Red nodded. "Laptop's working fine. Signal from the Beemer's GPS is strong."

Travis settled in his seat and buckled up. "We're about thirty minutes behind them. Any chance of making up some of that time?"

"Given their location," Red said, "looks like they're staying under the speed limit. Probably don't want to risk attracting attention."

"I can make some of that up," Fred said, punching the accelerator. "Depends on where they're headed."

Travis stared out the windshield. "That's the key question. Where *are* they headed?"

CHAPTER 45

Neither of us spoke. I couldn't tell if Tess was in shock. She must have known from my erratic driving and the sound of the crash that something bad had happened. But now the steady, quiet hum of the engine and soft hiss of the wind rush outside calmed and soothed my nerves. I assumed it was having the same effect on Tess. Eventually, she sighed. When I glanced over I saw she had finally settled into her seat, letting go of the tension that had left the imprint of her fingers in the leather console cover. In each hand she held a flat stone—one pink, one blue-black. She worried them between her thumbs and fingers.

We quickly left the suburbs behind and wound our way up into the foothills of the Cascades. The powerful car climbed without effort and ate the miles hungrily. Before I knew it, we'd wound our way up through Snoqualmie Pass and down into the Yakima River Valley. It was a while after that, maybe an hour and a half after our escape, that Tess finally spoke.

"Where are we?"

She said it so softly that I wasn't sure I'd heard her at first. I glanced over. She cocked her head expectantly.

"I'm not sure," I told her. "We passed Ellensburg not long ago."

"I know where to go," she said. She was silent a moment. "Pull up the GPS if you can, and look for a road that will take you to Wenatchee. Once you get there, take Route 2 north."

We crossed the Columbia River and got off the highway a few miles later, drove north through high desert that irrigation had miraculously turned into farmland. Then we doubled back west a little and followed the river up the valley to Wenatchee. From there, Tess's directions took us northwest, back into the mountains. She said no more about our destination, so I left her to her thoughts and enjoyed the gorgeous scenery as we wound up through the Cascades.

When we finally slowed to a stop at a light, Tess spoke.

"I've never come this way," she said. "Are we in a town?"

"Cashmere, I think."

She chewed her lip. "I think I know where we are. About ten miles to go."

Less than fifteen minutes later, we drove into what looked like a German village. Many of the buildings had been designed and built with Bavarian architecture, giving it a quaint, Old-World feel. Any minute I expected a sleigh drawn by eight reindeer to appear and complete the picture.

"We're in Leavenworth, right?" Tess said when I stopped at a light.

"Where's Santa?"

She grinned, a good sign. "Yeah, I know. Corny, but kinda sweet. Drive through downtown. On the other side, there's a gas station on the left. Can we stop? I'm hungry."

Hungry. Another good sign. My stomach growled, too.

Just as Tess had described, the gas station came into view a few minutes later. Inside was a small convenience store. I turned in and pulled up to a gas pump. While the tank filled, I poked my head in the car and asked Tess what she wanted to eat.

"I don't know. A sandwich, I guess. And chips. And something to drink. Water."

"Okay. You stay here."

"Wait. We need supplies. I should come in with you."

"What kind of supplies?"

"Well, enough food to last us until tomorrow at least. We need to figure out what to do."

"What are we going to do with it? There's no fridge in the car. And where are we going to stay? Camp out? Sleep in the car? Get a motel room?"

She smiled. "No. We're close. Only a few minutes from here."

I thought for a moment. "Okay, but I still think you should wait in the car. If people come looking for us and ask questions, a blind girl is pretty memorable. A single guy isn't."

"Okay, fine."

I could tell it wasn't fine, but she knew I was right. The gas pump shut off, so I holstered the nozzle, grabbed a receipt, and parked the car outside the door. I waited while Tess gave me a list of things she thought we needed, and went in. Five minutes later I came out with a sack of groceries and a couple of sandwiches to tide us over.

Tess guided me out of town down a side road a couple of miles, then told me where to turn off. An even narrower road wound down to the banks of a river and then split in two, one side running parallel to the bank and the other fork leading to a small bridge that crossed over. Tess directed me across the bridge, and we followed the road along the opposite bank as it curved through the forest. Pavement quickly gave way to dirt. When Tess felt and heard the change in road composition under the tires, she sighed.

"Not far now," she said. "I bet it's beautiful. Tell me what you see. Please?"

I described the scene out the windshield. High, fluffy clouds against an even higher ceiling of bright gray flecked with patches of blue sky. Douglas firs and spruce trees, along with maples and alders, lined either side of the road. Above them, in the near distance, rose a craggy mountain, the tops of its twin peaks still dusted with snow.

"About a mile to go," she said when I finished.

We drove the rest of the way in silence, me with a growing sense of restiveness. I wasn't sure what to expect. The road petered out a few minutes later in front of a lodge-style home that looked fairly new despite being weathered. I braked gently and we rolled to a stop a few yards from a massive door under a portico with columns of rough-hewn tree trunks. I sucked in a breath.

"Like it?" Tess said.

"Yeah. What is it?"

"Family vacation home. We're all—we *were*—all avid snowboarders. Mom and Dad built this place because it's about halfway between Stevens Pass and Mission Ridge ski areas, and a really pretty spot in both winter and summer."

She opened the center console and fished around with her hand, finally coming up with a key ring holding several keys.

"Come on," she said. "I'll show you around."

"Can we eat first?" I said. "I'm starved, too."

"Sure. Bring the food along. We'll eat, then take the tour."

She gave me the keys, told me which one unlocked the front door, and warned me that I'd have to disarm an alarm system inside. We got in without setting off any sirens. Tess reached out and found my arm, and we guided each other to the kitchen. I put the bag of groceries on the counter, fished out cartons of milk and juice, and put them in the nearly empty refrigerator with only a few lonely jars of condiments to keep them company. I put the sandwiches on the counter in front of two stools and left the rest of the supplies in the bag.

The windows darkened rapidly. A clock on the stove said we'd been on the road a little more than four hours, and the sun had already dipped below the mountains. I turned on some overhead lights and joined Tess at the counter. She'd already started in on her sandwich, chewing hungrily, but she had a thoughtful look on her face. She put her sandwich down.

"They came after me at *school*," she said. "They won't stop, will they?"

"No. Not as long as you have something they want."

She gave a small nod of confirmation and went back to her sandwich. When she finished, she patted the counter until her fingers found a paper towel I'd put there. She wiped her mouth.

"Are you ready for the tour?" she said.

"Sure." I stood and put her hand on my arm.

Behind the kitchen Tess showed me a laundry room and a small mudroom with a door to the garage. A staircase between the foyer and the kitchen led up to a bridge that overlooked both the foyer and great room and linked two bedrooms. She brought me back downstairs to the kitchen again. The kitchen opened up to a dining room, which in turn opened up on the left to a two-story great room with a vaulted ceiling. A wall of glass looked out toward the mountains, the twin-peaked crag now just a dark silhouette against a dusky smudge in the sky where the sun had dropped out of sight. Glass French doors opened to a patio outside, its far edge hidden in darkness. A large fieldstone fireplace dominated one wall. Behind that lay a master bedroom suite, and coming around in full circle led to a study next to the foyer. All of it was done in natural woods and stone, giving the large house a rustic, homey feel.

I noticed the quiet as we walked around the dark house, the lack of mechanical sounds, and a chill in the air suggested the furnace was either off or set at a very low temperature. A thin layer of dust covered the floors and furniture. I'd turned lights on and off again in each room as we toured, so the only illumination now came from the kitchen. Its reflection off the wood floor in the short hall and the stone tile in the foyer revealed our footprints.

"When's the last time you were here?" I said.

"More than a year ago. Winter break, I think. No one's been here since the accident."

"It just sits here?"

"Alice has someone check on it once a week. People come in to clean every few months."

"Travis doesn't mind? I mean, paying for heat and electricity when no one uses it?"

"Well, it's not like we can't afford it. He's never even been here. Probably hasn't figured out what to do with it now that my parents are gone."

"Maybe he's never gotten up the courage to ask you what *you* want to do with it."

She looked surprised at the suggestion.

"They'll figure it out eventually, you know," I said. "When we don't come back they'll think about where you'd go. They'll find us if we stay here."

She didn't say anything.

A dim, bluish glow emanating from the study drew me through the doorway. It seemed odd when everything else in the house was turned off. The dim light revealed a comfortable room with bookcase on one wall, a sitting area for reading, and a desk topped with a computer monitor and lamp. The glow came from a digital photo frame sitting on a shelf. I moved closer and watched as one picture dissolved and another took its place. A little girl in a yellow swimsuit hugged an inflated life ring next to the turquoise water of a swimming pool. The shot faded, replaced by a slightly older version of the same girl bundled up in winter clothes against a sea of white snow, face half hidden by goggles and a helmet.

"Is this you?" I said.

"Is what me?"

"Sorry. These pictures. There's a photo frame here with a slide show. Mostly photos of what looks like you. You know, cute little girl? Yellow swimsuit with a sunfish on the front?"

"Hey, give me a break. You were little once, too."

"Just teasing."

But through the doorway, in the glow of the photo frame, I could see that Tess looked like she'd seen a ghost. Her hand went to her mouth and she gnawed a knuckle.

"Oh, my god," she whispered. "It's me, my life history. Of course."

She reached out, her hands finding the doorframe, and felt her way into the room and along one wall toward the desk.

"Oliver—the memory card in the frame," she said as she touched the desk chair and sat down. "Bring it over here and help me boot up the computer."

My train of thought finally caught up with hers.

Dig deep inside yourself . . .

I turned on the desk lamp and the computer, then examined the photo frame and pulled out the memory card. Kneeling next to Tess, I inserted the card into a port on the computer. The monitor brightened almost immediately with a new window asking if we wanted to open the photos on the card. I leaned over Tess and navigated to the site Mark had steered us to for decoding software, downloaded it, and ran the program to look for an embedded file on the memory card.

"Find anything?" Tess asked.

"Give it a minute. I just started running the program." I paused to watch the screen. "Wait, here it is. Another file like the last ones."

Tess chewed a fingernail and quickly put her hand in her lap.

"Are we doing the right thing?" she said.

I hesitated. Part of me wanted the nightmare to end, but I couldn't say if the person on the other end of Tess's e-mail correspondence was good or evil.

"I don't know," I said. "It's your decision, Tess. All I can say is this person pretending to be your father isn't the one who's killing people. We've come this far . . . "

She thought about that. "Do it."

I signed into her new e-mail account. She had one e-mail waiting. All it contained was a link. Just like the other times, when I clicked on it, a prompt asked what file I wanted to upload. I selected the new file we'd created from the embedded code and hit "Send."

CHAPTER 46

The miles zipped by, nervous energy building inside Travis with each one, the feeling familiar and gratifying after a long year out of the field. He wasn't cut out to be an office drone, even though many aspects of running a company as large and strategic as the one James had built appealed to him. After all the months of physical inactivity, Travis was itching for a mission. This had all the earmarks of a potentially dangerous one, and the tightening in his chest and gut actually had a calming effect—it focused his mind on the tasks at hand.

He twisted in his seat. "Red, pull up everything you can on Leavenworth. I want maps, topographical info, satellite photos, whatever you can find so we know what the terrain looks like. Send whatever you find to Marcus in the other vehicle."

Travis briefly scanned the dark countryside out the window as he thought through their approach. He'd been stymied for nearly half an hour when the GPS signal from the BMW showed it leaving the interstate and backtracking up into the mountains. But he'd eventually realized where Tess was headed. Now that they were close, he wanted them all to be as prepared as possible for whatever lay in store.

He pulled out his cell phone and called Alice back at home.

"They're going to the Leavenworth house," he told her when she picked up. "Can she get in?"

"Of course. Sally kept keys in her car, and Tess knows the alarm code."

"I need the floor plans of the house. I've never been there. We're going in blind."

"I'll see if James kept a digital copy on his office computer. You expect trouble, I take it."

Travis heard concern in her voice. He knew she cared as much about Tess as he did.

"I'm not sure what to expect, but I want to be prepared. If they tried to take her from school, I'd say odds are pretty good they've got a lock on her location, just like we do. I could kick myself for not making sure the BMW was checked for bugs when it came back from the garage."

"It was my responsibility," Alice said. "I know the people who own the shop, and they're above reproach. But anyone could have broken in and put a homing device on the car. I should have anticipated it."

"Don't worry about it. You have enough on your plate trying to run the place, especially with a security team in the guesthouse. Gotta run. Send the plans asap."

"Will do."

"Oh, and Alice? Be careful. You and Yoshi keep your eyes open. They may try an end run while we're occupied out here and break in to search for what they're after."

Travis ended the call and dialed Derek's cell next.

Derek answered on the first ring. "Where are you?"

"Other side of the mountains. Look I need you to keep close tabs on Tess's e-mail and—"

"They're online now," Derek said. "I was just about to call you. Wait. Yup, there it goes! They just uploaded a file. I'm gonna try to catch it before this guy pulls the site down. Gotta go."

The line went dead, but Travis was already disconnecting and reaching for his satellite phone.

General Turnbull answered on the third ring. "Yes?"

"It appears things are coming to a head, sir. I may need some help running interference with local law enforcement."

"Where?"

"I'd rather not say. I just need to know if I can count on your support."

The general was silent for so long Travis wondered if the call had been disconnected.

"I warned you that once you left the army you were on your own," he said finally.

Not for the first time in the past few days, Travis wondered whose side Jack was on. It wasn't the answer that he wanted to hear, but Travis wasn't fazed. For most of his several tours in Afghanistan he'd operated independently, knowing that he'd be disavowed if he were caught. This was different. Now he was on US soil. But the people he was up against weren't playing by the rules, so he was damned if he'd let himself be bound by the law.

Not when it came to something like this. Not when it came to Tess's life.

"I understand, sir. We'll do our best to stay under the radar, but just so you know, things could get ugly."

"Duly noted." Jack paused, and when he spoke again, his tone softened. "I can't assert jurisdiction if the locals get involved, Travis. You know that. But if they're not in the picture and you need help with cleanup, I can send in a team like last time. In fact, I'd prefer it. I want to know who these bastards are."

"We're in silent mode. It might work."

"Good luck, son."

Travis disconnected and thumbed the throat mic on his tactical communications unit. Leaning forward, he glanced in the side mirror at the headlights following them.

"Marcus!" he barked. "You there?"

"Roger. Just got the maps Red sent."

"Good. Get ready. We're less then fifteen minutes out, and we're going in hot! Everybody hear that?" Travis looked around at the dimly lit faces in his vehicle. "I repeat. We're going in hot. Check your weapons and munitions, and be prepared for anything."

CHAPTER 47

I wasn't sure what I expected to happen after we'd uploaded the fourth and last piece of the program that someone had so desperately sought they'd enlisted the help of a blind girl and her somewhat clueless new employee. But I didn't expect *nothing*. No fanfare, no confetti, no congratulatory slap on the back—no nothing.

The disappointment, the letdown was just settling in when something *did* happen. The computer shut down and the lamp went out, throwing the room into pitch darkness. Momentarily confused, I stood and went to the doorway. The entire house was dark.

"Power's out," I said softly.

As I peered into the great room, my eyes adjusted to the darkness. Somewhere out beyond the glass, a faint green glow caught my attention. As I focused on it, I saw a flash of red, too, a ruby thread that sliced through the air as it moved toward me.

"They found us!" I shouted.

I ducked back into the study just as glass shattered in the great room, accompanied by the same muffled chatter of weapons fire I'd heard when Helen had been killed. Instinctively, I reached out in the darkness, my fingers finding fabric. I grabbed it and pulled Tess to the floor. The sudden silence was louder than the gunshots. Tess hadn't made a sound, and sudden fear gripped me with the thought that she might have been hit.

"Are you okay?" I whispered.

"Fine," she murmured.

I let out the breath I'd been holding and tried to slow my racing heart.

"I can't see a thing," I said. "I don't know how I'm going to get you out of here."

Tess scrabbled up onto all fours. "Can you see the door?"

A glittering red thread shot through the blackness, outlining the opening's black rectangle.

"Yes," I said.

"Point me there."

I turned her in the right direction.

"Follow me," she said. "I can get us out."

"We haven't got much time," I hissed. "By now they know we're unarmed. They'll storm the house any minute."

Without answering, she crawled through the doorway and turned right, making her way across the cold, hard stone floor of the foyer.

"Stay down," she breathed over her shoulder. "You coming?"

"Right behind you," I muttered.

I saw more flashes of red, and across the great room a green glow seemed to grow brighter as it bobbed up and down. Tess reached the other side of the entryway. I nearly bumped into her as she stopped and reached out with one hand to feel the wall. There was barely enough light to see the outline of a door. Tess's fingers found the edge and traced it up until they found a handle. She pulled herself up, opened it, and slipped inside.

"Come on!" she hissed.

I scrambled over to the black opening in the dark wall and dove through. Soft fabric hit me in the face, and I bumped into another wall. The door clicked closed behind me. When I tried to stand I kept bumping into Tess or walls and realized that we'd ended up in a coat closet under the stairs. Now the darkness was so complete that I couldn't see my hand in front of my face.

"We're in a freaking closet!" I grumbled. "You don't think they'll find us here?"

"Shut up!" she whispered.

Her back was turned to me, and I heard her hands brushing the walls, searching for something. Seconds later came the simultaneous sounds of shattering glass from the great room and a resounding crash close by as the front door was smashed in. I heard men shouting and boots stomping the hard floors as they spread out to search the house. Suddenly, Tess was gone.

Her whispered voice came from a few feet away. "Oliver, come on!"

I pushed past some coats and put my hands out to feel for Tess. In the pitch-black confines, my hands discovered that a wall had suddenly become an opening. The sounds of shouting and running feet still reverberated through the house around us. Tess reached out and felt me, grabbed my arm, and pulled.

"Watch your step," she said softly. "There are stairs here going down."

My groping hand found a banister, and I quickly stepped through and down a step. Tess stopped me with a touch, and I heard the click of the door panel moving back in place behind me. Tess took my hand, and we hurried down the stairs.

CHAPTER 48

The SUV's tires chattered over the ruts in the dirt road, trees close in on either side rushed past at breakneck speed. Fred was pushing the vehicle to its limits. When vehicles parked on the grassy shoulder loomed suddenly in the headlights around the next corner, Travis instinctively braced one hand against the door pillar as Fred stood on the brakes. The SUV slewed and fishtailed in the dirt and loose gravel. At the last second, Fred gave the four-wheel drive a shot of acceleration and wrestled the SUV around what had been impending disaster. He quickly brought the SUV to a halt. Fortunately, Kenny had seen Fred's brake lights, giving him more time to slow, and he pulled up right behind.

Fred craned his neck and peered at the vehicles parked half on the shoulder. "Fishermen?"

"This time of night?" Travis said. "Someone got here first. The kids are in trouble."

"Then let's go." Fred gave the accelerator some gas.

"Wait, wait!" Barney said, halfway out the back door.

Fred stomped on the brake, jerking the vehicle to a stop. Travis turned and watched Barney slither over to the closest empty vehicle. He crouched next to the front tire. A figure jumped out of the SUV behind them and ran to the vehicle parked in the rear. Now illuminated by the headlights, Travis saw that Luis had joined Barney at work on the parked SUVs.

In the backseat, behind Travis, Red peered at a map on the laptop screen. "There's a turnout around the next bend," he said quietly. "We can pull the vehicles into the trees under cover."

"How far to the house from there?"

"Less than a klick."

Barney moved to the rear tire on his vehicle, and a moment later Luis moved to the front on his. Travis glanced impatiently at his watch. Though it seemed like eons, it was only seconds later that Barney hustled back over and climbed in the backseat. He held out his open hand with a grin on his face, two valve stems nestled in his palm.

Red snorted. "Why didn't you just slash the tires?"

Barney gave him a hurt look. "Tires are expensive, man."

"We might need those vehicles later," Travis said. "Good thinking, Barney. Okay, let's go!"

Travis rolled down his window and waved to Kenny to follow. Fred quickly put the SUV in gear and drove around the curve. Travis scanned the terrain ahead and pointed to a break in the trees where they could hide the vehicles. Fred pulled in quickly, nosing the vehicle as far in as he could to give the other SUV room to maneuver in behind them. Travis hopped out before the SUV came to a full stop and waved the other vehicle in. As the men piled out of the vehicles, Travis checked over each one to make sure he was equipped with a communications unit, night vision monocular, and body armor. He knew all of them would have prepared as carefully as he had, checking and rechecking their equipment to make sure it would function as expected, but as their commander and employer, he was responsible for them.

They quickly opened the tailgates on each of the SUVs and pulled out automatic weapons and zippered vests with pockets for extra magazines and other munitions—grenades, flash-bangs, tear gas canisters, and whatever else each man favored. Travis had chosen the Heckler & Koch MP5SD3 submachine gun as the team's assault weapon. A little different than the modified M4A1 assault rifle he'd used in the army, the HK was more compact, even with the sound suppressor. Navy SEALs used the HK, and Travis found he liked it better.

Red kneeled on the ground with the laptop, and the group huddled around him while Travis gave out assignments.

"Marcus," he murmured, "you and Kenny take the right flank. Check the approach from the river. Luis and Red, take the left. Fred and Barney, circle around the back of the house, and be careful. I've got a feeling that if those vehicles back there indicate what we think they do, the main assault will come from that side. It's all glass. Anyone inside is easily visible from there. I'll go straight in the front. Okay, let's move!"

The men separated into their teams and headed out onto the road. Luis waited a moment while Red threw the laptop in the backseat, and as soon as they headed out, Travis fell in step as they broke into a jog. The other black-garbed teams were already invisible in the dark though they were only yards ahead. Travis flipped his night vision monocular down in front of his right eye to get a better sense of the road ahead, the green glow of his men popping into view in the lens. He saw the road curve into the trees, the house not yet in sight. He flipped the monocular up again so he could run more easily, and fell into a steady rhythm.

As they rounded the bend and the dark shape of the house came into view, the men split off into the trees on either side and made their way to their positions as quickly and quietly as they could. Travis slowed his pace as they disappeared, approaching more cautiously as he drew closer. Suddenly, Travis watched the crisscrossing red lines of laser sights lock in on the house, and the night erupted in muffled gunfire.

CHAPTER 49

At the bottom of the stairs, Tess paused and felt for the digital keyless lock pad. She punched in a six-digit code, a little surprised that she remembered it so easily. Her parents had insisted that none of their birthdates be used, so committing it to memory had been hard. The deadbolt unlocked with a soft click, bringing back memories of the drills her parents had run. As laid back and fun-loving as both of them had been, both also had harbored a practical side they'd constantly impressed upon Tess. "Be prepared," they'd said. "Plan ahead, and you'll be ready for whatever happens." That advice had extended to things like home fire drills and panic drills, though she had found them strange at the time. She turned the handle on a heavy metal door and pushed.

"Wait here," she told Oliver.

She stepped inside the door and hugged the wall to her right. Putting her hands out, she quickly found a small table and the battery-operated camp lantern sitting on it. *Be prepared . . .* She didn't need the light, but Oliver did. Though this room normally had lights, Oliver said they'd cut the power. She returned to the base of the stairs and put the lantern in Oliver's hand. She heard the click of the switch and Oliver's footsteps as he moved into the room. She closed the door and found the handle that slid the dual reinforced steel security bars into place.

"What is this?" Oliver said, his voice coming from the middle of the room.

Her mouth twitched up in a half smile as she imagined his reaction to the large room, an odd mixture of 1960s bomb shelter and comfortable rec room. A door in one wall led to a fully stocked pantry full of shelf-stable food and a small bathroom with a chemical toilet.

"A panic room," Tess said. "Kind of like the secret office at home."

"You mean your parents anticipated something like this happening? Your dad was that paranoid?"

Tess understood his incredulity. "I don't know what he thought might happen. I just know that he and Mom were always prepared. If I was hungry on the ride home from school, Mom always had an energy bar tucked away. If I skinned a knee at the park skateboarding with Dad, he came up with bandage from somewhere."

"Guess they were right. But what good does it do us? They know we're in the house somewhere."

"We're safe down here. They can't get through that door. At least not easily."

"We could be here for weeks."

"Help will come."

"No one's coming to help. No one else knows we're here, Tess."

"Well, there's plenty of food."

"There's no cell phone signal down here, either," Oliver said. "We can't even call for help."

"On purpose," Tess said. "My dad designed it that way, but I think he figured on having an Internet connection."

"Not without power."

"There's a generator somewhere, but I never learned how to use it. I was too little when they ran panic drills. I guess I never got around to learning."

"We can't stay here forever, Tess. The hidden panel in the closet is clever, but they saw us in the house. They know we can't have gone far. They'll find a way in, even if they have to blast the door down."

Tess reluctantly had come to the same conclusion before Oliver said anything. She knew all she'd done was buy them some time, but suddenly that was more important than anything else in the world.

Time . . .

She hadn't had enough time with her parents. And for many years, almost as long as she could remember, she'd wanted time to go faster, to rush her into adulthood, to be grown up, with all the privileges and perks that grown-ups enjoyed. The past year—and especially the last five days—had shown her the awful responsibilities that came with being an adult. Now, part of her wanted to cling to the safety and security, the carefree nature of her childhood.

But ever since she'd heard the awful, tinkling crash of breaking glass only minutes ago, something within her had changed. She felt it growing, filling her, giving strength to her limbs and her determination, adding clarity to her thoughts, her focus.

Rage. Blind rage.

She laughed at her own joke. No, it wasn't blind at all. It was clear as air after a storm, sharp as a scalpel. She'd held in her anger for the past year and now it coursed through her and she thought of all the people she wanted to direct it at: her parents for dying on her, Toby for leaving her, Travis for controlling her. Most of all, she was angry at herself for allowing herself to be a victim. Terrible things had happened to her, but she knew she still had a lot to be grateful for.

She listened to the muffled thumps of the men in the house overhead, destroying everything her parents had worked for. Not just the house they'd built, but their way of life. Everything they'd believed in, even the loyalty her father had felt to his country, as strong in its way as her uncle Travis's, she realized.

She wasn't a child anymore. And her parents weren't there to protect her. It was up to her to carry on. Finding and uploading that last software file had been a start.

It's time to finish this. The men upstairs have to be stopped. Caught and punished.

"There's another way out," she said quietly. "Two, in fact."

Tess suspected half the reason her father had gone to such lengths to design secret rooms and passages in their homes had been the child in him, not the adult. Whatever the reason, she was grateful now.

"Two? Why two?"

"Contingencies," Tess said. "Always have a Plan B. In the store room there's a ladder that leads up to the garage—escape by car. Over there..." Tess pointed at the sound of Oliver's voice and swung her arm about forty-five degrees to the right "is a passageway. At the end is another ladder that leads up to a trapdoor outside, closer to the river."

"The car's out front. Garage doesn't do us much good."

Tess nodded. "I agree. The farther away the better. Besides, if we can get across the river, there's a bed-and-breakfast down the road where we might be able to call for help."

"Okay, it's settled. Are you sure you're up for this?"

She swallowed hard and nodded. "Yes."

Oliver took her hand and walked her to the small, narrow door that Tess remembered thinking looked as if it had come out of the pages of *Alice in Wonderland*.

She ducked through the opening and gave his hand a tug. He didn't move.

"Are you sure there are no weapons down here? Bazooka, maybe? Rocket launcher?"

She smiled. "Sorry. Paring knife, maybe."

He sighed. "Well, at least I have you to protect me."

She felt her way down the passage, memories of running through it when she was little going through her head. Even without her sight, the distance to its end seemed much shorter than it had when she was young. Almost before she knew it, her fingers encountered the cold metal of the door at the end. The security bars were disengaged, as she expected. She turned the handle and the heavy door opened silently. Through the opening was a space the size of a large closet. On the far wall, a steel ladder's rungs led up a shaft.

"Why don't you let me go first?" Oliver said.

"You'd better leave the light here," she told him.

"Right." He put it in her hands. "I'll tell you when to turn it off."

His shoes scuffed the rungs with muffled clanks as he ascended. At the top, his fingers scrabbled with the latches on the hatch that opened to the outdoors. From the outside, it looked like a cover to a septic tank. She didn't think anyone would suspect them to emerge there, but she crossed her fingers.

"Okay," Oliver called softly. "Turn it off and come up."

She clicked the switch, set the lantern down, and gripped one of the steel rungs. Hand over hand, she climbed. When she reached the top, she extended an arm into the night air, expecting Oliver's help. But no one was there. She felt the lip of the shaft and pulled herself up.

"Oliver?" she whispered.

She strained to hear. Not far away, she heard the sound of soft grunts of pain and then the smack of fist on flesh. She crawled over the edge and scrambled to her feet as the speed and impact of the blows increased. Suddenly, there was silence. Her heart pounded in her chest. She wanted to call out to Oliver, but didn't dare. Even if she could make it to the river by herself—she could hear its burble and rush through the trees—she knew she'd never make it across without a guide. Heavy breathing close by intruded on her thoughts, and she steeled herself, closing everything else out of her mind. The breathing grew louder, closer, and someone grabbed her wrist.

"Just who we were looking for," a gruff voice said.

She was pulled forward. Rather than resist, she stepped in, twisted her arm in the man's grasp, and leaned toward him, bending her elbow and using it as a fulcrum against his own arm. The maneuver broke his grip. She pulled her arm away, took a half step back, and lashed out with an openhanded punch. The man grunted. Tess turned and ran, hands out in front of her to keep her from tumbling headlong into a tree. She'd only made it steps away before she was overtaken. Her attacker grabbed her shoulder and wrapped his other arm around her throat in a chokehold.

"Not so fast, girlie," the man said.

Tess smelled his rancid breath and was repelled. The anger inside her bloomed, hot and visceral. His hold tightened, cutting off her air. Pinpoints of light danced in her head.

Suddenly, two loud explosions ripped through the night air and muffled gunfire erupted from the direction of the house. The sudden noise distracted her attacker, and she felt him turn to look. She quickly stepped backward, putting her hip behind his, dropped into a horse stance, and swept her arm back against his chest. He let go and fell over her hip. Tess turned her head, trying to focus on the sound of water. When she got her bearings, she took off. Within seconds, though, the man once again caught up to her and roughly grabbed her arm.

"You little bitch!" he snarled. "Don't move!"

He pressed the hard barrel of a gun against her temple, ran his hand down her arm until he grasped her wrist, and twisted her arm up between her shoulder blades. Tess winced in pain, but she didn't cry out. She wouldn't give him the satisfaction. Rage burned fiercely inside her. The man spun her around and shoved her toward the bursts of gunfire still raging near the house, never loosening his grip. The gun barrel dug into her head, breaking the skin, and Tess felt a trickle of warm, wet blood snake down her cheek.

"Tess!" a voice shouted over the din of the gun battle.

The man holding her jerked her to a stop and turned her toward the voice. "Don't come any closer, or she dies."

"You kill her and you're a dead man," the voice said.

"Kenny?" Tess said. "Is that you?"

"Yeah, Tess," Kenny said. "Don't worry. We'll get you out of this."

"Not a chance," her attacker growled. "She's dead anyway. We just want her to talk first and tell us whatever she knows."

His words sent a chill up Tess's spine, but her rage seared the fear until it shriveled away to nothing. Without thinking, she spun toward her attacker, bringing the arm he still gripped with her. She curled her hand over his wrist, broke his grasp, and grabbed his hand with both of hers, bending it backward and forcing him down on one knee. She heard the *pop-pop* of a gun firing, and the man's arm went slack in her hands. She let go as if it was a snake. A moment later, Kenny's arm curled around her shoulders and he pulled her close.

"Tess, are you all right?"

"Oliver ... " she said, suddenly remembering the struggle she'd heard earlier. "He's hurt."

"We'll find him and see to him later," Kenny said. "I need to get you someplace safe."

Tess squirmed in his arms, but he held her fast and walked her away from the intermittent gunfire still coming from the direction of the house.

CHAPTER 50

Directly overhead the sky had cleared, unveiling a midnight-blue fabric stitched with glittering dots of light. Travis hadn't seen stars like that since he was in Afghanistan. He hadn't realized how much light pollution there was in the city.

No time for stargazing now, though.

He loped silently down the dirt road, staying close to one side along the trees for cover. He counted four men assaulting the front door of the lodge-style dwelling, and when the door crashed inward, three charged into the house, leaving the fourth to stand guard. Travis flipped the night vision monocular down and quickly scanned the edges of the circular parking area in front of the house and garage. There, in the cover of a thicket of bushes, crouched another sentry, just as Travis suspected. But his attention was riveted on the house and the motion inside.

Travis changed his angle of approach. Using the natural foliage as cover, he circled quickly and quietly behind the outer sentry. The kill had to be fast and silent. Travis rushed him from behind and put an unbreakable chokehold around his neck. He knew it would take just nine seconds for the man to pass out. He went limp in six, but Travis held the grip for another ten-count. He stripped the man of his weapons, his eyes on the movement in the house. Another team had breached the house from the other side. He counted at least six inside now, all still working without light. He glanced down at the man at his feet. He wore night vision goggles. Travis thumbed his throat mic.

"Fred," he murmured. "Flash-bangs. In the house. On my count."

The stun grenades normally would incapacitate a person's vision for at least five seconds, as well as disrupt hearing and sense of balance. Because night vision goggles amplified available light, flash-bangs would practically blind anyone wearing them for minutes—or even hours.

Travis quickly worked his way around the driveway circle and toward the front door, staying low and close to the building.

When he had a clear toss through the front door, he stopped and crouched low. The other guard stood facing the road, but the sounds and movement coming from inside kept diverting his attention. Travis waited until the guard turned and looked through the doorway, then breathed into the communications unit, "Three, two, one . . . "

He threw the stun grenade canister over the guard's head and into the entryway. He saw it bounce once. He immediately squeezed his eyes shut and waited for the blast. It came almost simultaneously with the explosion from Fred's. Before the echo even died away, Travis was up and running toward the door. The sentry turned at the sound of his footsteps, one hand pawing at his eyes. He raised his weapon. Travis fired. The guard wildly sprayed a volley of bullets into the night but collapsed in a heap as Travis's shots found their mark.

Travis sprinted through the open doorway and dove for cover behind a large couch in the great room. Twisting onto his back, he swung his weapon up toward the top of the stairs and fired a burst. One of the men tumbled forward, down the staircase. Another returned fire from the bridge, but came nowhere close to Travis, still blinded by the flash-bang. More gunfire came from the kitchen. Travis quickly slithered to the end of the couch, peered around it, and fired two quick shots. He swung the muzzle back up, sighted on the man on the bridge, and squeezed off a three-shot burst. The figure collapsed like a deflated balloon.

Someone let loose a volley from the dining room, bullets thudding softly into the stuffing of the couch. Travis heard return fire and saw the suppressed muzzle flash on the patio outside the smashed glass doors. Reinforcements.

He thumbed his throat mic. "Three upstairs, two of them out of action. Three downstairs."

"We've got two downstairs located," Fred said.

"That leaves two to find," Travis said.

He heard gunfire coming from outside, which meant the others were tied up. He, Fred, and Barney would have to clear the house. The open study door caught his eye. He brought his knees up under him and coiled in a crouch.

"Lay down some cover fire, Fred," Travis said. "On three. One, two, three!"

As Fred fired, Travis sprang to his feet and dashed across the open floor. As soon as he reached the cover of the study doorframe, he swung around and fired across the foyer at the shadow in the kitchen. The man went down without returning fire.

"Another down," Travis muttered into his com unit.

A burst of gunfire came from the dining room, bullets thwacking loudly into the wall just inches away. Travis fell to the floor, heart racing. *Too close.* Lying on the hard floor, he leaned through the opening and fired toward the spot where the volley had come from. Fred fired at the same time from his position, creating a withering crossfire. But he couldn't tell if they'd hit the man.

From the corner of his eye, Travis saw Barney slip through the shattered patio door and into the great room. He darted behind an easy chair, then pulled himself up onto one knee to get a better view into the dining area. He heard more gunfire from the woods outside, muffled, like kids playing with firecrackers.

Deadly firecrackers.

"Look out!" Barney shouted.

Travis twisted around and saw a dark figure emerging from the dark hall to his left, where the master bedroom lay. As the figure drew a bead on Travis, Barney fired and the man went down. Travis forced himself to breathe, heart hammering against his ribs.

He gave Barney a high sign and muttered into his mic, "Thanks. Okay, one left. Anyone have a lock on this guy?"

Fred moved inside in a crouch and shook his head. Barney did, too. Travis put his finger to his lips and listened intently in the silence. For interminable seconds, nothing.

Then he heard it.

A floorboard in one of the rooms above creaked. Travis silently pointed up and saw the other two nod. He sidled across the tiled entryway toward the stairs. Fred and Barney held their positions, both pairs of eyes trained on the top of the stairs. Travis rounded the banister at the base of the staircase and crept up the steps one at a time, careful not to make any noise. Halfway up, he moved toward the wall to avoid the body lying there, and one of the stairs groaned under his weight.

With a terrifying yell, a dark figure ran out of a dark bedroom onto the top landing and opened fire. Travis dropped to his stomach, arms extended, and pulled the trigger. The chatter of Fred and Barney's weapons joined that of his own. The man above him jerked one way and then another like a scarecrow learning to dance as the hail of bullets cut him down.

Travis raced up the stairs, leaped over the body, and checked the bedroom on the left. Empty.

"Clear!" he shouted.

He heard an answering shout from one of the Bedrock buddies downstairs as he raced across the connecting bridge to the other bedroom. It, too, was empty.

"Clear!" he called again.

He ran down the stairs, meeting Fred and Barney at the bottom. They all looked at each other, puzzlement clear on their faces.

"Damn it!" Travis said. "Where *are* they?"

He thumbed his throat mic. "Red, I need the floor plans, pronto!"

CHAPTER 51

"Tess!" The voice carried over some distance.

Kenny stopped abruptly, and Tess nearly stumbled. The voice had called from maybe ten or twenty yards away, she guessed. Though familiar, she didn't immediately recognize it.

"Are you all right?" the voice said.

"I got her, man," Kenny said. "I was just getting her out of here, taking her back to the vehicles where she'll be safe."

"Yeah, okay," the voice said, a little closer now. "That's cool."

"Let's go," Kenny muttered to Tess.

She felt him move and tried to match his pace so she wouldn't fall.

"Hey! No, wait!" the voice called again. "What are you doing?"

Tess heard a note of concern in it this time.

"What are you talking about?" Kenny said loudly. "I told you, man, I'm taking her back to the vehicles."

"No, wait! I see what you're doing. I can't let you get away with it, Kenny."

"Get away with . . . ? What the—?"

A muffled shot rang out, and something wet spattered Tess's cheek. *Blood.* She could smell it. Kenny grunted and fell away from her. She froze, heart leaping into her throat. She wanted to scream. Taking several deep breaths, she shoved aside the panic that threatened to overwhelm her. She would not freak. Not this time. Footsteps pounded toward her.

"Tess! Tess! Are you okay?"

The footsteps stopped in front of her and a little breath of air swirled past her, carrying a tropical scent like the coconut orchid Yoshi had brought to her room that morning.

Coconut. Marcus.

Her knees shook and almost gave way as it hit her with a wave of terror.

Marcus was the one who killed Helen.

She rarely missed a scent, and the one Marcus wore was the same one she'd smelled that day. Marcus was on the other side, not Kenny. And Marcus had just killed Kenny. They wanted to talk to her, though. Marcus wouldn't kill her—not yet. She had to get a grip on herself, think it through.

"Who's there?" she said, her voice quavering.

"It's Marcus, Tess. Oh, you poor thing. You must be scared to death. I'm sorry, I had to do that right in front of you, but Kenny wasn't who you thought he was. He wasn't getting you out of danger. He was taking you right into the lion's den. Are you okay?"

Tess shivered. Her fear was no act, but she couldn't let on that she knew.

Keep it together, buy some time.

"I g-guess so," she said. "I just want to go home."

"That's a great idea, Tess. Let me help you."

You do that.

She let him take her arm, her thoughts racing.

If I scream, he'll kill me for sure. But if I can get him to lead me back to the house, someone might help. If anyone's still alive after all that shooting.

She listened. The shooting had stopped.

Maybe they're all dead.

The silence was eerie. Then night sounds slowly returned to the forest, the river babbling over stones in its way, an owl hooting, the scurry of tiny feet through the brush as a small animal returned to its burrow.

"I . . . My purse," she said. "I left it in the house. Could we get it first?"

"It's not safe yet, Tess," Marcus said. "Let me take you someplace safe first. I'll go back and get it later, I promise."

He was smooth, she had to hand it to him.

No wonder Uncle Travis hasn't found out about him yet. Unless Uncle Travis . . .

No, she couldn't even think it. Marcus was the bad guy. She felt it in her bones.

Hang on.

She went along with him, but pretended to have Jell-O legs from the shock, slowing him down. She wouldn't make it easy for him. He pulled her a little more roughly, impatient.

"Ow!" Tess said. "You're hurting me."

"We have to get you out of here," he said. "It's not safe."

"Okay," she said in a small voice. "Just don't be so rough."

Make him think you're weak. Wait for your chance.

Every step she took filled her with more dread as he took her away from the house—away from any help she might get.

You don't need help. Remember what Yoshi taught you. You can overpower him.

Her brain worked furiously, thinking of all the ways in which she might incapacitate him if she got the chance. She would have to be patient. And maybe she could still make a break for it. Before he put her in a vehicle. On the road would be perfect, where the trees were close on either side and she could quickly get into the brush and hide.

You can do this.

She felt the rough, uneven terrain under her feet give way to the relative smoothness of the dirt road. She didn't have much time now.

"Wait, stop," she said, resisting his pull. "I think I have a stone in my shoe. It hurts."

"Okay, okay. Just get it out."

She heard the tension in his voice.

That's good. He's distracted.

She bent down and pretended to untie her shoe, visualizing how she would take him down. She let the anger simmer again, steeling her resolve.

Ready . . . set . . .

"Marcus!"

Above her, Marcus whirled. "Travis! I've got her. I found Tess!"

The lie came so easily to him that it was no wonder Travis didn't know what a snake he was.

It doesn't matter. I know.

Relief filled Tess. "Uncle Travis?" She stood and turned.

"Tess?" Travis scooped her up in a bear hug. "It's over, Tess. God, I'm so glad you're safe. I never would have forgiven myself if you'd been hurt."

She put her arms around him, her cheek against his neck. It could all change in an instant, she knew, but for the first time in a year she actually felt safe. She clung to him, making the feeling last a moment longer before he set her down. But he didn't let go. He still held her hand firmly.

"What gives, Marcus?" he said.

Tess heard the anger in his voice.

"Hey, I was just trying to get her out of the field of fire."

When Kenny had said it, she had believed him. She knew Marcus was full of crap, but she didn't let on.

"What's the matter?" Travis said. "Is your com unit broken? Why didn't you call it in?"

"Sounded like you guys were in the middle of a firefight."

"You should have told me you found her." He paused. "Where's Kenny?"

"He's dead," Marcus said. "Sorry to be the one to have to tell you this, Trav, but Kenny was a mole. I caught him trying to take Tess. He had a gun to her head. I had no choice."

The fury inside Tess threatened to burst out of her in a white-hot explosion. She clenched her jaw and tipped her face toward the ground.

"Damn!" Travis swore softly. "I hoped it wouldn't come to that. I'm sure you did what you had to, Marcus. I'm just glad Tess is safe."

"Uncle Travis?" she interrupted. "Someone needs to check on Oliver."

"Where is he?"

"In the woods. Near the tunnel entrance. I . . . I'm not sure . . . He might be dead."

"I'll get someone on it, Tess. I'm sure he'll be fine. Marcus, get out on the road and make sure no one gets in here. We've got a hell of a mess to clean up. I'll send Luis out to go through their vehicles and see if he can find out who hired these goons. He can relieve you after that. Tess, you're coming with me. I don't want you out of my sight for the time being."

Instinctively, her hackles rose. She was tired of being told what to do. Just as quickly, though, she realized that for the first time since Travis had taken over as her guardian, Tess didn't mind his overprotectiveness.

CHAPTER 52

Travis quickly assessed the situation. Nine dead altogether, only one from Travis's team—Kenny. Besides Kenny, Travis's team had experienced only two casualties. Barney had gotten a flesh wound in the firefight inside the house, and then there was Oliver.

If Marcus is right, Kenny hadn't been part of the team after all.

At least four of the attackers had escaped into the woods, including the sentry that Travis had choked unconscious. As much as Travis hated loose ends, part of him was glad that at least some of them hadn't died.

Such a waste.

He quickly issued orders, dispatching Luis to check on the vehicles and make sure those who'd escaped didn't try to sabotage the team's rides. He sent Fred and Barney out to find Oliver and retrieve Kenny's body. Red offered to bring in the other casualties. Travis felt he should go, too, but when Red glanced silently at Tess, Travis nodded, grateful. While the others started in on their assignments, Travis called Jack again, stepping onto the patio to keep Tess from listening in.

"Sorry to wake you, sir."

"I'm still up," Turnbull said. "Couldn't sleep after your last call."

"It's over," Travis said. "At least for now."

He briskly recapped what had happened, relaying the news that it looked as if Kenny had been the inside man.

"That could explain a lot," the general said.

"It could . . " Travis said slowly.

"You're not convinced."

"I had my suspicions about Kenny," Travis paused. "It's Marcus's call. He was there. I wasn't. If he says he had to take Kenny out, he must have had a reason. And I've always been able to trust Marcus."

The general was silent for a moment. "So, where does this leave us?"

"If your offer's still on the table, Jack, I'll take you up on it. No one's come nosing around yet, and I posted Marcus on the road in, just in case. We've got nine dead. It's a mess."

"I'll send up the same forensic team we used before. They'll be there within two hours. What else?"

"Tess uploaded the last file before we got here. We were too late, but so were the others."

"If only we knew who 'the others' were."

"Fred and Barney recognized a couple of them, sir. Hard core mercs that the boys say have seen action in places where no sane soldier would go. Fred said he heard rumors that both of them were involved in the theft of those Stinger missiles a few years ago."

"That's bad news, Travis. It confirms my worst fears. It means the world's most notorious arms cartel is after your little toy. Have you figured out what these software files actually do?"

"We think they're an intelligent kill command."

"That someone can use remotely to sabotage the prototype?"

"Yes," Travis admitted.

The line went quiet.

"The good news, sir," Travis went on, "is that I have someone who can crack the worm problem. I think we'll have the prototype up and running again well before the deadline."

"Well, that's something, at least."

"I trust you'll keep this between us, Jack. No need to tell Senator Latham about the files."

"I suppose not, since we don't really know what they are. Or who Tess sent them to."

"I have some ideas, sir."

"Oh? Care to share?"

"Not yet. I'll let you know when I do."

"All right. Good work tonight, son. Tess is okay?"

Travis glanced inside at his niece's silhouette, sitting on a couch in the dark. "She's tougher than I thought, Jack."

"She's a Barrett, son."

With that, the general disconnected. Travis turned and walked back inside to be with his niece until his men returned. It was time to tell her everything.

Well, almost everything. She deserves that. Hell, she's earned it.

CHAPTER 53

I dreamed that huge hands reached down through the darkness and lifted me in the air. They carried me somewhere, and though the ride was bumpy, it was not as uncomfortable as the cold, damp ground I'd lain on until they found me. Before I could make out where we were going, the world went black again.

I don't know how much time passed until I woke. I sensed a rocking motion again, but no one carried me this time. I gradually became aware of a smooth, pliable surface beneath my cheek. Leather. The same material hovered in front of my eyes, just inches away. When it started to spin, I closed my eyes again. A car. The BMW. Voices drifted over the seat backs. I concentrated, trying to hear the words. The effort hurt my head, and slowly I became aware of pain located elsewhere, too. Ribs ached with each breath. The top side of my face felt as if it had encountered a brick wall at high speed. One lip had ballooned up to the size of a sausage. I opened my eyes again to discover that the left one was actually swollen shut.

The words coming from the front seat sounded like some foreign language. I frowned. The voices were familiar, one high-pitched and female, the other definitely male. The man called the woman by name. *Tess.* Sure. Tess and Travis. And me. All in the BMW, headed home. I smiled. Still dreaming, I decided, but I was alive. That was a start. A school of questions swam through my head, flashing by too quickly to hook. None of them seemed big enough to be keepers anyway. My eyelids drooped and closed of their own accord, too heavy to keep open.

So tired.

The black void welcomed me back with open arms.

CHAPTER 54

The steady hum of the engine and the monotonous black night outside the windows lulled Tess into a torpor. The car was warm and comfortable, but she fought off the urge to sleep. She could do that once they got home. *Home.* It felt like weeks since she'd been there, and she was eager to get back. That she didn't dread it—the rooms with all their memories, the thought of school and the challenges she faced there—surprised her.

Maybe facing death changed me.

She would give that some thought later. She still had something important to discuss, especially after what her uncle had told her before they left the mountain lodge.

"Uncle Travis? You need to know something about Marcus."

"What's that?"

"You can't trust him."

"Why not?"

"I don't think he was helping me. I think he was trying to kidnap me."

Travis didn't say anything for a moment. "Okay, he didn't radio me the second he found you. But did he say or do anything that suggested he wasn't doing what he said he was?"

"No-o. But—"

"But nothing. There's your answer."

She wanted to scream at him, but she knew that the only way she would get through to him was to be calm, rational.

"Hear me out," she said.

She told him about what had happened when Marcus killed Kenny, that Kenny had seemed confused about what Marcus was accusing him of doing. And she told him about recognizing Marcus's cologne at Helen's. When she finished, Travis was silent for a long time.

"That's all you have?" he said finally. "A scent?"

"I'm never wrong about smells," she said. "Ask Yoshi."

"But isn't it possible that more than one man in the world wears a cologne or uses soap that smells like coconut?"

She knew she wasn't wrong, but Travis had a point. And she didn't know how to convince him.

"Yes, it's possible," she said. "But will you promise me that you'll think about it? Just keep an eye on him, please. For me."

He sighed. "Okay. For you."

He took her hand and gave it a squeeze. She settled farther into her seat and let some of the tension drain from her body. None of her friends would believe the day she'd gone through, even if she could tell them.

"Do you think we'll ever find out who sent me those e-mails?" she said.

He hesitated. "I couldn't say." After a moment he said, "You still think your dad sent them?"

"I don't know. I guess not."

"Why'd you do it, Tess? Why did you find those files and upload them?"

She thought about it long and hard and finally came to the awful truth. "I felt guilty," she blurted.

"Guilty? About what?"

She bit back the tears, but they came anyway. "I killed them, Uncle Travis. I killed Mom and Dad."

She told him everything. It poured out of her, about how she'd thrown a hissy fit when her parents had told her she couldn't go to the prom with Toby, how she'd argued with her dad about the music in the Range Rover on the way home, how she'd reached up between the seats to grab his iPod, distracting him just as the mountain descended on them. When she finished, the car filled with silence so thick it threatened to pop the windows out.

"You didn't kill them, Tess," Travis said quietly. "I did."

Stunned, she found she couldn't move. She must not have heard him right.

He couldn't have meant . . .

"I didn't protect them," he said quickly. "I didn't do my job. But I promise you, Tess, I'll never let anyone hurt you again."

She wondered if it was true, wondered who she could trust. Gentle snoring sounds from the backseat intruded on her thoughts.

Oliver.

Despite herself, Tess managed a small smile.

Acknowledgements

Authors don't write in a vacuum. Many of our ideas, plot twists and character quirks come from everyday life, from observing those around us, or by simply going about our day. A book like this one requires a lot of research—asking questions and looking things up. I know in the course of writing it that I absorbed a lot of information from friends, family, and experts. You know who you are.

I'm indebted to Graeme Base, author of *The Eleventh Hour*, for inspiring the way in which Tess solves clues left by her absent father, and for the bond his marvelous books have created between parents and their children.

I've tried to get all the details right. Any mistakes are mine and mine alone. But since this is a work of fiction, a lot of them are products of my imagination. I leave you to figure out which is which.

About the Author

Michael W. Sherer is the author of four books in the Seattle-based Blake Sanders series, including *Night Strike* and *Night Blind*, which was nominated for an ITW Thriller Award in 2013. His other books include the award-winning Emerson Ward mystery series, the stand-alone suspense novel, *Island Life*, and the Tess Barrett new/young adult thriller series. He and his family reside in the Seattle area.

Please visit him at www.michaelwsherer.com or follow him on Facebook at www.facebook.com/thrillerauthor or on Twitter @MysteryNovelist.

Photo: Valarie Kaye-Sherer

Made in United States
Troutdale, OR
02/19/2024

17812977R00189